By Rachel Nickerson Luna
Also from Emma Howard Books

The Eel Grass Girls Mysteries
Murder Aboard the California Girl Book 1
The Haunting of Captain Snow Book 2
The Strange Disappearance of Agatha Buck Book 3
The Desperate Message from Freeman's Island Book 4
Coming Soon:
The Eel Grass Girls Handbook

Darinka's Nutcracker Ballet
Darinka, the Little Artist Deer
Cape Cod Coloring Book
New York City's Central Park Color and Activity Book
Where Is Muffy Hiding?
The Thank You God Book

Visit our Web Site EelGrassGirls.com

THE EEL GRASS GIRLS MYSTERIES
BOOK 4

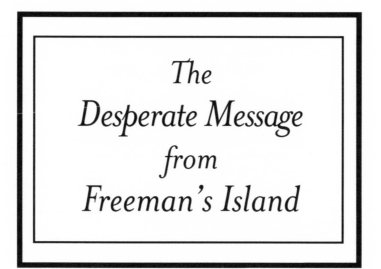

The
Desperate Message
from
Freeman's Island

RACHEL NICKERSON LUNA

Emma Howard Books
NEW YORK CITY

THE EEL GRASS GIRLS MYSTERIES
Book 4
The Desperate Message from Freeman's Island
By Rachel Nickerson Luna

© 2005 Rachel Nickerson Luna
Emma Howard Books, New York
Post Office Box 385, Planetarium Station
New York, New York 10024-0385

ISBN 1-886551-10-3
LOCCN: 2005905014

Illustration on Page 123 "All Dressed Up for the Captain's Ball"
by Moraiah Luna

The trademark name *Marshmallow Fluff* is used
with permission of Durkee-Mower, Inc.

Manufactured in the United States of America

Cover Illustration Armando Luna

Kiki Black, Copy Editor
Book Design by Ian Luna
Typeset in Mrs. Eaves Roman
Printing by
Patterson Printing
Benton Harbor, MI

Special thanks to

Leah Bennett
Kathy Casey
Antonio Luna
Emily Luna
Moraiah Luna
Ginny Nickerson
Jane West

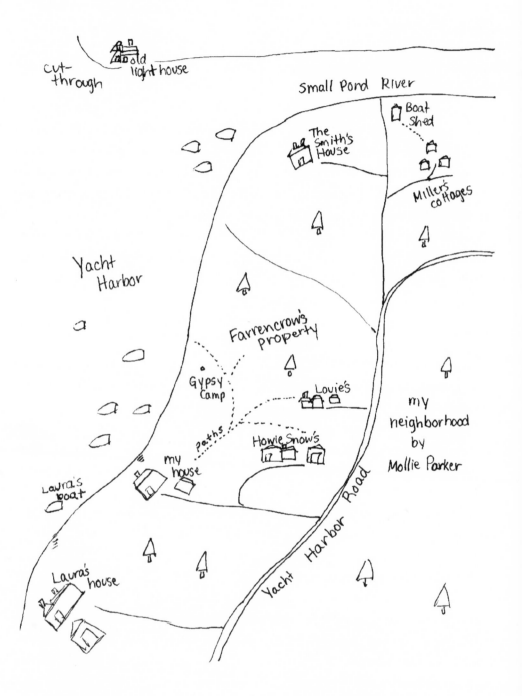

Chapter One

"August 15! That was a few days ago!" Laura exclaimed. "He must have been rescued by now."

She meant the person who had written the plea for help scrawled on a scrap of paper I held in my hand. I had just fished it out of a bottle I found floating in the harbor. We—the Eel Grass Girls—had come in from sailing and were mooring Laura's sailboat. The sails had been taken down, and we had boarded her dinghy to row to shore. That's when I had spotted the blue-green bottle bobbing in the murky water.

In case you don't know, I'm Mollie Parker, one of the Eel Grass Girls. There're four of us, and when we met at Yacht Harbor Sailing School back in July, we formed a mystery club, the Eel Grass Girls. Now we had encountered our fourth mystery, and since I was the one who found the message in the bottle, I'm the one who's going to tell you what happened. It all worked out so differently than we had expected.

I could see a note inside the bottle. After prying out the cork, I read the smudgy black message aloud: *Help me please. I am going to die out here. Please save me. Quick. August 15, Freeman's Island.*

"All he had to do was wave his arms at a passing boat," continued Laura. "Anyone would pick him up. Nearly every boat going to or from Nantucket or the fishing grounds passes right by Freeman's Island. I don't think he would still be there."

"Why do you keep saying 'he'?" asked Abigail, the lawyer's daughter. Sometimes she could be mucho technical. "It could be a woman who's stranded on that island."

"Who cares if it's a man or a woman?" I asked. "He, she, it. Someone wrote this note, and he's in trouble. We've got to help."

Muffy also wasn't convinced this was an urgent situation. "How could a person get stranded so close to the mainland? It's not as if Freeman's Island is in the middle of the Atlantic." She pointed her finger in the direction of the island. "It's right out there at the tip of Womponoy. The note couldn't possibly be real. It's someone's idea of a joke."

I let out a sigh. I didn't understand why the Girls wouldn't take the note seriously. It was our job to solve any mystery that came across our path. We'd already solved three mysteries in this Cape Cod fishing village. The note was obviously the beginning of a new mystery, and not just *any* mystery. Someone's life was in danger.

"How could someone end up on Freeman's Island anyway?" asked Laura, pulling deeply on the oars of her dinghy as we headed to shore. "I can't imagine a shipwreck in these waters."

"There was that rainstorm a few days ago. Was that on the 15th?" Abigail asked.

I shrugged my shoulders. I usually knew the day of the week, but not the date. It was summer. I wasn't keeping track of dates.

"He could have had engine trouble," she suggested. "Or maybe a shark attacked his boat, the boat sank, and he, or she, was forced to *swim* to Freeman's Island."

"If he could have done that, then he would have swum to Womponoy, walked to Deer Island at low tide, and then gone on home," said Muffy matter-of-factly.

"First of all, there're no sharks around here," I reminded them. "And second, there're riptides at the end of Womponoy, remember? No one with any brains would try to swim from Freeman's Island to Womponoy. He'd stay put."

"If he's a stranger, he wouldn't know about the riptides," said Muffy.

"What are riptides anyway?" asked Abigail.

"It's when two currents meet, and the water is all choppy," answered Laura, the only one of us who lived on year-round on the Cape.

"He'd still be there," I reasoned, continuing my line of thought, "because no one would pay any attention to a man on the beach waving his hands. They'd just think he was a real friendly guy, and they'd wave back. Look, there's Howie Snow in his dory. He's obviously finished with his fishing. Let's go ask him to give us a ride to the island on his boat. Come on!"

We were almost to the shore. "It's too far to row," Laura complained, resting her oars. "If we have to get to Howie, let's sail over. I'd rather rig the boat again than row all the way out to his dory."

"Never mind," said Muffy. "Howie's heading in." We turned to see Howie climbing from his huge dory into a crusty red rowboat, which was badly in need of a new coat of paint. "We can meet him on shore."

Laura rowed the rest of the way in, and we helped her beach the dinghy. The four of us ran along the water's edge to meet Howie at his landing. We arrived just as he was pulling his rowboat ashore.

He paused knee-deep in the water, gawking at us. "What's up?" he asked as if he really didn't want to know.

"Look at this!" I held the message under his nose. "Someone needs our help! We found this note in a bottle floating beside Laura's mooring."

Howie frowned. "It's not real."

"How can you say that?" I asked, putting my hands on my hips. Muffy had said basically the same thing. "It has a date and the exact location of the place where he's stranded. It *has* to be real."

"Well, it's not." Howie dragged his rowboat onto the beach. He was impossible! Earlier that very afternoon he had asked us to help *him*. It had been when we were out sailing. He had motioned us over to his dory to tell us about some mysterious voices he'd been hearing.

I was disappointed. Howie added, "I've seen a lot of stuff out there on the water. Believe me, this is nothing."

What did he mean by that? Whatever he saw or didn't see had nothing to do with this desperate message! "Thanks a lot, Howie!" I said sarcastically and turned my back on him, then stomped toward Laura's house. Howie was my next door neighbor. I considered him my friend, but he wasn't acting like one.

"I'm going to go to Freeman's Island one way or another," I shouted over my shoulder. "We're going to find out who wrote this message without your help!" The Girls hurried behind me.

"Don't be so upset," Muffy said, jogging alongside of me.

"How will we get there?" asked Abigail, catching up to us on the path leading from the beach to Laura's house. "It's so far."

"Billy Jones can take us," I suggested, pausing to wait for Laura, who had stopped to pick up her oars. "He can give us a ride in one of the yacht club motorboats."

"That wouldn't be right," said Laura. "But since he has a boat of his own, he could take us out in that. He might still be at the club."

"O.K. then. To the yacht club!" I shouted, racing across the lawn to Laura's barn where the Girls and I had left our bikes.

Chapter Two

After Laura tossed the oars into her barn, we pedaled down the driveway out to the road, turning right to the yacht club. It was a short distance along the harbor, but when we got there, the club-house was completely empty.

We circled the small wooden building, hoping that Billy was still around somewhere. Standing on the bluff, we scanned the beach and pier below. On one of the floats at the end of the pier, Billy Jones was loading something into a motorboat.

"We're just in time!" Muffy gasped as we bolted down the wooden stairs, dodged the club boats stowed along the narrow beach, and sprinted out onto the pier. Billy, one of our sailing instructors, is a real friend. He happens to have a truck too, which comes in handy when we have to go places in a hurry, especially at night. *And* he can be trusted.

Billy heard us approaching and looked up. "Here comes trouble," he joked.

"Aw, don't say that," I called out as we clambered down the ramp from the pier to the float where Billy stood. "You know you love all the excitement we add to your otherwise boring life. But never mind what we can do for you—we need your help."

"How did I guess?" He smiled. "What now? A severe zombie infestation?"

"Nothing like that!" Abigail giggled.

"It's something important. We found this message in a bottle." I showed him the crumply piece of brown paper with block letters scratched across it in charcoal.

"You're not taking this seriously, are you?" he asked, looking totally surprised.

I nodded. The Girls were silent. So much for support.

"Well, you're in luck. I'm just about to leave to check on my lobster pots. How about I drop you off on Freeman's Island, check my pots, then swing by to pick you up? If you find this Robinson Crusoe, we'll take him back to civilization—if he's willing to go."

"Huh?" I didn't understand the last part.

"Sometimes people enjoy the peace and quiet of an island retreat. They don't really want to be rescued, like in the book. Robinson Crusoe was happier on his island."

"That's absurd," I told him, using an adjective I love. "He wrote this note. He wants us to save him. Let's go."

We boarded Billy's boat, and he revved the engine. Laura uncleated the painter and pushed us away from the float. Just to let you know, the painter is a line, I mean rope, used to tie up a vessel. The day was a typical summer day on Cape Cod: blue sky, white fluffy clouds, and blue water with all kinds of boaters enjoying the harbor.

We cruised into the channel, and it wasn't long before we were plowing through the cut, past the old lighthouse. There were plenty of boats going out of the harbor. When we entered the Sound—that's the body of water separating Cape Cod from Nantucket Island—I was glad to see that the surface was calm. I didn't feel like getting tossed around the boat on our way out to Freeman's Island.

Abigail cheerfully waved to each passing boat. I imagined our castaway trying to attract attention, frantically waving to each boat that came near but never making contact, as every boater merrily waved back to him, never imagining he was in trouble. Wouldn't that be frustrating—no one understanding that he wanted to be rescued? Billy Jones was wrong. The note said the man was desperate to be saved.

Traveling the length of Womponoy Island, which stretched a couple of miles from north to south, we spotted Freeman's Island on the horizon. It looked small, but as we came closer we saw scrubby pines and low bushes surrounded by fields of beach grass. Rolling hills ended in cliffs of sand crumbling down onto beaches.

"Do you think his family reported him missing?" Abigail suddenly asked. "If they did, it's possible the harbor master and Coast Guard have already located the man."

"They couldn't have 'already located' him," I told her bluntly. "They don't know where he is and wouldn't know where to look, but we do. Let's do the authorities' work for them. Come on!"

12

Billy cut the engine, and his boat glided close to shore. I leapt into the frigid water and pulled the boat in to the shore. The island seemed deserted. I held the boat steady while the Girls jumped out.

"O.K., girls," said Billy. "I think you'll be all right 'til I get back. I'll check my pots and pick you up when I'm finished."

"Sounds good to me," I said, giving the bow of his boat a push away from shore. Billy waved as he headed off, speeding toward Womponoy.

"Where do we begin?" asked Laura, scanning the barren island.

"We'll split up," I said. "Muffy, you and I will go this way. Abigail, you and Laura take the other side. Look for footprints. When we meet at the far side of the island, we'll all go back together to the places where we've seen the prints and follow them to the castaway."

"You're sure we'll find footprints?" Laura asked skeptically.

"Of course! Let's go."

Muffy and I started toward the south side. There were lots of beer cans, rubber work gloves (the heavy-duty kind that fishermen wear), pieces of rope, and fishnet washed up at the tide line. Sandpipers raced along the sand where each wave receded. They made me wonder if there was any other wildlife on the island. Maybe fox, deer, coyotes? A tiny freshwater stream trickled over the sand, into the Sound. But there were no footprints.

"Over a hundred years ago, there was a settlement here, the same as the one on Womponoy," Muffy informed me.

"I can't imagine," I replied.

"Maybe we'll find some old foundations and the remains of houses. They'd probably be over there in the center of the island," she continued, but we couldn't see anything from where we were down on the beach. I kept glancing around to see if I could spot any sign of our castaway's efforts to get himself rescued, such as the remains of a fire on the beach or a white flag near the shore. They were oddly absent. Only the desolate sand, swept by waves, met our eyes.

"Hey, there're Abigail and Laura!" exclaimed Muffy. She called out to them, "Did you find anything?"

"Nothing," Laura called back. When they got closer to us, she asked, "What next?"

13

"You didn't see *any* tracks or evidence of a fire?" My theory about the marooned man *had* to be right!

"No evidence," said Abigail. Her father was a lawyer. She knew about evidence. "I rest my case."

But lack of evidence didn't discourage me. "No rest for the weary," I retorted. "Let's go inland and find him."

"People must visit this island from time to time, the way they go to Womponoy," said Laura. "If we find burned logs, it doesn't necessarily mean that it belongs to the castaway, does it? Besides, if he were ship-wrecked, he might not have had any matches to light a fire."

"Don't be so technical," I scolded her, turning to slog up the cliff. The Eel Grass Girls trailed behind me. When we reached the top, we immediately noticed a worn path through the stiff beach grass.

"Do you think animals made this path?" Abigail asked nervously.

"Either animals or humans," I answered. "Everyone who explores this island probably takes the same route."

I led the way. In the center of the island, several paths converged. I was about to tell Abigail and Laura to head north again, when I noticed a heap of driftwood peeking over the top of a hillock.

"Over there!" I pointed and dashed toward it. "Someone's built a hut!"

Chapter Three

In a clearing, we could see that someone had built the driftwood into a home. Bits of rope and handmade twine held logs and branches together to form an amazing structure. I marched forward, but Abigail held back. I don't know what she was afraid of.

"Be careful," she warned. "We don't know who's in there."

"It's our castaway!" I declared. "Hey!" I shouted.

"Quiet!" Laura hushed me as she caught up. "You don't really know who he is. We ought to be cautious."

"Oh, hogwash! Hey, you in there!" I yelled. "Come out!"

Though he looked just as I had imagined, I was startled to see an old man clothed in dirty rags poke his head out of the woodpile that was his home.

He blinked in the bright sunlight and shielded his pale eyes from the glare of the sun.

The Girls took a step back, but I bounded forward.

"Are you the one who wrote this note?" I demanded as I took the note from my shorts pocket and waved it in the air.

"Be careful!" Muffy called out.

"Did you write this note and put it in a bottle?" I asked again. "It says here that you want help."

The old man blinked again. He put one hand to his scraggly beard and reached for the note with the other.

"Yes, I wrote this," he admitted in a wavering voice, glancing at the note. He then handed it back to me.

"Well, we're here to save you," I announced. He stared at us and blinked a few more times. He didn't seem very excited about being rescued. The three girls edged up behind me.

"It's mighty nice of you to come out here to git me," he began, rather nervously. "But I ain't ready to go now."

"What do you mean?" I asked. I hadn't expected that response!

"Won't you come in?" he asked, motioning to his hovel.

Muffy peered into the hut. "I don't think we can all fit inside," she observed. "We'd better stay out here."

Large stones and logs had been placed around a campfire site. We sat down and waited for him to explain himself.

"I'm truly grateful to you," he began. "God knows I am, but I'm jest not ready. I thought I was when I wrote that note, but I'm not anymore."

He wasn't making sense. Maybe he *was* crazy.

"Were you shipwrecked?" asked Laura. The tone of her voice sounded kind. Her mother was a visiting nurse, so she had learned to be understanding and kind from her mother. That's what I thought, anyway.

"No, no. Nothing like that. I came here on purpose," he said.

"Huh?" Now that did not make sense! We waited for him to explain.

"A couple of months ago I took the Hyannis bus to town. Had an aunt here when I was a boy, so I know the place fairly well. So when I got here I walked down to the shore 'cause I thought I'd settle on the beach. I'd catch fish and shellfish to live on. I'd shoot rabbits and ducks." He pointed into his hut. "You can see I brought my rifle too, and enough ammunition to last a good long time."

We glanced inside his hut, but we couldn't see the gun, which was O.K. with me. Abigail's face was all scrunched up, and I knew she was thinking he might be dangerous. I was wondering about that too.

"But I realized I couldn't live on the beach—people'd hear my gun and run me off. So I waited for low tide and walked out to Womponoy. Then I saw those National Wildlife rangers swarming around over there like a flock of hornets. I knew they'd be trouble. I couldn't do any huntin' with them around."

He paused to catch his breath, then went on, "This island was near enough. I had my inflatable raft with me too, so I blew it up, put my gun and supplies in it, and rowed over here to Freeman's Island. I had to row in a wide arc to avoid the riptide, but I got here safe and sound."

He was smart for an old man. He blinked again and started to comb his long hair and beard with his fingers. Abigail squirmed on her log.

"Why did you leave?" Muffy asked. She liked research and gathering information. I just liked to know the answers.

"Couldn't take payin' all them taxes. I had land, plenty of it. And a big house with gardens too. I could keep it up all right, but with them taxes goin' up and goin' up, I couldn't make ends meet."

He continued combing his beard. "I don't mind the town buyin' a new ambulance and fire truck to take care of all the new folks who keep movin' to town, but why do I have to pay for four selectmen and a town manager? And for what? They don't know any more about runnin' a town than a horseshoe crab does!"

I didn't know the mental capabilities of the limulus polyphemus—I mean the horseshoe crab—so I kept quiet. He continued, "I didn't want to sell my vacant lot. Why would I want one of them developers puttin' in a hundred little boxy houses right next door to my house? I wanted to hold onto it—all of it. It was my granddaddy's farm. I had enough money to keep up the house and take care of my needs, but I jest couldn't pay them taxes. Then one day it sorta got to me all of a sudden. I couldn't see no way out. So I came here. All that confusion went away. I feel fine now—like a new man."

"So what happened to your house?" asked Laura.

"You'd better be goin' now," he said, looking nervous. Or maybe angry.

"Why did you write the note?" I asked. I wasn't going to leave.

"I don't remember. Good-bye."

"The note says something about dying. Are you sure you're all right?" asked Laura, with concern.

"Yes, yes. I'm fine." The old man seemed impatient. He stood and waited for us to leave.

"I demand an explanation." I stood my ground and stared him in the eye.

"Oh, I have no explanation," he answered calmly. "No explanation at all." He turned away and walked over to a basket of quahogs and slowly began to shuck them. He had quite a heap of shells accumulated beside his hut. When the wind shifted and blew our way, the smell was overpowering.

"Let's go," I said in disgust. Following the path north, we could see Womponoy and the mainland in the distance. It was astounding that the old codger had migrated to Freeman's Island to escape civilization.

"What do you make of that?" asked Muffy, leading the way through the beach grass and the dusty miller, with its yellow flowers encircled by dusty-looking green leaves.

"I think he's crazy!" exclaimed Laura. "He's a case for my mom. She makes house calls, but not all the way out here."

"Maybe she should," replied Abigail. "Someone ought to look in on him. If he's really crazy, he needs help."

"He doesn't need any help," I said. "He's sick of society and left it behind. There's no law against being a hermit if you feel like it. I'm just annoyed that we weren't able to rescue him. I was looking forward to it."

Muffy ignored my remark about the rescue and said, "There probably *is* a law against living on Freeman's Island. If we tell, someone will probably come out here and drag him off."

"Maybe we could bring him a fruit basket," suggested Abigail, changing the subject again.

"A *what*? The man wants to eat fish and clams. So let him."

We had reached the shore and nearly tumbled down the hill to the beach, where we saw Billy anchoring his boat. He saw us coming and waved.

"Look what I got!" he called out, pointing to a dark mass practically filling the cratelike structure in the center of his boat. I couldn't tell what it was.

"I guess your message-in-a-bottle sent you on a wild-goose chase," he laughed as we waded out.

"Not at all," I told him smugly. "We found our man, but he's perfectly happy living here. He changed his mind about being rescued."

"For real?" Billy looked at our faces, trying to tell if we were serious or not. "You really found someone?"

"Of course," I replied. "We found the man who wrote the note."

"Well, I told you so," said Billy. "He likes the peace and quiet here, I suppose."

"We think he's crazy," said Muffy. "But I guess we should leave him alone for now."

"Is he really crazy or just a little off?" Billy asked.

"We're not sure, but we ought to come back and check on him," said Laura.

"Sure," Billy said. "Just let me know when. I come out here a lot."

"What's that?" I looked into the boat.

"They're lobsters," said Laura.

"I thought lobsters were red," Abigail remarked. "Are those wild lobsters?"

"They're this color until you cook them," Billy explained as he helped us into the boat one by one. We gingerly peeked at the pile of lobsters.

"So who's your Robinson Crusoe?" asked Billy.

"He's an old man from Hyannis or somewhere," Muffy said. "He took the bus to town, walked out to Womponoy, and rowed over here in an inflatable raft, if you can imagine. And he has a gun."

"You're teasing me!"

"No, really!" Laura informed him. "He lives in a driftwood hut and eats shellfish. He'd probably appreciate one of these lobsters."

"Do you want to take him one?" Billy asked. "I have more than enough."

"I'm afraid to go back," said Abigail meekly. "Maybe we could come back here again, next week—with you, Billy."

"Do you think he's dangerous?" asked Billy. "Maybe we shouldn't bother him. Or maybe we should report him before he hurts someone, or gets hurt himself." Billy straightened up after securing a tarp over the lobsters.

"He uses his gun for hunting," I explained. "He doesn't want to leave. We can't force him to go if he doesn't want to. And we have to keep quiet about him and not mention it to the authorities. Otherwise they'll run him off and ruin his life."

"The police will capture him and lock him up," speculated Muffy.

"But he's living in a dream world," argued Laura. "He's lost his mind."

"Do you really think he'll be O.K.?" asked Billy. "He *did* write that note, didn't he?"

"He changed his mind, that's all," I said. I was no psychologist, but I could tell that the man had a problem. I thought we should let him figure it out for himself.

"Then let him be," Billy agreed. "We can come back here next week and bring him a lobster and some other stuff. What do you think he needs?"

"Blankets, clothes, ..." began Laura.

"Fruit," continued Abigail. "Vegetables."

"He looks perfectly healthy the way he is," I said. We didn't have to overdo it.

Billy pulled up the anchor and started the engine. Its roar broke the silence of that isolated place. Maybe the old man wasn't so crazy after all. Maybe he had made the right decision to run away from his previous life. But is running away a good solution?

We bounced over the gentle swells of the Sound, and before long, we were entering the harbor. Soon we found ourselves at the yacht club, pulling up to the float and tying Billy's boat to a cleat.

Muffy suddenly said, "We didn't even find out his name."

"It doesn't matter," I told her. Knowing his name wouldn't make any difference. We scrambled onto the float.

Billy held up a burlap bag. "Here're some lobsters for you. You'll have to split them up between the four of you. I only have one bag."

"Thanks, Billy," said Laura. "My mom will cook them for us."

"Good idea," I said. "My mother wouldn't know what to do with them."

"I don't think Grammy even has a lobster pot," Abigail said giggling. "She usually asks the fish market to do our lobster-cooking for us."

"Thanks for taking us out to Freeman's Island," I added. "We'll go out there again with you next week, when you check your lobster pots, if you don't mind."

"Sure. See you at sailing school tomorrow morning," he said as he untied his boat and putt-putted into the channel and toward his home.

"Now what?" I asked myself aloud. "Our mystery is solved."

"Let's go to my house for a lobster dinner!" exclaimed Laura.

"Sounds good to me!" said Abigail. We all agreed, jumped on our bikes, and pedaled toward Laura's house, though we outrode her because she was carefully holding the heavy bag containing our dinner.

Chapter Four

We rode past the harbor and up the hill. As we rounded the corner in the road, we almost ran right into Louie Stello, who was coming toward us from the opposite direction. He stopped his bike and we did, too, pulling over out of the road, facing him.

"What've you got?" he asked, eyeing the burlap bag.

"Lobsters," answered Laura. "Want to come over for dinner?"

Laura wasn't especially fond of Louie, but she knew how to be polite.

He didn't respond right away, but shifted his weight from one foot to the other, looking down. After all we'd been through, solving the mystery of Captain Snow's haunted house, it was surprising that Louie was still so uncomfortable with us Girls. All together, that is. He was fine with me—alone.

"Want to go fishing?" he asked me.

"When?"

"Now."

"I'm on my way to eat dinner at Laura's house."

"After. Meet you at the creek." He hopped on his bike and disappeared down the hill toward the harbor.

"What?" I asked the Girls, who were staring at me.

"I invite him over for dinner and he asks you to go fishing without even answering me!" exclaimed Laura.

"He's a boy. What do you expect?" I mounted my bike and rode ahead to Laura's driveway. The Girls followed close behind, through the pines to the Sparrows' old house and barn overlooking the harbor.

Laura's parents are always around. What I mean is, her father comes home every night for dinner. Even though her mother works too, she usually gets home first. They all eat together, go to church together, even do the laundry together. And Laura's dad takes her out fishing.

Muffy's family has plenty of togetherness too. Her parents are on vacation all summer long. They're always at home as well. Laura's and Muffy's families are so different from mine. My dad works in New York

City all week and drives up on the weekends. Even back home in New Jersey, he's never home for dinner.

Abigail spends the summer with her grandmother because her parents stay in Connecticut, where she lives in the winter. Her grandmother goes out a lot, but Abigail also has her Uncle Jack, who's visiting for a while. Another thing—the three of them are only children. I'm the only one with a spoiled-rotten sibling. Maybe that's why my mother is so distracted. Let's put it this way: Maxwell distracts my mother's attention from me.

When we got to Laura's back door, her mother came out to meet us.

"What's this?" she asked, giving the sack a suspicious look.

"Dinner!" exclaimed Laura, holding up the squirming bag. "Billy Jones gave us some lobsters to eat. Could you cook them for us, please? They're enough for everyone, but the Girls have to call home first."

"Lobsters! Yum!" Mrs. Sparrow took the sack. "Your dad will be pleased. We haven't had lobster all summer."

The Girls and I followed Mrs. Sparrow into the kitchen where Muffy and Abigail called home to ask permission to stay for dinner. My mom was out. Then we helped make a salad while Laura's mother put two pots of water on the stove to boil: a huge blue-speckled enamel pot for the lobsters and a smaller gray one for corn on the cob. Then she took long loaves of French bread from the freezer and popped them in the oven.

Out on the patio, we set the picnic table putting the plates on a red plaid tablecloth. We looked up when we heard Mr. Sparrow's truck tires crunching the quahog shells in the driveway. Mrs. Sparrow stuck her head out the back door and said, "Why don't you girls go to the beach? Dinner won't be ready for a little while yet. The water is taking forever to boil."

We crossed the lawn and filed down the narrow path between the huge wild rosebushes to the beach.

"Hey! What's going on here!" shouted Laura. We followed her gaze to her mooring. A gigantic fishing boat was tied next to her little sailboat!

In no time Laura was back in her yard, hollering to her father. We raced up behind her. Mr. and Mrs. Sparrow ran out of the house, their faces full of worry.

"What's wrong?" her father shouted as he bounded toward us.

"Someone's on my mooring! A big fishing boat! It'll wreck my catabout!"

Mr. Sparrow rushed to the edge of the bluff and looked down to the harbor. We stood beside him. The big, ugly boat, covered in fish guts and grime, was chafing against Laura's little wooden sailboat. Mrs. Sparrow ran up to us.

"Who would do a thing like that?" she asked.

"I don't recognize that boat," remarked Mr. Sparrow. "I'll call the harbor master right away." He returned to the house. In a few minutes he was back.

"We're fortunate the harbor master was still in his office. Apparently there're a number of strange boats in the harbor. All on private moorings. It seems they've decided to park their boats wherever they please."

"Why'd they have to pick my mooring?" moaned Laura. "Is the harbor master coming right away?"

"He said he was halfway out the door," answered Mr. Sparrow. "This will be his first stop."

"Doesn't the town supply moorings for visiting boats?" asked Mrs. Sparrow.

"Yes, but these people didn't bother to inquire about them," Mr. Sparrow said. He sounded disgusted. "It *is* August, the height of the season, so the harbor's full. There might not be any moorings left. And the town likes to know who's coming and when—reservations required."

"Sounds like the town's running a bed and breakfast," I joked. No one laughed. Laura was really upset. Understandably, she was worried about her boat.

The whine of a motorboat pierced the air. The harbor master appeared, coming from the direction of the town pier, which was next to the yacht club. The town had just hired a new harbor master. His name was Jake Rison. Mr. Sparrow disappeared down the path to the beach to get a better view of the proceedings. (That's another one of Abigail's lawyer words I've learned.)

"Dad would like to challenge those fishermen, I know," Laura said, as we watched Jake Rison pull up to the trawler, "but he'll have to let the harbor master handle it."

"Oh, no!" exclaimed Mrs. Sparrow. We looked at her in surprise. What was wrong with her? "The dinner!" She rushed back to the house. Abigail and Muffy followed her across the scrubby yard. Laura called it a "Cape

Cod lawn," which meant that it had grass, but not much. It was mostly weeds and brown patches. Mr. Sparrow never watered it. He said that would be a waste of time and water.

Our lawn, on the other hand, was the most unnatural shade of green—with fine, soft blades. Not a single weed. Full of pesticides and herbicides from a local lawn-care company. Muffy said that my brother and I would almost certainly die of cancer if we played in the yard. That was probably true, but it looked good.

I stayed with Laura on the bluff and watched as Jake Rison confronted the offending trawler. A group of strange-looking men had emerged from below deck. They wore colorful knit sweaters and caps. They looked more like gypsies than fishermen.

Jake was using exaggerated hand gestures to communicate with them. He pointed toward the cut-through, and the men nodded. Finally the fishermen untied their boat and followed Jake as he steered his boat toward the beach opposite Deer Island. They were heading to the left, or port, of the channel, near the cut. Mr. Sparrow reappeared, trudging up the path through the rosebushes.

"It looks as though the harbor master is putting them on a town mooring after all," he said. The wreck of a boat chugged along after the harbor master, veered out of the channel, and moored on a huge, neon-pink ball. When we saw that Jake was heading back, we tromped down to the beach to meet him. He guided his boat near the shore. Laura waded out and pulled him in.

"They don't speak English," he muttered, "and I don't speak whatever their language is. I can't tell where they're from either, but when I check out their boat registration number, I'll find out who owns that tub and at least where *he's* from."

"Is my boat O.K.?" Laura asked anxiously.

"No damage."

"How long are they going to stay?" I wondered aloud.

"They can't stay on a town-owned mooring for more than a few days. They'll have to move on. I think they're the same guys who were run out of Muddy River in July."

"Well, they'll have the best view in town while they're here," observed

Mr. Sparrow. "They get to live in the most beautiful town on the Cape rent-free and tax-free!"

What was it with adults and taxes? Mr. Sparrow and my castaway were obsessed with taxes, it seemed. I guess I'll find out all about them when I get older.

"Oh, they're not going to live on the boat," the harbor master told us. "We have a by-law against living on a boat. They'll have to stay in a hotel."

Mr. Sparrow raised his eyebrows. "Oh, really?" he asked. "Somehow I can't imagine them checking into the Inn on the Bay. Do you get to enforce that by-law?"

Jake smiled. "You guessed it. Now if you'll excuse me, I have two other squatters to confront." He threw his boat into reverse and headed over to another vagabond trawler on the far side of the channel, near Deer Island.

"Seems like those three boats might have come in together," remarked Mr. Sparrow. "I suppose they don't know any better. If they don't speak English, they would have trouble finding out our local rules and regulations. Well, all this excitement has made me hungry! Let's go eat those lobsters."

We climbed the path once more and crossed the lawn. Mrs. Sparrow and Abigail and Muffy were seated at the picnic table, where our plates were already piled high.

"Everything all right?" asked Mrs. Sparrow. Her husband explained the situation. "How odd!" was her reply. "Well, dinner is served! Dig in!"

We sure did. Since we were outside, we didn't have to be careful with the lobsters. Smelly lobster juice flew all over the place every time our nutcrackers broke into the hard shells of the lobster claws and legs. Mrs. Sparrow had split the tails so they were easier to open, but it wasn't easy getting the tasty white meat out. We tossed the empty shells into a big bowl in the center of the table.

"All this work makes the meat taste better," laughed Muffy, carefully pushing her hair out of her face with her wrist, so she wouldn't get any of the stinky lobster juice on her face. We ate in silence until we were stuffed. Then Mr. Sparrow gathered the bowl of lobster shells and corncobs and disappeared into the woods.

"He's feeding the skunks," Mrs. Sparrow whispered to us. It seemed a bit primitive to throw garbage in the woods, but what the Sparrows did on their own property was none of my concern. They lived far enough away from me that it didn't make a difference. My neighbor Howie Snow was another matter. I could smell his lobster pots and heaps of quahog and scallop shells every time I went to visit him, which I wasn't planning to do for a long time. He was a big creep to not give us a ride out to Freeman's Island!

Mrs. Sparrow brought a big chocolate cake out of the kitchen. As soon as Mr. Sparrow returned from the woods, we enjoyed thick slices of the moist cake, heaped with creamy frosting. I couldn't imagine my mother cooking like that.

"Girls, how about a sleepover?" I asked, feeling warm and fuzzy at the thought of having my friends around.

"Tonight?" asked Muffy.

"Not tonight. I'm going fishing with Louie, remember?"

"Wednesday night would be better for Laura," interjected Mrs. Sparrow. "She has a few chores around the house that have been neglected lately."

"That's two whole nights away!" Laura made a face, but turned it into a smile. "What time?" she asked me.

"How about coming over for dinner?" I suggested.

"When is your tennis lesson?" Abigail asked me.

"Tomorrow afternoon. It won't interfere with anything," I assured her. "Why don't you all come over for dinner tomorrow night too?"

"Your mother won't mind everyone coming over two nights in a row?" Mrs. Sparrow asked.

"No. She won't mind," I assured her.

We agreed on the sleepovers, though the Girls would have to ask permission.

"I didn't know that you like to fish, Mollie," said Mr. Sparrow as he stacked plates to take into the kitchen. He had remembered that I was planning to meet Louie later.

"The truth is, I don't," I confessed. I didn't know exactly how to answer Mr. Sparrow. It wasn't the fish that mattered, it was just that I liked to fish with Louie Stello. At his favorite spot on Snow Pond, no one else is ever around. It's peaceful and quiet. "We don't talk. We just fish."

"That's the way it's done," said Mr. Sparrow, heading toward the back door.

I was afraid he was going to ask me to go fishing with him and Laura. I liked to fish with Louie, but I didn't like fishing enough to go out with the Sparrows in their boat. That was a whole different story. Anyway, I think that Laura and her father like to fish alone too.

After clearing away all the plates and leftover food, the Girls and I washed the dishes. Then we headed home, going our separate ways.

Chapter Five

I rode south a short distance along the deserted road to my driveway. Howie Snow's driveway branched off from mine to the right. I wanted to ignore him, but I didn't want him to ignore me, so I rode my bike up to his house. I had time before I met Louie. Howie's truck was parked near his barn. He sat in a battered plastic chair, fiddling with a fishing reel. Because his usual loud music wasn't blaring, his place seemed eerily silent. He looked up at me.

"Hey, little friend."

"You didn't seem so friendly when you refused to take us out to Freeman's Island today," I said, giving him an angry look.

"Did ya go out?"

"Yes. Billy Jones took us."

"Didn't find anyone, did ya." That was a statement, not a question.

"As a matter of fact, we did. There's an old man living out there."

Howie stopped his fiddling. "Well, I'll be! Who is he?"

"He's from Hyannis, I guess. Ran away from his taxes." Then I remembered that I didn't want to tell anyone about him. Oops! But we could trust Howie. He would never tell.

"So?"

"So we left him there. He didn't want to be rescued, anymore. He changed his mind."

"Told ya it was nothin'."

He was *impossible!* He turned his attention back to his reel. I watched him, but I couldn't figure out what he was trying to do with it. He tinkered a little more, then said, "I hear voices. Music too. It comes and goes. As soon as I turn my radio off, it stops. Sometimes it's from the south, sometimes from the east. You're the only one who lives around here, 'cept the Stellos, but they're on the other side. The Farrencrows are my only abutters."

"Your only *what?*"

"The Farrencrows," he repeated.

"I heard that. What is it they are?"

"My abutters. That means their property's next to mine."

"Then it must be the Farrencrows," I said. "Or it could be Louie Stello and his brother."

"The Stellos are too far away—and besides, them boys don't make no noise. And the Farrencrows ain't here. They're all the way in Michigan. There's no house on the property. Never has been. The family bought land here over 75 years ago and just left it."

"Your point being?"

"Who's talkin' and playin' music?" he asked.

"Could the sounds be blowing in from a boat in the harbor?"

"Might be, but that's never happened before," he replied.

"Did you go look around?"

"Not yet. I thought you and your friends might go check it out for me."

Did he think we had nothing better to do than creep around in the woods looking for talking trees and musical mushrooms? What was he thinking? If he was so bothered by the voices, he ought to go see who was making them himself. Why should we help him?

"All right," I heard myself saying. Drat! Why did I do that? I guess it was because I couldn't forget that he had saved us from a dangerous situation just a few hours ago. (You'll have to read *The Strange Disappearance of Agatha Buck* to find out about that.) I decided that the Eel Grass Girls wouldn't mind exploring in the woods. We could check out Howie's auditory hallucinations tomorrow evening when we had our sleepover.

I got on my bike and pedaled back to my driveway. As I approached my house, I could see that Mom's car wasn't home yet. I assumed that she was playing tennis and Maxwell was with her or on a play date. I parked my bike in the empty garage and began looking for my fishing tackle.

Louie had given me a piece of wood with line wrapped around it and a fishhook on one end. It was the same kind of fishing tackle he used. My dad had only the latest and fanciest fishing gear, but Louie could catch more fish with this simple contraption than my dad ever dreamed of catching. I heard Mom's car coming up the driveway. She pulled into the garage. Maxwell was in the back seat.

"Oh, hi, Mollie," Mom called out. "How was your day?"

"Fine," I said. She hurried out of the car and disappeared into the house. Maxwell gave me a scowl as he trailed behind her. I scowled right back. He was such a pain!

I cut across our greener-than-green lawn to the steps leading down to the beach, where the creek was. The creek was a freshwater stream flowing through a little marsh to the beach and was full of the perfect size of minnows we liked to use for bait. Louie wasn't there yet. I decided to go back up to my yard and cut through the woods. There was a path leading to Louie's house. I would probably meet him on the way there.

The scrub pines that made up the woods were spread out, with small oak trees filling in the spaces between them. Long, feathery grass lined the path and covered the forest floor, springing up among the pine needles and last year's brown oak leaves.

Then I heard it! At first I wasn't sure what I had heard, but I knew I wasn't alone in the woods. I froze. The pine boughs danced up and down, dappling the grass with sunlight.

"Ah, aaah, ah." What was it? Was someone being strangled? Murdered? I was ready to bolt out of the woods, but which way should I go? Back to my house or toward Louie's?

"Aaaah, la-la." It was singing! I relaxed, even though it was the strangest-sounding song I had ever heard. As I strained to listen and tell from which direction the sound was coming, it stopped as suddenly as it had begun! All I could hear was the echo of the song in my mind. The sound had drifted through the woods, floating on the breeze, and was now gone. Who was it? Where was he? Why was he singing in the woods? Now was my chance to find out, but without any sound to follow, I didn't know where to look.

I stood still, listening to the swish of pine needles in the tops of the trees. Would I meet the mysterious singer if I continued on to Louie's? I jogged quietly along the path.

The woods were deserted. When I reached Louie's yard, no one was at home. A knock on his door brought no response. I waited. I turned to follow the path home, scanning the trees as I went, searching for the singer, but I saw no one and heard no more of his song.

Whoever the singer was, he wasn't trying to hide his presence. Howie had been hearing the singer, so maybe he was staying in the woods. Why? And who was he? And where was Louie?

I thought I'd wait for him on the shore. I took the path to my yard and cut across it to the stairs. When I reached the beach, I saw Louie looking out over the water. I wondered how he got there. He was amazing, but I wasn't about to tell him that.

"I've never seen those boats before," he said as I walked over to him.

He was gazing at the three fishing boats that had been escorted to the town moorings by the harbor master.

"One of those boats had the audacity to tie up to Laura's mooring," I told him.

"The what? Uh, where're they from?"

"No one knows. They don't speak English, so the harbor master had trouble communicating with them."

Louie handed me his net, and we walked to the creek in silence. I scooped up minnows and dumped them into his bucket. It didn't take long. I wanted to ask him if he had heard the singing on his way to the beach, but I would wait. We'd talk about it later. He might have heard something, might even know who it was, or at least have some ideas.

"Where's your bike?" I asked.

He nodded in the direction of his house. "Meet you on the road," he said.

I went back up the steps and, after getting my bike, rode to the end of the driveway and waited. When I saw Louie coming, I headed in the direction of the yacht club. He caught up to me, and we pedaled over the bridge, parking our bikes in the woods near Captain Snow's house. We hiked over an old path through the bayberry bushes, brambles, and towering silver leaf trees to Snow Pond.

Louie took the lead, crossing the narrow beach and carefully stepping over the splintered planks of a rickety pier. We sat down at the end of the pier, hooked minnows on our lines, and let them fall into the dark water. Some kind of white bird, almost like a stork, circled near the opposite shore and landed on an old piling. A pair of fishermen docked and began to unload their catch of bluefish. Then all was quiet.

A light breeze kept the nosee'ems away. Louie caught a couple of flounder. I hooked a big crab, a freaky sea robin, and a bluefish. I threw the crab and sea robin back, but I tossed the bluefish into the bucket for Louie to take home. My mother couldn't cope with a fish right out of the water—and neither could I.

After a while, we let the leftover minnows go free and hiked back up the path. We had to pass through Captain Snow's yard again. The house was creepy, but ever since Laura's father had begun to fix it up for the current Mr. Snow, a very distant relative of Howie, it didn't seem quite so bad.

When we were almost to our bikes, Louie stopped and said, "I heard something."

"Just now?" I asked, looking around at the tall, somber bushes and looming trees. I glanced back toward the old house. What could it be? I hadn't heard anything.

"Near my house. In the woods."

"Like what?" I asked. So, he had heard it too!

"Voices."

I waited for an explanation, or at least an elaboration, but none came.

"What kind of voices?"

"Talking. Singing."

"I heard something too, on the path in the woods while I was on my way over to meet you, before I found you on the beach," I said.

"What?" he asked.

"A man singing, I think. At first I thought he was being murdered." I laughed. It seemed silly now. "Have you heard of the Farrencrows?"

"Yeah. They own the woods between me and you and Howie Snow, all the way down to the beach and over to the point, near the Smiths. Why?"

"Nothing. Only that Howie Snow said that the woods belong to the Farrencrows. There's no house on their property, so no one lives in there. Someone else is in the woods."

"Sounds can carry," he said confidently. I knew that, but I wanted to hear what he thought about the voices. He told me, "I was thinking a new house might be going up, and it was workmen, 'cause I've never seen any-one or heard anything in those woods before. Funny thing is, as soon as I

32

hear something and stop to listen, there's nothing. It goes all quiet."

"That's what happened to me!" I shouted. "And Howie Snow said the same thing! Why do you think that is?"

"Don't know."

"Howie didn't say anything about a new house being built," I said. "We've got to investigate!"

"Not tonight. Mom's invited Aunt Lydia and her boyfriend over for rhubarb pie. Tomorrow."

I wasn't sure if we could wait, but if the Eel Grass Girls didn't get a chance to snoop around on our own, we'd wait for Louie. So I said, "All right. You can meet us at my house after dinner then. The Girls are coming over for dinner tomorrow night and sleeping over on Wednesday night too."

Louie didn't answer, but that's how he is. He would be there. He didn't have to say it. He balanced the bucket of fish on one of his handlebars and started down the old sand driveway to Lowndes River Road. We pedaled our bikes through the lengthening shadows, over the bridge, and turned left, up the hill past the yacht club. Fireflies flickered in the fields. Wild rosebushes smothered the split-rail fences separating the fields. Lights shone through the windows of the old gray-shingled houses, making them look cozy.

The harbor was calm. I glanced toward the cut. I wondered if those fishermen would really check into a hotel. No matter what the harbor master said, we all knew that plenty of people lived on their yachts the entire time they were moored in the harbor. I guess as long as they didn't break any other laws, the harbor master would look the other way. No one wanted trouble, but it seemed the gypsy fishermen didn't know how to avoid it.

When Louie and I reached my driveway, I turned in. He kept on going toward his house. I parked my bike in the open garage and put my fishing tackle on the workbench. The sun was about to set, but I wanted to check out who was making all that ruckus in the woods. Neither Howie, Louie, nor I had seen anyone, yet someone was in there somewhere, talking and singing.

According to Howie Snow, the Farrencrows were out of town and had never lived here. They were holding on to the land for whatever reason. Someone else was using one of the paths. Passing through the Farrencrows' land on their way to a rented cottage along our road, just the way Louie and

I cut through the woods. I walked to the edge of the trees. It wasn't completely dark yet. I could see the path leading to Louie's house, though his house was quite a way off and hidden behind trees. I would just go a little way.

I followed the path, looking back toward my house every few yards. Mom had all our lights on as usual, so I couldn't get lost even when it became totally dark. All I had to do was look at the lights, and they would guide me home. Louie's house was straight ahead, and there was a fork in the path; that I knew. But I hadn't counted on a fork in the fork. I had never bothered to follow any of the other paths in the woods, and there were quite a few. Which way? I turned left. I could hardly see my house anymore. Then I heard it. Chills went down my spine.

"Ay-ai! Ai!" It was as if the trees were being tortured, but it wasn't the trees. The sounds came from somewhere just beyond me. "Arghhhhh! Ah!" Silence. Then "Ay! Ay! Ay!" It was men's voices all right. It must have been the ones Howie, Louie, and I had heard before. But who was it? Was it campers or teenagers partying? It was definitely someone who couldn't sing!

They were wailing and talking. No big deal. So why was I spooked? I wanted to get out of there. I didn't want to meet up with a group of strangers in the dark woods.

I turned around to go home, but I could no longer see the lights! My house had vanished into pitch blackness. I couldn't see a thing. Stay calm, I told myself. Just walk in a straight line. The path to Louie's house couldn't be far. I realized I had been holding my breath when I caught a glimpse of the lights again and started breathing. I hurried along the path. When my feet hit the lawn, I raced across it to the safety of my home.

Later I peered out of my upstairs window. I couldn't see anything except darkness and a dim glow from Howie's house. There was no trace of flashlights or a campfire. Those men were a minor mystery, but I didn't like them being in my woods. What were they doing there? Were they camping or partying? Those woods belonged to the Farrencrows, according to Howie Snow, so the men were trespassing. Technically I was trespassing too, but I was a neighbor. I had a right to pass and they didn't. It made me feel unsettled.

Chapter Six

The next morning I quickly dressed and headed down to the kitchen. Mom and Maxwell were gone. My brother had swimming lessons on Tuesdays. I grabbed a granola bar and hunted for some orange juice in the fridge. There was a jug way in the back behind numerous "doggie bags."

I munched and chugged while I tried to locate my life preserver. I was afraid that I had left it at Laura's house the day before, but I saw it hanging near the kitchen door. I didn't remember putting it there. Then it occurred to me that Mom must have found it in the garage, or wherever I had left it. She had brought it in and hung it up for me.

Sometimes I thought that Mom only cared about Maxwell, but little things like this reminded me that she did care about me too. I was slightly annoyed with myself for not knowing where my life jacket was though. I have to have it for sailing school. I have to keep track of it.

Dashing back upstairs, I brushed my teeth. In the hallway I paused to look out the window again. This time I thought I saw someone on the path in the woods, but whoever it was vanished. Maybe it was just an animal, or morning light on the rustling oak leaves. It could have been a tourist who had wandered off the road onto one of the paths, or come up from the beach. It couldn't have been Louie or his brother; they would be at work by now, mowing lawns. I peeked into Mom's room to see what time it was. I was early! I had some extra time, so I decided to walk to the yacht club by way of the beach.

I looked out into the harbor and saw Howie Snow rowing out to his dory. Nearby was an older couple rowing from their yacht to shore. I knew the type: They would probably walk into town for a cup of coffee and a copy of the New York Times. I saw the fishermen on one of the gypsy trawlers hanging their laundry out to dry. Hmmm. Did they just get back from a night at the Inn on the Bay? I doubted it.

Several men and a woman were scratching for clams. They stood waist-deep in the still water, long rakes resting against their shoulders. One shellfisherman had his metal bushel basket set in an old inner tube tied to his waist.

I passed Laura's house and climbed over the revetment, or protective embankment wall next to her house. Since the last bad hurricane, some families had dumped boulders on the beach to protect their homes and property, but it didn't really seem necessary in the harbor. In my opinion, we were well protected, but you never know.

Soon I was crossing the yacht club beach and heading up the wooden staircase. Lots of kids were on the deck. Billy Jones was drawing racing diagrams on the board. I could see Muffy sitting alone on one of the gray wooden benches. I sat beside her.

"I heard those voices in the woods," I said, "the ones Howie's told us about. Louie's heard them too. I want to check them out tonight."

"O.K., but who do you think it is?" Muffy asked.

"It sounds like men or teenagers," I explained. "They're camping out in the woods, or partying and drinking. It's peculiar that they've picked that spot."

"Peculiar?" laughed Muffy. "Whoever it is, they're not trying to keep it a secret. If everyone's hearing them, they must be loud. Don't you think it's just some kids playing around? It could be Jeffrey Silva and his friends."

"Jeffrey Silva's a strange kid, I'll admit, the way he likes to poke around in the woods looking for dead animals to stuff, but he's not the loud, singing type," I said.

Laura and Abigail rushed up to us, panting. The two of them squeezed onto the bench, almost pushing me off the edge.

"I almost didn't make it!" exclaimed Abigail, fanning her face with her cap. "Uncle Jack's friend Freddy wants to go into real estate. He's so excited about it that we got excited too, and I almost forgot about sailing school."

"He's becoming a developer?" I was shocked.

"Who's developing what?" Billy Jones was suddenly hovering over us.

"No, no, no," gasped Abigail. "It's nothing like that! We're talking about my Uncle Jack's friend Freddy Frisket."

"Freddy who?"

"Freddy Frisket. But he's not going to be a developer. He's only going to sell old houses. He'll buy broken-down houses, fix them up, and fill them with beautiful antiques."

"Uh-huh." Billy directed his attention to Judy, another instructor, who had just come out of the clubhouse to begin our class.

"My dad would like Freddy's idea," said Laura. "Too bad he's so busy with his regular work and the new work on Mr. Snow's house. He's also going to be repairing the old lighthouse on weekends."

Laura's dad loved old houses, such as the house they lived in. It was centuries old and had been built by her great-great-grandfather, or someone. Mr. Sparrow worked as a carpenter and was a real Cape Codder.

"Shhh! Class's starting." Muffy shushed us. Judy announced that we would be having mock races. What else was new? We always had mock races, when we weren't having capsizing drills.

"Good!" whispered Laura. "I want to sail near those fishing boats and see what they're up to."

"Why would they be up to *anything*?" I asked. "They'll be moving on soon, so you don't have to worry your little head about them."

She didn't look so sure. Billy Jones went over some starting tactics on the board. The design of blue, red, and green boats and the dotted lines representing their courses around the marks looked like a big multicolored furball. If you hadn't been listening, no one would ever be able to decipher his drawing! When he gave the order to rig, we charged down to the beach to get our favorite Sprites.

"Laura!" I called out. "Shall we take the *Chubby Quahog* or the *Minnow*?" These were the best boats, in our opinion, which was always correct.

"Muffy," she asked, "which boat do you and Abigail want to take?"

Laura and I ended up with the *Chubby Quahog*. That was fine with me. The *Minnow* is the best boat in the fleet, but it had had an accident recently, you may have read about, and I wasn't sure it was as good as new. Sometimes we all sailed in the same boat, but I had to admit it was too crowded with the four of us. The sailing instructors always tried to split us up, but we would sail near each other so we could talk.

Judy was heading out in one of the motorboats to set up the racecourse. The boat carried a couple of huge, neon-pink balls that would act as our markers.

They were easy to see—you couldn't miss them, not even from a mile away.

We quickly rigged our boats. The Sprites had a mainsail and a jib, which is a smaller sail in front of the mast. I could tell that Laura was glad to see that Judy was dropping the markers near the cut, not far from the visiting trawlers.

"Let's go!"

Some of the instructors and other kids helped us carry our boat down to the water. Abigail and Muffy had rigged their boat so they were ready to go too. Together we tacked back and forth past the town pier until we were clear. I was at the helm and skimmed past the yacht club float as we sailed out toward the cut. It felt great to be out on the water with the breeze in my hair and sun on my face.

"Get close to those boats," said Laura. "I'm still mad at them for using my mooring."

"Forgive and forget," I instructed her. "They're off your mooring now, and they didn't do any damage."

"They could have ruined my boat! They didn't care about it. I want to see who they are and keep an eye on them. You don't know what they'll try next!"

Dodging motorboats and a long, sleek sloop cruising out for a day trip, we crisscrossed the channel. Soon we were approaching the moored trawlers. The *Minnow* was close beside us as we passed the offending trawler.

"*Ocean Rose!*" Laura read the name handwritten across the stern. "There's no homeport written underneath. I'm curious to know where they're from."

"From where," I corrected her. "It doesn't make any difference."

Two men were working on gear while a third hung some rags to dry on the railing. The men looked scruffy, as if they hadn't shaved or bathed in weeks. They gave us a cold stare as we tacked and sailed by the second boat. It was named *Wind Dance*. A fisherman threw a bucket of garbage overboard almost on top of us!

"Hey!" I yelled. "Watch out! What do you think you're doing?" He glared at me but didn't respond. "Did you see that?" I shouted to Abigail, who had maneuvered the *Minnow* alongside of us. "Who do they think they are—dumping their garbage into our harbor? I'm going to tell Judy to radio the harbor master right away!"

We both rounded the third boat, the *Sea Song*, in an effort to zigzag our way over to Judy, who was moored on the starting line of the mock racecourse. When we arrived, we turned into the wind and came to a stop on either side of the *Sea Calf*, the smaller club launch. Laura grasped the motorboat, as did Muffy on the opposite side. Abigail explained what had happened.

"I'll call Jake Rison right now," she said, picking up her radio. "They can't get away with polluting the harbor!" After a quick chat with the harbor master, she turned back to us and said, "Jake will be over pronto. You go on and start the race. I'll blow my whistle for you if he needs to talk to you. You'll probably have to give an account of what you saw."

"O.K.," I agreed. "But tell Jake that it was the *Wind Dance* who did it, even though the other boats are probably dumping garbage too. The muck is floating on her port side."

I felt a little too preoccupied with the pollution to concentrate on the race. It made me angry too, but I tried to focus. We studied the race board which Judy had propped up on the side of the motorboat. "R, Q, 2" followed by a red square. R was the mark near the beach, to the port of the cut, and Q was a pink ball dropped further to port. We would round both marks to port (that's what the red square meant) two times, then finish.

Because Laura owned a sailboat, a catabout, her sailing had improved over the past few weeks. I didn't own a boat, neither did the other Girls, but I was determined to become a better sailor and racer too—and win. Enough of this wimpy "coming in last except for little kids" for me!

"What's your strategy?" asked Laura. "Are you going to start at the windward end of the line or try for the middle?"

"It seems that we're faster on port tack," I observed, "so I think I'll start at the leeward end and hope I can shoot across the starting line fast enough not to collide with any of the other boats."

"Hmmm. Might be kind of risky, but it could work," Laura speculated.

"It'll work."

Judy blew the airgun to announce that we had three minutes until the start. Abigail waved as we passed her. It seemed as if Muffy was giving her advice too. Two minutes. One minute. Thirty seconds. I was passing the pin. Wait—wait. Quick tack. "Ready about—hard to lee! Pull in the jib!" Twenty. Ten. "Head up! Head up!" Three, two, one, beep-beep-beep-beeeeeep. We hit the starting line right at that exact moment. Three other boats were stacked up at the *Sea Calf*, at the opposite end of the line, all of them starting on a starboard tack, which gave them the right of way over me. Abigail was the middle boat. We cut in front of them.

"Starboard!" the first boat yelled. It was cousins Gilly Wagner and Harvey Seymore. "Get out of our way!" they screamed. Gilly's red curls stuck out from under her blue Yacht Harbor Yacht Club hat.

"Hold your course," I bellowed back. They weren't anywhere near us. No one was going to hit me—and I wasn't planning on hitting anyone either. We were off!

"Great start!" Laura complimented me. "I didn't think it would work!"

"I thought you said 'it might,'" I teased her. "You have to have more confidence in your captain."

"I'm glad we made it without a major collision with those other boats," Laura said, sounding relieved. "We would have been in the wrong and we'd have to pay a penalty."

"I'm not wasting my time with penalties," I boasted, not even looking back to see how the others were faring. I set my eyes on the first mark.

I tacked up to R ahead of the others and rounded the mark. We were on a reach as we steered toward Q. Billy Jones was just off of Q in one of the other club motorboats, monitoring the race.

Gilly and Harvey were gaining on us. Abigail had fallen behind. I could see that Jake Rison was approaching Judy. I hoped Jake wouldn't call me back, not when I was going to win this race! He drove his boat over to the *Wind Dance*. We saw him fish some garbage out of the harbor just as we rounded Q. Billy gave us a wave.

"It's back to R," I said to Laura.

"Go, go, go, Mollie!" she cheered.

We were on a reach back to R. It was a strange course—only two marks. There were usually three, but if there were only two, one was usually windward, as R had been from the start, and the other directly downwind. But whatever it was, it was good practice for me.

I was still in the lead as we rounded R again and headed back toward Q. The other boat had fallen behind, but Abigail was catching up. The third boat had hit Q and had sailed off, away from the other boats, to pay their penalty (sailing in a complete circle) before continuing the race. Around Q again and I was on a run toward the finish line.

"Pull up the centerboard!" I ordered Laura.

"I was just going to," she replied. With one hand she pulled up the metal centerboard and cleated the line. With the other hand she held the jib out on the opposite side of the mast from the mainsail. Because the wind was directly behind us, we wanted to catch as much of it as we could.

"Abigail's overtaking us," said Laura, looking behind us.

"Oh, no she's not!" I took a quick look. Though we had the right of way and Abigail had to keep clear, I didn't want her to block our wind. I wanted to charge at the finish line and get out of her way. Pushing the tiller away from the mainsail, I headed off, but the wind caught the mainsail at the out-side edge. With a terrific "whoosh," the wind whipped the big sail across the boat in an accidental jibe! The Sprite pitched to leeward as the boom almost took Laura's head off.

"Hey!" she hollered from behind the sail. "What happened?"

"Sorry! Are you all right?"

"Barely! " She ducked out from under the boom and moved to wind-ward, stabilizing the boat.

"I was trying to get away from Abigail. She was going to blanket us."

"I don't think she was. But whether she was or not, you have to be more careful," Laura warned me. "You can't change course without thinking about what's going to happen. I'm too young to die."

She was right. If the boom had hit her head, Laura would have been seriously hurt. I knew that sailing can be dangerous, but I hadn't real-ized that such a slight movement could make the boat jibe that way. At least the wind wasn't blowing very hard. We could have capsized as well.

I had learned my lesson. "I'm really sorry," I repeated. Then, under my breath, I said, "We're almost there." I felt like blowing on the sail,

41

wiggling the rudder, anything to make us go faster. The finish line was only yards ahead. Abigail was bearing down on us, veering to port and starboard, whichever way I turned, trying to take my wind!

"Back off!" I turned to yell at her.

"Don't take it personally," Muffy called to me. I knew she was coaching Abigail. Abigail wouldn't be so aggressive on her own.

"How should I take it?" I called back as I slipped over the line. Abigail was a few seconds behind me.

"That was close!" Laura let out a sigh of relief.

"Ha, ha! I won!"

"But you almost lost your crew!" laughed Muffy. It was no laughing matter. I felt bad about that jibe. Amateur sailors could be dangerous, and I didn't want to be placed in that category.

"Thank you!" I said to Judy as we sailed by. "Where's Jake?"

"He's behind the *Sea Song*, still talking to the *Wind Dance*, I suppose. Go on over, if you want to. You may have to testify."

"Let's go!" I headed toward Jake. "Good race!" I called to Abigail.

"You too. I didn't think the *Chubby Quahog* had it in her."

"Yeah," giggled Laura. "She may be chubby, but she can run."

"Ha, ha." Her pun was corny, but that was O.K. I was happy that I came in first. I didn't mind beating Abigail, but I was thrilled that Gilly and Harvey were way behind both of us. I was happy to leave them in my wake!

"Where're you going?" Abigail asked me as we let our sails out again and headed downwind.

"We're going to find Jake Rison. Come along." She followed, but this time she kept to our port, being careful not to steal our wind. We rounded the *Sea Song* and saw something unpleasant.

Chapter Seven

Jake Rison was standing in his boat facing the *Wind Dance*. His face was red and flushed. One hand was on his hip and in the other he was holding something really disgusting-looking. Jake caught sight of us and turned toward us as we sailed in. Our mainsail was out to port, so all I had to do was head up. Laura grabbed hold of Jake's boat. Abigail had to jibe and come up alongside me, but her jibe was easy and controlled, unlike mine.

"These guys have no idea what they did wrong!" Jake was exasperated and really upset. "They don't speak English. I guess wherever they come from everyone dumps their garbage in the water."

"What language *do* they speak?" asked Laura.

"That's a good question," he replied. "They're out of New Bedford, so you might think they were Portuguese, but they're not. I need an interpreter."

"Parlez-vous français?" I asked. There was no response.

"Hablas español?" asked Muffy. The men stared at us blankly, somewhat angrily. What was their problem?

"So what are you going to do?" I asked Jake.

"I'm trying to get ahold of the guy who owns these boats so he can pay the fine. But in the meantime, I don't want these guys to go on polluting."

"Ah, ai-ya!" What was that weird sound? Singing? It sounded similar to the noise I had heard last night in the woods.

We whizzed around to see one of the men approaching in a rowboat. Anyway, he looked like one of them—scruffy yet colorful. He continued "singing" or wailing in another language, oblivious to the trouble his comrades were in.

He rowed up to the stern of the *Wind Dance* and tossed the painter, up to his friends, and climbed a rope ladder to the deck. He faced Jake.

"What wrong?" he asked.

"Plenty!" Jake replied, trying not to lose his temper. "You and your buddies can't throw garbage in our harbor." He held up the handful of gook he had fished out of the harbor and pointed to the rest of the debris floating on the surface of the water between the boats.

The fisherman's face contorted in frustration and he fiercely confronted his companions. They shouted back at him, flailing their arms until I thought a fistfight would break out! Three of the men reluctantly descended into the rowboat and pulled away from the trawler, scooping garbage from the oily waters as we watched.

Finally the one who had rowed up said to Jake, "We not do again."

"Well," Jake began, "let this be a warning to you. And don't let it happen again or you'll be paying, big time. You guys are pushing your luck. Remember, you've got to be out of here in two days. It's time to move on."

"We go," he said, nodding his head, holding up two fingers. "Two days. We go."

"Where are they from?" asked Muffy, unable to keep her curiosity under control.

Jake turned to her and said, "They're from New Bedford."

"But what country?" she asked.

One of the men on deck was listening and answered, "Europa!"

"Europe isn't a country," I said loudly. Where had he gone to school?

"We from Ireland," he said boldly.

"It's no use," said Jake. "I've got work to do." He pushed away from the *Wind Dance*, and Laura let go of his boat. "You girls had better get back to your sailing class and keep away from these guys. They're shifty characters."

Muffy let go of our boat. The other Sprites were sailing back to the club already, and we could see Judy motoring over to pick Q out of the water. The pink balls are what we call "dropped marks" because they're dropped into the water before each race and picked up afterwards. Abigail set off, and we stayed on a run all the way back to the yacht club pier, then jibed very carefully to reach the shore.

After pulling our boats ashore, we derigged and put the sails and rudders away in wooden bins at the base of the bluff. We climbed the steps to the clubhouse to discuss the races (the other students had completed two races) and the rules.

I was more interested in the rules than I had been in the past, now that I had just won my first race. Though there hadn't been any incidents in that race, such as protests or collisions, another time there might be. I needed to know the rules a little better just in case.

"I'm hungry," remarked Abigail.

"You have to wait," I told her. "We can't eat until class is over." That was obvious.

"I'm in the mood for the Clam Bar," she added in a dreamy tone.

"Me too," said Muffy.

Billy Jones was explaining how to handle a collision. Then he startled us by saying, "And don't forget the Captain's Ball coming up the weekend after next. Tell your parents to make their reservations now."

"The Captain's Ball?" asked Abigail. "What's that?"

"I'll tell you as soon as class is over," Laura said.

As soon as Billy Jones finished the lesson, he approached us.

"What's up girls?" he asked.

"We're starved," Abigail said.

"What is the Captain's Ball?" I asked.

"It's a big party for all the yacht club members," Billy explained. "You have to come and bring your families. It'll be fun."

"The Clam Bar is calling us," Muffy said.

"Oh, yes," Billy smiled. "Mrs. Pitts wants to feed you."

"Ugh!" I grunted. Mrs. Pitts had been our enemy just weeks ago.

"She's had a rough time," said Laura. "She was O.K. the last time we saw her, so let's just forget about the past."

"But she was mean and hateful and tried to kill us," I reminded her.

Abigail said, "Cooky's keeping her under control, I hope."

"Yeah, sure," I muttered. We said good-bye to Billy. It was then I remembered I hadn't ridden my bike to the club. Why hadn't I? Now I'd have to walk all the way to the Clam Bar! The other Girls pulled their bikes out of the blackberry bushes.

"Hey!" exclaimed Muffy. "Where's your bike?"

"I left it at home. I don't know why I decided to walk! I came by the beach."

"You can ride with me," offered Abigail, so I sat on the seat of her bike while she took the handle bars and stepped onto the pedals. We coasted down the hill. Muffy and Laura rode ahead of us to Lowndes River Road

45

where we turned right. Past the marina and just before we reached the bridge, we pulled off the road and parked our bikes at the Clam Bar, a little gray-shingled shack that sold hamburgers and hot dogs.

We marched up to the window to place our orders. Mrs. Pitts was there, her blank expression better than the menacing looks she had given us when she had been involved in a witches' coven. She had never been friendly, but she had been extremely unfriendly not so long ago. Cooky was working over the grill. He ignored us, but we didn't care. We didn't want any trouble with either of them—we just wanted food.

The riverbank was quiet. Tourists were fishing from the bridge, and boats were going in and out of Lowndes River, which connected the harbor to Snow Pond. Soon our lunches were ready, and we sat on the grass to eat.

"Tell us about the Captain's Ball," I said to Laura. "Billy didn't give us much information."

"I've heard it's a big party with dancing and food," said Laura. "The yacht club has it every year. I saw it on the calendar."

"Then why didn't you say anything about it before?" I asked. "Are we going?"

"Of course we are," replied Muffy, taking a sip of her juice. "We can't miss a yacht club event."

"But who will we dance with?" Abigail asked. She opened her grilled cheese sandwich and peered inside, then closed it up. I don't know what she was looking for.

"Certainly not Harvey Seymore!" scoffed Laura.

"That's for sure!" I said. "We'll dance together, or by ourselves. Who needs boys?"

I thought of Louie Stello and Billy Jones. Some boys could be O.K., but we didn't really *need* them. I did have to admit they came in handy at times.

"Why are there so many bad fishermen?" Abigail wondered aloud, changing the subject as she munched on her sandwich.

"Haven't we already had this discussion?" Laura asked.

"There aren't so many bad fishermen," said Muffy. "Most of them are good, like society in general."

"Society in general?" I repeated. Where did she get these phrases? I

46

pushed a potato chip in my mouth and savored its salty crunch.

"There are bad people, or not-so-bad people," she continued, "but some of the men who fish see the isolation of the water as an opportunity to commit crimes they might not otherwise commit."

"How poetic!" giggled Abigail. "'The isolation of the water.'"

"Lovely!" I said, but I didn't mean it. I didn't have time for poetry. Or maybe it was patience I didn't have.

"Those men from New Bedford might not really be so bad," Muffy offered. "Probably they don't know any better. They don't know our rules and regulations. They're not trying to do anything wrong."

"So you say," I said.

"All fishermen know that you don't tie your trawler to the same mooring as a little wooden sailboat," said Laura with emotion.

"And what kind of people throw garbage in the water?" I asked.

"They said they were Irish," Muffy said. "My mom's Irish, and they don't look anything like her."

"I should hope not!" I joked, thinking of those scruffy men. "But you're right, they don't look Irish. They're different-looking."

"Like gypsies!" exclaimed Abigail.

"Yes! That's it!" cried Laura. "They're gypsies! I've heard that they're all over Europe. Maybe they really *are* from Ireland."

"I'll find out," Muffy assured us. "I'm sure they're not, though, but I can stop by the library on my way home. I'll let you all know what I find out when we meet at your house, Mollie, for dinner."

"Great!" I said. "Try to find out what language they speak. Then we can eavesdrop on them."

"That's not nice!" said Abigail, frowning.

I didn't respond. We finished eating. There was still time before I had to be home for Mom to take me to my tennis lesson, so I asked "How about going to the Eel Grass Palace?"

"Good idea," agreed Muffy. We tossed our paper plates into the green-painted oil drum that served as the Clam Bar's trash can and placed our juice bottles in the recycle box next to it. I grabbed Abigail's bike. This time I pedaled while she sat on the seat.

Soon we were at the intersection of Lowndes River Road and Yacht Harbor Road. We turned right, then left onto a dirt road. At the end of the road, we laid our bikes in the high grass out of sight. You never knew who might come along. We didn't want anyone to know where our secret palace was, but someone was very close to finding out!

Chapter Eight

I led the way along the path going through the bushes to the tangle of grapevines that made up our Eel Grass Palace. First we entered our clubhouse to observe the solemn ritual of the marshmallow roast.

We each had a stick that we kept in the ceiling of our meeting room. The rooms, or houses as we usually called them, were like igloos made of vines, rather than ice and snow. There were no leaves on the inside, just twisted brown vines. And there was just enough room for the four of us to squish inside. We sat on the sandy floor around a campfire that was made of twigs and always ready to be lit.

Before I had the honor of lighting the match (we kept the matches in an old rusted tin), we opened and handed 'round an empty vanilla extract bottle, deeply inhaling the pleasant aroma. Marshmallows, stored in another tin, were also passed around and pushed onto the sticks. Once the fire was burning, we roasted and silently ate the sticky treats—a strange combination of sweetness and the bitter taste of charcoal.

After carefully dousing the fire with sand and laying down new twigs for next time, we returned the roasting sticks to their place in the ceiling and put everything back into the tins. As we were creeping out of the clubhouse on our way to continue our rituals, we stopped short. Voices!

Oh, no! We didn't want anyone to discover our secret place! We strained our ears to hear, but couldn't make out the words. It was coming from beyond the old abandoned cranberry barn, not far from our palace.

"I know what it is," said Muffy, relaxing. "My parents were talking about it."

"What?" asked Laura. How could Muffy be so calm?

"Someone wrote a book about cool places to go walking. Now the tourists have a list of every out-of-the-way path and trail in town. The cedar swamp, right behind the barn, was probably mentioned in the book. It's just some tourists."

"What are we going to do?" asked Laura. "We can't have tourists creeping around the cedar swamp! Next thing you know, they'll find the barn, and it won't be long after that they'll be hiking through the Eel Grass Palace, leaving their pink and purple coffee cups and beer cans all over the place!"

"Let's see who it is for sure," I said. "We don't want any tourists finding this place!"

"Who wrote that book?" asked Muffy. "He ought to be run out of town!"

Ah, that was a good idea, especially if he would take all his confounded books with him!

We crept over to the barn and carefully peeked around the corner. A path led into woods thick with blueberry bushes and scrubby oak trees. Poison ivy and brambles climbed the tall pitch pines. Carefully we wandered down the path, wondering where it would lead us—and whom we might find along the way.

The brush became thicker as we went along. The path headed away from the cedar swamp rather than toward it. All we could hear were our own footsteps tromping over the pine needles and snapping twigs. Maybe the voices *had* been tourists enjoying the beauties of the cedar swamp. Then we saw something up ahead. There were figures moving among the trees! Men in brightly colored sweaters and caps! We crouched behind a clump of bird berry bushes.

"Oh, my!" Muffy whispered. "Look familiar?"

"I'll say!" said Laura. "What are they doing here?"

"I don't think they're sightseeing," I answered, figuring they weren't bird-watching or on a garden club tour.

"Seems like they're looking for something," said Abigail. "Don't let them see us! They might be doing something illegal."

We crept further off the path and hid ourselves behind a thick blueberry bush laden with blue-black berries and watched the men, five of them in all, standing in a small clearing. They talked, gestured, and looked around them as if they were in fact taking in the scenery. One of them began to pile up stones in the center of the area, while another picked up pieces of fallen wood and twigs. A third man cleared the small bushes, pulling them up by their roots!

"Hey! They can't do that!" I stood up to go tell them off, but Abigail held my arm.

50

"Shush!" Muffy commanded. "The bushes will grow back. Don't worry about it. Let's see what they're going to do."

"I've seen enough!" I retorted. "Let's get the police! They can't go around ripping up the wildlife!"

"Bushes aren't exactly 'wildlife,'" Laura corrected me.

"O.K., Nature Girl! But are you just going to sit here while they pull the forest apart?" I hissed. Their blasé attitude was getting on my nerves.

"We're not sit—" Abigail began.

"Hush!" Muffy put her finger to her lips, and we saw that the men were leaving, moving further away from our hiding place. We waited a minute, then crept out to the path to follow them.

"Why didn't we ever notice this path before?" asked Abigail as we hurried along.

"Because we've never explored this part of these woods," said Laura.

"I'm sure Louie knows this trail," I said.

Louie knew every trail, path, abandoned property, and fishing spot in town. It seemed that these fishermen, who were newcomers, knew the path too. But how? The men were walking fast now. We kept far enough behind them so they wouldn't notice us. I wondered where they were going.

The path wound on and on, then suddenly ended in a field. We could see beyond the field to houses and recognized Yacht Harbor Road. The Girls and I halted behind the trees. The men continued, crossing the field and road, then ambling down to the beach where they had probably left their rowboat.

"They must be planning to camp in the woods tonight!" said Muffy. "But why?"

"It's cheaper than the Inn on the Bay," Abigail answered.

"Of course!" I said. "But I suppose there's no law against it." I knew that was the wrong answer as soon as I said it.

"Oh yes there is," said Lawyer's Daughter, Abigail. "It's called 'trespassing.'"

Right. Trespassing. It was one of those laws you ignore when it's convenient, such as when I want to get to Louie's house in a hurry.

"Should we tell the police?" asked Muffy. "We don't know whose land this is, but they would know."

51

"Camping is illegal in this town," Abigail added. "It could be dangerous too, if they're not careful with their fire. We know *we're* careful with our fire at the Eel Grass Palace, but if *their* fire gets out of control, our Palace could go up in smoke! Besides, living on someone's land is different—worse than just crossing over it. They ripped up those bushes too, remember?"

"Leave them alone," Laura said. "Let them camp out. It'll be easier to spy on them here, than if they're on their boat. We could come back after dark."

Then I had an idea and asked Muffy, "Does your mother know Gaelic?"

"A little bit. Why?"

"If these guys are really Irish, they could be speaking Gaelic. Your mom could translate for us. Then we'll know what they're saying."

"I doubt if they're saying anything important," said Laura. "Probably just 'Let's moor next to that puny sailboat' or 'Shall we dump our garbage off the starboard or port side of the trawler?' or 'Rip up some more bushes.'"

She was most likely right, but we could find out more about them if we knew what they were saying. They were being a nuisance, and who knew what other evil plans they were concocting?

"I've got to get to my tennis lesson," I said. "I'm halfway home, so I'll walk the rest of the way on the road."

"Go ahead," said Muffy. "See you tonight."

"Meet me at my house later," I said. "Come prepared. We have work to do."

I cut across the field to Yacht Harbor Road, and the Girls headed back to get their bikes near the Palace. We hadn't been able to finish our rituals because of those fishermen. From the road I could see them rowing out to their trawler. I didn't appreciate them pushing themselves into our lives.

As I strode along the narrow road, I thought about our castaway and how people camp out for different reasons. Some set up camp out of necessity, others by choice, others just for pleasure. It would be fun to sleep in a tent. I had never tried it. The Eel Grass Girls and I had attempted to sleep on lawn chairs on Laura's patio, but it hadn't worked out very well. The fog rolled in—and, well, we ended up inside.

When I got to my house, I saw Mom wasn't home yet. Her schedule was hectic, but she never forgot my tennis lessons! Tennis was the most important thing in her life next to Maxwell.

I entered the house, took my tennis racket from a hook near the back door, grabbed a metal basket full of neon pink-balls, and went back outside. I would whack balls against the side of the garage until Mom got home.

After a while I felt warmed up enough and ready to go, but Mom still hadn't returned. Maybe she had left a note. I reentered the house and looked on the kitchen table and counter, the places where she usually left notes, if she bothered. Nothing. What was I supposed to do? I had no idea where she could be, and there was no one I could call to find out. She didn't carry a cell phone. Supposedly a cell phone would complicate her life. At that moment it would have made my life easier if she had one.

I didn't know what to do, so I decided to go upstairs to prepare my room for the sleepover on Wednesday night. My twin beds would be enough. The sheets were probably clean. Mom always took care of that sort of thing. A flashlight might come in handy. I checked the bedside drawer. It was there—and it worked. Good. I placed it beside the lamp.

I looked out the window facing the harbor. The three trawlers were still on the town moorings. Hmmm. That was weird. Why hadn't they gone out fishing? I hadn't thought of that before when we saw them dumping garbage and preparing their campsite.

Why were they even in our harbor if it wasn't to fish the waters? If they were coming and going, the harbor master might even allow them to stay a little longer, but if they were on a mooring day in and day out, they would surely have to leave when their two days were up. But what did I care? I wanted them to go. They were causing too many problems—to local boats, to the cleanliness of the harbor, and to the wildlife.

Where was Mom? I was getting annoyed. Though I didn't love tennis, I was fairly good at it. If I had to take lessons, I wanted to get better. I wanted to take my lesson and be done with it. I didn't like this waiting around. I crossed the room and looked out the window that faced Howie's house. I could see his chimneys peeking up above the tops of the pines. A small airplane was whining across the sky, following the contour of the beach. I looked down to the driveway.

What was that? A slim figure staggering up our driveway! Long hair. A dark jacket held tightly around him. The person lurched forward, looking back toward the road every few steps. He halted, then turned and ran headlong into the woods!

What should I do? Was the person hurt? The way he clutched his jacket and staggered, he could be wounded. Or was he being chased? He kept looking behind him as if someone were after him.

If he had been hurt, he should have come to the house for help. If he had been pursued, he should have come to the house as well. It was as if he hadn't even seen our house. Oh, fiddlesticks! I ran into my parents' bedroom and dialed 9-1-1.

"Hello? This is Mollie Parker. Someone just ran up our driveway and disappeared into the woods...No, I don't know who it was...A long-haired man about twenty years old I guess...No, I couldn't tell...He's gone now...I should have expected as much from you!"

I slammed down the receiver. The local police made me furious! Didn't they care if someone were hurt and afraid of someone who was chasing him? Maybe it would have been a waste of time to send a cruiser over and have an officer search the woods, but maybe not. All they had to say was, "Thank you for being such a good citizen and being so observant and concerned. We can't send a cruiser over right now, but we will as soon as possible. And we'll make a note of your report and check it against any other reports that might come in."

I dashed downstairs and ran out of the house. I would have to do the policemen's job for them! But then I had an unpleasant thought: If someone were after the man, they might be the ones to show up next. I paused. I didn't want them to come after me. But it seemed that the man had escaped them, whoever they were, and they weren't following him now. No one was in my driveway or on the road beyond. If the man had been hurt, at least he wasn't bleeding. As I headed toward the road, I noticed that there were no spots of blood on the white quahog shells covering our driveway.

Halfway down, I turned into the woods. The man had entered here, but he was long gone. I saw and heard nothing. This whole area had once been farmland, but when the farms had been sold and the land parceled off, pine trees had sprung up. Lots of them. This land beside our driveway, which I now knew was the Farrencrow property, had probably been kept clear longer because the pines were more sparse than deeper in the woods where Louie's path was.

I looked over the long, feathery grass growing beneath the trees. There was no path, no trail, no evidence of the man's flight through the woods. I jogged in a straight line, perpendicular to the driveway. Soon I came to the path going to Louie's house. Which way had the man gone? To Louie's? To my house? I turned toward Louie's and took the left-hand path at the fork, the one I had taken the night before. Before I got very far, I heard a car horn honking. It was Mom. Rats! I couldn't stop now.

I ran a little further, but the man had vanished, if he had even come this way. I turned back, then stopped. Was I doing the right thing? Shouldn't I keep looking for him? But what if he didn't want to be found? I wondered if that could be be possible. I gave up my search and went home.

Chapter Nine

"Where were you?" asked Mom in an impatient tone. She was in the car. "You're going to be late."

I passed by her into the house, where I had left my racket. She was the one who was late. I had been ready for hours. Besides, I had been trying to help someone, but I didn't mention that. I didn't say anything at all as I got into the back seat beside Maxwell, who gave me a smirk.

"We had such a lovely time at the Natural History Museum, didn't we, Maxwell, honey?"

"Uh-huh," he replied. I wanted to smack him. We drove in silence the whole way to Muddy River, where the tennis camp was located. Silence except for the children's tapes Mom was playing for Maxwell. The idiotic lyrics were enough to drive me crazy.

When we pulled into "Tennis for Teens," I bolted from the car and found my instructor, Lizzie Winkle, who was about 16. Her long blonde curls bouncing up and down, she was picking up balls on one of the courts.

Lizzie had been my teacher for most of the summer. I had begun with Jim Stern, who could play tennis, but couldn't teach. He never explained anything. The only thing I ever heard from him was a groan whenever I missed the ball.

But I didn't miss the ball often. Not anymore. My lesson this afternoon was constructive, concentrating on my backhand. I don't know what Mom and Maxwell did for the entire hour. By four o'clock they were back, standing outside the fence, licking ice cream cones.

"Mrs. Parker," Lizzie addressed Mom, "could Mollie come on Friday morning? We have to change the schedule again because of the Round Robin."

"Oh, that would be fine," Mom replied. "But when can you fit Maxwell in?"

"Jim could take him tomorrow, I think. Let me check the chart."

"But what about you? He likes you, you know," said Mom, smiling. Maxwell stared at Lizzie. She giggled nervously, frantically scanning the lesson chart. Even though the camp was called "Tennis for

56

Teens," they gave lessons to younger kids too.

"I'm all booked up. See? Jim's free. How about eleven?"

Mom wrote our lessons in her date book. On our way home I told her, "The Girls are sleeping over tomorrow night and coming over for dinner tonight."

"Tonight? Don't you remember the Meiers have invited us to their barbecue?"

"The Meiers? I don't know who the Meiers are. I've never heard of them. Why don't you and Maxwell go to the barbecue, and I'll order a pizza for the Girls and me."

"All right." We drove on in silence. Correction: No one spoke, but I had to listen to squawking songs all the way home. I began to think about how I could arrange for the tapes to get lost.

When we finally arrived home, I stayed outside and practiced my backhand for a while, whacking balls against the side of the garage. My thoughts drifted to the man I had seen earlier. Who was he? No one had pursued him, but he kept looking behind him. Hmmm. He hadn't been bleeding, but he seemed to be hurt. Possibly he could have been in a fight, and someone had punched him in the stomach.

"Mollie!" It was Laura. She must have walked from her house to mine by way of the beach. She strode across the lawn. "Why are you so angry at that poor little tennis ball?"

"I had a great lesson! If you ever want a good tennis teacher, go to Lizzie Winkle. She's the best."

"I can't get over to Muddy River twice a week to take tennis lessons. My parents work, remember?"

"What about your grandparents? Don't they live in Muddy River?" I asked.

"Yes, but they're old and they don't run a taxi service. They drive, but not much, except to church. Besides, I have enough going on with sailing school, my boat, and the Eel Grass Girls."

"I wish the others would hurry up!" I said. "I have something to tell you guys."

"Tell me!" Laura moved closer. "You can tell the others as soon as they arrive."

I told her about the man who ran into the woods.

"That's kind of creepy," she responded.

"Yeah," I said. "And now he's hiding in the woods next to my house!"

"Why is everyone in your woods all of a sudden?" she asked. "Did he look like one of the fishermen?"

"No, he didn't. He was skinny. His hair was kind of long, but somehow he looked more clean-cut. He was wearing a long jacket. That was weird too, because it's summertime and it's so hot. It doesn't make sense!"

"He could be one of the men you heard last night, don't you think?"

"Yes. That occurred to me. Look! Here come Muffy and Abigail."

"Hey! I've got news!" called Muffy. They rode up on their bikes and parked them in the garage next to mine.

"I went to the library and found out that gypsies *do* live in Ireland!"

"Really?" I found that hard to believe. "I thought they lived in Romania or somewhere."

"They do. Romania and everywhere else. Originally they came from India. Their language, Romani, is similar to one of the Indian languages," Muffy continued, trying to catch her breath. "They migrated to every country in Europe. And now they're all over the world. They're in the United States."

"I heard they're from Egypt," Abigail interjected. "A girl at my school did a report on them and said that the name 'Gypsy' came from the name of the country 'Egypt.'"

"They do call themselves Egyptians and Gitano, but they're from India," declared Muffy, the Eel Grass researcher and expert on many topics. "I hate to tell you, Mollie, they probably don't know Gaelic any more than I do."

"Don't be so sure," I said. "I've got something even more exciting to tell you!" Then I told them about the long-haired man I had seen.

"We've got to investigate!" said Laura. "We can't let him disappear into your woods."

"He's probably gone by now," I said.

"You might be right," Abigail considered. "But we ought to be careful just in case he's still lurking around."

"Come on!" Muffy said, ignoring Abigail's warning. "Let's get started."

I stowed my racket and balls on the bench just inside the back door. The four of us crossed the yard and set off along the path to Louie's. It was becoming a little dim among the trees. At the fork, we veered left.

After a short while, I said, "This is where I was when I heard the voices and that strange singing." We proceeded along the path, but we found nothing. The woods went on and on. There was nothing unusual. The endless pines, oaks, and bushes all looked the same.

"There's got to be something," said Muffy. "If they were here at night, they must have made a campfire."

"I didn't see one," I said. "It was pitch-black. But it's logical that they would have one. Let's spread out."

We fanned out and scoured the woods on either side of the path.

"I found something!" called Abigail after only a few minutes of searching. She was leaning over something lying on the pine needles.

"What is it?" asked Laura, coming up beside her.

When I got to them, I could see a clearing and the remains of a fire. There was a ring of small stones with burnt charcoal in the center. Several sardine tins and a bread wrapper lay strewn about, as well as lots of cigarette butts.

"Who was here?" I asked. "No beer cans, so it probably wasn't teenagers."

"Why do you need beer cans? Do all teenagers drink beer?" asked Laura. "And do they have to camp out in the woods just to drink beer?"

"Of course!" I answered. "If they were of drinking age, they would have gone to the Nor'easter or at least built a bonfire on the beach and done their drinking there. That would have been more fun. But no, they were hiding in the woods, so it has to be for a reason: They're underage, too young to buy alcohol."

"But if there're no beer cans, does that mean they're not teenagers? What about all the cigarette butts? There's such a thing as underage smoking. Then why were they in here?" asked Muffy. "It looks as if they were only eating sardines and bread. Nothing illegal about that."

"They were trespassing," began Abigail. "Could it have been the gypsy fishermen?"

"It was them, I'm sure," Laura announced.

59

"They," I corrected her. "Wonder why they decided to make a new camp near our palace."

"Do you think they heard you last night?" asked Abigail. "If they did, they might be afraid to stay here again tonight."

"They have only one more day to stay in the harbor," I reminded them. "Those men didn't hear me last night. And they couldn't have seen me in the dark. There're three boats of them, with too many men to stay in one place. They probably decided each crew should make its own camp in a different place."

"So do we think the gypsies are camping out because they can't afford to stay in a hotel?" asked Muffy.

"It seems so," answered Laura. "And they leave their garbage wherever they go! It's gross! I've seen enough."

We found our way back to the path. "I want to see where this path leads," I said.

"It probably leads to the beach," said Laura. We followed the path for a while and found out that she was right. Before long we were at the edge of the woods, on a bluff overlooking the harbor. We looked out to see the fishing trawlers, the old lighthouse, and Womponoy Island beyond.

"Look at all the footprints down there," cried Muffy, glancing at the beach below the bluff. "Your long-haired man and the sardine-eating campers probably went down this hill to the beach." She descended carefully, making sure she didn't disturb the footprints. "Look! Here on the beach!"

We also avoided the footprints and tumbled down to the shore where we saw what Muffy was hollering about—imprints of a smaller shoe in the sand. They were deep. The small-footed man must have still been running when he made these prints. Further on they were swallowed up in a mass of larger prints. Then they all disappeared at the water's edge!

"This is interesting," remarked Abigail, carefully walking around the edge of the mess. "It looks as if the man ran into the sardine-eaters, and they all rowed away in a boat."

"Could he have something to do with the gypsies?" asked Laura.

"No," I answered. "The gypsies probably left early this morning in their own rowboat. The man I saw showed up later. It was low tide, I'm fairly sure, so he could have easily waded out to any boat and taken it."

"But they're all motorboats," observed Abigail.

"And motorboats are supposed to carry at least one oar," Laura said.

"Let's go tell Howie what we've found," I suggested.

"Why?" asked Laura. "He's no help."

"We owe it to him to tell him who's crooning in the woods," I said.

"But we don't know who it is for sure," Muffy said. Then she added, "I guess we can tell him what we do know."

We took the path back to the main trail going to Louie's house. "There should be another path cutting through to Howie's," I said. How was it that I had never paid any attention to these other paths? I should have been curious enough to investigate them, but before this time, I had always gone straight to Louie's house and back. Now I wished that I had explored them all.

We came across a path shooting off to the right and took it. Just as I suspected, it led straight to Howie's barn, but Howie wasn't home. His truck was gone. We rounded the barn and heard a crash. There was the sound of breaking glass, then clanging metal!

"Wwwwhat's that?" whispered Abigail, grabbing the back of Laura's T-shirt.

"It came from Howie's house," I said. We crept along the side of the barn and peeked around to the back. The screen door of the house flew open, and a red fox whizzed out and vanished into the woods!

"Holy mackerel!" I cried. My heart was pounding!

"What was a fox doing in Howie's house?" asked Abigail. "That's not normal!"

Muffy answered, "Looking for food, I'd say."

"Shouldn't we check inside to make sure everything is all right?" asked Laura.

"I don't think we should," I said. "How much damage could a little fox do? He just wanted a snack."

"It sounded as if he did a lot of damage," Laura said. "He probably wrecked the place!"

"Shouldn't we at least leave a note for Howie?" asked Abigail.

61

"No paper. No pencil," I said.

"Aha!" Muffy announced, as if she knew something we didn't. In a jiffy she had her backpack open and had produced a notepad and pencil. "*Voilá!*" She jotted down a brief description of our encounter with the fox and a promise to stop by tomorrow morning to give Howie the news about his mysterious voices. After pinning the note under the front door-knocker, we left by way of the driveway.

"All this excitement has made me hungry," said Abigail.

"You don't need any excitement to give you an appetite," I said. "But I'm hungry too." We all were.

We walked to my driveway and headed toward my house, where life was normal—or so I thought.

Chapter Ten

Mom's car was gone. She had taken Maxwell to the Meiers' barbecue, whoever they were. There was a twenty-dollar bill on the counter and a note with the phone number of the pizza parlor, as if I couldn't have looked it up in the phone book myself.

I dialed the number and put in an order for a large pizza with everything on it. The Girls could pick off whatever they didn't like and give it to me. Half an hour? We'd starve before it got here! I began rummaging through the cupboards and fridge. I didn't want another granola bar. Neither did the Girls. We had to keep our minds off our stomachs for a while. What could we do?

"Let's go upstairs and help you pick out a dress to wear to the Captain's Ball," Laura suggested. The Girls and I climbed the stairs to my room. First we looked out the window to see the trawlers. Were those fishermen really gypsies? Why had they come here in fishing boats if they weren't going out fishing?

"It makes sense that they would camp out in the woods," Muffy said.

"It's cheaper than the Inn on the Bay," added Laura. "They would be forced to keep quiet there. No partying or loud talking or bizarre singing allowed."

"Let's look in your closet, Mollie," Abigail said, opening my closet door and going through my dresses, of which there were not many.

The rest of us sat down on the beds and watched Abigail display each dress.

"This is the prettiest," she proclaimed, holding up a green print with orange rickrack around the neckline and hem.

"Fine," I responded. It didn't matter to me.

"I don't have a ball gown," Muffy said. "But I do have a really pretty dress."

"We could wear the same dresses we wore to your grandmother's party," Laura suggested.

"I don't want to wear the same dress," said Abigail. "But I have others that are similar."

Muffy said, "But a ball is special. We need lace and diamonds."

"Ha!" I laughed. "This is Cape Cod—in the summer. No one is going to wear diamonds!"

"Well, I am!" exclaimed Muffy. "We all are! Fake diamonds, that is. My aunt has the most beautiful tiaras that just came in at her shop. Each of us could wear one. And she has long gloves that go all the way up to your armpits, with feathers around the edge. We'll look gorgeous."

"I'm not sure if that's my style," I protested. Who needs feathers in their armpits?

"Oh, come on!" Laura said, gently poking me in the arm. "It'll be fun."

Just then we heard a knock downstairs at the front door. We stampeded down the stairs. Laura opened the door while I leapt into the kitchen to get the money, but it wasn't there!

"Hey, Girls," I called. "Where's the money?"

"It's on the counter," Muffy called back to me.

"No, it isn't. Did one of you take it?" I asked, reentering the hallway where the pizza delivery guy was standing, holding the huge box.

"We didn't touch it," said Abigail, looking to the others for confirmation. "It was on the counter. I saw it right before we went upstairs."

This was exasperating! If Maxwell had been home, I would have blamed him for taking the money. He would do that just to annoy us, but he wasn't around, and we were the only ones at home.

"Just a minute," I said to the man. I motioned to the Girls to follow me into the kitchen.

"O.K., let's be logical," I began. "We came in the back door. The money was on the counter, right?" The Girls bobbed their heads in affirmation. "No one touched it." They nodded again. "But the money is no longer here." Their heads turned to one side and then the other: No.

"The wind could have blown it onto the floor," suggested Abigail, looking down at the floor, where no money was to be seen.

We had to admit it—the money was gone.

I went back into the hallway.

"My mom left us a twenty for pizza," I explained. "It was on the kitchen counter half an hour ago, but now it's gone."

He said nothing. I prayed he wouldn't take the pizza away and leave us to

64

starve. He took a pad of paper out of his pocket and wrote a note, dated it, and asked each of us to sign our names. The pad had a piece of carbon paper in it, so he had a copy as well. He left the top copy with me.

"Your parents are going to have to pay for this pizza."

"Yes, yes. They will, don't worry. They'll pay you and give you a nice tip too," I assured him. "Thank you! Thank you so much!" I took the warm box from the man and closed the door.

We rushed into the kitchen and ripped open the box, each of us grabbing a slice. Muffy quickly picked off all the mushrooms and flung them back into the box before cramming the steaming slice into her open mouth. Abigail did the same thing with her anchovies, and Laura removed the green peppers. That was fine with me. I had already gobbled up half of my slice. I planned to scoop up all their rejects and plonk them on my second slice.

"What do you think happened to the money?" asked Muffy, as she worked on her second slice. "You know it didn't just walk away."

"It must have caught on someone's clothing as we walked past the counter on our way upstairs," I surmised.

"You know that didn't happen," Laura insisted. "It's gone."

"Well, what do you think happened to it, then?" I asked, piling discarded toppings on my second slice.

"Obviously someone got in the house while we were upstairs, and they stole it," remarked Muffy.

"Really?" cried Abigail nervously. "Who could it be?"

"It's not the first time we've had this problem," said Laura, referring to our mystery involving Mrs. Pitts, when she sneaked into our houses to steal the clues (and other things) related to the mystery we had been working on.

"But who is it this time?" asked Abigail. "We don't have any enemies. And we're not working on any mystery."

"Stealing money is different," observed Laura.

"It's something a teenager would do as a prank," I said.

"You shouldn't go around blaming teens," advised Muffy. "That's what adults do, and I don't like it. But would an adult break into your house and walk off after only stealing a twenty? They'd steal something else too."

"So maybe they have," Abigail answered, her voice rising. "Let's look around, quick. He might be hiding!"

I was too busy eating. "Let's finish the pizza first, then we'll look." I didn't really believe that anyone had stolen the money. It must be around somewhere. Besides, I didn't have the sort of feeling I thought I would have if someone had just robbed us. I felt perfectly fine.

"Well, I can't eat if there's a burglar in the house!" exclaimed Abigail.

"Hold your horses," I said, as patiently as I could. "There's no burglar." I stuffed the last bite of my second slice into my mouth. "I'll prove it to you," I said as I put my hand over the back of her shoulder and nudged her from one room to the next. "See? No one's here. Nothing's missing."

Muffy and Laura followed us. I was confident, but as we entered the living room, I saw that the sliding glass door was open. My family always keeps it shut, or if we do open it, we make sure that the screen door is closed to keep the bugs out. But both the glass door and the screen door were wide open. Abigail saw it too, and she clutched my arm.

Then we saw the bag. My mom's big canvas beach bag lay on the floor, its contents scattered over the carpet.

"Uh-oh!" gasped Abigail. "It's her again!"

"You mean 'she,'" I informed her, "but who do you mean?"

"Why, Mrs. Pitts, of course!" exclaimed Abigail.

"And why would she be creeping into our houses again?" I asked. If you want to know the gory details of the Clam Bar lady sneaking into our houses, you'll have to check out Laura's mystery which she calls *The Haunting of Captain Snow*.

"You don't think it's Mrs. Pitts?" Abigail asked.

"It's got to be someone else," said Muffy, "but who?"

"Those gypsy fishermen!" Laura exclaimed. "You've seen them roaming around the woods. They're probably the ones who're camping illegally. Let's call the police!"

"It may not be the gypsies," said Muffy.

"Call 9-1-1, Mollie," said Laura. "Officer Nick will help us sort it out."

Officer Nick had helped us before. He knew that we solved mysteries, and he was apt to take us more seriously than the police chief or some of the other officers.

"Don't touch anything," Abigail instructed. "Leave it just as it is for the police."

I picked up the phone and dialed. After a brief conversation, I announced, "The police are on their way. I hope Officer Nick will be the one to come."

"Are we going to tell the police that we suspect the gypsies?" asked Muffy. "You know we don't have any evidence. I read that gypsies have been persecuted for hundreds of years. They get blamed all the time for things they didn't do. I know they shouldn't camp in the woods, but it's not such a big thing. Couldn't we just keep quiet? They'll be gone soon."

"But if they took the money," Laura argued, "they shouldn't be allowed to get away with it."

It was obvious that Laura was still angry with the gypsies for tying up to her mooring. She was willing to blame them for this crime as well. Were we obligated to tell the police our suspicions? I wasn't sure. I hoped that the police would be able to figure it out on their own, but I doubted it.

A siren wailed in the distance, and soon a police cruiser pulled up to the house. We ran outside to meet it, but what we saw through the cruiser's windshield filled us with disappointment.

Chapter Eleven

To our dismay, the female officer who was usually on desk duty, Officer Personality we called her, rolled down the car window to greet us. She had a very young officer, what the locals call a "rent-a-cop" (young recruits from the academy who don't carry a weapon yet) in tow.

"What seems to be the problem, ma'am?" the woman asked, sliding out of the cruiser.

Ma'am? I was insulted, but I coolly answered, "As I said on the phone, someone broke into my house." I led the way into the kitchen and showed the officers the countertop where the money had been and explained that we had been upstairs waiting for the pizza man to arrive, when the twenty-dollar bill disappeared. Then we entered the living room, and Abigail pointed out the ransacked beach bag and the open door. "You'll want to dust for fingerprints," I said.

The female officer reacted as if she hadn't thought of that and wasn't so sure it was necessary. When she noticed us staring at her, she reluctantly asked the young policeman to do the job. I wondered if he had ever dusted for prints before. He went out to the cruiser and came back with a little kit. He fumbled around with it for a while, spilling the powder on the floor.

"I got something," he claimed. "But we'll have to fingerprint these kids, so we can tell their prints from the others."

"All right, girls," said Officer Hutton, which was her name according to the badge on her chest. "Get in the cruiser. We're taking a ride down to the station."

We did as we were told. As we drove out onto the road, Mom and Maxwell were just about to pull in on their way home from the Meiers'. They stopped in the road when Mom saw the police cruiser, and I could see the look of shock on her face. She stared at the four of us piled into the back seat, wondering what on earth we had done wrong.

"Stop!" I commanded. "That's my mom!"

Officer Hutton rolled down the window and explained to Mom why we were being taken to the police station. She asked Mom to follow her so she and Maxwell could be fingerprinted as well. It was a short drive down Small Pond Road, through the rotary at Main Street, and left at the ball field. The police station and the firehouse stood side by side on a hill overlooking the ball park.

When we arrived, Mom rushed over to us and worriedly asked, "Are you girls all right? Tell me exactly what happened!"

I filled her in on the break-in.

"That's terrible!" she wailed. "I've always felt so safe! It's awful. Poor little Maxwell will be frightened."

"Poor little Maxwell" looked as if he were ready to steal Officer Hutton's gun, so Mom took his hand and led him into the station.

We were fingerprinted, one at a time, by the young rent-a-cop, whose name was Officer Lopez. After we wiped the black ink from our fingers, Mom asked me, "Who do you think could have done it? I can't imagine that anyone in this town would break into our house!"

"We don't know," I said.

Muffy whispered in my ear, "I didn't want to accuse the gypsies yet, but I'm not sure what's the right thing to do. It was easy to blame them, even though somehow it seems unfair, since they don't speak enough English to defend themselves."

"We were upstairs when it happened," Abigail said, "and we didn't hear a sound."

"I was thinking it might have been those teenagers who've been hanging around," Mom said.

"What teenagers?" asked Officer Hutton, who had been hovering over the fingerprinting process.

"I don't really know," began Mom. "I've never seen them. I've only heard them a few times—when I'm watering the flowers or taking Maxwell down to the beach. I hear them talking and howling. I suppose they're singing—in the woods that surround our house. The voices actually come from the area between our driveway and the harbor."

I gave a sidelong glance at the Girls. They looked back, but we said nothing.

"Let's go have a look-see," replied Officer Hutton. A 'look-see'? Was that some kind of police talk? Maybe she watched too many cops and robbers shows on TV, or maybe it was a real police expression. It sounded corny to me. We split up between the cruiser and Mom's car and drove back to the house. Officer Lopez came along too.

We parked near the garage.

"Where'd you say those voices came from?" Officer Hutton asked Mom, glancing around at the pines.

"From over there," Mom answered, pointing to the woods, the Farrencrows' woods, with the paths leading to the Stellos' and Howie Snow's.

I whispered to the Girls, "Should we show them the campsite we found?"

"Of course we should," Laura whispered back. Abigail agreed, but Muffy didn't respond.

"Excuse me, Officer," I interrupted. "We found a campsite in the woods earlier today. Would you like to see it?"

"Campsite?" Officer Hutton asked. "There're no campsites in this town."

"Not an official campsite," Abigail explained. "Someone's been camping in the woods."

"They built a fire and left their cigarette butts," Laura added.

"I want to see this," said the officer. "Come on, Lopez," she called to her sidekick, who had been awkwardly standing beside her.

I led the way. I was annoyed that Maxwell was coming along too. I didn't want him to know about the paths going through the woods. They were *my* paths going to *my* friends' houses. But there was no way to get rid of him. He hadn't said a word, though, and that was good. Maybe he was in awe of the police.

We trudged along the path towards Louie's, then took the left side of the fork toward the beach. A bit further along we spotted the area where we had found the campfire. The officers quickly left the path and began snooping around, bent over almost double, their faces downward. Maxwell ran over to a wad of paper and snatched it up as if he were on an Easter egg hunt and had found the golden egg.

Officer Hutton saw what Maxwell had done. "Drop it!" she sternly commanded. He let it go, like a hot potato, his mouth open and his eyes wide in fear. I thought he would cry, but he didn't. Instead he ran and hid behind Mom, his lips quivering. He was told by the police not to touch anything and to stay out of the way. For the first time in his life he obeyed. I was glad that someone was able to put that little brat in his place.

Lopez produced a handful of plastic bags, and the two officers carefully picked up the paper and other garbage, sealing each item in a bag. They were very interested in the cigarette butts and sardine cans.

"This could tell us something," Officer Hutton said, holding the bags up for us to see. All it told me was that the campers had bad taste!

"This path goes on down to the beach," Abigail announced. I knew she was thinking about the footprints leading to the water. What would the police think of them?

When we reached the edge of the woods, Officer Hutton stood on the bluff and looked down at the path leading to the beach. It wasn't really a path, just a deep rut full of footprints. She descended on the side and asked us to do the same, not to disturb the evidence, as she called it.

Once on the beach she asked Mom to hold Maxwell's hand and keep him from "contaminating the site." Hutton whispered to the young cop as they followed the set of small prints to the water's edge. There they pointed at the larger prints.

"A missing person's call came in a day ago," Hutton said, approaching us. "Of course, we don't routinely let people file a missing person's report on anyone right away, because they usually show up within a day or two. But it was the girl's mother who called. Even though she was up-Cape, she was calling every police station on Cape Cod. Says her daughter was at a friend's house in the evening and left early to come home, but she never made it."

I wondered why she was telling us about that. What did it have to do with anything?

She cleared her throat. "These look like a young woman's footprints. And it looks as if there was a struggle. After that, she was picked up and taken away in a boat."

I felt my scalp tingle! A girl? Kidnapped? From the look of the trail of footprints, we had considered that the person might have left in a boat, but a struggle and a kidnapping? That changed everything. It was scary. Very scary! More scary for the girl who had been kidnapped and taken away against her will. And scary for me too, living in the neighborhood where it had happened. Scary for everyone in town! I was sure I knew—the gypsies!

"A call came in earlier about a long-haired man in the woods somewhere around here," Hutton continued. That was my call! The officer on duty probably hadn't bothered to take down my name, though I had given it. He certainly hadn't asked for any details, so I was very surprised that Hutton knew anything about it.

"I wish we knew who made the call about the man," Hutton was saying. "The girl went missing 15 miles away, but she could be the one. The kid who put in the 9-1-1 call said 'long hair'."

I had to speak up. "I made the call," I admitted. "I thought it was a man I saw."

"But it could have been a young woman," Hutton interjected.

"Yes, it could have been," I said. "His—her head was down, but she kept looking behind her, as if someone were chasing her."

"Tell me more," she said, scribbling on her police blotter.

"She looked as if she were about twenty, maybe younger, about the age of the older instructors at our yacht club. He—or she—had a long jacket, shorter than a trench coat, wrapped around her."

"Around her shoulders?" asked the officer, crossing her arms and clenching her fists on her upper arms as if holding a garment around her shoulders. She was insisting that the person I had seen was female. Maybe so, but since I didn't know for sure, I went along with her.

"No, she had it on, but not buttoned, held together in front of her, like this." I demonstrated by clutching my T-shirt.

"Why didn't you tell me about all this?" asked Mom, stepping up. Maxwell still hid behind her, holding her skirt.

"When could I have told you?" I asked. I suppose I had had a chance to tell her, but the truth is, I never talk to my mom. That's just the way it is.

I turned to the police. "I thought she might be hurt because of the way she was holding the coat around her. She staggered. And all the while she kept looking back toward the road."

"She was escaping her captors," Hutton replied. She conferred with Lopez. "Is there a quicker way to get back to your house?" she asked me, looking down the beach.

"Yes, along here," I answered, leading the way along the shore. Soon we were at the base of the steps going up to my house. Officer Lopez climbed up ahead of us and headed toward the cruiser. We crossed the lawn as he quickly returned carrying a small box shaped like a briefcase.

"He's going to make casts of those shoe prints," Hutton explained. Lopez traveled back toward the beach and disappeared down the steps. Officer Hutton lingered.

"My goodness!" exclaimed Mom. "That poor girl! Do you really think she was kidnapped? In broad daylight? Who could have done it?"

"The party that made that camp probably did it," Hutton stated. Then she asked. "You haven't seen anyone in these woods?"

"I thought I saw someone early this morning," I admitted, "but it could have been the oak leaves blowing in the wind."

Mom added that she hadn't seen anyone. She'd only heard their voices.

I wondered about my theory. If the gypsies had left earlier, I suppose they could have returned. Should I tell Hutton our suspicion of the gypsies? A girl's life was in danger. Before I could say anything, I was distracted by Maxwell!

He was still clinging to Mom, but suddenly he began to howl. He couldn't stand not being the center of attention. And he got what he wanted. Mom scooped him up into her arms and lugged him into the house. In the meantime, Hutton retreated to follow Lopez to the beach.

I had a thought. Turning away from my friends, I jogged up to the policewoman. "Officer Hutton?" She stopped and faced me. "Uh...have any other missing person reports come in?"

She gave me a hard stare, then rubbed her chin. Was that a police thing? They all seemed to do it.

"Nothing recent," she said. "We did get one quite a while ago from Hyannis. Some old codger ran away from home. Packed up and left without a word to his daughter, so he's not technically missing. Probably went to Las Vegas or Florida. Why?"

"Oh, I just wondered if it happened often," I answered, not wanting to give away the whereabouts of our castaway. He didn't want to be found.

73

I walked back to the Girls and told them what Hutton had said about the castaway. Now we were alone, so we went over to the patio that overlooked the harbor and sat down for a conference. We weren't worried about the old man, but the girl's situation was different.

"Do you think the gypsies kidnapped that poor girl?" asked Abigail, her voice trembling.

"Looks like it," said Laura. "Shouldn't we tell the police about them?"

"I think we should," I said. "I was going to do just that when Maxwell started to holler."

"But we don't have any proof," Muffy stated.

"Let the police find the proof!" I said. "The gypsies will probably write a ransom note. They'll want money. They look as if they need it. They work for someone else, remember? Jake Rison said the owner of those boats lives in New Bedford."

"Fishermen make plenty of money," said Laura, "whether they look like it or not."

"Just because they're gypsies doesn't mean that they did it," argued Muffy. "But maybe we should tell the police what we know. The gypsies could have seen something and are staying quiet about it. They keep getting into trouble, so they don't want any more of it."

"You're right," I said. "Besides, the police don't have a clue. They don't know it's the gypsies who've been camping in the woods. They'll never be able to figure it out without our help. We have to tell them!"

"Of course we do!" Abigail said with emotion. "For the sake of that poor girl! We should tell them about the new campsite too."

"O.K.," I said. "To the beach!"

We raced across the lawn and thundered down the wooden stairs to the beach. We could see the police in the distance, so we jogged along the shoreline to meet them.

"We have some more information," I gasped between deep breaths. "There're gypsies on those trawlers out there." I pointed to the three boats moored near the channel. "We think they did it."

"Why do you think that?" asked Hutton, appearing only mildly interested.

Laura explained her run-in with the gypsies over her mooring, Jake

74

Rison's confrontations with them, and the fact that we saw them in the woods near the old barn.

"Not your favorite people," observed the officer. "Wouldn't mind giving them some more trouble?"

What was she saying? That Laura was accusing them only to get back at them?

"You've got no proof to link them to this kidnapping," she said flatly.

"But we...we saw them in the woods..." Laura spluttered, then fell silent. I could see that Laura thought she was wasting her breath trying to convince the police. "It's no use," she mumbled.

"What about stealing our pizza money and my mom's cash?" I questioned. "Can't you go out to their boats and confront them about that? If you get a search warrant, you can look for the girl at the same time."

"We've got nothing to connect those fishermen with any crime," explained the officer. "Mooring problems and dumping garbage are the harbor master's domain. From what you've told me, he's handling them."

"Hmph!" I exclaimed. I lowered my voice. "We'll take care of them ourselves, Laura."

The police finished up and nodded good-bye before they strode up the beach toward the stairs.

I thought of Howie Snow.

"Let's go see if Howie's home yet," I suggested. "We can fill him in on who's been making the noise in the woods and get him to help us."

"We don't know who it is for sure," Muffy said. "But I have to admit it's probably the gypsies. I'm not accusing them of kidnapping, though."

"We have to find out," Laura said. "The police aren't going to follow the lead we gave them. We have to make sure whether they have the girl or not."

"You're right about that," I agreed.

We charged up the bluff and along the path. At the fork we turned left and continued on until we reached the branch leading to Howie Snow's place. He was sitting on a crate, intently cleaning a lobster pot. He looked relaxed, but did he have a surprise for us!

Chapter Twelve

"Got your note," he said without looking up. "My kitchen was a real mess."

"I guess a hungry little fox can make a really big mess," I remarked.

"Real clever the way he opened the refrigerator and was able to find the cash in my cookie jar!" he continued.

"Huh?" What was he talking about?

"Didn't you see it?" Howie asked, finally raising his eyes to meet ours.

"We saw the fox," I said. "When we were coming around the barn, we heard glass breaking and metal clanging. We crept around back just in time to see the fox run out of your kitchen."

"We thought we might go in," said Laura, "just to check on things, to make sure your house was all right, but then we didn't think we ought to."

"How did the fox get into your refrigerator?" asked Abigail.

"I don't think he did," I muttered. "Howie's trying to tell us that some-one else was in his house. A two-legged fox."

"That's strange!" said Abigail.

"*Very* strange," Howie repeated. "You didn't see no one else?"

"No, we didn't," I said. "But they must have broken in, left the door open, and that's how the little fox got in. Someone broke into my house, stole our pizza money, and went through my mom's beach bag. It must be the same people."

"I've got to call the cops!" Howie exclaimed. He put down the lobster pot and began to stand, ready to head inside to make his phone call.

"Wait, Howie," I said. "There's more."

We proceeded to tell him about the gypsies and their campsites, the one near the beach and the one not far from the old cranberry barn.

"So I've been hearin' singin' gypsies, have I?" asked Howie, shaking his head. "That's a good one!"

"Yes, but that's not all!" Laura continued our news. She told him about her problem with the gypsies tying up to her mooring and how they had dumped garbage in the harbor.

"Dirty dudes," mused Howie going back to his work, waiting for what else we had to tell.

"Wait 'til you hear the rest of the story!" said Abigail. She related the tale of the missing girl and our theory of how the gypsies had kidnapped her.

"What's with our town havin' so many problems?" he asked no one in particular. "You say them trawlers is from New Bedford? I was wonderin' where they was from. I thought they looked like bad news the first time I seen 'em!" He scraped some barnacles off and paused. "How'd the girl git here from up-Cape?"

"We don't know," I admitted. "She must have been kidnapped near her home, escaped, and was recaptured. That's when they took her to one of their boats. We found the girl's footprints in the sand on the beach. They went right down to the water's edge."

"And?" he questioned.

"And we don't know," Abigail answered. "Her prints got confused with the gypsies' prints, but we didn't see them anywhere else on the beach. So she must have been dragged into their boat."

"Or went for a swim," he chuckled. We didn't laugh. It wasn't funny.

"We've got to help her," Muffy said. "The police won't listen to us."

Howie suddenly became diligent with his cleaning and didn't say a word.

"I don't like to accuse them," began Muffy. "And I'm not. We would just like to talk to them. To see if they know anything or saw anything, such as who did it."

"They're the ones who did it!" said Laura. "We can be sure of that."

"They don't speak English either," Abigail informed Howie. "It's not going to be easy to interrogate them."

"Interrogate?" asked Howie, probably wondering why Abigail would use that word.

"Her father's a lawyer," I told him. "Do you have any ideas, Howie?" I asked. I don't know why I asked him. It was worth a try, though.

"I'm not happy about singin' gypsies campin' in the woods an' stealin' my cash and beer!" he retorted. "And I don't appreciate them tearin' up my kitchen. The police can handle that part, but this girl's another story. She needs help, especially if she's been taken by them bums. If the police won't go after those fishermen, I'll do it all right. And I'll be on the lookout for the girl."

"Does that mean you'll help us?" I asked, not really sure of his intentions. "If we come up with a plan, would you really help us?"

"I s'pose," he mumbled. Why was it so difficult for him to just say "yes"? We had solved the "case of the mysterious voices" for him. The least he could do was help us find the girl.

"You'd better call the police now," I told him. "Hopefully they'll listen to you and put two and two together. With two robberies in the same neighborhood, they ought to take it seriously and go out to visit those trawlers. Let us know if you hear anything more or see anything, here or out on the water. And keep an eye on those trawlers." It was a lot for him to do, but he could handle it. He nodded.

We thanked him and said good-bye.

The Girls and I walked back to my house through the woods. It was more scenic than the driveway. The fireflies, or lightning bugs, were just coming out with the evening dew. Clinging to the long blades of the pale grass, they looked like fairy lights. I can't believe that I thought that, but it was true. The grass felt damp as it brushed against my bare legs.

The woods were turning gray. The darkness and quiet made it creepy.

"Couldn't we walk along the beach?" Abigail suggested.

With thieves and kidnappers lurking, I thought it wouldn't be a bad idea to cut to the trail to the beach. Soon we found ourselves out of the woods and standing on the bluff overlooking the harbor. It was brighter and made us feel safer.

We took the beach back to my house. It wasn't that far. We could see a few boats coming in from fishing or a day trip to Nantucket. We went up the wooden stairs and over the lawn. Laura bent down to catch fireflies, whose luminous bodies glowed in the dew. Others glided through the darkness.

"Look at this one!" She held up the biggest firefly I had ever seen. It stayed in the palm of her hand as if it were tame, then lifted off and twinkled over the lawn.

Through the glass doors, I could see that the living room was brightly lit. Mom was talking on the phone, Maxwell crashing his miniature cars on the rug. She hung up as we walked across the patio and slid open the glass doors. The inside handle was still covered with fingerprint-lifting powder, as was the floor.

"That was your father on the line," Mom said, looking up. "He's driving up tomorrow night with an old high school friend."

"Really?" I was surprised. "Doesn't he have to work?"

"You know your father never takes a vacation. His friend has time off and was able to persuade your father to take a few days off too. They ran into each other in the city during their lunch breaks. Even though they hadn't seen each other since graduation, they found out that they have so much in common they just couldn't stop talking. Then when his friend— Frank Picardi is his name—discovered that your dad has a house on the Cape, he didn't want to wait. Frank wants to buy a house up here."

"Sounds weird," I replied, glancing at the Girls. Muffy shrugged her shoulders. They wouldn't understand. This kind of thing never happened in my family. We have a schedule. My dad always works and comes to the Cape most weekends. Why was he suddenly taking a vacation for the sake of some guy he hadn't seen in twenty years when he never did it for us, his wife and kids?

"Dad's friend isn't staying here with us, is he?" I asked, not wanting a houseguest to interfere with my plans.

"Well, probably. We have plenty of room." Oh, well. Maybe having his buddy around would keep Dad occupied while I solved our new mystery with the Eel Grass Girls. I changed the subject.

"Howie Snow had a break-in," I told her.

"Howie too?" Mom was shocked. Her face turned white. "What is happening to our neighborhood? The Cape is supposed to be a safe place! What will become of little Maxwell with all these robbers around?"

I didn't care about "little Maxwell." I rolled my eyes as I led the Girls through the house. We climbed the stairs to my room and plopped on my beds. I lay back, my hands behind my head. Louie was supposed to come over. He should have been here by now. I thought we ought to wait for him before we did whatever it was we were going to do.

Laura stood up and looked out the window. It was considerably darker now. There was nothing to see. But she surprised us by suddenly asking, "What's that?"

"What's what?" Muffy joined her at the window. Abigail and I jumped up and crowded around her to see.

"I saw a light moving in the woods. Down there." She pointed to where I knew the path was.

"It must be Louie," I said. "He's supposed to come over tonight. He can help us prowl around. He knows his way around this town better than anyone."

We clambered downstairs to meet him. I got to the back door first and peered out through the screen. No one was there! We waited, but no one came. The Girls and I stared at each other.

"If it wasn't Louie," Abigail said, "then who was it?"

Just then a form materialized at the screen, right in front of our faces! My heart leapt into my mouth as I stared out, trying to recognize who it was. Was it one of the gypsies—or the girl, escaped from her captors again? Suddenly the screen door jerked opened and the figure burst into the kitchen! What the...?

"Boo!"

It was Louie! Who else? I should have known.

"Did I scare you?"

The Girls didn't reply, but they were breathing hard, looking really annoyed. He had scared them—scared us all. The Girls didn't like Louie. I knew that. He loved to play tricks on us, especially in the dark. This wasn't the first time he had scared the eel grass out of us, but we played cool as our pulse rates returned to normal.

I calmly answered, "We were expecting you. You're late."

"Saw the police down on the beach. Some kind of trouble."

"We know all about it," replied Laura, who had known Louie for years and wasn't the least bit impressed by him. They were in the same grade at the local school. She found him useless and couldn't understand why I wanted to be friends with him.

"Did you notice anyone in the woods when you came over?" I asked.

"Nothing," was his reply. "Didn't hear anything, either."

I filled him in on the gypsy camps, the robberies, and the missing girl.

"Let's check out the woods here first," he suggested.

I didn't like him trying to take over, but checking our woods was exactly what I had been thinking of doing. So I said, "Yes, first we'll show you where the campsite is. It's near the path that juts off from your path. It's on the left before you get to the beach."

"Yeah," he responded. "I know where you mean."

I continued, "If the gypsies aren't at that camp and don't have the girl with them there, we'll have to see if she's on one of the boats. If she's not, we'll have to check out the camp near the Eel...l...old cranberry bog. They may have taken her there, if they didn't leave her on a boat."

Whew! That was close! I had almost said "Eel Grass Palace!" The Girls were glaring at me. Big deal. Louie wouldn't pick up on it even if I had said it. He was a boy.

"I'll get my flashlight," I announced and raced upstairs.

Muffy had followed me up to get her backpack, which she had left in my room. I grabbed the flashlight from the bedside table, and we bolted back downstairs to the kitchen. Just then Mom entered.

"Oh, good evening, Louie," she said. "How are you?"

He grunted and looked at the floor.

"We're going out," I told her.

"Maybe you shouldn't, with that burglar around," she said. "And a kidnapper."

"Louie will protect us," I answered. Not that I believed it, even for a second. We didn't need any protection, and I would never really consider Louie any kind of protection, but I thought my mom would fall for it, and she did.

"The grass is wet so be careful," she called out as we cut through the house and exited by the sliding glass door.

"Be careful of what?" I muttered as we headed out. "How could wet grass hurt us?" No one bothered to answer as we swiftly crossed the damp yard.

Fireflies still dotted the grass. From the way Laura hesitated, I could tell that she wished we had time to catch them, but we didn't. We were in a hurry. We were the Eel Grass Girls. We had work to do. There was a young woman who, at that very moment, was being held prisoner by a band of singing gypsies. It sounded more comical than dangerous, but it *was* dangerous. And it was our new mystery. We had to solve it.

Louie took the lead. Onto the path he sped, into the thick darkness of the woods. I had to admit that I felt safer with him leading the way. It wasn't because he was a boy, but because he knew the woods and all the paths better than we. He also knew how to handle situations. Anyway I hoped he would know how to handle the "situation" we were about to confront.

Chapter Thirteen

Louie could see in the dark, or so it seemed. I had my flashlight, but he asked me not to use it. He moved through the inky blackness like a cat, and before I knew it, he was veering to the left, and we were headed toward the campsite. We almost lost him, even though we were tagging him as closely as we possibly could. No one wanted to get lost in the woods at night, especially with robbers and kidnappers on the loose.

Louie slowed his pace, but we could see and hear absolutely nothing. I was sure the gypsy camp was to our left, but there was no fire and no light of any kind.

"No one's here," he stated.

"Rats!" I whispered, though there was no point in whispering in the deserted woods.

"Maybe they set up camp in a new place every night," Muffy speculated. "And that's why they were looking around the woods near the old barn."

"Let's go out to the trawlers now," I said. "We know the gypsies will be off the boats and camping near the bog and maybe somewhere else too, so we won't have to worry about anyone being onboard. When we find the girl, we'll call the police. They'll catch those guys, and it will all be over for them. Abigail, did you bring your cell phone?"

"How did you know I had my own cell phone?" she asked, sounding puzzled. "No, I didn't bring it—I left it at home."

"Great!" I said with sarcasm. A cell phone would come in handy, but only if we had it with us. "Hey! Where's Louie?"

Louie had disappeared in the blackness!

"He must have gone on to the beach," said Abigail. "Let's go. I don't like standing here all alone."

"You're not alone," I said. I made sure I was still on the path. "Follow me."

"Since when do you have your own cell phone?" Laura asked Abigail as we stumbled along in the dark.

I wished they would stop chattering. Our mission was serious, but Laura wasn't exactly high tech. Her parents didn't even have a clothes dryer! I guess that's why she was so curious about the cell phone.

"After all the trouble we've been having," said Abigail, "Grammy ordered me a cell phone of my own. She gave it to me just this afternoon when I got home. I was going to tell you all about it, but so much has been happening, I didn't get the chance."

Louie met us on the bluff.

"How're you going to get out to the trawlers?" he asked. I was perturbed that he had ditched us in the woods. Our plan would go more smoothly if we stayed together, but I didn't want to say anything to him. That would mean admitting that we needed him to navigate the woods.

"We'll think of something," I assured him. The beach below looked like a gray scarf draped along the edge of the dark harbor. I looked out to the black shapes on the water. Not a single light. The three trawlers were in total darkness. No one was onboard. Now was our chance. We needed to get out there.

"Looks like they're deserted," Muffy observed.

"Don't you think they left a guard on duty?" asked Abigail.

"Maybe not if they tied the girl up and locked her in the hold," Laura speculated. "They might not bother to leave a guard if there's no way for her to escape."

"I don't like this," Abigail informed us.

"Shouldn't we scout out their other camp first, before we make the trip out to the boats?" asked Muffy. "If the girl is with them, it'll save us the bother of getting ourselves out there to the trawlers."

"We're almost there now," I said. "The boats are right in front of us. All we have to do is go out, take a look around, and if she isn't there, we'll still have plenty of time to check the camp."

"There's no wind," observed Laura. "Otherwise we could sail out. I'm afraid we'll have to row."

Abigail sighed. "It's so far."

"We can take turns rowing," I suggested. "Howie's boat and oars are just down the beach. We can borrow them." I moved in the direction of Howie's landing.

"Are you sure?" asked Muffy, following behind me. "He's so weird. If anything should happen to his boat, we'll really be in trouble!"

"It's an old custom," Laura informed us. "You're allowed to borrow anyone's rowboat, as long as you bring it back when they need it."

"A custom from when?" Muffy asked. "A hundred years ago?"

"Howie won't need his boat tonight," I said, picking up the oars from under the boat.

Louie helped us flip the rowboat over and drag it into the water. I steadied the boat as the Girls hopped in, piling into the bow and stern. Louie and I sat on the middle thwart, side by side, each taking an oar. We pulled hard, making good headway out to the channel. Laura and Muffy directed us.

If you've never rowed before, you might not know that when you row, you sit with your back toward the direction you're going. You face away, so you can't see where you're going. Some people row the other way around, so they can see where they're headed, but that way you wouldn't be able to pull as hard on the oars, making your travel slower.

"On your starboard," Laura called out in a husky whisper. I had to think which side was starboard. My right oar hit the glowing hull of a motorboat.

"Oops!" I twisted around to see boats everywhere! We had to weave in and out, zigzagging through the maze of obstacles: buoys, motorboats, sailboats, channel markers, moorings, and fishing boats, to get to our destination.

Louie was going strong, but I was getting tired. There was too much weight in the boat. Four Eel Grass Girls and one Louie Stello made the boat drag. Halfway to the channel, I confessed, "I can't do this anymore! The tide must still be coming in. Who wants to row?"

"I will," volunteered Muffy. The boat wobbled as we exchanged places.

In the stillness, the harbor was silent. There were lights on a few yachts, long sailboats, and grand motorboats moored in the deep waters.

Beyond the channel, Laura took over. Was Louie stronger because he had been doing yard work with his brother all summer? Probably, but I was glad he was strong. It made it easier for us. I wondered how we would get back to shore. I was pooped. My arms ached. I wasn't complaining, though.

We were almost there. There were more important problems at hand.

"What's our plan?" whispered Abigail. "We can't board an unoccupied boat. That would be trespassing."

"I know, I know," I answered. "The missing girl's most likely tied up and stowed below deck on one of these hulks, but how can we get to her if we can't go onboard and search?"

"Knock," said Louie.

"Huh?" I didn't understand.

"Knock on the hull. If she's in there, she'll answer."

"What if she's gagged?" asked Laura, not thinking much of Louie's idea.

"She'll answer," he insisted. "She can kick or bang her head. Put your ear to the hull. You'll hear her."

It sounded reasonable to me. We glided up alongside of the *Wind Dance*. Laura caught hold of a thick line hanging down over the edge. Muffy and Louie pulled the oars in and secured them under the thwart.

"O.K., knock!" I instructed. Muffy gave a tap on the side of the boat that sounded like a pat on the back. "Not like that! Harder!"

"My hands hurt!" she said. "It's not that easy."

Louie had picked up one of the oars and gave the boat a few good whacks. Maybe they were too hard. I would have been worried about damaging the paint job, if the boat had been in good condition, but it was in serious need of a new coat of paint.

Abigail, Louie, and Muffy all put their ears to the side of the boat and listened while Laura and I balanced the rowboat. We couldn't all listen at the same time. If we moved to the same side of the boat, it would tip over. But there was no sound. Nothing. Louie whacked again. Still no answer, only the gentle lapping of the current against the side of the trawler.

Abigail switched places with Muffy to take her turn at rowing. Silently we moved through the black waters to the *Sea Song* and repeated the process.

"Are you sure this will work?" asked Laura. "If she's in a cabinet or something, how do you know we could hear her?"

"We could," Louie stated. He didn't have a boat, but his brother did. Maybe he knew. He knew a lot. There was still no sound. There was only one more boat for us to try.

Chapter Fourteen

We had to round the *Sea Song* to get to the *Ocean Rose*. I wondered what secrets these boats held. If only we could understand the gypsies' language, we could have learned a lot about them from the argument we had overheard earlier in the day, when Jake had accused them of dumping their garbage into the harbor. But as it was, we knew nothing except that the boats were from New Bedford, and they would be leaving tomorrow.

As it was, the *Ocean Rose* came up on my side.

"Let me try," I said to Abigail.

She handed me the oar to do the honor of giving the hull a few whacks. I reached out for the oar and felt it with my hand, but it was so dark that before I had a good grip on it, Abigail let go! A big splash let everyone know what had happened. The oar had dropped into the water!

"Oh, no!" she wailed. "I'm sorry!"

"Get it, quick!" I practically shouted, but the current had taken it beyond the side of the rowboat. In an instant, I could no longer see it! Louie was still holding the other oar, so he quickly began to paddle hard. I thought I saw it floating alongside the trawler. Louie brought us to within reach of the runaway oar. Muffy stretched out her hand to grab at it, but it slipped away again!

"Curses!" I exclaimed. The oar disappeared into the dark shadow of the *Sea Song*, making it impossible to see where it had gone! I dreaded trying to get back to shore without it. Then we heard a gentle clunking sound. It came from midway along the side of the *Sea Song*. Paddling over, we caught sight of the oar, trapped against the boat's long hull.

Laura was now seated on the center thwart. She expertly caught hold of the oar and pulled it in. We all breathed a sigh of relief. Laura then helped Louie row back to the *Ocean Rose*.

"I'm really sorry," Abigail apologized as we covered the short distance. "I didn't mean to drop it."

"Forget it," I said.

"It was an accident," Muffy consoled her.

"Technically, an accident is something that can't be avoided," I said. "Letting go of the oar was a mistake. And we're detectives, so we can't afford to make mistakes."

Oops! I hadn't meant to say "detectives"—not in front of Louie! He would think that I meant that we were acting like detectives, I hoped.

Louie had helped us with one of our mysteries, but we didn't want him to know that we were the Eel Grass Girls, real detectives solving real mysteries. It was our secret. Of course our parents and Billy Jones knew a little about our mystery club, but we didn't want anyone to interfere. We liked having their help when we needed it, but we didn't want anyone to bother us about our work when we wanted to be left alone. Does that make sense?

"We've got to act like professionals," I continued. "The water is no place for 'accidents' that can be avoided. Next time wait until you feel that I have a good grip on the oar before you let go."

Abigail meekly uttered, "I will, I promise."

"Don't be so hard on her," said Laura. I ignored her. We had an important job to do. There was no room for coddling.

We were at the *Ocean Rose* now, and the boat was on my side again. Abigail and Laura had traded places. This time I carefully took the oar from Abigail and gave the side of the battered trawler a couple of good whacks. Abigail and I listened. Laura, in the bow, put her ear to the peeling paint of the hull as well. Only silence. The second series of whacks didn't produce a response either. Short of boarding the boats, there was nothing left to do.

For some reason, Laura must have still been trying to listen to the hull, because she suddenly said, "Wait! I hear her!"

"Huh?"

"Listen!" I put my ear back to the peeling wood, as did Louie. Laura was right—we could hear a faint tapping! The girl had responded. She was trying to communicate with us. We had found her!

Louie and I paddled the rowboat to the stern of the *Ocean Rose*. There we saw a rope ladder hanging down. Laura held onto it while I climbed up. When I reached the deck, I looked toward the hold. The girl was down there, but it was pitch-black. I wasn't going in there without a flashlight. Where was it? Just as I thrust my hand into my shorts pocket to get it, two gleaming eyes appeared!

Was that the girl? A piercing bark broke through the darkness! I stepped back, almost falling backwards into the water. A huge, black beast came bounding across the deck, straight at me!

"Holy Cow!" I cried and flung myself over the edge of the boat, missing the ladder and falling heavily into the rowboat below. The boat rocked violently as I screamed, "Shove off! Shove off!"

Louie pushed away just in time. The animal leapt up, its two front paws grasping the railing. It looked as if it would jump off the trawler right into our rowboat, but the big dog stayed on deck. It peered down, barking viciously.

"That was close!" I gasped, trying to collect myself. I was actually trembling. "Let's get out of here."

"What about the girl?" asked Abigail. "Aren't we going to rescue her?"

"I don't think she's there," said Muffy.

"What do you mean?" Abigail was confused.

"It was the dog's tail-wagging that we heard," said Laura.

Muffy said, "Let's knock on the boat again, just to make sure."

We moved in a wide arc around the bow of the boat, to keep away from the dog. We had to get close to the boat again, but we didn't want the dog to try to leap overboard onto us. We came in under the bow.

This time Abigail hit the boat with an oar. The dog barked, but we heard no other sound. Laura was right. It had been the dog we had heard. I imagined that Fido must have been sleeping, and when he heard us, he thumped his tail on the floor, making the tapping sound.

"Head for shore," I commanded. "It's time to find out where those gypsies have taken the girl."

Abigail and Louie pulled away on the oars. I shook myself to stop shaking, if that makes sense. Boy, did that dog give me a scare! I didn't know if he would have bitten me or not, but I was sure glad I didn't have the opportunity to find out. Who ever heard of leaving a watchdog on a boat? I hadn't, but maybe next time, it was something to consider.

The current was flowing in the same direction as we were,

sweeping us back to Howie's landing. In no time we were pulling the row-boat ashore and replacing the oars.

"Where's your bike, Louie?" I asked as we jogged down the beach to my stairs.

"It's at home," he said. "I can go with one of you."

"You can go with me," I offered. "There's a path leading from a field near the yacht club to the Snows' old cranberry barn."

"I know," Louie said simply. We skittered across the lawn to the garage where our bikes were parked. I let Louie pedal my bike, while I sat on the seat. I didn't care if he did all the work.

Soon we were at the field. We stashed our bikes in the bushes, hopped over the split-rail fence, and cut across the long grass. It was really dark and I didn't like the looks of the woods, but Louie barged right in and we blindly followed.

He wove through the trees, his shirt a gray smudge bobbing up and down ahead of us, leading us deeper and deeper into the darkness. Finally, there was a light up ahead. We slowed down and crept closer. We could see the campfire. Loud voices broke the silence—raucous laughter, boisterous howls, and bizarre singing. It was the gypsy fishermen all right. There they were, sitting around their fire, eating out of tin cans, leaning against the pines or on blanket rolls. But there was no girl!

"Where is she?" asked Abigail in a hushed whisper.

"We know she's not on any of the boats," Muffy answered. "Where could they have hidden her? On one of the islands? In an abandoned building? The old cranberry barn!"

"That's got to be it!" Laura exclaimed. "That's why they're camping here. It's near the barn. Come on!"

Louie didn't say a word, but suddenly he was ahead of us, leading the way to the barn. We shifted off the path to get around the camp. Fortunately, the gypsies were so loud, they didn't hear us stepping on twigs as we thrashed through the brush. Soon we reached the dilapidated barn and slipped inside the back door. We stood in the big, musty space with zero visibility.

"Do you think they left a guard here?" Abigail asked. "Or another guard dog?"

90

"I hope not," I said, switching on my flashlight. We waited, but saw and heard nothing. I assumed they would have left the girl tied and gagged without a guard. I hoped that I was right.

"We have two flashlights, don't we?" asked Laura.

Louie produced his, but we decided to stick together rather than split up. We tiptoed around the barn, poking into every corner and behind every pile of junk. The barn contained an assortment of antique cranberry harvesting equipment and stacks of wooden boxes which had been used for packing the tart red berries. Then we heard it—a faint rustling! Oh no! Was it one of the fishermen guarding the girl? Or was it the girl herself?

Louie boldly stepped forward, toward the sound.

I panned the beam of my flashlight into a heap of old boxes and burlap sacks, where we could still hear the sound. To our surprise, we could see a series of little beady eyes peering up at us!

"What are they?" asked Abigail, leaning forward and gripping my arm at the same time.

"A nest of baby raccoons!" exclaimed Laura.

"We don't want to meet Mama Raccoon," warned Louie. "We'd better get out of here."

"We can't leave until we finish searching the barn," Laura told him.

I have to admit that my heart was still pounding as we continued our search. We wanted to find the girl, but I hadn't expected the baby raccoons, even though they were better than finding a kidnapper.

We made our way around the barn, but found nothing. No one. No one else besides the raccoons, that is. Where had the gypsies hidden the girl? We slid the big door open at the front of the barn and walked outside. I sat on the fence beside the dirt road which led out to Yacht Harbor Road.

"We'll never find her," complained Abigail. "Maybe they did leave her on Womponoy or Freeman's Island or somewhere like that."

"Don't be ridiculous," I said. "She could walk off Womponoy at low tide, and our castaway would have found her if she were on Freeman's Island."

"But what if she were tied up?" Abigail persisted.

"The National Seashore rangers are all over Womponoy. They would find the girl in no time," I told her. "They're always snooping around out there, looking for something to stick their noses into and meddle with." I was thinking of the sea gulls they had poisoned and coyotes they had shot—all to protect a certain kind of shorebird. Their new crusade was to prevent local shellfishermen from fishing on the island. If killing one kind of wildlife to protect another doesn't make sense to you, I know how you feel. We couldn't figure it out either. You would think they would protect *all* wildlife.

"What do we do now?" Muffy queried.

"Let's go home and sleep," I said. "Maybe we'll get some bright ideas while we're sleeping."

"Why would the gypsies want to kidnap the girl?" asked Louie as we groped behind the barn and back into the woods.

"Keep your voice down!" I whispered. "They want ransom money."

"Wouldn't they send the ransom note to the girl's parents?" Laura asked.

"Sure, I suppose," I admitted.

"That would mean the police would be contacted by her parents, and it would be up to the police to handle it," added Muffy. "We can tell them what we know, which is where the girl isn't."

We fell silent as we neared the camp. The men were still partying and seemed awfully happy for men who were kidnapping and stealing. I guess they were pleased with themselves for pulling it off and having hidden the girl so well we couldn't find her. We trudged on until we reached the field. Soon we were pulling our bikes out of the bushes and riding along the harbor.

"Hey! What's that?" Louie stopped suddenly and we almost had a pile-up collision! He wasn't trying to kill us all in a late night bike crash. He'd seen something really strange that complicated our new mystery!

Chapter Fifteen

"What's what?" Muffy asked, looking around.

"I saw a light on one of the fishing boats!" he answered.

"Which one?" Laura asked.

"I think it was near Howie Snow's dory," he said. "But it's gone now."

"It was probably just a reflection," I said.

"I saw it," he insisted.

"We're not going to row out there again, are we?" Abigail asked with a definite whine in her voice.

"Should we?" Muffy asked, looking around at our faces.

"Why?" I asked. "People come and go from their boats at all hours. It wasn't one of the gypsy boats, so why should we care?"

"There's a lot going on in the harbor because of those guys," said Laura. "We can go down to the shore and watch. We don't want whoever it is to see us spying on them. We'll take cover, just in case."

"Just in case what?" I asked, dumping my bike in the bushes once more. The others did the same, and we cut across a lawn and down some wooden steps to the beach. We crouched behind a boathouse and some beached dinghies. This time we all saw the fishing boat light.

"I told you so," growled Louie.

Soon we saw a boat glide away from the fishing boat and could distinguish two figures seated in a small motorboat. We crept along the beach and watched as the duo boarded several other boats in succession. From their posture, we could tell that they were off-loading equipment or supplies of some sort. We couldn't go home now. We had to try to find out what they were doing and who they were, but we had strong suspicions.

At last the boat traveled across the channel to one of the trawlers. We thought it was probably the *Sea Song*.

"It's two of the gypsies!" Laura's tense voice pierced the darkness. "We should have known! What more proof do we need?"

"But what exactly are they doing?" asked Abigail.

"Stealing, of course!" I said in disgust. "While the rest of them are partying in the woods, they've sent two of them out on a stealing spree!"

Muffy asked rhetorically, "What is this world coming to?"

"They've been stealing from houses along the harbor, why not from boats?" asked Laura.

"I'm glad we weren't out there at the same time," Abigail said. "It would have been terrible if they had caught us on their boat! Shouldn't we call Jake Rison?"

"He won't appreciate being awakened at this hour!" I said.

"But he'll be able to catch them red-handed if he comes now," Laura argued.

"Abigail, you've got to learn to bring your cell phone," I scolded her.

"I know, I know," she wailed.

"So let's go to my house and call the police from there," I suggested. "Laura's house is closer, but mine is safer. Mom won't ask any questions, even if she wakes up." Mom was only concerned about Maxwell. I was basically on my own.

We scurried back to our bikes and headed to my house. Louie stopped at my driveway.

"See you tomorrow night," he said and vanished.

I was glad to have my bike back to myself. The house was pitch-black by the time we got there. Mom and Maxwell were sound asleep. We quietly entered the kitchen to call the police. I flicked on the light as Muffy picked up the phone and dialed 9-1-1. She gave all the information about what we had seen.

"Do you want us to meet you on the beach?" she asked, breathlessly. There was a pause. "Don't you want our phone number so you can call us back when you catch them?" We waited. "Then I'll call you."

When she hung up the phone, she looked upset. "I don't think they're taking me seriously! I'm going to call Jake Rison. Where's your phone book?"

I fished the phone book out of a drawer and she dialed. By the way she was talking, I knew she had gotten an answering machine.

"Did you call his office?" I asked.

"Yes," she replied.

"Try his home phone then," said Laura.

Muffy found the phone number but had to leave another message on an answering machine. "What if they get away?" she moaned.

"They won't," I assured her. "Maybe we should go back and see what happens. The police might show up any minute, and Jake will try to find those thieves as soon as he checks his messages."

"I think we'd better get home," said Abigail. "It must be late. Grammy won't worry because she knows that we're together, but I can't stay out all night."

"Let's meet in town tomorrow morning," Laura suggested. "How about the bandstand at ten? Then we'll stop by the police station and see who they've caught."

We agreed on the plan.

"You have the longest way to go home, Muffy," remarked Abigail.

"I'll ride with you as far as your house," Muffy said to Abigail. Laura lived just a few houses away from me. I watched the three of them set off into the dark, then I shut the back door. I was looking forward to crawling into bed.

As I crept up the stairs, my mind drifted off to thoughts of the castaway. I could forget about him now. He didn't want to be rescued and was perfectly happy camping out on Freeman's Island. The gypsies were our only problem now. They were committing little crimes of illegal camping and polluting and the very big crime of kidnapping. And tonight we had witnessed more robberies!

I couldn't think straight anymore. After brushing my teeth, I threw myself, fully clothed, onto my bed and knew nothing until the bright sun awakened me the next morning.

Chapter Sixteen

I lay in bed remembering what we had seen the night before. As I dressed, or rather changed my clothes, I hoped that the police had caught the gypsy thieves. Then the police would be sure to search the gypsies' boats and get them to confess to the kidnapping and tell where the girl was hidden.

I headed downstairs and grabbed a granola bar on the way out to the garage. Mom and Maxwell were off someplace. Maybe they were on the beach, but that didn't bother me. I had work to do.

I biked out to the road and decided to go down Pine Street and pass by Small Pond. It was probably a little longer than going by the yacht club, but I wanted a change. Main Street was still quiet. A few tourists were buying coffee and big-city newspapers from the handful of variety stores in town.

It was almost ten by the time I parked my bike next to the bandstand that stood in the middle of the park in the town center. The green grass sparkled in the morning sunlight. I stretched out on the bandstand steps and waited for the girls. I couldn't help thinking about the kidnapped girl. Where were the gypsies keeping her? How could she be found before it was too late?

Soon Abigail rode up.

"Hi, Mollie!" she called out. "How did you sleep?"

"Huh? What kind of question is that?" I asked. "I fell asleep with my clothes on and woke up feeling great, only I can't get that kidnapping out of my mind."

Before Abigail could answer, Laura appeared from the left side of Main Street and Muffy from the right. Muffy was prepared for today and tomorrow with her backpack and life jacket.

"Hey, Girls," I called to them. "Hurry up!"

They coasted down on their bikes and joined us on the bandstand steps. The bandstand was a gazebo-like structure where the town hosted a concert every Friday night. It was an Eel Grass Girl favorite.

"O.K.," I said, huddling them around. "We've got to focus on this kidnapping. The gypsies have stashed the girl somewhere, and we have to find out where."

"I say we wait until they send their ransom note. The police will get clues from it," said Laura. "Then we can go from there."

"The police won't notify us when the note comes in," said Abigail. "I doubt that they ever called back last night. Am I right, Mollie?"

"Of course," I said. "But Officer Nick will tell us what's going on."

"The police chief might not tell him everything," Muffy said. "But we can let him know we need the information. He may be able to find out the details and give us some clues. Until then, I don't think we can do much to help, except pray."

"That's a good idea," said Laura. "Let's pray."

"Don't include me," I said, moving away to the far side of the bandstand. "But go ahead. Pray, if you think it will help."

"Pray with us," begged Abigail. "The more people pray, the more likely it is to work."

"Won't God listen to you three?"

"He'll listen," Muffy said. "But it would be nice if we *all* participated."

"I don't believe in God or in prayer. Besides, God won't really appreciate it if I pretend to believe in order to manipulate Him."

"You're talking as if you do believe," said Laura.

"Well, I don't. Hurry up and get it over," I commanded them. They tried to drag God into all our mysteries, but I didn't get the point. The Girls never considered that if there were a God, we wouldn't have to solve mysteries. He, or She, or It, would take care of all the problems in the world. Hmmm. But then, what kind of world would that be? No problems would mean no surprises, wouldn't it? Might be boring. Well, He didn't exist and that meant we had plenty of problems to solve on our own.

"Please, God," I could hear Muffy saying, "help us find the kidnapped girl. Protect her and keep her safe until she can be found. Catch the bad guys. Amen."

It sounded good, but the truth was, we couldn't sit around waiting for God to answer that prayer. We had to do the work ourselves. Muffy wasn't even giving God any clues, so how could He help? She hadn't even told Him that the bad guys were gypsies.

But let's say that God *could* help, that is, if He were real. What did Muffy expect him to do? Come down out of the sky with a big sign saying, "The girl is in an old shack on Womponoy" or "Look for the robbers at the Nor'easter"? Now that would be helpful, but it was ridiculous to expect it to happen. I let them have their prayer meeting. It made them feel better and didn't do any harm.

"If church is over, we've got to get to the police station and talk with Officer Nick," I said. Muffy gave me an exasperated look.

I gave her a blank look and asked, *"What?"*

We jumped on our bikes and made our way down Main Street. There were a few more cars on the road by now, but it was a good day for the beach, and most of the vacationers were going there, so the traffic wasn't too bad. We were careful anyway. There was no need to get whacked by some tourist opening a car door in front of your bike.

At the rotary, we made our way past the ball field to the little hill where the police station was situated. A few patrol cars were parked outside next to a fire truck in the process of being washed. We entered through the screen door and looked at the officer on duty. He had a buzz cut and didn't look familiar. I marveled at the fact that such a small town had so many police officers. He looked up.

"Uh...Hi!" said Laura. "Is Officer Nick in?"

"Nick Eldredge?"

"Yes, I guess so," she answered. "Unless you have another Officer Nick." He gave her a suspicious look, then checked what I presumed was a schedule.

"He's not here."

"Where is he?" I asked. "We have to talk to him."

"I can't give you that information," he said. It seemed as if he thought we were the enemy, instead of good citizens trying to do a good deed.

"How about the chief? We'll see him instead," I told him.

He seemed to soften a little and sighed heavily. "Who shall I say wants to see him?"

I was impressed: He used correct English! "Mollie, Laura, Abigail, and Muffy."

"Huh?"

"He knows us," I assured him. He clicked on the intercom. Instantly the chief came to the doorway of his office, which was at the back of the station house. He wore a tired and irritated expression. I suppose he thought it would be easier to give us a few minutes of his precious time rather than instruct his flunky to get rid of us.

"Girls! Come into my office." He sounded polite, as if he might really want to talk to us. We entered the tiny office.

"Have a seat," he offered.

We squeezed onto two chairs as he seated himself behind his metal desk.

"I heard you gave us a lame tip last night."

"Lame?" I shouted at him, jumping up and leaning over his desk. "It wasn't lame! We saw those two gypsies going from boat to boat! They were unloading stuff, and we saw them take it back to one of their trawlers! If you had gotten there sooner, you would have been able to catch them! Didn't you find the goods?"

"Oh, we sent someone out there, all right," he answered, unfazed. "Jake Rison visited the trawlers this morning and he didn't find a thing, I mean not a thing out of the ordinary."

I glanced at the Girls. It was *déjà vu*. This couldn't be happening to us again! But it was.

"I suggest you girls spend your evenings playing board games and getting a good night's sleep," he said with a benevolent smile.

"Thank you, sir," said Abigail.

I wanted to kick her, but I stamped out of the office instead. I was steaming.

"Of all the idiotic…!" I blurted out as soon as we were outside the station.

"Take it easy, Mollie," said Muffy. "If Jake Rison couldn't find anything, what was the chief supposed to do?"

"It just proves that those gypsy thieves are smarter than we think," said Laura. "We have to outsmart them. They must have taken the goods to the trawler first, then taken them and hidden them somewhere else later last night. Maybe they're hiding the girl in the same place. Officer Nick will help us, and Jake will too. A robbery on the water is his department, and he might have some ideas."

"Crumpets!" I said as angrily as possible.

"What?" asked Abigail. "Isn't that some kind of food?"

"You and food!" I said. I was running out of good expressions to use to express my frustration. But I certainly wasn't thinking of eating. Not at a time like this.

"What's next?" asked Muffy. "Should we talk to Jake?"

"Let's talk to him later. We should go to my house now," suggested Abigail. "Maybe Grammy's made another coconut cake."

"What?" I asked. "Are you serious?"

"It will help us think better," Abigail said. "We can't think straight if we're hungry. Let's go."

"Let's stop by my grandparents' house first," said Muffy. "I want to see my Grammy too." We agreed to make the stop. I didn't have any grandparents, but it was obvious that the Girls liked their relatives, and spending time with them was part of our routine.

I had calmed down and was glad to be out on the road again, pedaling away from the police. We went toward the rotary, to Main Street. Muffy's grandparents' big summer house sat atop a terraced lawn a little way down the street on the left. Mr. McLaughlin was asleep in a wicker chair on the front porch. We entered the driveway, parked our bikes near the garage, and climbed the back steps to the kitchen. Mrs. McLaughlin was there, making lunch.

"Oh, girls! How nice to see you all!" she said. Muffy moved forward to receive a kiss on her cheek. "You're just in time for lunch. Would you like some nice ham sandwiches on rye?"

It sounded horrible to me, but we said yes.

"Muffy, why don't you pour the milk for everyone and take this out to Grandpa? He's on the front porch."

We helped get the glasses and plates ready, and within minutes we were seated on the steps of the front porch eating our lunch. Mrs. McLaughlin had joined us, and her husband had awakened. We watched Main Street activity as if we were watching a movie.

It was the usual parade of tourists in loud clothing pushing baby strollers, kids on bicycles and skateboards, and a continuous stream of cars inching now along the narrow way. We accepted the bumper-to-bumper traffic, but it seemed so out of place in a small fishing village like this. Yet, it was August, the most popular summer month for vacationers. The scene was amusing, but then we saw something truly interesting!

Chapter Seventeen

Officer Nick! There he was, patrolling Main Street! We had to talk to him. I excused myself and thanked Mrs. McLaughlin for lunch as I bounded down the terraced lawn to the street. Laura was close behind me.

"Hey! Officer Nick!" I called out.

He turned and smiled at us. "You girls have been up to your old tricks, I've heard."

"They're not tricks!" I said defensively. "We've been trying to help you guys fight crime, but it seems that your police chief isn't interested."

"What can he do when we can't find the culprits, the stolen property, or any evidence of a crime having been committed?" he asked, smiling sympathetically at us. At that moment, Abigail and Muffy joined us. We moved off the sidewalk into a little park with a Civil War memorial in the center of it. At least we were out of the way of the pedestrians, but we were in full view of the McLaughlins and the entire town.

"Hasn't anyone reported anything missing from their boats?" asked Abigail.

"Not a single person," responded the young officer.

"That doesn't mean much," I said. "A lot of people don't use their boats every day and might not go out until the weekend. You'll have complaints about missing equipment sooner or later."

Laura said, "We know it's those gypsies—the ones who're on those fishing boats moored in the harbor. You do believe us, don't you?"

Officer Nick nodded and waited for her to continue.

"They've been camping out in the woods at night, and we clearly saw them stealing from other boats last night, but the police chief told us that when Jake Rison searched their trawlers, he found nothing."

"That doesn't mean that they didn't do it," Abigail put in. "But we don't have any proof, except what we saw."

"You girls have telescopic night vision?" he asked.

"We saw them," I repeated very slowly, so he could grasp the meaning. "There were two of them. They went from boat to boat. The one who boarded came back carrying something each time, bending over with the weight. What do you think they were doing if they weren't stealing? They had no right to board anyone's boat one way or the other." The fact that I boarded one of the trawlers came to mind, but that was different. I had been searching for a kidnap victim, not stealing.

"I believe you," he said earnestly. "But you need evidence. Give us something concrete, and we'll take it from there. In the meantime, what do you girls want from me?"

"Let us know if you get any new information," Muffy answered. "Then we can piece it all together."

"And put a stop to all this stealing," added Laura.

"Any new leads on the kidnapping?" I asked.

Officer Nick looked shocked. "You know about the kidnappings?"

"Officer Hutton told us about the old man and the girl yesterday afternoon when she came over to investigate the robbery at Mollie's house," Abigail informed him. "We could see that the girl was kidnapped by the gypsies."

"Her footprints were trailing across the beach," Muffy stated. "They went from the woods near Mollie's to the edge of the water. There were lots of other prints there too. Big ones. That's why we think the gypsies kidnapped her."

"I heard they're still checking on the prints," Officer Nick said. "Then there were all those robberies too. Yours, Snow's, and the Smiths'."

"The Smiths'?" Muffy asked in surprise.

"Yes. Your neighbors, Mollie," said Nick. "They called in late last night. When they came back from the theater, they discovered that someone had broken into their house and taken some money, jewelry, and liquor.

"Aha! Those fishermen are all over the place stealing everything they can get their hands on," I said. "There are enough of them—three boats full."

"And we got a new report about another woman missing," the officer continued.

"A woman from town?" asked Muffy.

"Yeah, from town," he replied, shaking his head in dismay. "Mrs. Bartles. We don't know what to make of it. We've got three missing persons. It's rare for the Cape to have one missing. Even though two of them are

103

from Hyannis, the fact that one of them was seen in town after she disappeared makes the two cases connected. The man's gone off-Cape, we think."

"Wow!" I exclaimed. "Three victims!"

"Kidnappings are committed for a reason," said Officer Nick. "We're expecting to hear any time now that ransom notes have been received by the families."

"I think it's very scary," Abigail said.

"Three kidnappings is serious!" I commented.

"What should we do?" asked Abigail.

"Keep your eyes and ears open," said Officer Nick. "We suspect the kidnappers have the women hidden away somewhere in town. This is a very urgent situation. You girls and I can share information, but whatever I tell you can't go any further. The chief wouldn't appreciate me telling you anything, even if you're helping with the investigation."

"We understand," I said. "Thanks, Nick—I mean, Officer Nick. You're a true friend."

We said good-bye and turned to go back to the McLaughlins'. Muffy led the way back to the front porch where her grandparents were still sitting, enjoying the view.

"What a handsome young officer," commented Mrs. McLaughlin as we sat down on the wide, gray-painted steps. "It's so nice that you've made friends with him."

"He's one of them rent-a-cops," observed Mr. McLaughlin.

"Oh, don't say that, dear," Mrs. McLaughlin chided him. "He's from the academy, and this is his summer job. It's similar to an internship. He's learning how to be a policeman while he's on the job."

"Not much good that'll do us," Muffy's grandfather complained. "He doesn't even carry a gun. No crook will respect him."

"The policemen in England don't carry guns," Muffy informed him. "And England is surviving."

"Barely," he responded grimly.

"Do you have a new mystery going on?" Mrs. McLaughlin asked her granddaughter.

"Uh, there's always something mysterious going on in this quaint little fishing village," Muffy joked, avoiding the mention of the gypsies. Then she quickly changed the subject. "How about some dessert?"

"I don't think we have a thing in the house," her grandmother replied, jumping up from her chair to conduct a search of the pantry and refrigerator.

"Oh, Grammy, don't bother," said Muffy. "We can go to the ice cream shop. We wouldn't mind, and we were headed to Abigail's house anyway."

"Well, thank you for stopping by," she responded. "It's always so good to see you, dear, and all your little friends." She smiled warmly.

We thanked her for lunch. It wasn't that bad. In fact, the sandwiches were quite tasty, considering they were made of ham and rye bread. After saying good-bye to Muffy's grandfather, we exited through the kitchen and went down the back steps to get our bikes.

The Girls and I pedaled down Main Street to the ice cream shop and leaned our bikes against the   side of the picturesque building of gray shingles and pink trim. Inside we placed orders for ice cream cones in our favorite flavors. Soon we had our desserts and were back outside on weathered gray picnic tables under flowering trees. We licked away, concentrating on eating, but we couldn't help picking up snatches of conversation from the table next to ours, where two middle-aged women were close together eating huge chocolate sundaes.

"... Bartles is missing!" said one, whose hair was dyed an unnatural shade of black.

"I heard! Her husband Jeff said she went out for a walk on the beach last night and never came back!" said the other woman, whose pudgy face was rimmed in hair that had been the recipient of a very bad perm.

"Where do they live?" asked Black Hair.

"On Deer Island. That's where she disappeared," responded Frizzy.

The four of us were listening intently by now. The women didn't seem to notice that we were eavesdropping.

"Poor Jeff!" lamented Frizzy. "He must be worried sick."

"You know he is! And I heard that the police can't find a single clue. There's not a trace of her. Seems like she vanished into thin air."

Frizzy had an idea. "Aliens!" she nearly shouted. "They always show up during the summertime."

"What do you mean, 'they always show up'?" Black Hair gasped and paled noticeably. "They've been here before?"

"Oh, yes," her friend replied knowingly. "I see them most every summer. The alien space ships, I mean. Up there in the sky, twinkling like stars, hovering over the harbor, just waiting for someone like Millicent Bartles to go off walking alone."

Black Hair gave a shudder, and they fell silent. Then they went on to talk about a new outlet opening up in Muddy River, the next town over.

The Girls and I exchanged glances. "This must be the woman Officer Nick told us about. She disappeared from Deer Island, right on Yacht Harbor!" I said in a low tone. "That's not far from where the trawlers are moored. Those gypsies have gone too far! That frizzy-haired woman's theory isn't going to help us, unless we're prepared to investigate aliens."

"The gypsies are aliens, technically," said Abigail. I rolled my eyes.

"And so are you," laughed Laura. "All of you are, except for me. I'm the only local Eel Grass Girl."

"O.K., O.K.," I intoned. "Are we aliens going to visit Abigail's grandmother or not?"

"We are," answered Abigail. "Come on."

We threw our paper napkins into the trash barrel and hopped onto our bikes, riding toward the lighthouse. I felt unnerved by the new information about another kidnapping. The gypsies were out of control. It was one thing to tie up to the wrong mooring and dump garbage into the harbor, but it was atrocious to rob boats and go crazy stealing innocent citizens!

Turning off Main Street, we wound our way to Abigail's grandmother's house, near Snow Pond. When we arrived, Uncle Jack and his friend Freddy Frisket were seated on the porch beside Abigail's grandmother. They were enjoying Mrs. Lincoln's famous coconut cake.

"Here come our little mystery-solvers!" Mrs. Lincoln exclaimed as we entered her circular driveway. "Please join us."

"I'll get more plates and forks," said Abigail, parking her bike and dashing up the porch steps and in through the screen door to the kitchen. The other Girls and I seated ourselves on the mismatched chairs which lined the old porch. I tried to keep calm, but my mind was whirling around, trying to form a plan of action.

"Have you heard about my new career?" Freddy asked us.

"Oh, yes," Muffy replied. "You're going to fix up old houses and sell them."

"That's right!" he proudly said. "I can stay here in this gorgeous town and still do my day job over the Internet—that is, as long as Mrs. Lincoln will allow me to stay."

"I love having you around." Mrs. Lincoln doted on him. "You and Jack are so much fun, and I approve of your new girlfriend!"

"I have a new girlfriend?" asked Freddy, looking around for verification. We giggled. Both he and Uncle Jack had begun new relationships during our last mystery.

"The more young people the merrier," Mrs. Lincoln continued as Abigail returned with a plate-and-fork-laden tray. "It was quite a lonely winter without my dear husband. Even though I traveled for much of the time, visiting my friends, I felt the loss."

"Grandpa is in heaven," Abigail stated. "We do miss him, but he's waiting for us. One day we'll all be there with him, and we'll never be separated again."

She sounded so sure. That kind of thinking amazed me. Heaven, hell—it was all a big fable. A fairy story. I had trouble understanding how so many people, even smart people, could believe it.

I had to admit that we had seen some strange things this summer, some of which could not be explained, but I wasn't ready to admit that they proved that there was a God who had something to do with our lives. The supernatural occurrences had been coincidences. Still, the older I got, the more I noticed that some things have no rational explanation.

Abigail served the coconut cake. Even after my favorite ice cream cone, I had room for a piece of that cake. Everyone did. It was the best cake in the world. We ate in silence. Uncle Jack and Freddy were talking.

"It's the news all over town, Mother," Uncle Jack was saying. "They say a woman from Deer Island is missing too."

I assumed that they were talking about the girl, the old man, and the Bartles woman, but it was someone else entirely!

Chapter Eighteen

"It says here that the man is quite respectable. His wife is going crazy," Freddy said.

"What happened?" asked Mrs. Lincoln, obviously stunned by the news. We were too! The Girls and I listened attentively.

"He went out for a stroll after dinner last night, and his wife hasn't seen him since," said Uncle Jack.

"And who is he?" Mrs. Lincoln asked. "Where was he when it happened?"

"Let me see." Freddy picked up one of the papers on the little table beside him. "His name is Otis Wilton. And he lives on Sea Gull Way. Where's that?"

"Why, it's on the other side of the lighthouse, off the dyke road leading to Deer Island!" Abigail's grandmother answered. She was horrified. This was strange news. "It's so near!"

"You mean the island isn't an island?" asked Freddy.

"Oh, you know, Freddy," said Uncle Jack. "When we take the boat out of the marina, it's that causeway to the left. It's the strip of land they filled in so people would be able to live on the island and get on and off at all times, rather than waiting for low tide."

"Excuse me?" I asked. I hadn't heard that one before.

"What he's trying to say," Mrs. Lincoln continued, "is that Deer Island used to really be an island, but after a while the harbor changed, and the island became accessible by foot and car, but only at low tide. At one point, maybe thirty years ago, a causeway, or dyke, as some like to call it, was built. Once the island was connected to the mainland, it was developed. I suppose the developer had the road put in. Otherwise, no one would have bought the lots or built homes out there. You would think the dyke road was a perfectly safe place to go for an evening stroll."

We were always out at night and usually considered every place in town to be safe. But I had to admit that certain residents or visitors could make the place quite dangerous, as we had found out in the course of the summer.

"The woman who disappeared lived on Deer Island," observed Uncle Jack. "It seems quite a coincidence."

"It is!" Mrs. Lincoln was quite upset.

Freddy rustled the papers again. "I read about two others who are missing also. Here it is. A girl, last seen near the beach at Yacht Harbor. And an old man. But the police think he's in Las Vegas."

"I've never heard anything like it!" exclaimed Mrs. Lincoln. We'll all have to be cautious if we go out alone, especially you girls."

"We will, Grammy," Abigail responded.

The Eel Grass Girls had to talk. This was too much. Four missing persons was way too many. Of course, the old man was our castaway and he was fine, somewhat, but it seemed that the gypsies were on a terrible kidnapping rampage!

Abigail caught my eye. "We're going swimming," she announced.

"Did everyone wear a swimsuit?" her grandmother asked.

"Probably not, but I have enough extras," Abigail said. We stacked our plates on the tray, and after thanking her grandmother and excusing ourselves, we headed to the kitchen.

"What do you think of that man disappearing?" Muffy asked. "It's really incredible that he and that woman both vanished last night!"

"I'll say!" agreed Abigail as she hurriedly loaded the dishwasher. "That can't be a coincidence. If no one heard anything, the gypsies must be using guns or knives to threaten their victims so they won't scream. Then they tie them up and drag them away in their boat. Isn't it just awful?"

"We've got to stop it!" declared Laura. "But aren't the gypsies supposed to leave the harbor today?"

"They're supposed to go," Muffy answered. "But if they've kidnapped all these people, do you think they'll just go away?"

"We have to think of something to do," said Abigail. "Jake Rison and the police should be patrolling the harbor. If they had responded right away to our call about the boat robberies, maybe they could have prevented these other two kidnappings."

"But they wouldn't listen to us," I complained. "We're too young to be taken seriously."

"Let's go swimming and maybe we'll be able to think of something we can do to help," Abigail suggested.

"We're not really going to swim in Snow Pond, are we?" asked Muffy. "It's so muddy and covered with an oil slick from all those motorboats moored in there."

"It's not that bad," Abigail replied. She continued with another thought. "I know what we can do. Tonight we can keep an eye on the harbor from your house, Mollie. I think that's the best way to help. Maybe we can prevent someone else being kidnapped." We all agreed it was the best, most logical, and possibly the only thing we could do.

After we trotted up the back stairway to her bedroom, Abigail rummaged in her drawers until she found a swimsuit for each of us. Fortunately we were all about the same size.

Abigail handed us beach towels from the linen closet in the hallway and grabbed a tube of sunblock. We went downstairs and out the back door. The gardener, Slim H., had pulled up in his old truck and was unloading his lawnmower. He nodded to us as we passed by. We had questioned him when we had been solving our other mysteries because he knew the town and most everyone in it, but he wasn't easy to talk to—and I doubted that he would have any information for us on this mystery.

"Hi," Abigail greeted him. "What do you think of all the kidnappings?"

"Them summer people're always gettin' theirselves into trouble," he responded. With that, he yanked the cord on his old lawnmower, drowning out any further conversation with the roar of its engine.

We passed by him and went out to the lane and down the hill to the narrow beach. So much for our informant. When we reached the pond, we walked along the water's edge until we came to an old pier.

"This is where Louie and I go fishing," I said. We walked to the end of the pier and sat down, dangling our legs over the edge, into the water. Abigail let herself down and then vanished below the surface of the pond. In a second she popped back up.

"It's deep! It must be high tide."

I dove in, making a big splash, so the others were sure to get wet. Laura and Muffy jumped in after me and soon we were playing games and having fun, forgetting our mystery for a short while. We couldn't think about it every second. We needed a break, and sometimes we came up with an idea when our minds were on something else. But that didn't happen this time. We swam between the motorboats and sailboats, pleased that the changing tides had cleaned the oil off the water a little. Abigail's idea to watch the harbor tonight was good enough.

One by one we climbed back onto the pier and stretched out on our towels. Abigail shared her sunblock with us. We absorbed the warmth of the sun and lay there on the pier without talking, just listening to the gentle lapping of the tide against the boats. Wisps of conversations carried across the pond. We could hear the peeps of shorebirds as they scurried through the sea foam, looking for dinner.

When I noticed that the sun had shifted, I sat up. "Let's go to my house," I said. "If the gypsies are still moored in the harbor, we can get ready to scout around tonight. Louie can help us. If those gypsies haven't left yet, they're sure to try something again."

"Like trying to kidnap us?" asked Abigail, picking up her sunblock and towel. "Can't we watch them from your window, Mollie?"

"No. We have to at least go down to the beach."

"Then we'd better be careful," Abigail warned. "If they can kidnap all those adults, they won't think twice of trying to grab us."

"What about your dad coming up?" asked Laura. "Is that going to interfere with our investigation?"

"Why should it?" I asked. "I'll be at home, basically. What more could he want? Anyway, he can't be thinking of spending 'quality family time' if he's bringing his old school friend along with him."

"You're right," Muffy said. "Let's go."

We followed the path along the beach and back to the lane. When we got to Abigail's, we rinsed off in her outdoor shower. Her grandmother must have heard us because she met us at the door with clean towels to dry ourselves off and wrap up our dripping hair. We raced upstairs to change back into our clothes. Abigail stuffed her pajamas and toothbrush into her backpack for the sleepover.

"Don't forget your cell phone," Muffy reminded her.

"It's already packed!" Abigail replied smugly.

"Program the police and Jake Rison's numbers into it," I suggested as we clambered down the front staircase.

At the foot of the stairs she stopped at the telephone stand and looked up the numbers in the phone book. After she put the numbers into the phone's memory, we were all set.

On our way out of the house, Abigail dropped our wet suits off in the laundry room and grabbed her life jacket. Out on the front porch we said good-bye to Mrs. Lincoln. She told us that Uncle Jack and Freddy had gone off to look at an old home that had just been put on the market.

The shadows lengthened as we rode down Lowndes River Road and over the bridge. Tourists were still fishing, and Cooky was closing up the Clam Bar. Mrs. Pitts was already gone. I wondered if she were the one stealing from our houses, but her previous thefts had been linked to the mystery we were solving at the time and had nothing to do with money or beer. She couldn't be a suspect in this case, I decided.

After we pedaled by the yacht club, we rode along the harbor and looked out. The three trawlers loomed near the cut. Obviously they weren't going away. I wanted the gypsies to leave, but not if they had three people stashed away.

We stopped off at Laura's house to get her things for the sleepover. When we got to my house, Mom and Maxwell were still out. We climbed the stairs and dumped everything in my bedroom and stretched out on my beds. Just as we were getting comfortable, the phone rang.

"I've been trying to reach you all day!" It was Jake Rison.

"What's going on?" I asked breathlessly. "Did you catch the gypsies? Did you hear they've kidnapped two more people now? What are you doing about it?"

"Wait a minute, wait a minute! And hold your horses! What's all this about kidnappings?"

I filled him in on the missing girl, how she disappeared in the woods, and how we found her tracks on the beach, tracks surrounded by men's footprints, all leading to the water.

"The police didn't tell me all that!" he responded. He had heard about the other two disappearances and thought that it was strange the way they had all occurred on Yacht Harbor. "But I wanted to tell you what's going on with the off-shore robberies. The gypsies showed up at my office first thing this morning. They say that they were robbed, too."

"What?" I was incredulous!

"Vital equipment missing. We have to let them stay until we can find it," he was saying.

"Are you sure it's really missing?" I asked.

"The items they reported stolen are not on their boats. They can't leave or go out fishing without it. There's nothing we can do. The town can't send them away," he reasoned.

"And you believe them? You think they were really robbed?" I asked, aghast. "They made the whole story up because we suspect them. If they say that they are victims too, you'll stop investigating them. Am I right?"

"Miss Parker," Jake began, "you ought to be able to admit that you're wrong."

"I'm not wrong," I protested. "Don't you see that they're making a fool of you?"

"Fool or not, we have to follow procedures. I want to get those trouble-makers out of town more than anybody, but if they're stealing and kidnapping, the place for them to go is jail. Now tell me exactly what you saw."

I told him that we had seen two gypsies go from boat to boat. "I wish I knew where they're hiding the things they stole. If they were locals, they would use their garage or barn, or they'd know some abandoned property where no one would ever look. But where would the gypsies hide all that equipment, if it's not on their boats?"

"I'm sure a walk around any neighborhood could turn up a good hiding place," said Jake. "I was caught off guard when they appeared this morning saying they had been robbed, but I think you're right about them trying to get me off their trail. As long as their hiding place isn't too far from the shore, those men are strong enough to haul off all the equipment they've been stealing. But we're supposed to presume they're innocent until we can prove them guilty."

"We saw them do it!" I said. "Isn't that proof enough?"

"They say they're victims too, and their boats are clean," said Jake.

"Clean?"

"Figuratively speaking. Help us find the proof, and we'll nab them. All this crime is bad for business."

"Business?"

"The tourist business."

"Who cares about that?" I argued. "As far as I can tell, tourists just get in my way, try to run me off the road, and throw their litter around when they leave. What good are they?"

"I bet your family first came to town as tourists," he said gently.

"We'll keep our eyes open," I concluded. I didn't need any more lecturing. I hung up the phone and told the girls everything that Jake had said.

"The gypsies were robbed too?" asked Abigail.

"Of course not!" said Laura, bitterly. "They're just saying that so no one will suspect them."

"But we saw them!" said Muffy. "I don't want to blame them, but we know it was them."

"They," I informed her. She wrinkled her nose at me.

"What's for dinner?" asked Abigail. "Pizza again?"

"I doubt if Mom remembered to leave us any money," I lamented.

"Why don't we pool our money?" asked Abigail. "Maybe we have enough."

The Girls pulled open their backpacks and searched their pockets. We scraped together enough money for a plain pizza so I called the local pizza parlor. When I gave my name and address, I was glad to hear that Mom had stopped by earlier that morning to pay for last night's pizza.

We lounged around on the beds talking about the Captain's Ball until we heard the pizza man knocking at the front door. We greeted him with handfuls of coins and dollar bills. It was the same delivery man who had come last night. He smiled, though, and didn't complain.

"Your mother gave me a big tip!" he told me. I took the steaming box from him and he left, whistling as he went. The four of us stampeded to the kitchen, where we piled around the table to dig in.

"What do you have to drink?" asked Muffy, jumping up and looking into the refrigerator. She pulled out some sort of carbonated juice that I had never seen before. I supposed that Mom had gone shopping and remembered that my friends were coming over and decided to buy something new.

When we finished eating, we moved into the living room to play a board game, as the police chief had suggested. Of course our playing the game had nothing to do with him—we would have done it anyway. After a couple of rounds, Louie appeared at the glass door, scaring me half to death. I really wished that he wouldn't do that. The Girls weren't pleased with his behavior either, but no one made a comment.

"Louie, come in," I said. He opened the screen door and entered. I began to update him on the robberies and kidnappings.

"I heard about those people," he said. "They say it was aliens."

"We heard that one too," Laura said with a smirk.

"Have you heard anything else?" I asked him. Because he was a local kid with a teenage brother, it was possible that he could have found out something important.

"Nah." Oh, well. This was not an easy mystery.

"After it gets really dark, let's go down to the harbor and see if they try something again," I said.

"It's getting dark now," Abigail said, motioning to the glass door, where the lights on the harbor were now shining, as well as a few stars. "Do you think Jake questioned all the people who are staying on their yachts?"

"He must have," Muffy remarked. "You have your cell phone with you?"

"In my pocket," Abigail proudly replied.

We were all ready. "Then let's go."

Once outside, we crossed the lawn. The grass was slightly damp with dew. The fireflies were gliding slowly through the warm air. Down to the beach we went and settled on the sandy point between my house and Laura's, where we had a good view of most of the harbor.

"We should have brought a blanket," said Laura, settling into the damp sand.

"Yes, it's kind of cold," added Muffy, "but let's be brave."

"What if they see us sitting here?" asked Abigail. "We're so exposed."

"Don't worry," I assured them. "Just relax. Enjoy a beautiful evening on Cape Cod. Look! We have the water, a clear sky, no bugs. What more could you ask for?"

"I could ask for a warm blanket," muttered Laura.

We sat there and waited. Before long, our efforts were rewarded.

Chapter Nineteen

As I said, we were waiting. Exactly for what, we didn't know. The gypsy trawlers were dark, that was for sure. We assumed most of the gypsies would be in the woods camping. It was the others that we hoped to see.

We watched for activity. There was a rowboat moving out toward a yacht. A fisherman rowing in from his "gill netter" to the town pier. A motorboat cruised in through the cut, as well as a two-masted sailboat under power. Night fell, and the activity continued. Someone was hosting a party at a house beyond Laura's. The sounds of laughter and voices drifted toward us.

"We came out too early," complained Muffy. "The thieves won't strike until later."

"How late was it when we saw them last night?" asked Abigail.

"Not very late," said Laura. "But there're too many people on the harbor now. The crooks will wait to strike."

"What is that over there?" I asked, pointing to Deer Island. A small motorboat cruised out of the marsh toward the gypsy trawlers.

"It's them!" whispered Abigail. "Do you think they just kidnapped another victim on Deer Island?"

"Could be," I said, watching anxiously. The boat approached the trawlers. Even though it was dark, we could see one of the gypsies as he held onto the trawler while the other one boarded. I wondered if the new victim was tied up in the bottom of the boat. Soon the gypsy onboard reappeared. He seemed to be carrying something heavy!

"Hey! They're unloading the things they've stolen!" Laura exclaimed. "Let's see what they do with it."

"They sure are slick," I muttered.

"Slick?" Abigail asked, not understanding my term, which meant slippery or slimy.

"Dial Jake Rison!" I almost hollered. She fumbled in her pocket and produced her new cell phone. She dialed his work number first.

"He won't be there, but I'll leave a message," she explained while

116

the phone was ringing. "I'm sure he calls in to check his messages. Then I'll call his home."

Unfortunately, Jake wasn't at either location. Abigail left the information along with her cell phone number. We continued watching as the motorboat headed across the harbor.

"They're heading for Small Pond," said Louie. He hopped up and started for the steps.

"Did you bring your bike?" I asked him, hoping he had. I didn't want a repeat of the night before. Louie was my friend, but sharing a bike with anyone is no fun.

"Yeah" was all he said as he sprinted across the lawn. We jogged to the garage where we all grabbed our bikes and pedaled down the driveway to the road. Louie led us past his house to Smith's Landing. The road ended in a tiny parking lot on the very edge of Small Pond River, which flowed into Small Pond.

"Look!" Muffy gasped. A small motorboat was mooring a few yards away from us. "Get back!" she whispered.

We quickly hid our bicycles in the thick bayberry bushes bordering the parking lot, and we crouched down behind the same clump to continue our vigil. A boat shed stood to our right, and cement guard rails were lined up in a row on the landing straight ahead. We crept along the side of the parking lot, hoping to blend in with the bushes and trees to the left. Had they seen us? Or heard us? It seemed that they hadn't, because the two gypsies began to silently unload their cache into a waiting rowboat.

"Whose boat are they using?" mouthed Muffy. I shrugged my shoulders and continued watching.

Before long, the two gypsies rowed ashore. In the dim glow of the lone street light, we could see their colorful knit sweaters and caps. The two of them hoisted their loot out of the rowboat and onto the beach. I was thankful there wasn't another kidnap victim among the goods.

After pulling the boat up as far as possible, they clunked an anchor into the sand. One of them moved to the boat shed where he put a key into the padlock on the door. How did they get the key? They lugged the goods into the shed and stashed them inside, locked the door, and cut across the beach grass beyond the shed. Where were they going?

Louie nimbly bounded across the parking lot, paused at the corner of the shed, then disappeared after the two men into the dark. We cautiously followed. Soon the thieving gypsies and Louie were lost in a maze of scrub pines. We halted, not wanting to get lost ourselves, but before we knew it, Louie was standing in front of us!

"Where did the gypsies go?" Laura demanded.

"They disappeared at Miller's Cottages!" Louie panted.

"Where's that?" Muffy asked.

"Who's Miller? Fill us in," I demanded.

"Mollie, keep calm. Bob Miller has a bunch of little cottages he rents out over on River Lane," said Laura before Louie could answer. She pointed in the direction from which Louie had appeared. I had heard of River Lane and knew it was somewhere in the neighborhood. Laura added, "Mr. Miller usually rents to college kids working in town for the summer."

"Yeah, nice work they're doing," I murmured, sarcastically. "Do you think they're working with those crooks?"

"They must be," Laura said. "The kids must be letting the gypsies use their motorboat and the shed, and they're selling the stolen goods for them! What a bunch of creeps!"

"Abigail, call Jake, quick!" I commanded.

"But he's not home," she answered. "Remember?"

"Then call the police," said Muffy.

Abigail dialed, but looked up at us, puzzled. "The call's not going through!"

"What?" I grabbed the phone from her and dialed 9-1-1. Nothing. "It must be the battery."

"Or it could be the location," Laura speculated. "Let's get to your house, Mollie, and call from there."

So much for technology! We rode furiously back toward my house, but at Louie's driveway he said good-bye.

"I'll call you tomorrow," I yelled over my shoulder as we pressed on. "Or just come over," I called out, my voice piercing the summer night.

Barreling up my driveway, I was shocked to see the house lit up like a Christmas tree. I almost stopped short, but I kept going. I had forgotten that my dad was coming up with his "new" old friend.

"Your mom's still up?" asked Muffy as we parked our bikes in the garage.

"Houseguest, remember?" I answered. "My dad's old high school buddy."

"We forgot," said Abigail.

"So did I," I said, pulling open the back screen door.

Loud laughter and voices came from the living room. It sounded like a party!

"What's going on?" I asked, peeking into the living room.

I was shocked by what I saw: Maxwell was having a toy sword fight with another monster his own age, Mom was seated on the couch chatting with a bleached-blonde woman who was wearing way too much makeup, and Dad was sitting across from Mom talking to a loud, overweight man with curly brown hair. A girl, about our age, was seated alone on a footstool off to the side. She had black shoulder-length hair and black eyes. She didn't look very happy. In fact, she looked downright disagreeable!

We ducked back into the kitchen. The police had to be called. I dialed. Officer Hutton was at the desk.

"This is Mollie Parker. We just came from Smith's Landing. We saw two of the gypsies in the harbor, robbing boats. We followed them and saw them stash the goods in a boathouse on the right, and then they went to Miller's Cottages."

"Slow down, ma'am," she replied.

"Don't you remember me?" I asked, exasperated. "You were at my house yesterday! After you left, at night, we spotted two gypsies stealing from moored boats and called the police. Now they've done it again, but this time we know where they hid everything they stole."

"How'd you know they weren't just moving stuff off their own boats?" she placidly asked.

"Tonight they were taking things from one of their own boats, but last night we saw them board other boats as well!"

"Where did you say they put the stuff?"

I repeated the information.

"What'd they look like?"

"Two gypsies. Knit caps and colorful sweaters. Will you let us know when you catch them?"

She didn't give me any promises. If she didn't contact us, we'd call her. I hung up feeling satisfied.

"They'll catch them soon," I announced. "Those gypsies sneak around the harbor every night, so the police ought to station a lookout there. Then maybe they can catch the rest of them the next time they rob someone's boat or try kidnapping again."

"I thought people were basically honest," Abigail mused.

"Ha!" I responded. "Well, we'd better meet those people in there." I indicated the strange family in the living room.

Mom suddenly appeared in the doorway.

"Oh, there you are!" she said. "We were beginning to worry about you!"

My friends greeted Mom, and she led the way into the living room to make the introductions.

"This is our daughter Mollie and her friends Mora Cortez, Abigail Lincoln, and Laura Sparrow," she said to the fat man and the bleached-blonde, who I presumed were my dad's friend and his wife.

"Do you always stay out so late?" the man laughed, looking up.

"Only when we have a sleepover," Muffy answered before I could open my mouth. It was just as well because I couldn't think of a smart answer to his dumb question. Of course, we often stayed out late, but that wasn't public information.

"This is Frank Picardi, his wife, Mrs. Picardi, Georgie, and Brittany. She's just your age," said Mom, as if I cared. "She'd love to be included in your sleepover."

The girl looked as if it was the last thing on earth she wanted to do. It was certainly the last thing I wanted.

"Oh, Brittany loves sleepovers, don't you Brittany, honey?" the mother cooed. Brittany grimaced. I hoped she would speak up and say she wasn't interested and didn't want to stay with us, but she kept quiet.

"Maybe it's time for us to hit the hay," remarked Mr. Picardi, standing up and stretching his legs. "Are there any hotels in the area?"

"There are quite a few in town, but please stay here with us, why don't you?" offered Dad. "We have plenty of room."

"Oh, no. I'll see who's got a vacancy. Give me a name," insisted the man.

"The Inn on the Bay is lovely," said Mom. "Let me telephone them for you."

Mr. Picardi already had his cell phone out and information on the line. He was connected in no time and fortunately they had room. Mrs. Picardi had stood up by now, and Brittany was whispering in her ear.

"We'll see you at the inn for breakfast, Eddy, say 7:30?" Mr. Picardi was obviously a control freak. And my father's name was not "Eddy." He preferred "Ned" or "Edward," but definitely not "Eddy."

"Uh, that's a little early for my family," said Dad. "How about nine?"

"Eight o'clock it is." He shook Dad's hand. "Great to see you again after all these years! What luck to run into you yesterday and just imagine—here we are on old Cape Cod! Who'd a thunk it?"

"Brittany's going to take a rain check on the sleepover," Mrs. Picardi told Mom. "She's a little shy."

"Oh, come on, Brit!" her father practically shouted. "We came all this way to see the place. You gotta make friends. She'll stay. I'll get her bag out of the car."

"Would Georgie like to stay over with Maxwell?" Mom asked.

"Sure," said Mrs. Picardi, without even asking Georgie. He and Maxwell were still play-fighting, yelling, and stumbling into the furniture. I already hated this family. Brittany gave us a sour look. Why did she have to be such a wimp? Why couldn't she insist on going with her parents? We didn't need this. The Eel Grass Girls had work to do, a mystery to solve. Brittany would be in our way.

"It might be nice to have breakfast here, rather than at the inn," said Mom.

"Meet us at the inn," said Mr. Picardi, who had already returned from their SUV with the kids' bags. He seemed used to getting what he wanted. Mom and Dad gave in. Then I had an idea, a way to get rid of Brittany, I hoped.

"Mom, the Girls and I have sailing school first thing tomorrow morning," I said as meekly as possible, trying not to show my real intentions. "Brittany won't be allowed out in a sailboat. It won't be any fun for her."

"In that case, you can stay onshore with her," Mom suggested.

"But I need the practice!" I implored.

"Missing one day won't hurt," she said.

Rats! My plan had backfired! It would be agony sitting on the yacht club deck with Brittany while my friends were out sailing. The Girls gave me sympathetic looks. I felt so aggravated. I wished I could think of a way to get her to leave, but I couldn't.

"We're really tired, Mom. Could we go to bed now?" I asked.

"Certainly. Good night."

Dad kissed me on the cheek. I ignored the boys. The Girls and I said good night to the adults, and we headed up the stairs. Brittany trailed behind us.

When we got to my room, I realized that there was no place for Brittany to sleep. I only had two beds, and there was hardly room for us with two girls in each bed. When Brittany saw the situation, she bolted back downstairs. I could hear her telling her mother that there was nowhere for her to sleep. Mom came up to my room.

"Mollie, you and one of your friends will have to sleep on the floor so Brittany can have your bed," she explained. "Where's your sleeping bag?"

I got it from the closet and spread it out on the floor.

"I don't mind sleeping on the floor," said Muffy.

Brittany was back, inspecting my bed.

"Are these sheets clean?" she asked no one in particular.

How was I supposed to know? Changing the sheets wasn't my department. Mom had already begun stripping the bed. I knew this girl would be trouble. Her scowl was worth a thousand words, as the expression goes.

Abigail helped Mom make the bed. I pretended to be fixing my sleeping bag. Muffy and Laura unpacked their backpacks.

"Where do you live?" Muffy asked Brittany.

"New Jersey."

"Which town?" Laura queried.

"You wouldn't know it."

Mom could sense the tension, so before I could even open my mouth, she said, "The bed's all made. Why don't you girls wash up and go to sleep? We have to get up early tomorrow."

"I know," I groaned.

As we headed for the bathroom, Muffy whispered, "Something good will come of this."

I rolled my eyes.

"Have you ever been to Cape Cod before?" Abigail ventured.

"What do you think?" Brittany asked with a sneer.

I had had enough. I faced Brittany and stood so she couldn't pass me in the hall. "O.K., Picardi! It's time for you to shape up or get out of my house!"

A look of shock swept across her sallow face, but it didn't last. A defiant smirk quickly replaced it. That irritated me even more.

"Get the point?" I asked, putting my hands on her shoulders so she was pinned against the wall. "I don't want you here any more than you want to be here. My friends are trying to be nice to you, but if you don't want to stay with us, leave. Your parents are still downstairs. If you can't stand up to your old man and tell him you want to go with them to the hotel, then shut up and put up."

Brittany straightened her shoulders as she considered her options. She said nothing and sauntered into the bathroom and began to brush her teeth. The Girls were startled, but kept silent. Laura gave me a questioning look. I was disgusted with Ms. Picardi and didn't even want to use the same bathroom as she, so I detoured into Mom and Dad's. Muffy followed, but the other two Girls stayed with Picardi.

We began brushing our teeth. "You sure know how to treat a house guest," Muffy mumbled, her mouth full of toothpaste.

"The sooner they go back to New Jersey, the better," I said, brushing furiously. I then attacked my face with a soapy cloth. "No wonder my dad doesn't have any friends from his high school days. If they're all like Mr. Picardi, I'm glad he's lost touch with them. Too bad he had to run into Mr. Picardi yesterday."

"The whole situation is awfully strange," Muffy said. "Your dad doesn't seem like the type to take a trip all of a sudden, without any planning."

"Dad's not the type to take a trip. Period. We come up here for the summer, but Dad comes up just on weekends. We never go anywhere else as a family. It makes me angry that this Picardi guy could talk Dad into bringing him and his horrible family up here when Dad never takes us anywhere. It doesn't add up."

Muffy shrugged and finished flossing her teeth. "Tomorrow's

another day," she said, in an attempt to cheer me up.

"I'm really looking forward to it," I said as sarcastically as possible.

"The police haven't called us back," she remarked. "I'm going to call them and see what's happening."

We entered Mom and Dad's room and sat on the edge of the bed. Muffy dialed the police non-emergency number.

Muffy explained who she was and why she was calling. She didn't like whatever the police officer said to her.

"I beg your pardon?" she almost screamed into the phone. "That can't be true! You sent them to Miller's and no one was there?" I looked intently at her anxious face and waited. "Did you search the shed?" There was a pause. "But we saw them! They unloaded the stolen property right in front of us!"

I mouthed, "What's going on?" She put her forefinger to her lips to tell me to be quiet.

"I understand that you need a search warrant," she said, "but the shed has to be guarded until you can search it, or it'll be empty by the time you get there!"

Frustration changed her face into a frown. She replaced the receiver. "Can you believe the gypsies got away? Everything they stole will be gone by the time the police get a search warrant—if they ever get one! They'll never catch those guys!"

"Unbelievable!" I was so disappointed. We had given the police all the evidence they needed to arrest the gypsies on robbery charges, and now they had let the two men escape.

"Where could those two men have gone?" asked Muffy.

"I don't know," I responded. "The police must have arrived too late, or maybe the gypsies ran off into the woods when they saw the police cruiser. How will they find the kidnap victims now? Arresting the gypsies for robbery is the only way to get them into the police station and make them talk!"

"We'll talk to Officer Nick again tomorrow after sailing school," said Muffy. "He'll help us."

"I hope so, but he may not be able to do much" was my summation of the situation.

We returned to my room, where Brittany was already in my bed. Ugh!

Abigail was in the other bed, and Laura was rummaging in her backpack. They didn't see the disappointed look on Muffy's face, and we couldn't discuss our case now, not with Brittany there.

"See you tomorrow," I said as I turned out the lights. The floor beneath my sleeping bag felt hard, but I didn't care much. I was tired. Muffy settled in, and we fell asleep soon enough. I wasn't looking forward to tomorrow. As it happened, tomorrow *did* have some surprises in store that would complicate our lives, to say the very least.

Chapter Twenty

"Girls! Wake up!" Mom called to us in a hushed voice. Why was she whispering if she was trying to wake us? I rolled over and pulled the sleeping bag over my head.

"Dear, you have to get up. We're supposed to meet the Picardis at the inn."

"But we have sailing school," I told her, sitting up. "We can't be late. It's an important lesson, and I'll miss half of it because of *her*." I indicated Brittany with an icy stare in the direction of my bed. Then I remembered something, "I'm running out of money, Mom. We ordered a pizza last night."

"All right, dear, I'll leave you a few dollars on the kitchen counter." She tiptoed out of the room. I immediately closed my eyes and went back to sleep.

"Wake up! Wake up!" It was Laura. "We're going to be late!"

"What time is it?" asked Abigail, sleepily sitting up and stretching.

"It can't be morning yet," Muffy mumbled as she shaded her eyes from the sunlight flooding into my room.

"Time to rise and shine!" Laura continued, ripping the covers off Abigail and pulling down the top of my sleeping bag. "We don't want to miss roll call. Come on!"

We reluctantly got up and dressed. Brittany didn't budge. No one wanted to wake her, or touch her, so we left her and clambered downstairs to hunt for food. Mom and Dad and the boys had apparently left to meet the Picardis at the inn. I found granola bars and orange juice. The Girls made faces, but I ignored their looks. Food is food.

"Are we going to call the police to find out what happened to the gypsies?" asked Abigail.

"They weren't able to catch the gypsies!" Muffy said. She explained her conversation with the police the previous evening.

"Will they call us after they search the shed?" Abigail wondered.

"Of course not!" I said. "Did they call us after they went to the cottages? No. Will they tell us anything? No. Not unless we go to them and ask. And we're going to look for Officer Nick as soon as sailing class is over."

We had finished our breakfast. The kitchen clock said that we had enough time to brush our teeth, so we raced back upstairs.

Brittany was coming out of the bedroom when we thundered down the hall. We stopped short when we saw her.

"We're going to sailing school," said Abigail. "Would you like to come?"

"I suppose," Brittany said without any enthusiasm.

"We have to leave now," I added, ducking into Mom's bathroom to brush my teeth.

The Girls and I brushed while Brittany dressed. They took their backpacks and life jackets. On our way out the door I grabbed the money Mom had left on the counter and a granola bar for Brittany.

"You can ride Maxwell's bike," I told her as we approached the garage.

"I don't ride bikes," Brittany stated. I supposed that translated into "I don't know how to ride a bike."

I sighed. "Then you can ride with me. I'll pedal."

"I don't want to," she responded, sulkily.

"Then stay here," I retorted. I angrily put my hands on my hips.

"Mollie, you and Brittany could walk," suggested Muffy, trying to make peace.

Brittany nodded in assent.

"Fine! Then we can walk on the beach," I said. "It's shorter. You go on," I instructed my friends.

The Girls pedaled down the driveway. This was a fine kettle of fish. I don't know exactly what that expression means, but I think it means that things are a big mess. I turned toward the beach and led Brittany across the lawn to the steps. I sighed as we descended to the beach. I handed her the granola bar. She did not say, "Thank you, Mollie."

We trudged through heaps of eel grass, seashells, and brittle horseshoe crab shells. Brittany was careful not to step on any fish bones or in any of the muddy areas around the beach grass.

She was definitely not a country girl. Muffy was from New York City and was more countrified than Brittany, a New Jersey girl. Heck, I was a Jersey girl myself, and I didn't mind getting my feet wet or dirty. Maybe if her time with me was miserable enough, she would spend the rest of the weekend with her parents. Then we wouldn't have to deal with her. Maybe the whole family would go home early.

We walked on in silence. I walked quickly because I didn't want to be late. Brittany baby-stepped and toe danced, but she kept up. I supposed that she didn't want me to leave her behind all alone on a strange beach. Finally we reached the yacht club. I heaved another sigh. My day was ruined because of Brittany! If only my foolish father didn't have such a poor choice of friends!

Up the stairs we climbed, from the beach to the deck. The Girls were there waiting for us. They were talking to Billy Jones.

"Hey!" called Billy. "Is this your friend from New Jersey?"

Friend? Not exactly. "This is Brittany Picardi," I said, introducing her to Billy. "Her father went to high school with my dad, and they haven't seen each other since graduation until they ran into each other in the City just the other day." I wanted Billy to know that Brittany was no friend of mine.

Gilly Wagner and Harvey Seymore sat on the bench in front of us. Gilly was applying sunblock to her freckled face and bouncing her red curls all over the place.

Harvey seemed lost in thought, then suddenly spun toward us and exclaimed, "Picardi? From New Jersey? My dad says they're into money laundering!"

Gilly covered her opened mouth. "What's that?" she asked in horror.

Harvey went on to explain, in a loud voice, how illegal money was "laundered" through legal businesses, making it appear to be legitimate. I couldn't quite understand how that would be done, but I did notice that Brittany had turned white as a sheet. She stared straight ahead and said nothing.

Billy turned to Harvey. "I'm sure there are lots of Picardis, and besides, New Jersey is a big state. Also, your information could be classified as slander. You shouldn't say something like that unless you know it's true."

"It's true if my dad says it," countered Harvey. The cousins stared at Brittany.

"That's such a mean thing to say," Abigail scolded them.

"Not to mention rude," added Laura. "Turn around and mind your own business."

"You don't know what our business is," said Gilly, but she saucily turned back and focused on roll call, which was just beginning.

Brittany fidgeted with the long sleeves of her shirt. She was trembling from Harvey's accusation. Whatever Harvey heard his father say, Harvey was sure to get wrong. Still, I was surprised to see Brittany so upset by what he'd said.

Billy and Judy were describing our exercise for the day, a capsizing race.

"Huh? What's that?" I murmured, trying to tune in.

Judy explained, "You'll sail out towards R, where the starting line will be. Same course as Tuesday, only once around. You'll start the race as usual, but between the start and R, which will be the first mark, you have to capsize your boat—and I mean *capsize*. No taking on a little water, then recovering. You have to go down all the way, sails in the water."

Billy took over. "Then right your boat and go on with the race."

Surprisingly, no one complained. Usually we all hated capsizing drills, but this was different. It sounded fun, only I would miss it, because of *her*.

"Any questions?" asked Judy.

Some of the kids had stupid questions, which were such a waste of time, but what did I care? I had all the time in the world. Judy gave the kids a quick review of things to remember about righting a boat after it capsizes. Then we were dismissed, and the kids swarmed toward the stairs and down to the beach to rig up.

The Girls looked at me. "Go on, or you won't get a good boat," I said.

"Maybe we can sail together," said Abigail.

"What's the holdup?" asked Judy, striding over to us.

"I have a guest," I explained.

"So? Let's get her a life jacket, and we'll put her on the committee boat with us."

"Yes!" I exclaimed. I avoided looking at Brittany, not wanting to give her the chance of messing up the opportunity that had just presented itself.

We raced down to the beach, and I went straight to the bin where extra life jackets were stored. Judy took Brittany under her wing, and they ambled down the stairway after us. I pulled out a mildewed and slightly damp blue model that would be just right for my pal Brittany. I tossed it to her and rushed to the *Chubby Quahog*, but I could see that the cousins Gilly and Harvey were already rigging her.

"What the—?" I began. The two kept their eyes on their work, refusing to make eye contact with me.

"First-come, first-served," Gilly said in an annoying singsong voice. She was so prissy it made me want to vomit.

"You think you're smart, don't you, Wagner?" I said. "We'll beat you no matter which boats we get."

I scanned the beach. Someone else had the *Minnow* too! That's what a moment's hesitation got us! The Girls were rigging the *Albatross*, which was known to be one of the slowest Sprites ever built. We had Brittany to thank for this disaster as well. Only one boat was not rigged, *Greased Lightning*. *Greased Pig* was more like it! Abigail came over to join me. She gathered a set of sails while I found a rudder. We rigged her without saying a word.

"It's nice that Judy and Billy are taking Brittany on the committee boat," she said. I didn't answer. We finished rigging and made sure that we had two bailers tied securely to the mast. We would be needing them.

With help from some of the other kids, we carried our boat down to the water's edge. Once all the boats were in the water, we pushed off with Abigail at the helm. She tacked past the docks and pier to the channel.

It wasn't such a bad day after all. I was able to sail with my friends and get away from that girl. Billy and Judy stood on the pier with Brittany and called out directions to the kids, until all had cleared the piers and were in the channel sailing toward R. Brittany looked miserable in the spore-ridden life jacket.

We tacked through the boats moored opposite the club dock. Before long we were passing the three gypsy trawlers and noticed several men hanging out their laundry and dumping basins of water overboard. I guess that was allowed, as long as no sewage or garbage was in it. The big black dog was peering over the railing, eying us. Did he remember us from last night or was he just curious?

"Where do you think they're keeping that girl and the two adults?" asked Abigail.

"I don't know," I answered. "I hope the police hear about a ransom note soon."

"But if those gypsies don't speak English, how will they be able to write one?" she wondered.

"One of them speaks enough to say, 'Pay or she dies' or something like that."

"That's just terrible!" she shuddered. "I hope they won't hurt them."

"I don't think they're that dumb."

We tacked and kept our course, which was heading toward Laura and Muffy. When we were within earshot of them, Laura called out, "What's your strategy?"

"We're going to be the first to get our boat up," I boasted.

"I'm not asking you," she teased. "I'm asking Abigail."

"It's a secret," she called back.

"Oh, I thought so," laughed Muffy, who was at the tiller. "I don't know what to do either."

Abigail stuck out her tongue at Muffy.

"I hope those kids who took the *Minnow* and the *Chubby Quahog* take care of them," Muffy added. "I hate to think of someone else capsizing our boats. I hope they'll be all right."

"Yeah," I agreed. "They'll have to answer to us if they damage them. Of all days for someone else to take our boats!"

We sailed away from the *Albatross*, but our paths kept crisscrossing until we reached the starting line. Judy and Billy had anchored at the starting line after dropping a big, neon-pink ball. Brittany sat sulking in the bow.

The *Greased Pig* handled like a barge, so Abigail kept her away from the other boats when she tacked. The horns had been sounding, and it was thirty seconds until the start. I guess our instructors thought that the capsizing was enough to think about. That's why they gave us a course we already knew, but this time it was only once around.

We were near the committee boat. I could see Brittany gazing into the deep water with half a smile on her face. Her eyes met mine, but I didn't know what that look of hers meant. I would find out right after the race.

Chapter Twenty-One

Abigail came up at twenty seconds. We were on a port tack, which meant we didn't have the right of way. Several other boats were bearing down on the starting line, headed straight toward us. Ten seconds. Abigail headed below them, then tacked onto starboard at the center of the line. Gilly and Harvey were above us.

"Starboard," Gilly yelled.

"Leeward!" Abigail shouted back.

"Good girl!" I was impressed. "How did you know to say that?" She was right: When two boats are on a starboard tack, the leeward boat has the right of way over the windward.

"I listened in class," she replied as the beeps sounded, followed by a long blast, indicating that the race had begun. We crossed the starting line on the dot. A horn sounded, and Billy shouted to Gilly that she was over early. We heard her swear as she sailed up and tacked to get out of the way of the other starting boats in order to restart.

"I'll get you for this, Abigail Lincoln!" she screamed. We ignored her. The fact that they were over the line early had nothing to do with us.

"Where are you going to capsize?" I asked, watching some boats capsize nearby, almost as soon as they cleared the starting line.

"You'll see," she said, as she sailed on. I was surprised at her. She was usually so nervous and scared of everything. I think sailing in a tub like *Greased Lightning* gave her the confidence to take some risks. It was strange how something like a slow boat could make such a difference in her.

The boats toppled over, one by one. We were the last boat to remain upright. As we neared R, Abigail gave the warning, "Ready to capsize." Then, "Capsize ho!" I knew that "Jibe ho" was a real nautical phrase, but I wasn't so sure about "Capsize ho." Anyway, I knew what it meant and held onto the coaming, or edge, as we went over. Abigail held the sail in as tightly as she could, causing the boat to gracefully lean until the bilge filled with water and the boat became so unstable that over it went.

The sails hit the water. I hoped that the boat wouldn't turtle. That's when the mast goes straight down, and the hull rears up out of the water like a diving duck. The danger is that the mast could get stuck in the mud, but even if it doesn't, it is much more difficult to right the boat from that position.

We didn't turtle or duck-dive or whatever. As soon as the top of the mast hit the water, Abigail and I tore around the boat to climb up on the centerboard, which projected outward from the middle of the hull. By standing on the centerboard, holding onto the coaming, and pulling backward, we were able to get the sail out of the water. We righted the boat, but it kept on coming! With the bilge full of water, the boat was so tippy that it capsized once more, this time on top of us, trapping us under the sail!

Abigail and I were still side by side. I reached out for her and grabbed her arm, pushing toward the boom, where I knew the sail would end and we could come up for air.

"That was close!" she spluttered, gasping for breath. "I'll try again, but this time you stay on the other side of the boat to keep it from going over another time."

"Well, you'd better hurry!" I warned her. "Two boats are approaching."

Abigail saw the boats and splashed around *Greased Lightning* to climb out of the water and stand on the centerboard. I waited at the stern, holding my head above water and kicking my legs out to keep from sinking. When Abigail pulled on the coaming, I quickly moved to the side coming out of the water and held on, keeping the Sprite from going over onto Abigail.

The bailers, which were bleach and detergent bottles cut out to form scoops, were floating on the surface of the water in the hull. I untied one as Abigail untied the other. Careful to keep the boat balanced, we began to bail, furiously scooping and dumping the water out of the bilge. Before long, the boat was only half full.

"Let's get back in the boat," said Abigail, nervously surveying the competition, meaning the two boats headed for R. They were gaining on us.

"I'll go first and get more water out before you get in, O.K.?" I said. "I don't want the boat to capsize again."

I carefully pulled myself over the stern and sat in the center of the boat. "It's still wobbly," I observed.

After I had bailed like a madwoman, it was safe for Abigail to enter. I helped pull her aboard. The two boats were already rounding R, and Gilly and Harvey were coming up fast.

"It's them!" I uttered in disgust. Of all the students to be gaining on us!

"Cleat the jib," Abigail ordered, as she trimmed the main and we set off. "But keep bailing, please."

I obeyed her commands and took the opportunity to look behind us. Gilly was overtaking us and, in an instant rounded R just ahead of us. The two other boats were speeding toward Q.

"Having trouble?" Harvey asked as snidely as possible. We didn't bother to answer. *Greased Lightning* followed close behind them, further back, but we fell away as we rounded R to port and pointed toward Q. The course was simple, but not simple enough.

"You can do it, Abigail, old girl!" I shouted.

"We won't even get third place at this rate," she groaned.

Now that the first two boats had rounded Q and were headed toward the finish, I could see who it was. Two older girls were in the first boat, and two older boys in the second. The cousins weren't far behind them.

I kept bailing, hoping that we would speed up as we lost the extra water weight. We plowed through the water as we rounded Q, going a little faster. Muffy and Laura suddenly appeared. They rounded Q and sailed above us, taking our wind. They bore down on us and swept ahead.

"Curses!" I yelled at them, shaking my fist.

"Calm down, Mollie. It's only a race."

"Only a race? How can you say that? Our lives depend upon this race! You can forget those girls and the older boys ahead of us, but we'll never hear the end of it if you let those cousins beat us."

We headed toward the finish line. Gilly and Harvey held their place ahead of the *Albatross*. There was no way we could catch up to them. Several boats were still capsized and would probably never finish the race. Muffy and Laura sailed further ahead of us and took the advantage. Second place wouldn't have been bad. Third wouldn't have been either, but we were looking at fifth place. We glided over the line two boat-lengths behind the Girls.

"Thank you," Abigail called out to the race committee (that is, Judy and

135

Billy) when they acknowledged our finish by calling out, "Over. Good race."

Brittany looked us in the eye. She was still smirking about something. As soon as the Picardis left the Cape, I was going to have a real heart-to-heart talk with my Dad. He could not go around picking up long-lost friends off the street, especially if they had such rotten eggs for children.

"Go on in," hollered Billy, so we kept on sailing until we were well away from the finish line. We caught up to the *Albatross* near the *Ocean Rose.*

"You did well!" Muffy called out as we approached.

"Congratulations!" Abigail rejoined. "You came in fourth place!"

"I liked your strategy," Laura said. "We couldn't get the *Albatross* to capsize and then once she was down, we couldn't get her up. It's so different when you have to sail a boat you're not used to."

"That's for sure," laughed Abigail. "This boat handles like a tug. You deserve an extra pennant for doing so well in that boat. I hope our favorite boats make it back in good shape."

"They'd better," I said. "Those kids will hear from me if anything happens to our boats." Of course, the boats weren't really ours. We merely preferred them and were usually able to sail them. But the yacht club staff discouraged students from having favorite boats. And it was true that all of the boats were supposed to be equally good, but the fact was that all Sprites were not created equal.

"Looks like Judy and Billy have their hands full," I said, looking back at the boats still flailing in the water. Brittany sat like a statue in the *Sea Cow,* that is, the committee boat.

We sailed through the trawlers, straining to see on-board, but there was nothing to see. The gypsies were busy working on their nets and cleaning up, though the boats didn't appear any cleaner. Soon we were rounding the end of the club dock and heading for shore. Other Sprites were coming in too.

We lowered our sails and carried them over to the dock, where we laid them flat on the ground. I grabbed the hose and rinsed the sails with fresh water while Abigail put the rudder away. Together, we helped the other students carry all the boats back onto the beach. Dragging them across the sand damages the paint on the bottom of the hulls. We mounted the stairs and sat on the deck.

By now the *Sea Cow* was docking at the end of the pier. Brittany disembarked and came along the pier with Judy, who took her life jacket and plunked it back into the bin as they passed by.

When they got to the deck, Abigail asked Brittany, "How did you like watching the race?"

"I didn't watch the race," Brittany answered with a toss of her hair.

"Then what did you do the whole time?" Muffy wanted to know.

"I just looked at all the sharks," she said, her eyes meeting mine.

Abigail paled. "Sharks?" she gasped. "Where?"

"They were all over the place," said Brittany. So that's why she was smiling! She was just waiting for us to be eaten alive! The skunk!

Muffy folded her arms over her chest. "There aren't any sharks around here," she said defiantly.

"Oh, yes, there are," countered Brittany. "I saw them, plenty of them."

"How big?" asked Laura, not showing any emotion.

"As big as you. Absolutely huge!" Brittany exclaimed, unable to hide her excitement.

"Dogfish," said Laura blandly.

"What?" My haughty houseguest had never heard that term before.

"Those were dogfish," Laura explained. "They're harmless."

"They didn't look harmless to me," Brittany said, not willing to let it go.

"Was anyone bitten?" Laura asked. "Even with all the movement going on in the water? The thrashing and kicking of kids treading water and trying to get back into their boats. No. They look like other sharks, but they're not. They won't bite or attack."

Brittany tried to hide her disappointment.

"Sorry to spoil your fun," I said, not able to keep quiet. I had given her a moldy life jacket to wear, but that wasn't as bad as hoping that we would be eaten by a shark! Muffy says that I have no feelings and say just what I think too much, which hurts other people's feelings. But at least I know right from wrong!

Brittany scowled at me, and we all directed our attention to Billy Jones, who was announcing the winners of the race. "I'd like all the winners to tell the other students what they did to get their boats up so quickly," he said.

The first-place-winning girls stood up and said that one of them was on the centerboard in no time while the other stayed in the water to stabilize the boat as it came out of the water. That's just what we did—the second time around. The boys told about some special sailing formula of the wind ratio on their sail compared to the angle of the mast or some baloney, which had nothing to do with the capsize, and the cousins said they won because of the wonderful way they worked together as a team. Yuck!

"I'm hungry," whispered Abigail. "Could we eat before we go to the police station? Please?"

"How about coming to my house for peanut butter and Flu—" Laura didn't get to finish. Just then we saw Brittany's father barging through the clubhouse, straight toward us. Parents were discouraged from interfering with sailing lessons. Class was just about over, but if it had been my father, I would have been embarrassed to death.

Mr. Picardi waved at Brittany, who looked straight ahead and pretended not to notice him. Probably my father was not far behind him.

"Oh, hogwash!" I mumbled under my breath. "I bet I'll get stuck spending my precious time with these people until they leave Cape Cod!"

The moment Billy Jones said that class was over, Mr. Picardi pushed his way through the crowd of retreating students to greet his charming daughter. Gilly and Harvey stood stock-still on the deck, staring at him. They began whispering and moved to a corner of the yard, where they called their friends over to them.

A little crowd formed around the cousins. They continued chattering away, presumably telling their friends all about Mr. Picardi's sordid laundry business. They were blatantly pointing at the big man and his daughter. Mr. Picardi didn't notice, and Brittany pretended not to. I would have thought the cousins would be more interested in bragging about their third-place win than spreading a rumor, but there was no figuring out those two.

"Where's my dad?" I asked.

"Out in the car with the boys." Mr. Picardi motioned toward the street. I cut through the clubhouse and found Dad sitting at the wheel of his car. Georgie and Maxwell wrestled in the backseat.

"Dad," I called, moving to the open passenger window. "What's up? The Girls have invited me to go with them for lunch."

"Frank and I thought you two girls would like to go fishing with us. If we go out to Womponoy, we could catch some blues for dinner."

Oh, no! I couldn't think of anything I would hate more! This was *not* going to happen to me! The Eel Grass Girls had important work to do! And even if we hadn't, I wasn't going to spend any more time with Brittany Picardi if I could help it.

Chapter Twenty-Two

Besides the fact that my father couldn't fish and had never cleaned a fish in his life, there was nothing I would enjoy less than an afternoon at sea with the Picardis. I smelled disaster, not to mention the fact that I would loath spending one minute more with Brittany. And I couldn't bear the thought of missing out on a field trip to the local police station.

"Brittany was on the committee boat all morning," I informed Dad. "I think she's had enough sun and water for one day."

"Fishing is different," Dad replied. "We're taking the boys too. I bought some new lures I want to try."

I had to manipulate Dad as fast as I could. "Then Brittany and I definitely shouldn't go, Dad. You and Maxwell need to spend some quality time together. Brittany wants to go shopping with her mother. I just know it. And I have to go with the Girls."

"We had it all planned!" my father lamented.

"Dad, trust me. Fishing is a man's sport." Of course I didn't believe that for a minute—fishing is gender-neutral—but I was determined not to spend the rest of the day with either the Picardis or Maxwell. "You can take me out another time. Alone. And we can...um...play mini-golf together. Just the two of us. That would be great!"

"You're right, sweetie. I haven't spent much time with Maxwell, and Frank doesn't get much time with his kids, either. But we're all going to the Nor'easter for dinner. We'll have fun together then."

"Sounds wonderful!" I stretched the truth a bit. In reality, it was wonderful not to have to go fishing with that crowd.

The Girls were peeking out of the clubhouse, eavesdropping. I turned to them and winked. I could see smiles spread across their faces. They didn't want to lose me for the afternoon.

Mr. Picardi appeared with Brittany around the corner of the clubhouse. He had his arm draped around Billy Jones's shoulder, but Billy was looking very uncomfortable.

"Eddy!" he called to Dad. "Look here! I got a real-estate scout. Says he'll find me a place."

"I said I don't know of any places for sale other than the houses I've seen with 'For Sale' signs in front of them," said Billy, trying to shake off Mr. Picardi's arm.

"You can do better than that, son," the man said. "There's a big commission in it for you. I'm sure you could use the money for college. It'll be more than you make working at this dump." He glanced at our little clubhouse and the sparse grass surrounding it.

Billy stiffened up and said, "I don't do real estate." Then Billy caught sight of Abigail in the clubhouse doorway.

"Abigail," he called out. "Isn't your uncle's friend selling real estate?" He seemed desperate to get out of any association with Mr. Picardi.

"Uh...um..." she stammered. "Freddy is interested in fixing up old houses."

"Old houses?" roared the large man, "We don't want an old house! We want something big and brand-new! Your friend can do that for us. Give me his name."

"Freddy Frisket. He's staying with us," Abigail offered meekly.

"I'll get his number from Eddy. Thanks for the lead, kid," he said to Billy. "You'll get your cut." He winked at Billy, who stared in silence, upset by Mr. Picardi's manner.

"Nice to see you, Mr. Parker," Billy said to Dad. Then to everyone in general he added, "Have a nice day," spun around, and disappeared inside the clubhouse. My opinion of Mr. Picardi was lowering by the instant.

"Nice kid," he remarked. "He'll go far."

I saw something flash across my dad's face, but I couldn't quite tell what it was. It wasn't outright surprise or dislike, but it was something negative. He said, "The girls have made arrangements for lunch, so our fishing trip's going to be for men only."

"Sounds great to me," said Picardi, getting into the car. I was glad that he gave in easily on this one. "See you later, Brit!"

Off they drove with a wave of Dad's hand. It wasn't a perfect plan. The major flaw was that I now had to put up with Brittany until I could deposit her with her mother. But at least I wouldn't be stuck on a motorboat out in the middle of the ocean with her, her father, Georgie, and Maxwell for the rest of the day. I wouldn't mind being with Dad. Now all I had to do was get rid of that girl.

"I'd better check in with Mom," I announced for Brittany's sake, as if it were something I did several times a day. I needed to cinch my plan. I entered the clubhouse. Off the main room there was a wall phone the students were allowed to use. I hoped beyond hope that Mom would be home—and she was.

"Hi, Mom. What's happening?"

"Mollie? Are you all right?" she asked. I never call home. She thought it was an emergency.

"Yeah, no problem. Brittany wants to go shopping with her mother, I think, so I thought I could bring her home."

"That would be fine. We just came up from the beach for lunch. The boys are having so much fun together. Your dad just called on Mr. Picardi's cell phone to say they're getting the boat ready to take the boys out fishing. Isn't that nice?"

"Wow. That's really kind of Dad and Mr. Picardi to do that."

"I like Joan a lot," she rambled on.

"Who?"

"Joan, I mean Mrs. Picardi. See you soon."

"I'm going home," I said, giving the Girls a "don't ask" kind of look.

"Meet us at my house," said Laura, but not loud enough for Brittany to hear. She didn't want to seem rude, I'm sure, by excluding her, but we had important work to do, and Brit was *not* part of our plan.

Laura and the other two Girls hopped on their bikes and cycled off while Brittany and I ambled along, following the road past rambling Cape houses facing the harbor. She didn't say a word. Neither did I.

Before long we were plodding up my driveway and entering my back door.

"Brittany!" called out Mrs. Picardi. "How was it? You want to go shopping?"

Brittany shrugged her shoulders.

"You coming too?" Mrs. Picardi asked me.

"I have something to do," I said. "Bye!"

I bolted toward the door, but Mom rushed after me. "Mollie, wait a moment. A man named Jake something called for you. Who's he?"

"What did he say?"

"He asked to speak with you. When I said you weren't home, he said he would like you to call him back."

"O.K." I grabbed the phone book out of the drawer. Mom stood there while I dialed. "It's something to do with the harbor," I told her. When Jake didn't answer, I left another message.

"Dear, we're meeting the Picardis at the Nor'easter at seven for dinner."

"I'll see you then," I called over my shoulder as I headed toward the garage. I pulled out my bike and rode down the driveway without looking back. I did it! I'd escaped!

Soon I was at Laura's house. Her home was almost next door. The Girls sat around the kitchen table eating sandwiches that oozed peanut butter and white, gooey Marshmallow Fluff. There was one already made for me, beside a tall glass of cold milk.

"Jake Rison called earlier and left a message for me to call him back, but he was out when I called," I announced.

"They must have arrested the gypsies," said Laura. "That's good!"

"And found all those people they kidnapped!" exclaimed Muffy.

"We'll find out soon enough," I said, washing my hands. I seated myself at the table and attacked the sandwich. "Yum!"

"Where's Brittany?" asked Abigail.

"She's going shopping in town with her mother," I explained.

"Why is she so grumpy all the time?" Muffy wondered. I didn't know and I didn't care.

"It may be because of those stories about her father being mixed up in money washing—laundering—whatever it's called," Laura speculated. "She seemed really upset by what Harvey said."

"That's baloney!" I exclaimed with my mouth full. "She's just that way."

"How do you know?" asked Abigail. "She might be worried about her father."

"Maybe," I said, but I didn't want to think about her. "We'll go to the police station and get the scoop."

143

"As soon as we're finished eating," said Abigail. "The important things come first." She smiled. I can't understand why she likes food so much. She loves to eat and always likes something fancy. Food is food as far as I'm concerned.

We finished eating and started off to town to find our friend Officer Nick. We agreed we should ride our bikes along Main Street to look for him before we tried the police station.

"What if we meet up with Brittany and her mother?" asked Muffy.

"I have to go to dinner with them tonight. That should be enough," I replied. "I shouldn't have to spend twenty-four hours a day with her."

We rode past the yacht club and toward town. It turned out that we were correct in our assumption concerning the whereabouts of Officer Nick. He was near the candy store, giving a ticket to an irate tourist who had parked his car so that the rear end was sticking out in the middle of Main Street. It seemed obvious to me that that wasn't the right way to park, even if there hadn't been traffic, huge delivery trucks, and kids on bicycles squeezing along the narrow street at the same time.

The Girls and I parked our bikes in front of the candy store and patiently waited for the tourist to stop screaming at Nick. The man then reparked his car, and Officer Nick approached us.

"Don't you kids ever sleep?" he asked.

"How can we when the good citizens of our town are disappearing right and left and thieves are stealing from our homes and almost every boat in the harbor?" I countered.

"All I can say is that your thieves are pretty smart," he answered cryptically.

"What do you mean by that?" Laura crinkled up her nose.

"I was surprised, but the chief got a warrant for that boathouse. They found plenty of goods in there."

"They did?" exclaimed Abigail, her eyes widening as she wondered what the police had actually found.

"Three pairs of oars, an oil drum or two, a broken outboard motor, four kayaks, a leaky dinghy, some rusty chains, and a smattering of lobster pots," he answered with a perplexed look.

"What?" I almost shrieked. A tourist family stared at us in horror and hastily swept their children into the candy store.

"But we saw them!" exclaimed Laura.

"You saw them," repeated Officer Nick, "but you assumed they were doing something illegal, and they weren't."

"They skulked from boat to boat," Abigail persisted. "They carried things off right in front of us. Hasn't anyone reported any thefts?"

"Yeah. Your gypsy friends and a few other folks," he replied.

"All those stolen things have to be somewhere," said Muffy.

I was losing my temper. "You know about the robberies, and we told you who it was and where they put the goods. Why can't you catch them?"

"No one was at the Miller's Cottages when we got there, and we don't have enough to go on to question all of Miller's tenants. Since there was nothing out of the ordinary in the boat shed," he said, giving us a sympathetic gaze, "there was nothing more we could do."

"You policemen have to get to the scene of the crime faster, that's what I think," said Laura. "Then you would have caught them."

"Or," I added under my breath, "we'll have to catch them ourselves."

Officer Nick heaved a heavy sigh. "Ah, don't say that! We'll apprehend whoever it is who's doing this. You have to stay out of police business. You might get hurt."

"This is ridiculous!" I said. "You can't catch them even when we call you and give you all the information. And don't you see? The sooner you catch them on the robberies, the sooner you can find all those kidnapped people."

"We appreciate your leads. Keep trying," he said encouragingly. "We're doing all we can. The town is really pressuring us too. All these troubles, especially the kidnappings, have made a big problem for the local businesses."

"I think it must be a bigger problem for the kidnap victims," Laura muttered.

"Has there been any news about them?" asked Abigail. "Any ransom notes?"

"Nothing," replied Nick. "Not a word, which is very strange. We've got to solve this case! The selectmen and the commercial organizations are giving us a hard time. News like this scares people away."

"Really?" I exclaimed in mock surprise. "Come on, Girls!"

I was frustrated. Officer Nick was our friend, but he wasn't in a decision-making position on the police force. Though he could give us information, he couldn't do much else to help us.

"Thank you," Abigail said to him as we pushed our bikes down the sidewalk. "What will we do now?"

At that moment we saw Billy Jones's truck pass us and turn into the Nor'easter parking lot. Billy worked in the kitchen of the Nor'easter on his off hours from the yacht club. I had an idea, so I motioned to the Girls, and we pushed our bikes across the street, on the crosswalk, of course, and entered the driveway of the restaurant. We walked around back, where Billy was just getting out of his truck.

"Look who's here!" he exclaimed. "I can sense trouble."

We ignored his remarks. "Billy, do you know anyone who lives at Miller's Cottages?"

"Let me think. Hmmm. Yes, one of the busboys does. Why?"

"We need to know everyone who lives in those cottages, where they work, and if any of them has a motorboat," I said.

Billy appraised us. "Is this...? I won't ask. O.K., I'll see what I can find out."

"I'll be having dinner here tonight," I informed him. "I'll stop by the kitchen."

"I can't promise you anything by then, but I'll try," said Billy.

"When do you go out to check your lobster pots?" I asked. "I have tennis in the morning."

Billy answered, "After lunch, about one o'clock would be good. Is that O.K. with you girls?"

The Girls all said "Yes."

"Let's make a nice care package for our castaway," Laura suggested.

"I'll give him a lobster or two," offered Billy.

"I think he could use a blanket," said Abigail.

"Matches in a plastic bag," Muffy added.

"Got to get to work," Billy said, heading into the kitchen. "See you tomorrow."

"I'll see you tonight," I reminded him.

"Thanks!" Laura called out as Billy disappeared, and the screen door slammed shut. "That was good thinking, Mollie. Maybe we should spy on those cottages."

"How?" Abigail asked.

"We could stop by and ask if anyone needs a babysitter," Muffy suggested.

"For college kids?" I asked.

"We don't know who they are for sure," said Muffy, her eyes sparkling. "And they don't know that we know they're college kids. And we might be able to discover which one owns the motorboat the gypsies are using."

"But when should we go?" Abigail queried.

"They'll be working now and partying (or stealing) at night," began Laura. "Early morning would be the best time to get them."

"It will be interesting to meet our suspects," I said, imagining sleepy college kids being awakened at the crack of dawn. It made me chuckle.

We pushed our bikes onto the sidewalk and heard something awful that stopped us in our tracks!

Chapter Twenty-Three

A roaring noise came from our left. It was frightening. We listened as the sound grew louder and louder. We craned our necks to see down the street. A bright red convertible sports car came whizzing toward us, a little too fast for the crowded conditions of Main Street. It whipped into a tiny parking space right in front of the Nor'easter.

We stared as two men casually climbed out of the car, sauntered up to the Nor'easter, and entered the door leading to the bar. Two men going into the bar was not unusual, but the way they were dressed was. One of them wore a crisply ironed yellow Hawaiian shirt tucked into a fancy belt and white linen slacks.

His friend's tan linen suit with a narrow tie looked very out of place. They both wore Panama hats. The men were too crisp and fancy for Cape Cod. Palm Beach or the Riviera, maybe, but not Main Street in our little fishing village. We watched them enter the bar.

"They look suspicious," said Abigail. "But we have to presume they are innocent until proven guilty."

"Thank you, Lawyer's Daughter!" I joked. We could always depend upon Abigail to be legally correct.

"How about some ice cream?" she asked, changing the subject to her favorite subject, food.

We pushed our bikes along the sidewalk and across the street to our beloved ice cream shop. We ordered our cones and I treated, since I was the only one who had any money left. We sat at the picnic table and wished some gossipers were there to give us new information.

"Why don't we go to my aunt's shop?" asked Muffy. "We can look at the tiaras and plan what we'll wear to the Captain's Ball."

"Weren't you going to be in a fashion show?" asked Laura. "I seem to remember you going in there for a fitting a while ago."

"It's next week at the Inn on the Bay," Muffy informed us. "I'll show you the outfits I'm going to wear."

Just then we saw Brittany, her mother, and my mother walk by. They went into the ice cream shop and didn't even notice us sitting at the table. The second they were inside the shop, I jumped up.

"Let's get out of here!" I said, creeping over to my bike. I didn't want any of them to see us if they happened to look out through the windows. Luckily they were too busy looking at the boards of flavors and specialty listings. We hopped onto our bikes and sped up Main Street to Muffy's aunt's shop.

We entered the driveway, which took us under a shady maple tree to a small parking lot surrounded by a white picket fence. Muffy boldly led the way through the "employees only" back door. Her aunt was seated at her desk in the air-conditioned office.

"If it isn't the 'mystery girls'!" her Aunt Ella exclaimed. "The workmen just finished giving my office a new coat of paint."

We looked around the office. It seemed the same as always, but maybe a little neater. It had suffered a serious accident during the course of one of our previous mysteries, but as I said before, that's Laura's story, not mine. You would have to read *The Haunting of Captain Snow* to find out all about it.

"Would you girls like to help with our fashion show next week?" she asked us.

"Yes," Laura replied. "But what do we have to do?"

"You can meet us at the Inn on the Bay, down at their beach club," she began. "You'll help dress the children in their outfits, brush their hair, hide the tags on the clothing, make sure the children are lined up in order. Quick changes are the most important."

"Sounds like fun," Abigail said. Muffy's aunt, that is, Ella McLaughlin, gave us the date and time to be at the inn. I had never been to a fashion show, so this would be interesting. The Picardis would be gone by then, so we wouldn't have to worry about seeing them at the inn.

"What are you doing now?" Aunt Ella asked.

"I'm going to show the Girls the new tiaras that came in," said Muffy. "We need tiaras for the Captain's Ball at the yacht club."

"Why don't you each pick one out, and I'll give them to you for helping with the fashion show," Aunt Ella replied. "How does that sound?"

"Fantastic!" exclaimed Muffy. "I already have one, but I noticed some new styles, and I'd love to have another."

"Thank you!" we chimed in. I wasn't crazy about wearing a fake diamond crown, but I supposed it wouldn't be that bad. If the Girls wanted to do it, I would go along. I knew they would be disappointed if I refused.

We passed through the dressing rooms, sale racks, the boys' room filled with jackets and ties, shorts, and polo shirts, into the big front room filled with dresses, toys, and jewelry. The shop was in an old, old home where Muffy's great, great grandmother had been born and raised. I couldn't imagine it, but she said it was true.

Muffy was already displaying the glittery tiaras. "I like this one," I said, picking up one with a pale pink diamond among the clear, white ones.

After trying them on, and each of us choosing one, we looked around the shop and tried on some clothes. I would have to come in one day and let my mom buy me some new clothes for school. Muffy's aunt had a great selection of really different-looking clothes. I didn't care that much about fashion, but I didn't want to look generic. I liked different, but not trendy or wild clothes. Do you know what I mean?

Muffy had a twinkle in her eye as she beckoned us to follow her to a narrow stairway leading up to the shop's second floor, that was off-limits to customers. I held onto the banister as we carefully climbed the steps up to the dim rooms. Old-fashioned wallpaper of large pastel flowers covered the walls of the small rooms.

"Aren't these cute?" She pointed to a miniature pair of skis and bamboo poles with crumbling leather straps and bindings. There was an antique tricycle in one corner, complete with an upholstered seat. Behind racks of winter coats and boxes was a wooden butter churn. We lowered our heads as we passed under the eaves. Laura had paused to look out a window facing behind the store.

Her mouth fell open, so we quickly gathered around her at the open window to see what was so startling.

Beyond the shop's picket fence were the parking areas of the various stores lining Main Street. We could see all the way over to the Nor'easter parking lot. It was here that we saw the two men we had seen entering the

Nor'easter. They were in the middle of a discussion with a young man wearing an apron.

"Look!" said Laura. "It's those fancy men."

"And talking to a dishwasher or someone," observed Muffy. The man in the Hawaiian shirt took something that resembled a wad of money out of his pocket and gave some to the boy. They smiled at each other, shook hands, and walked off toward the restaurant, disappearing from sight behind another building.

Abigail asked in a whisper, "Why are they giving money to that boy?"

"Maybe he gave them a tip about where to catch the biggest striped bass," speculated Laura.

"Probably," Muffy said.

I told them. "It's nothing that concerns us."

"You don't know that," Abigail countered. "I think we should store it in our files." She tapped the side of her head.

Muffy guffawed. I rolled my eyes. Muffy led us from room to room until we reached another stairway that twisted downward to the other side of the shop.

"This was a pretty big house," remarked Abigail. "Where was the kitchen?"

"Out here." Muffy pointed to a room filled with baby cribs, knitted items, and silver bowls and spoons. We meandered back through the shop, carrying our tiaras with us. When we reached the office, Aunt Ella asked Muffy to put the tiaras in a bag with our names on it. She then tucked the bag away beside her desk.

"Where are you girls off to now?" she inquired.

Muffy shrugged. I was ready to take a nap. It wasn't sleeping on the hard floor that bothered me, but staying up late was the thing that did it. We thanked Aunt Ella and said good-bye. Back outside we leaned against the white fence to talk.

"Let's prepare our package for the castaway," suggested Abigail.

"Why don't we each go home and get something to give the old man?" I asked.

"Good idea. Then we'll meet tomorrow," Muffy said. "I'm feeling tired."

"Me too," Laura and Abigail replied in unison.

"But what about tonight?" I asked. "Those robbers and kidnappers might be prowling around the harbor. They do their work at night. Are we just going to ignore them?"

The Girls looked from one to the other. I couldn't believe that they were too tired to watch for the crooks! They gave me their most pitiful expressions.

"Take a nap and meet me later," I said.

Abigail began to whine that she needed a break.

"O.K., O.K.," I acquiesced. "But tomorrow morning come over early so we can get over to Miller's Cottages to apply for babysitting jobs. Then I have a tennis lesson, so maybe you could hang out at Laura's until I get back. You might as well bring your donations for the castaway because we meet Billy at the yacht club at one."

"You sound like a tour guide," giggled Abigail. "We have quite an itinerary!"

I liked to keep moving and get things done. I was also the logical Eel Grass Girl, but at times like this, I felt like a sergeant major.

The Girls and I said good-bye to Muffy, who rode her bike in the opposite direction, toward the rotary and her home. Laura and I pedaled through Main Street with Abigail and dropped her off at her grandmother's house. We continued behind the lighthouse, down Lowndes River Road. When we neared the marina, we could see the bright-red sports car parked across the street. We slowed down to observe the two fancy dressers in a motorboat moored at one of the docks.

"What do you think they're doing?" I asked Laura as we pedaled toward the yacht club.

"They certainly aren't dressed for fishing!" she noted. "Even if they do know where to get a good catch."

Who cared about them, anyway? We had only noticed them because of their noisy car and out-of-place clothing, but they weren't acting strangely. People tipped restaurant workers all the time. Just because the tipping had gone on in the parking lot didn't really make any difference, as far as I was concerned.

Laura and I continued along the harbor, past the yacht club and on toward our homes. I really did feel sleepy. I hoped that Mom was still out, because that would mean no one would be home. The thought that either of my parents, and hence the Picardis, might be at the house made me feel queasy, but I hoped none of them would be there and I could sleep in peace.

I said good-bye to Laura at her driveway and rode on to my place. I was relieved when I saw the driveway empty. Ah! Peace and quiet. But as I entered the kitchen, the phone rang.

Chapter Twenty-Four

It was Jake Rison on the line.

"Mollie Parker? This is Jake Rison. I heard that you and your friends saw some action on the harbor last night."

"We did, but the police told us they didn't find anything in the boat shed or anyone at Miller's Cottages," I answered.

"Be that as it may, I want you to keep your eyes open. We've been getting a lot of calls about thefts around the harbor, and we want to put a stop to it. The gypsies reported another robbery, though I'm not ready to count those troublemakers out just yet. I'd like to arrest those bums. I guess you've heard there're no leads on the kidnappings. Those gypsies have caused me so many problems I'd like to get this resolved and fast."

It was now my turn to complain. "For one thing," I began, "when we telephone you, you never answer. And the police take so long to show up they let the gypsies get away. They're kidnappers and they're on the loose. No one in town is safe. We're trying to help, but our efforts are being wasted." I thought that sounded very adult.

"Keep trying," he said in a very serious voice. "I've asked the Fishermen's Association to instruct all their members to be on the lookout. It's amazing that we're having so many problems at once. The kidnappings are baffling. Can you tell me again everything you saw, starting from the beginning of this mess?"

I went over the episodes again and ended by recounting the tale that led us to the boat shed and Miller's Cottages. I was fed up with the authorities, but the Eel Grass Girls are supposed to do the right thing. That was our motto, but when things didn't work out, the right thing sometimes could become cloudy. Like now. We had to take things into our own hands, but what should we do?

Before I hung up the phone, I promised to keep Jake informed if we saw anything unusual. It seemed that we were seeing a lot of out-of-the-ordinary things, but a few of them were not related to our mystery.

Therefore, I wasn't going to mention the two "fancy dressers."

As I was about to head upstairs for a nice, peaceful nap, I heard a car drive up. I leaned to see out the back door. I tensed up as I recognized the Picardis' car.

"Oh, no!" I exclaimed to myself as I raced up the stairs to my bedroom in an effort to avoid them. I was about to flop onto my bed when I remembered that Brittany had slept in it. Eeeew! I shut the door and lay down on my spare bed, pretending to be asleep. Mom wouldn't notice that I was home unless she looked in the garage and saw my bike. I didn't care about anything at the moment, except a little bit of sleep. I shut my eyes and drifted off.

"There she is!" Brittany's brassy voice jolted me awake. I felt as if I were Goldilocks being discovered in the baby bear's bed. I looked up to see Brittany, her mother, and my mom peering through the open door.

"Oh, there you are, dear!" Mom came into the room. "Do you feel all right? You don't have a fever, do you?"

"I'm just really tired," I said, wishing I could tell her, "I have a bad case of Picarditis."

Mom sat down on the bed and felt my forehead. "You feel awfully warm. Maybe you should stay home tonight."

"No staying in bed!" Mr. Picardi's voice boomed from the hallway as he pushed his way into my room. I guess the men had come home from fishing. "Everybody's going to dinner tonight 'cause we didn't catch a thing! Not even a minnow." He laughed at what he supposed was a joke. I guess those four going fishing was a joke, and it seemed that Dad's new fishing lures hadn't worked either.

"But Mollie may be sick," my mom said.

"She's not sick, she's just groggy from waking up from a nap," he said. I wished he would get out of my room. He was so loud and reeked of fishing bait.

"Why don't you all go downstairs?" Mom suggested. After they left, she asked, "How do you really feel?"

"I'm fine," I replied. "As long as Brittany doesn't sleep over again."

"She's invited you to stay at the Inn on the Bay with her tonight," said Mom. "They've invited Maxwell too. You and Brittany will have your own room."

I knew what that meant! Brittany hadn't invited anyone to do anything.

Our mothers had made a decision for us, and I was sure that neither one of us wanted the sleepover.

"The Girls are coming over early tomorrow morning, so I can't," I said. I hoped that this sleepover issue wouldn't reoccur every night the Picardis were in town!

"Brittany will be so disappointed," Mom said, but I doubted it. I was sure she would be as glad as I was to not have any more togetherness.

"We'll be eating dinner with them tonight," I said. "And there's always next summer." Of course I hoped that the Picardis would never return.

"The Picardis will probably go back to the inn now so Frank and Georgie can clean up. We won't be meeting them at the Nor'easter until seven," Mom informed me. "So, why don't you go back to sleep? I'll wake you in about an hour or so."

It sounded good to me. She shut my door, and I fell back to sleep. When I awoke, the room felt dark and cold. The windows were open, and I could hear the waves outside. I shivered as I sat up and lay down again. The next thing I knew, someone was shaking me. It was Mom, I supposed. As I opened my eyes, the bright light made me close them again. Mom was leaning over me. I was feeling a little dizzy.

"Mollie, dear, please wake up."

"I feel so cold," I shivered.

"It's time to get ready," Mom said, placing her hand on my forehead again. "You might have a slight fever." Her face showed concern, but I knew it would be easier to go along to dinner, no matter how I felt. Maybe Billy Jones would have some information for me. I would enjoy leaving the Picardis' dinner party to sneak into the kitchen to talk to him.

I shivered again and rubbed my arms. The breeze coming in off the harbor seemed unusually cool, so I changed into long pants and a sweater. The Nor'easter might be super air-conditioned anyway, and I didn't want to suffer from being cold on top of being bored.

Downstairs Mom and Dad were herding Maxwell through the house. We got into the car, and as we drove to town, Dad said, "I'm concerned about all the robberies and kidnappings, Gabby."

"We shouldn't discuss it in front of the kids," Mom quietly responded.

Maxwell was crashing two plastic cars together and wasn't listening.

I spoke up. "I already know all about it."

"I want you to always travel with your friends and not wander away by yourself," said Dad. How could I promise that? I was always alone when my friends weren't around. I didn't answer, rather than make a promise I couldn't keep.

"The robbers came right into our house!" Mom said with a shudder. "Not even our home is safe."

"Maybe we should get a dog," Dad suggested.

"Maxwell's allergic, remember?" Mom reminded him.

"Oh, yes." He paused, then continued, "Just be careful."

Soon we were on Main Street and pulling into the Nor'easter's driveway. We could see the Picardis on the sidewalk with all the other patrons waiting to be seated. We parked out back and walked around to meet them. Mr. Picardi barged up to the hostess to announce that the rest of his party had arrived. We were swiftly ushered to our seats at a large, round booth table in a front corner. The dark interior, ship's lanterns and steering wheels, heavily varnished captain's chairs, and marine paraphernalia gave the room a nautical but hokey ambiance.

The smells of fried clams and seafood filled the room. I concentrated on the menu. Clam chowder and Caesar salad took my attention for the moment. After our orders were placed, I excused myself to wash my hands. Of course they were perfectly clean, but I had to find out if Billy Jones had any information or clues for me.

I darted away from the table before Mom could arrange for Brittany to accompany me. I couldn't do a thing if she tagged along. Weaving through the crowded restaurant, I reached the back of the room and entered the hallway connecting the restaurant to the bar. I poked my head into the big, steamy kitchen. It was quite a contrast to the dark dining room, with its bright overhead lights and the chefs in white aprons, their assistants, and the waiters all yelling at once.

Through the hubbub I could see Billy preparing food of some sort, at a far counter. There was no way I could get his attention, and I couldn't just barge into the chaos without risking my life. I turned to go back to my table when I was startled to see the two fancy men coming straight toward me! They must have been in the bar area. I melted into the kitchen wall, just inside the doorway, as they passed by, then I popped out again and followed them. To my surprise, they made a beeline to our table!

Chapter Twenty-Five

"Frank Picardi! What are you doing here?" the man in the designer suit asked, extending his hand to shake Mr. Picardi's.

"Elbert! I didn't expect to see you on Cape Cod," responded Mr. Picardi. "And Silverson! You know the wife and kids. And this is my high school buddy, Eddy Parker. And this here is his family."

The two men shook hands with Dad and nodded to the "wives and kids." I was still standing somewhat behind them, waiting. Then Hawaiian Shirt said, "Why don't you step into the bar and have a little drink with us before your dinner?"

"Good idea," Mr. Picardi said without even asking my dad. He stood and pushed his way out of the booth and took my father by the arm. Dad started to protest, but Mr. Picardi put a "don't say a word" index finger to his lips and dragged Dad through the packed restaurant to the bar. They hadn't noticed me. I slid into the booth. Mom had a bewildered look on her face.

"So much for a 'family dinner,'" she laughed nervously.

"Oh, men!" chuckled Mrs. Picardi. "You might as well get rid of them when they're going to talk business."

"Those men do business with your husband?" asked Mom.

Mrs. Picardi was flustered and as if she thought she had said something she ought not to have. "I...uh...don't know...Look! Here come our drinks."

The waitress stood at our table with a tray of sodas, wine, and beers. As she placed them on the table, I discreetly asked her to let Billy Jones know I was there and that I would be stopping by the kitchen door soon, so to be on the lookout for me. She nodded, amused at my request I'm sure, but I didn't care.

Mom and Joan were yapping, and the boys were poking each other in a violent way. Brittany was wedged in the middle with an unpleasant look on her face. I sipped my ginger ale and remembered that I hadn't put anything aside for the castaway yet. I would have to find time after my tennis lesson tomorrow morning. What would a castaway like? Hmmm. I knew—Granola bars and a blanket! We had extra blankets in the garage. I hoped they wouldn't be musty.

Brittany was perusing her menu now, even though we had already ordered, so I saw my chance to sneak away. I slithered to the kitchen and hovered in the doorway, stepping aside every few seconds not to block the way for the waiters and busboys rushing in and out. I noticed the boy who had taken money from the fancy men. Billy caught sight of me, slowly edged around the room, and slipped into the hallway beside me.

"I've got news," he whispered, glancing back into the kitchen. "That kid I told you about, the busboy, lives at Miller's with a bunch of his friends. They're from all over, but a couple are local kids. One of them and a summer kid both have motorboats. Is that what you wanted to know?"

"Yes," I answered. "Which cottages do the kids with the boats live in?"

"One is staying in the cottage called *Bluebird*. They say—"

"Billy Jones, get your carcass back in here!" a voice rumbled from the kitchen.

"Got to go!" Billy whisked back into the kitchen. It wasn't much information, but it was enough to give us a start. The *Bluebird* would be our first stop tomorrow morning. Our waitress rushed by with a huge tray loaded with food that looked as if it might be our order, but instead of going back to our table, I turned toward the bar. I wanted to see what was going on with the menfolk. The fact that those fancy men were doing business with Mr. Picardi made that trio suddenly suspicious.

I sauntered along the softly lit hallway and peeked around the corner into the darker bar. It was too loud in there, with music blaring and people laughing and shouting, to be heard above the din. I searched around for my father. I noticed a few of the fishermen we had met earlier in the summer. No gypsy fishermen here. They were hiding in the woods and doing their drinking there, getting ready to pillage our town.

Finally I spotted my father at a tiny table in the back, squeezed in with his new "friends." I wasn't exactly ecstatic with the way he let those men drag him away from his family without putting up much of a fuss. Children weren't allowed on the bar side, but the waitresses and bartenders were too busy to notice, I hoped, so I made my way back to Dad.

"Hi, Dad," I said cheerfully.

The conversation died, and the men looked at me in an odd way.

"What's up?" asked Mr. Picardi in what could have been perceived as an annoyed manner.

"I was just going to ask the same thing," I said with a smile. "I think the waitress is serving our dinner."

"Yeah? Well, we're not finished talking yet," said Mr. Picardi. He was being rude.

Dad stood up and excused himself.

"Hey, where're you going?" Mr. Picardi seemed shocked.

"I want to be with my family," my dad stated simply. "It isn't often we have a dinner together." He put his arm around my shoulders, and we walked back into the dining room.

"What were you all talking about?" I asked, as if I didn't really care.

"Frank and his friends want to buy property in town," he answered, but he didn't sound very happy about it.

"Were you and Mr. Picardi good friends when you were in school together?" I queried.

"We weren't in the same classes, but we were in the same grade. He was very popular. Always had something going on," Dad answered vaguely. "When we met in New York, it seemed that we had a lot in common."

I thought so. Frank Picardi hadn't really been my father's friend. Oh, well. He was entitled to make one mistake in his life, but I wished he could correct the problem before my entire weekend was ruined.

"Where's Frank?" asked Mrs. Picardi as we sat down at our booth again.

"He's still talking to his friends," said Dad, dipping a spoon into his chowder. "I think he'll be a while, so we might as well eat."

I started on my chowder as well. Maxwell spilled his soda as he attacked Georgie with his straw. Family time wasn't always fun, but at least Maxwell was bothering his new friend and not me. I was proud of Dad for standing up to Mr. Picardi.

I was also glad that Brittany was keeping to herself. It would have been much worse if she had been a chatterbox. I concentrated on my dinner. When I had eaten almost all of my fried-clam plate, Mr. Picardi returned to the table.

"What kept you so long?" Mrs. Picardi inquired.

"The guys got big plans," he said, sitting beside his wife. "This place is a real goldmine, I tell you."

I had heard that term before, and I didn't like the idea of Mr. Picardi thinking of the town in those terms. It told me that he didn't appreciate the smallness and quaintness, the qualities that usually draw people to the Cape.

"Edward Parker? I'm John Seymore." A strange man loomed over our table, extending his hand to my father. "My son Harvey goes to sailing school with your daughter."

I contorted my body to look around the room. Not far from our table I saw Harvey Seymore, Gilly and her red curls, and a few adults I didn't know. I turned back to the last delectable clam.

Dad introduced Mr. Seymore to everyone at our table. Then Mr. Seymore said, "Edward, I'd like to introduce you to my family." He led Dad over to his table. They talked for a while. When Dad returned to our table, he seemed a little subdued, but didn't say anything. Mr. Picardi noticed nothing, but Brittany didn't miss a trick. After Mr. Picardi finished his meal, we walked down the street to the ice cream shop for dessert. We ate our cones on the way back to the parking lot.

Mom and Mrs. Picardi were trying to make a plan for the following day. Maxwell would spend tonight with Georgie, and my parents would meet the Picardis for breakfast at the inn. Mom would then take me to tennis while the men and boys went out fishing with a group from the inn, Brittany and her mom would go shopping, and the whole bunch of us would meet at the band concert at night. I could slip away with my friends at the band concert, so I didn't complain.

Mr. Picardi caught a glimpse of Billy Jones in the kitchen door. He stalked up to the screen door and hollered, "Hey, boy! You got any leads for me?"

Billy looked out in alarm. It seemed that at first he didn't recognize Mr. Picardi. "No, sir," he called back. Everyone in the kitchen was staring at Billy. He added, "That's not my line of business. Sorry," and turned back to his work.

Dad didn't seem embarrassed by Mr. Picardi's boisterous behavior, and his buddy Frank couldn't tell that he made other people uncomfortable.

Maxwell got into the car with the Picardis, and everyone said good-bye to everyone else, except Brittany and me. I was relieved to be delivered from her, and Maxwell and Georgie, for an evening. After they drove away, Dad sighed and we got into the car.

"What's the matter, Ned?" Mom asked.

"John Seymore told me that the Picardis are into some..." he quickly glanced at me in the rearview mirror. "Uh...funny business in New Jersey."

"Money laundering?" I asked.

"How do you know about it?" asked Dad, stopping the car just before he pulled out onto Main Street.

"How do you know what money laundering is?" Mom asked, giving me a worried look as if I practiced it myself.

"Harvey Seymore was talking about it at sailing school this morning," I informed them. "It made Brittany really upset."

"I should think so!" Mom said. "Why would Harvey say a thing like that?"

"Apparently it's true," Dad said, "according to John. He wanted to let me know because Harvey told him that I had recently run into Frank. He assumed that I might not really know Frank all that well. Harvey must have overheard you say something about me running into Frank after many years, Mollie."

"Yes, Dad. He did eavesdrop," I said. "So Mr. Seymore says it's true?"

"He did, but I'm asking you not to repeat it. I didn't like Frank's friends we met at the restaurant. They want to buy up property in town. They say they're only interested in investing, but I have a feeling that there's something more to it. Maybe money laundering."

"But where are they getting the money?" asked Mom.

"I don't have any idea," said Dad. "And I don't want to know." We drove past the lighthouse and he continued, "I'm thinking that it was unwise to invite the Picardis to town without knowing more about them."

"But I like Joan," said Mom. "I doubt if she knows what her husband is doing."

"Maybe, maybe not," said Dad. As we drove past the yacht club and along the harbor, he gripped the steering wheel so tightly his knuckles were white. "The thing that bothers me is that I feel that I don't like his friends because they're different."

163

"No, dear," Mom soothed him. "It's because their morals are different from yours that makes you uncomfortable. You were willing to accept them. It's obvious that they're not like most of our other friends, but if you felt they were honest, we wouldn't be having this conversation now."

Dad turned into the driveway and parked in the garage next to Mom's car. For a minute I pretended that I was like my friends, an only child. It felt nice, but it was too bad that Dad was so preoccupied with the Picardis. I'd had it. I was Picardi'd out.

We entered the house. My parents walked into the living room. I stayed behind to use the phone. I had promised to give Louie a call. His mom called him to the phone, and I filled him in on the kids living at Miller's Cottages and Dad's new "old friend." We made a plan to meet at the band concert the next evening.

I joined my parents in the living room. They were sitting on the sofa having a relaxed conversation. Not something that usually happened at our house. Dad stunned me by asking, "How about a board game?"

Mom was flabbergasted. She quickly recovered and said, "All right. We have a new game I bought a few days ago for Maxwell. The object is to think of different categories that all begin with the same letter."

"I know that game," I said. "I've played it at a friend's house in Jersey."

"Sounds like fun!" said Dad, perking up. I felt happy. Dad was here and Maxwell was gone—the Picardis were good for something after all. We settled down on the living room floor. It was one of the best times I had ever had with my parents. I was thinking that maybe this was going to be a good weekend after all, but I was wrong—very wrong.

Chapter Twenty-Six

I awoke next morning to Muffy's voice. It seemed far away, but as my head cleared, I realized that I was indeed in my own room and that the voice came from downstairs. She was talking to Mom. I hurriedly dressed and dashed downstairs to meet her. She was sitting at the breakfast table with my parents, who were drinking their coffee.

"There's my little sleepyhead," said Mom. I gave her an unappreciative look and grabbed a granola bar from the cupboard. Mom poured me a glass of orange juice.

"So what important business are you girls attending to this morning?" asked Dad, thinking that he was making a cute joke, never realizing that we *did* have important business.

Muffy just shrugged and smiled. She could not tell a lie.

"We're off to the inn," said Mom, placing the coffee cups in the sink. "I'll be back in time for your tennis lesson, but are you sure you won't join us?"

"The other Girls will be here any minute," I said. "See you later."

Dad was dressed for his fishing trip in shorts, a fishing vest with shiny lures stuck all over it, and his lucky hat. If you went by his gear, you might think he knew what he was doing. Maybe he could learn something from the other fishermen. Muffy and I said good-bye to Mom and Dad. They exited the kitchen and drove off to the inn. I offered Muffy some breakfast while we waited for Laura and Abigail, but she said she had already eaten "real food," whatever that meant.

Soon the others were at the back door. "Come on, let's go," Laura said, tossing her backpack and life jacket inside the door. I noticed that Abigail hadn't brought her life jacket.

"Abigail, you forgot your life jacket," I said. "But you can pick one up at the yacht club before we go out with Billy."

"I can't go," she replied. "Grammy says I have to have tea with a friend of hers whose granddaughter is visiting from out west."

"So you're not coming with us to Freeman's Island?" asked Muffy, obviously disappointed.

"I can't. But next time." She was disappointed too.

I shrugged. What could we do? There was no way Abigail could get out of it. We headed toward the garage. "Those college kids probably sleep until noon."

"I'm sure," Laura said, shaking her head. We couldn't imagine it.

"Billy Jones told me two of the kids have boats, and I know which cottage one of them lives in," I said, leading the way across the lawn. "But he never got to give me all the information he had. We'll have to find out where the other kid lives. One is local, and one is a summer kid."

"If they're helping the gypsies, won't they be dangerous?" asked Abigail, already apprehensive.

"Not at this hour of the morning," Muffy snorted. "Don't worry, Abigail. You don't have to be afraid."

"And you'll never guess what happened last night at the Nor'easter!" I told them about the fancy men wanting to buy property in town and how Mr. Seymore told Dad about Mr. Picardi laundering money.

"What is your Dad going to do now?" asked Muffy.

"I don't know," I answered, pulling my bike from the garage. "But my Dad has some serious thinking to do. He can't be friends with a man who's a crook." Dad had to make a decision about Frank Picardi, but for now, we had our own decision to make, which was to get on with our plan.

We rode single file toward Smith's Landing, but before we got there, we took a right onto River Lane. After dodging potholes, we were confronted by two dirt roads. Nailed to a pine tree was a hand-painted sign that said "Miller's Cottages" with an arrow pointing left. We pushed our bikes through the deep sand to a small clearing where three little cottages stood. Each one had a different color trim. The *Robin* was red, the *Finch* was yellow, and the *Bluebird* was, you guessed it, blue. Several economy-size cars were parked between the cottages, as well as a beat-up old truck.

"Billy gave me a tip last night, when we had dinner at the Nor'easter," I told the Girls in a hushed voice. "We should try the *Bluebird* first."

"What did you eat?" asked Abigail.

I made a face at her. Now was not the time for chitchat.

"What if they really do want a babysitter?" asked Muffy. "I've never done it before, except for one of my cousins, and that was when at least six adults were present."

"Shush!" I hissed. We approached the blue-trimmed cottage and wondered how more than one person could possibly live there. The entire cottage was considerably smaller than my bedroom. The front door stood open, but a screen door was closed to keep the bugs and skunks out. I peered into the darkness within, but I couldn't see much. Bed sheets covered the windows. I gave a firm tap on the door. There was no response.

I knocked harder and shouted, "Hello! Anybody home?" Still nothing. "Hello in there! Wake up! Hello!"

Finally we heard mattress springs creaking. A young man in a grubby T-shirt and boxer shorts stumbled to the door. His hair was all rumpled and his eyes were half shut.

"Huh? Whad'ya want?"

"We're your friendly local babysitters," Laura said brightly. "We're at your service. We babysit day or night, any quantity of children, any age, from one to one hundred and one. We're—"

"Hold on a second," he yawned. "I don't need a babysitter."

"What about your roommates? Maybe they need a babysitter?" Muffy inquired politely.

"They don't need one either."

"This is such a lovely spot," I said. "So near the harbor. It would be nice if you had a boat so you could enjoy the water."

"I *do* have a boat," the young man answered. "It is kinda nice here."

"Didn't you graduate from the local high school?" Laura asked.

"Yeah! How'd you know?"

"I live down the street. I thought I recognized you," Laura replied. "Do you take all your friends out in your boat?"

"Katie Hinckley has a boat too," he said. "She lives in *Finch*. Then Sammy Boucher uses his relatives' boat. We all go over to Womponoy once in a while." He yawned again. "Uh...if you don't need me anymore, I'm going back to bed."

"Thank you for your time," Muffy called to him as he disappeared into the darkness of the cottage.

"I think we can eliminate him," said Muffy as we moved on to the next cottage. "He's too talkative and gave us too much information."

"What if he's trying to trick us?" asked Abigail. "He could have misled us on purpose."

"But I know him, even though I can't remember his name," Laura said. "I agree with Muffy. He wouldn't have told us anything if he were working with the gypsies."

"I think you're right," I concurred, as we walked up to the *Robin*.

In the process of offering our services, we discovered that four young men lived there, one of whom was the boat-borrower Sammy Boucher. The *Finch* contained five college girls including boat owner Katie Hinckley. No one needed a babysitter, but we now knew our suspects. One of these three had to be the person lending a motorboat to the gypsies.

Pushing our bikes back through the deep sand of the driveway, we discussed what we had found out.

"They must use that old truck to haul the stolen property away," speculated Abigail. "I wonder how they sell it?"

"It has to go out of town," Muffy said. "Otherwise someone would recognize it. Our town is too small for them to sell it locally."

"Don't forget the gypsies have a key to that boat shed," I said. "Either the owner of that shed is also involved, or the gypsies know how to pick the lock."

"They picked the lock," said Laura.

"I keep thinking about those poor kidnap victims," Abigail said. "What are the gypsies going to do with them? It's been days since the girl was captured. She must be so frightened! And that other woman. The man too. Do you think they're feeding them?"

"I'm sure they are," said Laura. "But I wonder why they don't send ransom notes? Why are they waiting? They must want money. Why else would they do it?"

"They could have sent the notes already," I said. "Or maybe they telephoned the families. Kidnappers don't want the police to get involved. Maybe the families are paying up. The girl might even have been released by now. The others too."

"Really?" asked Abigail. "That makes me feel better. I hope we get a call from Officer Nick telling us the good news. Then we could concentrate on helping the castaway. I wish I didn't have to go to that tea party! I want to go to Freeman's Island with you."

"No use crying over spilt milk," I said. Muffy gave me a weird look. I changed the subject. "I'd like to have a look at that boat shed in the daylight. Let's go!"

We rode down River Lane, turning right to Smith's Landing. There were two trucks and a car parked in the small lot, but no one was around. I put my kickstand down and surveyed the shed. There were two windows in it, one on either side, but they were obstructed by the junk piled up against them inside. We couldn't see exactly what was in there. Presumably the stolen goods were gone.

"So, you think they picked this lock?" I asked Laura, as I inspected the padlock.

"Sure," she replied. "But it wouldn't hurt to find out who owns this shed."

"The town offices!" exclaimed Muffy. "The three of us can make them our next stop, while you're at your tennis lesson. It won't take long."

"Good, because I've got to get going," I told them.

"Meet you back at your house in a couple of hours," Muffy called out as they rode off.

The Girls headed toward town by way of Pine Street and Small Pond Road to Main. I rode back home to wait for Mom. I got my tennis racket from its hook inside the back door and stayed outside to whap a tennis ball against the side of the garage until Mom arrived. It wasn't long before she drove up.

Soon I heard her car enter the driveway, but when I craned my neck around the side of the garage to see, it wasn't Mom. It was a red convertible!

Chapter Twenty-Seven

I waited for the car to approach. The two fancy men were taking their time. They kept looking into the woods and pointing on one side and then the other as they gabbed away. I kept hitting my tennis ball, not knowing exactly what I should do.

The car stopped in front of the house, and the fancy men got out.

"Hello, little lady, I'm Mr. Elbert," said the man in the suit, when he saw me. I wondered if it were the same suit he was wearing yesterday.

I hit the ball again. What did they want?

"Your father home?" asked the other man, who sported a red Hawaiian shirt today. At least one of them changed his clothes.

"Maybe," I said. "Who wants to know?"

"I'm Mr. Silverson," the Hawaiian shirt said with an insincere smile. "I met your father last night at the Nor'easter. We have a business proposition to discuss."

"What is it?" I asked.

"A business proposition is—" he began.

"I know what it means," I replied. "I want to know what is *your* business proposition."

"It's for your father, not you," said Elbert, sneering. "Is he home or not?"

"His car is here," remarked Silverson, looking into the open garage.

"I'll go inside and get him," I said. I thought I would use the occasion to telephone the Inn on the Bay and see where Mom was. Why did she have to be late for my tennis lesson again today? In the kitchen I quickly looked up the phone number and dialed the inn. When the receptionist finally reached the dining room hostess, I was told that Mom had already left, but that Mrs. Picardi was there.

"Mollie? What's up?" she asked when she was on the line.

"Hello, Mrs. Picardi. Is Mom on her way home? I have a tennis lesson."

"She should be there any minute. The men and boys had a little bit of trouble getting off on their fishing expedition," she laughed. "I hope you won't be late."

"Thank you," I said, looking out the kitchen window. "Here she is!"

I hung up and sprinted outside to Mom's car just as she pulled in beside the garage. I wanted to get to her before those men did. "Mom!" She parked, and I rushed up to her window. "Those creepy men are looking for Dad," I whispered. Mom nervously eyed them as they moved toward us.

"Morning, Mrs. Parker," said Elbert, tipping his hat. "We're looking for Mr. Parker."

"He's gone fishing for the day," replied Mom.

"We'd like to look around the lot," he said, motioning toward the Farrencrows' property. "If you don't mind."

"But that's not our property," Mom said. "The owners are away."

"Who are they?" asked Mr. Silverson.

"I...um...don't really know," Mom stammered. "Why don't you call Ned tonight and you can talk to him about it? My daughter has a tennis lesson now, and we have to leave."

"Then we'll just look around on our own," said Mr. Elbert.

"I would prefer that you leave," Mom said firmly. I was astonished. She was generally wishy-washy and she always gave in to Maxwell. I have to say that I was proud of her for standing up to those bums.

Mr. Elbert opened his mouth as if he were going to say something, but he changed his mind. "Let's go," he mumbled to Mr. Silverson. They got into their convertible and nodded to Mom as Silverson shifted into reverse, turned the car around, and left.

Mom let her breath out. "Those men give me the willies! I hope they won't come back again. We'd better hurry or you'll be late for your tennis lesson."

On the way over to Muddy River, Mom chattered away about her new friend Joan and her wonderful life in New Jersey. "They don't live very far from us. Joan plays tennis too. We're going to play this afternoon. The inn has a lovely clay court. We can get together on the weekends when we're back in Jersey, except your Dad will have to make sure that Frank's business is legitimate and all that. But even if he *is* into money laundering, it's not Joan's fault."

"She married him," I said.

"He may have been all right when they got married, dear," she pointed out.

Eventually we arrived at "Tennis for Teens" tennis camp. Lizzie Winkle was at the desk waiting for me. I realized that I hadn't practiced much since my last lesson, but I was a busy Eel Grass Girl.

The lesson went smoothly. I had some good volleys, and Lizzie gave me some tips. When we finished, I followed her back to the office to confirm my next lesson. One of the other teachers, Jim Stern, was there.

"You got a call from a Sammy Boucher," he said, handing her a note and giving her a knowing look. "New boyfriend?"

"Hardly!" She snatched the note from Jim.

That name sounded familiar. My ears perked up.

Lizzie fingered the note nervously and read it.

"You know Sammy?" I asked.

"Uh, yes. Do you?" She seemed shocked that I would know him.

"Not really. I know someone who works with one of his friends," I explained.

"We met at a party," Lizzie said. "Actually, one of my college friends lives in a cottage next to his and gave him my number. I wasn't very happy about that! Sammy's a total jerk! Oh, sorry. I didn't mean to say that, but he keeps calling, and I don't want anything to do with him."

My head was spinning. I had to think fast. "Lizzie, could you do me a big favor?" I explained that we needed some information about the kids living at Miller's Cottages. "If you could find out what Sammy does in his spare time, it would really help. I know you don't like him, but could you ask him what he does for extra money and who his friends are?"

"Why do you want to know more about him?" she asked quizzically. "He's not a great guy, and I don't think he's anyone you would want to know."

"I can't explain now," I said. "But it's really important. Please?"

"You're a cute kid and one of my most serious students," Lizzie said, considering my request. "O.K., I'll see what I can find out. I'll call my friend right now and see what I can do. I could tell you when I see you next, but you don't have another lesson until Tuesday. I'll call you if I find anything out. I have your number."

"Thanks, Lizzie. I really appreciate it."

Mom appeared and chatted for a minute with Lizzie while I took a drink of water at the fountain. This was quite a coincidence, Lizzie knowing Sammy. Mom and I joined a long line of traffic, inching along all the way from Muddy River to the rotary in town.

On the way I wondered what the Girls might find out at the town offices. I thought of the fancy men and hoped we wouldn't see any more of them, but that wasn't likely. I saw the Girls seated on the back step as we turned into our driveway. The second Mom stopped the car, I bolted out and joined my friends.

"Pizza?" she called out after us.

"Sure." The Girls and I raced around the side of the house to the patio. We sat on the plastic lawn chairs and got to business.

"Wait 'til you hear what we found out," Muffy said, leaning forward. "The boat shed belongs to John Seymore and Granville Wagner!"

"Now that's something!" I muttered.

Laura said, "It proves that the gypsies are picking the lock! The police searched the shed, so they must have notified Mr. Seymore about it. Now he knows the gypsies are using it to stash their loot. And even if they change the lock, it won't help. They'll still find a way to get in."

"Mr. Seymore and Mr. Wagner should booby trap the shed," Muffy suggested.

"Let me tell you who came to visit this morning, just before I went to my tennis lesson—those two characters in the red convertible!" I said.

"What did they want?" asked Muffy, obviously puzzled.

I explained, "They want to buy the Farrencrows' property. Mom asked them to leave, but I have a feeling that they'll be back. I wish Dad had never met Mr. Picardi."

Abigail gave me a sympathetic look.

"Time to pack our care package," said Laura. We opened the sliding glass door and filed across the living room. We could hear Mom in the laundry room—washing my sheets, I hoped. I shuddered to think of Brittany sleeping in my bed.

The Girls dragged their backpacks upstairs to my room while I slipped out to the garage to find an extra blanket. There I found a canvas bag that would hold everything.

173

"The pizza will be here any minute," Mom called out to me as I passed through the kitchen.

"Give us a holler when it arrives," I called back. Upstairs I was astounded by the array of supplies the Girls had brought for the care package. There were candy bars, cookies, pasta, canned beans, a can-opener, an old pot, socks, a sweater, deodorant, toothpaste, two bars of soap, matches in a plastic bag, and a nail clipper! Holy Cow!

"It's great, isn't it?" Abigail exclaimed. "Everything he needs."

"Yeah," I agreed. We stuffed it all into the canvas bag along with the blanket. "Billy will give us some lobsters, too."

"The old man needs fruit and vegetables," said Abigail.

"I doubt if we have any," I replied, considering the usual state of our refrigerator.

"I do," said Laura. "We can stop by my house on the way to the yacht club."

"Pizza!" Mom called up from the bottom of the stairs. We raced headlong down the steps to the kitchen, where a nice hot steamy pizza was waiting for us. We dug in and enjoyed the tasty, doughy slices. It was heaven! Not literally, of course, because I don't believe in that place, but I do know the concept and can appreciate the experience of heaven on earth in the form of a pizza, the best food known to humankind.

Mom poured us glasses of soda. She had changed into her tennis dress, so I assumed she would be leaving soon for her match with Mrs. Picardi. As soon as we finished eating, we tossed the pizza box into the trash, grabbed our life jackets, and bolted out the door, carrying our bag and backpacks.

"Hey! This bag is too heavy," I said, trying to balance the big canvas bag on my bike. We divided up the supplies among our backpacks and headed off.

Our first stop was Laura's house. She barged in the back door and marched toward the big fruit bowl standing in the middle of the kitchen table. A note was lying there, held in place by a beach stone.

"What's this?" she asked, picking up the note. "Uh-oh! Miss Deighton wants me to do some weeding for her this afternoon! Mom promised her I'd be there at two. How could she do this to me?"

We slumped into the chairs around the table. What was happening to our plan?

"That means that Muffy and Mollie will have to go to Freeman's Island all by themselves," Laura concluded. She stood up, gathered some apples and oranges, and raided the fridge, loading my backpack with a crown of broccoli, a bunch of carrots, and an onion. Muffy and Abigail packed Laura's supplies into their backpacks.

"Well," she said sadly. "This is good-bye."

"Cheer up! We'll see you tonight at the band concert," Muffy said. "Meet us at our regular place behind the bandstand."

She stood in her driveway and waved good-bye to us. We hopped on our bikes again and rode out onto the road. The ride to the yacht club was quick.

Abigail rode on to her grandmother's house, after unloading her backpack and saying good-bye to us.

"Have fun at your tea party," Muffy called out after her. "And see you tonight."

Muffy and I parked our bikes in the blackberry bushes and looked down to the dock, where Billy Jones was loading his boat. Together we lugged the canvas bag down and joined Billy at the end of the pier.

"What'd you bring the old coot?" asked Billy by way of a greeting.

"Nail clippers and deodorant," I said simply, glancing at our heavy bag. Billy laughed out loud.

"That's not all," said Muffy. "We brought food and candy too. And a sweater and blanket."

Billy smiled, but made no comment. "Come on. Hop aboard."

We untied the painter from the cleat as soon as Billy had the engine going, and pushed off. Soon we were following the channel toward the cut-through.

Muffy said, "We checked out the cottages this morning. Thank you for the lead."

"Find out anything?"

"Plenty! Now we have three suspects, instead of only two," I told him. "The boy in *Bluebird* talked so much we might eliminate him. Then there's Katie Hinckley and a kid named Sammy Boucher. "

"Sammy Boucher? I didn't think of him," Billy said as we cruised at five miles an hour, observing the "no wake" restriction. "I didn't know

175

that he was living at Miller's too. He's John Seymore's nephew."

"The plot thickens!" Muffy said in a mysterious tone. She was right about that.

I couldn't believe it. "You mean Sammy Boucher is related to Mr. Seymore?"

"Yes. And to the Wagners too. They all live in a compound near the dyke road to Deer Island. But I think I know why he's at Miller's. I heard that he had some trouble with his parents. Maybe they asked him to move out."

"He's a problem child?" asked Muffy. I hadn't had a chance to tell her what my tennis teacher, Lizzie Winkle, had said about him.

"He's a crummy bum," Billy said. "His uncles are decent enough—his father too—but he's a bad seed."

"A what?" I wanted to know.

"The whole clan is fine, except for him. I guess that's why he's living at Miller's Cottages." Billy steered his motorboat around a channel marker. "But he doesn't have a boat."

"We think he's using his uncle's boat," Muffy said. "But we don't know to which uncle the boat belongs."

We told Billy the details of what we had seen two nights before. "The gypsies don't have access to a small motorboat," I said. "They only have those huge trawlers and some little rowboats."

Muffy continued, "They probably met Sammy and made a deal to borrow his uncle's boat to haul the things they steal. Sammy's relatives own the boat shed at Smith's Landing, so Sammy may even have lent the gypsies his key! Maybe Sammy even loads the goods into his truck and takes them off somewhere to sell."

"It sounds logical," Billy said, but he didn't sound convinced. "John Seymore moors his motorboat at Smith's Landing, but I'm not so sure of your theory. Sammy Boucher may not be my favorite person, but don't you think that the gypsies could be hot-wiring the motor and picking the lock of the shed? It's possible Sammy doesn't know a thing about it."

"But the gypsies disappeared in the direction of Miller's Cottages!" I almost shouted.

"Circumstantial evidence," Billy said. When he noticed our perplexed expressions, he explained. "What you saw, or think you saw, doesn't prove anything. I want those robbing kidnappers apprehended as much as you do, but proof is what we need."

"We need a police force that responds more quickly when we tell them where the stolen goods are," Muffy muttered.

The gypsy trawlers were coming up, to port. They were still tied to the town moorings. Their time was up, but they couldn't leave now. We wished they would leave, but they were guilty of so many crimes, we should have been thankful that they were staying, giving us more time to find the evidence that would convict them.

The gypsies were on deck, placidly scrubbing the decks and hanging out their wash. How could they appear to be so domestic and innocent by day and be so corrupt by night?

We didn't notice any garbage floating on the water. Were the gypsies outwardly behaving well? Was it all for show, to appear law-abiding and avoid any more trouble with the authorities? They were headed for big trouble, though. We would find the evidence needed to convict them. I didn't know how, but we would.

One of them peered out at us. Without removing his gaze, he called his buddies over to the railing and pointed at us as we cruised by. They scowled. I scowled back.

"Just look at them!" Billy exclaimed. "Cool as cucumbers! Who do they think they are?"

"And what have they done to their victims?" Muffy wondered.

"It's all over town," Billy remarked. "My brother works at the Nor'easter, you remember, and he hears more than I do since I'm stuck in the kitchen all the time. He told me people are making speculations about aliens! The cops are really stumped this time. Four people missing already and not a word about any ransoms."

"One of them is our castaway," I reminded him.

"I know. But why haven't they written any ransom notes for the others?" asked Billy.

"The gypsies probably can't write," I speculated.

"Then why do they keep on kidnapping?" Billy asked.

"They want the ransom money," I began, "but don't know how to get it."

"If Sammy Boucher is their accomplice," Muffy said, "why don't they ask Sammy to write the notes?"

"Kidnapping is much more serious than stealing boating equipment," answered Billy. "Those bums are probably trying to figure it out on their own."

We passed a small sloop under sail and waved to some yacht club members in their big motorboat. We passed through the cut and into the Sound, carefully gliding over the sandbars surrounding Womponoy.

"I'll check a few pots first, so I can harvest a couple of lobsters for your friend," Billy said.

We neared Womponoy, where we could see Billy's yellow and black wooden markers bobbing in the water. Billy cut the engine and pulled a marker into the boat. After Billy hauled up a long length of line, a big lobster pot rose up through the blue-green water.

"Aha! Here's the old geezer's dinner!" Billy announced, opening the top of the pot and dumping two mottled black and green lobsters into the bottom of the boat. I noticed that the pot contained a red brick. For weight, I supposed.

"Help!" cried Muffy, giggling. "They're going to bite my toes!"

Billy laughed too as he deftly swept them into a burlap bag. "There you go." He handed the bag to me, and I carefullly placed the burlap bag next to my canvas bag.

Billy rebaited the pot with some kind of horrible-looking entrails and dropped it down into the water again. Then we held on as he sped off to Freeman's Island.

Chapter Twenty-Eight

It felt great to feel the sun and the salt air on my face. I felt so free. This was the way summer should be. Sun, wind, and waves. I usually didn't give much thought to these things. I took them for granted, but they are such a big part of my summer.

The best part of the summer was that I had made three good friends, and we had formed the Eel Grass Girls Mystery Club. Already we had solved three major mysteries including a dead body that disappeared, a haunted house, and a coven of witches, but now we faced another serious mystery.

Robbery was one thing, but the kidnappings were another. The gypsies' days as free men were numbered, as they say in crime stories. It was only a matter of time before they would be caught.

I was sure that if the police could convict them of the robberies, they could get the gypsies to reveal the hiding place of their victims. If only they would approach the families and ask for ransom money, maybe then they could be caught. Possibly they thought they had botched their plan and didn't know what to do next. As long as they didn't panic and hurt anyone, I hoped this case would have a happy ending for the victims and their families.

Freeman's Island loomed on the horizon like a big sea turtle. I guess that doesn't sound very picturesque. Soon Billy had reduced the boat's speed, and the motor puttered as we drifted close to shore. Muffy and I disembarked with our bags.

"See you back here when I'm finished with my lobster pots," said Billy as he gunned the engine and headed back toward Womponoy.

We climbed the cliff of crumbling sand and then followed the trail that led from the crest of the bluff inland through a sea of beach grass.

"I hope he doesn't act weird again," I said.

Muffy reminded me, "Remember, he does have a gun."

"Oh, hooey!" was my response to that. "The gun is for hunting food. There's nothing to worry about."

We trudged along. The lobsters began to feel heavy. It was probably because I was carrying them somewhat away from my body for fear of being snapped by their claws through the old burlap sack. Muffy and I lugged the canvas tote bag between us. Eventually we came to the little hollow where the castaway had made his camp and saw the top of his driftwood shack sticking up above the beach grass.

"Hello!" I shouted. "You have visitors!"

There was no answer. We drew nearer. It looked the same as before. The campfire had burned out. Heaps of shells stood stinking beside the hut. But the place was deserted!

"Maybe he's out fishing," suggested Muffy, but she approached the hut anyway, and peeked in.

"Oh, no!" she gasped

"What?" I rushed to her side. In the dark hut, on a pile of rags, lay the old man.

"He's dead!" I concluded.

"He couldn't be!" Muffy sobbed.

I pushed past her and entered the dim structure. Muffy was at my elbow. We leaned over the form of the old man. He lay on the rags, his eyes closed and his mouth open, his gray hair and beard matted and damp, a thin, threadbare blanket pulled up to his chin.

"He's breathing!" I said. "He must be sick. Looks like a fever."

"We've got to get help!" Muffy said, frantically turning toward me with her eyes full of tears. "I don't know what to do first!"

"If only we had Abigail's cell phone." I felt frustrated. If only I had a cell phone of my own! "Billy won't be back for a while. I'll go to the shore and make a fire. That will get his attention."

"All right," said Muffy. "I'll come with you. I don't want to stay here alone."

"You have to stay here. One of us should wait with him. You don't have to be afraid of him in this condition," I said.

"I'm not staying," said Muffy. "It might not be right to leave him alone, but I'm frightened."

I didn't say anything, but I found the matches in the canvas bag and stuck them in my pocket. "There's plenty of driftwood and dry grass on the beach," I said.

Muffy pulled the blanket out of the bag and covered the old man with it. His own blanket wasn't doing him much good. Muffy and I then ran back to the shore.

When we reached the beach, we dragged pieces of driftwood into a huge pile. We stuffed dry eel grass into the middle and lit match after match, trying to get the fire going. I gathered some more beach grass and twigs. They finally caught fire and the whole thing began to blaze.

"Too much salt in the wood," said Muffy. She took off her sweatshirt and fanned the flames, generating a big billow of dark smoke. "Someone will see this."

We ran over the sand, picking up every thing that would burn: paper cups, scraps of line, mostly wood.

"Hey! Look! Someone's coming!" cried Muffy. She jumped up and down, waving her arms and sweatshirt in the air. I looked out to see not Billy's boat, but Howie Snow's huge wooden dory.

"What ya doin'?" he shouted across the water. "Havin' a clam bake?" As he drew nearer, he saw the frantic looks on our faces. "What's wrong?"

"Our castaway is sick!" Muffy hollered. "We need help!"

When he was close enough, I waded out into the water to meet him. Muffy was right behind me. Howie tossed his anchor over the side of his dory and pulled the line taut until the anchor was secure.

"Let's go get him," he said. Howie climbed overboard, and we started for shore. "How'd ya git out here?"

"Billy Jones. He's harvesting lobsters off Womponoy," Muffy said, looking over toward the other island. It seemed that Billy was so engrossed in his lobster pots that he hadn't noticed our bonfire.

Muffy and I led the way, and Howie lumbered up the bluff behind us. We jogged along the path until we reached the hut.

"He's in here," said Muffy, trying to catch her breath.

Howie stooped down and stuck his head inside the door of the little hut. "Where?" he asked.

"Where what?" I asked him, pushing forward and peering around him into the interior. The blankets lay on the heap of rags, but the old man was gone!

Muffy squeezed into the cramped space. "Where is he? What happened to him?"

She looked at me, but I had no answers. "He was too sick to move," I told Howie. "He couldn't have gone anywhere on his own. He must have been... must have been..."

"Kidnapped!" whispered Muffy. "Oh, no! The gypsies must have kidnapped him!"

"But how?" I asked. "They couldn't have escaped. They must still be on the island! We've got to find them!"

"What's going on?" asked Howie. He was clearly clueless.

"The old man was here, just minutes ago," I said as calmly as I could. "He was almost dead, hardly breathing. Now he's gone. The only explanation is that the gypsies were out here, on the far side of the island, lying in wait. The moment Muffy and I ran down to the shore to build the bonfire, they came in here and kidnapped the old man. They would have had to carry him, so they might be loading him on-board their boat right now. We have to go!"

We hurried along the path heading south, until we reached the shore. A number of boats were in the water, coming and going. We saw a couple of boats not far from shore, with groups of men in them, but it was difficult to tell if they were the gypsies or not. We presumed that the castaway would be lying on the bottom of the boat bound and gagged.

"Do you really think they'd kidnap him in broad daylight?" Howie inquired.

"They must have!" said Muffy with emotion.

"We should circle the island," I said, "in case they're hiding on the other side, waiting for us to leave."

Howie sighed, but he accompanied us around the entire island. It turned out to be not such a great idea. We didn't find any trace of the old man or the gypsies. There were even more boats passing by in the Sound and carrying passengers who looked as if they could be the gypsies.

"Howie, we have to see if any of those boats really are the gypsy kidnappers," I said with a sweep of my arm, encompassing all the boats in the Sound between Freeman's Island, Womponoy, and the harbor.

When we came to our bonfire, we covered the burning embers with sand. Howie climbed into his dory, hauled us on-board, and gave his old dory all the power he could.

"We need to tell Billy what's going on," Muffy said. "Can you take us over to him?"

He nodded and veered toward Womponoy, where we could see Billy still working.

"Billy!" I shouted when we were close enough for him to hear me. "The castaway has been kidnapped!" We told him the details of what we had found on the island, or rather, hadn't found. "We have to tell the police and maybe the harbor master and the Coast Guard."

"I'll go look for him," said Billy. "They may still be hiding somewhere on the island. Are you coming back out here?"

"We're goin' to check out some of them boats goin' into the harbor," said Howie. "Them gypsy folk may have got the old man, and they're takin' him for ransom. Be careful!"

Billy said, "Those gypsies sure are heartless to kidnap a dying man!"

Muffy yelled a thank-you to Billy, and we sped away to try and find the gypsy kidnappers. Nearing each of the boats in turn, we found groups of sport fishermen and day-trippers, families and a dog or two. No gypsies, but we had to admit that they could have gotten away while we were walking around the island—my dumb "bright idea"! We chugged through the cut and into the harbor.

"Howie, could you please drop us off on the beach near my house? I'll run up and make the phone calls there."

"Then I'll moor my dory, and we can take my other boat if ya want to go out ta Freeman's again," he said.

"Not your rowboat?" Muffy asked, horrified.

"I got a skiff." He chuckled at her wrong assumption. "I'll be here and ready when ya git back."

"Thanks, Howie," I said as Muffy and I raced up the steps and across the lawn. No one was home when we got there. I ran for the phone and called Jake Rison first. He answered right away.

Chapter Twenty-Nine

"Jake! It's Mollie Parker. There's a castaway on Freeman's Island. I mean he was there, but he's not anymore. He's really sick, and as soon as Howie Snow arrived, the old man disappeared. He's the man who's been missing from Hyannis. You have to call his daughter."

"Hold your horses, missy," he said. "What's all this about a castaway?"

"He's half dead!" I screamed. "The gypsies have kidnapped him." I tried to relate the entire story, but I had a feeling it was confusing. "Billy Jones is out there on Freeman's Island right now, looking for him. But the gypsies either have him there or they've dragged him away in their boat!"

"Ruben Dill? You mean to tell me you found old Ruben Dill? I read in the local paper just this morning that his daughter Connie is beside herself with worry. Hasn't heard from him for weeks. The police thought he was in Vegas."

"I'm telling you he was on Freeman's Island just minutes ago, but now we can't find him at all. You have to send help right now!" I pleaded. "Will you call his daughter?"

"Better let the police take care of that," he said. "I'll notify them immediately and get the Coast Guard out there. They'll find him, wherever he is. I'd better get going on this."

"We'll meet you at Freeman's Island," I said.

"Why don't you and your little friends stay put?" he said. "This is a serious situation."

"You can't cut us out of this," I replied indignantly. "We're the ones who found Mr. Dill." Muffy gave me a questioning look.

"Let's not waste any time. Good-bye." He hung up. I was furious.

"Jake doesn't want us to go back out there to help," I told Muffy as I flipped through the phone book, searching for Mr. Dill's phone number. "But he gave me the old man's name, Ruben Dill, and his daughter's name too. Connie." I found Ruben's number. Right above it was one for Constance Dill. I dialed.

"Hello?" It was a woman's voice.

184

"Hi. This is Mollie Parker. We found your father on Freeman's Island, off of Womponoy. If you come over right away, my friend Howie Snow can take you out to him."

"You found my father?" She was incredulous. "Is he all right?"

"You'd better get here right away." I gave her directions to my house. The second I hung up, Muffy and I raced back down to the beach to tell Howie the news. He was on his way over in his skiff.

As he neared us I shouted out, "His daughter is on her way. We'll wait for her at my house. It'll probably take her twenty minutes to half an hour to get here."

"Dependin' on the traffic," he shouted back. "Go ahead. I'll stay here." He brought the skiff in almost to shore.

Muffy and I went back up to the house. "What should we do with ourselves while we wait?" I asked.

"We should get some water for Mr. Dill. He's sick, so he may be dehydrated, and fresh water would be good for him."

I looked in the fridge and took out an almost empty soda bottle. After pouring its contents out in the sink, I filled it with tap water and put it in my backpack, which I was still wearing.

"Do you think it's wrong for us to do this?" Muffy asked. "Jake Rison is the harbor master and he told us not to get involved. The Eel Grass Girls are supposed to do the right thing and—"

I cut her off. "Don't worry about it. We're helping the authorities and they should be thankful. Let's go out by the road and wait for Connie."

We walked out to the road over the crushed quahog shells of my driveway. I sat on the split-rail fence, and Muffy sat on a boulder that Dad had asked the builders to place at the end of the driveway for some reason I'll never understand.

"You didn't tell Connie that her father is missing," Muffy said.

"The Coast Guard will find him before she gets here," I responded. "They'll be able to search the gypsy trawlers and any boat they come across." Then I had an uneasy thought. "But they haven't been able to find any trace of the other victims." I squirmed. "Oh, let's not think about it."

From Muffy's expression, I could tell that it was all she was thinking about.

185

I directed my thoughts to hoping Connie would hurry up and arrive soon. I sprang up when I heard the sound of a speeding car, but I was embarrassed when a red convertible screeched around the corner!

"It's them again," I said to Muffy. We tried to act cool and calm, but I'm afraid that it was obvious that we weren't.

"Your daddy home yet?" asked Silverson.

"No," I rudely replied.

They both laughed as if I had just told the funniest joke in the world and they floored the gas pedal, making ugly black marks on the pavement as their tires spun. They lurched forward and recklessly careened toward Smith's Landing.

I shook my head. "Some people!"

"Those men really make me uncomfortable," Muffy said.

She took her place on the rock again, and we continued to wait. Soon we heard another car racing up the hill. A small blue sedan came toward us and stopped just before the driveway.

"Mollie Parker?" asked the thirtyish woman as she hurriedly swung the car door open and stepped out. "I'm Connie Dill. Where's my father?"

"My friend Howie Snow is waiting down at the beach with his boat. Let's drive to my house," I said, pointing up our long driveway. "It will be faster." Muffy and I hopped into the back seat. The car pulled into my driveway and sped toward the house. We all jumped out and sprinted across the lawn to the beach. Howie saw us coming and got out of his skiff to help us board.

I made introductions. Howie seemed self-conscious all of a sudden, and Connie kept giving him a sideways glance. She sat on a middle thwart while Muffy and I shared the bow. Howie steered the boat from the stern.

"Saw the Coast Guard goin' out," he said nonchalantly as he started the engine. "And Jake Rison."

"Tell me what's happening," Connie said, nervously. "Where is Daddy?"

Howie helped Connie securely fasten a life jacket around her and got under way. Muffy glanced at me, then she blurted out, "We have to tell you the truth." Connie tensed up, expecting the worst. "We saw your father, just an hour or so ago, but somehow he disappeared. He was on the island, so the only way he could have left was for someone to have taken him away."

"Who would take him?" she asked, her eyes filling with tears. "I don't understand any of this. Please tell me how he got out to an island in the first place."

Muffy related the whole story of how we found Ruben Dill on Freeman's Island.

"He put a message in a bottle?" Connie asked. "And he's been living in a hut on an island? That's incredible! I can hardly believe it. It's not like him at all. He has a huge, beautiful house near Hyannis, with sprawling lawns and lovely gardens. Are you sure it's my father you found?"

"We're sure he is," Muffy said aloud, then whispered in my ear, "but what if he isn't? What if he's someone else? He didn't tell us his name. Wasn't it Jake Rison who said he was Ruben Dill? What if Ruben Dill *did* go to Las Vegas and our castaway is someone else altogether?"

"Oh, hush!" I told her and said out loud to Connie, "Your dad said he ran away because of the taxes."

"Oh, my goodness! Is that the reason? I feel just terrible!" she said, hanging her head. "Oh, dear! Poor Daddy. If only I had taken over paying the bills for him, then none of this would have happened. I knew he was upset about the high taxes. It's all my fault."

"Don't blame yourself," Howie said tenderly. He no longer seemed ill at ease. "Hindsight is always twenty-twenty. It ain't your fault. He wouldn't let you help him."

"How do you know?" she asked Howie, astonished at his comment. "You're absolutely right. Daddy is so stubborn. He won't allow me to do one single thing for him."

"There ya go!" said Howie, whatever that meant. "When ya git yer dad home agin, you'll set it all straight."

"Are you sure we'll find him?" she wailed, wringing her hands. She seemed to be growing more nervous by the minute. "Do you have any idea who could have taken him off the island?"

"We're hoping that the Coast Guard has found him," I said, though I wasn't sure at all. Those sneaky gypsies could have disguised themselves. If they had taken off their brightly colored sweaters and hats, we could have seen them and passed by, not even recognizing them. We had no idea where they were stashing their victims, either. Had we done the right thing by telephoning Connie and dragging her out to Freeman's Island?

We had already plowed through the cut and were now more than halfway to Freeman's Island. The white and orange Coast Guard cutter and Jake Rison's launch were anchored near the island. Billy's motorboat was there too.

Soon we were anchoring close to the beach and tossing our life jackets in the boat. "This way," I said splashing into the cold water and racing up the dune. As we cut across the beach grass, we saw one of the Coast Guard officers coming toward us.

Connie ran up to him. "Where's my father?" she cried frantically.

The petty officer answered plainly, "We don't know. We still can't find him."

Chapter Thirty

"Can't find him?" Connie looked as if she were ready to fall apart. "But you must!"

"Any clues?" I asked.

"Someone has been in a hut over there for weeks, I'd say," the officer said. "But we can't find any evidence of anyone else out here, except a canvas bag of supplies recently brought out."

"We did that," Muffy said. "Were there any other footprints, or marks of a boat coming close to shore?"

"The footprints are pretty unreliable by now," he said. I knew what that meant. We had all been tramping around in the sand without thinking. How could we have been so stupid? We had circled the island looking for the gypsies, but we weren't looking for their footprints!

I tried to assess the situation and think straight. I asked, "Where's Billy Jones?"

"He's on the beach or somewhere, helping us look for the old man," replied the officer.

I introduced the castaway's daughter. "This is Connie Dill. We'll show her the hut."

"I'll go with you," the officer said and led us along the path to the clearing. Connie was clearly shocked by the scene that met her eyes—the driftwood hut, the campfire, the piles of shells. On the other hand, Howie Snow seemed fascinated by the way the hut had been constructed and what the camp revealed of the way Mr. Dill had survived.

Connie followed me into the hut, where she snatched up the old blanket that had covered Mr. Dill.

"This is the blanket from his bed at home!" she cried. "Oh, where can he be?"

"I hate to tell you this," I said, "but he was sick when we found him earlier today. He had a fever, we think."

"Could someone have taken him off the island to get him to a doctor?" she asked hopefully.

"I hope so," Muffy said, but she sounded as if she doubted it.

"Let's find Billy," I suggested. "He's our friend who brought us out here, and he looked for your father while Howie took us home to contact you and the authorities."

The petty officer walked with us to the north side of the island, where Jake Rison was talking with Billy and a couple of other petty officers on the shore.

Billy looked puzzled. He seemed relieved when he saw us coming down the bank. When Howie reached the group, he extended his hand toward Jake, then Billy, and the other men in turn. "Connie Dill," he said, introducing her to everyone.

"Billy, didn't you find anything?" I asked.

"When I got to the hut, no one was there," he said. "I saw the blanket, your care package, and the bag of lobsters, but the old man had vanished, as you said. Mr. Rison, the Coast Guard, and I have covered every inch of this island. He's gone, but we can't figure out how or where."

"I'm surprised to see you girls out here," said Jake mildly. "But I'm glad to meet you, Miss Dill. We have some questions for you about your father."

"I'll tell you anything you want to know," she replied.

"Miss Dill," began one of the petty officers, "have you heard about the kidnappings that have been going on?"

"Yes," she replied anxiously. "I've heard about them and read about them in the newspapers. The police thought that my father may have been the first victim, but then they decided that he had gone to Miami or Las Vegas or Atlantic City, even though he's not that type. He would never dream of gambling."

"Well," continued the petty officer, "we think that your father may be the latest kidnap victim. We—"

"No!" she sobbed. "The girls said he was so sick! Oh, no! No! Why would they kidnap Daddy? Where have they taken him? Oh, no!"

Howie Snow took her in his arms and she cried on his shoulder. I looked at Jake Rison. This was a fine mess.

Howie offered Connie his handkerchief, and she dabbed her eyes. "Who do you think is doing the kidnapping?" she asked between sobs.

Jake acted embarrassed and looked down at the sand. "We don't exactly know," he said. There was an awkward silence. I could hear gulls calling overhead and waves lapping on the beach.

"It was those gypsy fishermen who're moored in the harbor!" I exclaimed. "And we all know it. Isn't this proof enough? Can't you arrest them?"

"This isn't proof," said Jake. "But proof is something we need very badly."

"Can't you do anything?" Muffy asked the petty officers.

"Harbor Master Rison is right," one of them responded. "We need more proof than we have."

"We're heading back in," another officer announced. Jake nodded and thanked the officers. They walked along the shore back to their launch.

"We might as well leave too," said Jake. "Where can we reach you, Miss Dill?"

"You can call me," said Howie. "Connie, you can stay at my place until they find your dad."

"You can call me too," I added. Jake frowned. I guess it wasn't likely he would share any information with me, but we were in the middle of this investigation. He ought to appreciate our help and keep us posted.

Billy looked apologetic. "I have to get to work at the Nor'easter," he said. "I don't know what else I can do to help."

"You were great! Thank you," Muffy said. To Connie she added, "Billy is the one who brought us out here and gave those two lobsters to your dad."

Billy smiled shyly and turned to walk with Jake toward their boats.

"I want to go back to the hut," said Connie. Howie put his arm around her, and the four of us climbed up the hill and over the path to the hut. I picked up my canvas bag with all the food and things in it. Howie saw the burlap bag move and peeked inside, expecting to find the lobsters, I'm sure.

"There's Daddy's gun," Connie said, pointing to the shotgun leaning against the side of the hut. "I don't know if we should take his things. What if he comes back?"

Howie didn't say anything. How could the old man come back? He had been carried away and was in no condition to return, even if he could somehow escape his captors. Howie picked up the gun and a knife. He left the old raft. Then he ducked under the doorway and went back outside. Connie came out a moment later with the blankets. She looked inside again, not knowing whether to stay or leave.

"Oh, Daddy!" She began crying again. "I've been so worried about him, and now this! I almost found him, but now he's gone again!"

Howie patted her on the back. It was weird to see him doing that. He was the type to throw fishing nets around his dory and clean lobster pots, not the type to pat someone on the back.

"Who are these gypsies that you suspect of kidnapping Daddy?" Connie asked.

"They came into the harbor 'bout a week ago," Howie explained. "Tied up on anyone's mooring they pleased, dumped garbage overboard, camped in the woods, stole my beer, now they're stealin' offa boats in the harbor and kidnappin' old men! I'd like to run 'em outta town myself, only we got to find their victims first!"

"That's just awful!" Connie grasped Howie's hand. "You don't think they'll hurt Daddy, do you?"

"Don't have ta worry 'bout that. They won't dare try with me around."

I wondered how Howie thought he could protect Mr. Dill, but Connie obviously believed he could, because she seemed to relax a little. Howie led her to the path. They walked hand in hand ahead of Muffy and me.

"I'm confused," Muffy said. "Why *did* the gypsies take him? What would they want with a sick old man anyway? I don't want to wrongfully accuse them. I wish they were innocent, but who else would do this?"

"They're the only crooks in town," I stated. "Of course, Mr. Picardi and his pals could be considered crooks, but they're in the washing business."

By then we were on the bluff, going down to the beach. The Coast Guard launch was gone. Billy and Jake could be seen in the distance, following it into the harbor. Howie helped us into his skiff and started the outboard. It was a long and silent trip back.

When we cruised into the channel after coming through the cut, our scenic view was spoiled by the gypsy trawlers. They sat on the town moorings off to starboard. I couldn't stand the sight of them. Why wouldn't the Coast Guard search their boats? Why didn't Jake arrest them?

I felt that the world had gone haywire. What ever happened to logic and sensibility? How were the victims ever going to be found if the authorities didn't arrest the crooks who were sitting right under their noses?

Howie steered toward my beach. "How about dinner at my place?" he asked all of us.

"Thank you, Howie, but we have plans for tonight," I told him.

"I don't really feel like eating," said Connie.

"As I said, you can stay at my place," offered Howie. "Jake Rison might give ya a call if he gits any leads."

Howie drifted into the shore, just below my steps. "Connie, you could come with us now to get your car. Howie lives right next door. We'll show you where."

We disembarked and thanked Howie for all his help. He had done a good job of assisting us this time, and I was really appreciative. We would forgive him for all past annoyances and disappointments. Muffy and I led Connie up the steps, and we started across the lawn. Connie suddenly stopped and stared straight ahead of her with a look of panic on her face.

"What's wrong?" Muffy asked.

"Whose car is that?"

I looked toward the house and driveway. Dad's car, the Picardis' car, and a red convertible!

"Do you mean the red car?" I asked.

"Yes. Does it belong to two creepy real-estate developers?" Connie asked in an alarmed tone.

"Creepy is a good word for them," I answered. "They're friends of an old buddy of my dad, who has recently wormed his way into our lives. I don't know exactly what their scheme is, but I don't like it."

"They were pestering Daddy and me, right before Daddy disappeared. They wanted us to sell our property to them so they could build an enormous housing development. We had a terrible time trying to get rid of them. After the tax burden, that was the last straw. Those men contributed to Daddy feeling overwhelmed. He just couldn't take it anymore."

We traversed the lawn, and when we got to the driveway Connie said, "I hope you don't mind if I just leave. I'm in no mood to deal with those awful people. Not now, not after what I've been through."

"I understand," I told her. "Muffy and I will go with you to Howie's house. He's right next door, but you should take your car." We got into the blue sedan. Connie backed up and drove to Howie's driveway, which branched off of ours. He wasn't there yet, so we parked near his barn and got out. We sat in his plastic lawn chairs to wait for him.

I noticed that his truck wasn't there either. I wondered where he left it. Was there a landing near his dory? And when he wasn't hauling equipment to and from the shore, did he use one of the paths through the woods to get to his boat? He hadn't mentioned hearing the gypsies lately. Were they still coming to our woods to camp for the night? Just then a rumbling sound made us turn to see Howie's truck coming up his driveway toward us.

He parked and took some gear from his truck and tossed it in his barn, then came toward us. "Might as well eat them lobsters you girls left out there," he said, taking the sack and my canvas bag from the back of his truck.

"Have you heard the gypsies lately?" I asked as we followed Howie into the house.

"Ain't heard nothin' and ain't had no problems, but some guys in the harbor are pretty mad they're missing stuff offa their boats. They want them gypsies out of here, but rumor has it they've been missin' stuff too."

"It sounds as if those gypsies are causing all sorts of trouble," Connie said. "Why won't the Coast Guard and police just arrest them? Surely they have enough evidence that they're committing these crimes. And how difficult can it be to find the kidnap victims? It seems as if they're just sitting around waiting for Daddy and the others to show up at the police station!"

"You could say that," I replied. I knew how she felt. Well, no. Maybe I didn't. Her own father was missing—and he was old and sick. I didn't know how to help, but the Eel Grass Girls would follow any lead we could get.

"Have a nice dinner," said Muffy. "Please let us know if the police call you or if you get any information from Jake."

Howie nodded, and Muffy and I said good-bye to them. We ambled down Howie's driveway toward my house.

"I can't wait to tell the Girls what's happening," said Muffy. "But how are we going to find Mr. Dill? I can't imagine what they would want with a sick old man anyway."

"He's got plenty of money, or at least plenty of land, which is worth plenty of money," I said. "The gypsies were very clever to anchor their boat out of sight, kidnap Mr. Dill, and get away before we came back with Howie."

"It hardly seems possible, but it must have been, because they did it," Muffy said. "Mr. Dill is definitely gone."

We strolled toward my house. "How can we have fun tonight at the band concert when all these people are missing?" she asked. "I feel upset!"

"We'll use our time tonight to come up with a plan," I assured her. "Don't worry."

"But what will we do? We don't have a single clue!"

"The gypsies will make a mistake. They're not that clever. They'll have to leave a clue sooner or later." That's what I hoped, anyway. And there *were* mistakes made, *big* mistakes, that turned our mystery upside down!

Chapter Thirty-One

All the cars were still in the driveway. I let the back door slam behind me. I could hear the Picardis and the fancy men laughing and talking in the living room. I hated having those nasty men in my house, sitting on a sofa where I liked to sit. It made my skin prickle just to think of it! I would ask Mom to have the house exterminated as soon as they left.

"There they are!" shouted Mr. Picardi when we came into the room. Muffy and I sat together on a footstool, the only seat in the living room still available.

"What've you been doing?" asked Mrs. Picardi.

"We were out with our friends," I replied.

"Brittany would have loved to go with you," she said with feeling.

Brittany sat in an armchair, scowling.

"Brit, show them what we bought in town," her mother said, but Brittany didn't move.

"Let me make you girls a drink," said Dad, getting up. As he walked by us he said, "Come with me into the kitchen and let me know what you'd like to drink."

Muffy and I hopped up and followed.

"Did you have a fun day?" he asked.

"Sure," I said. "Uh...how about you? How was fishing?"

"We didn't catch much. I used my new *purple popper, guaranteed to catch a whopper*. Didn't get a bite, but it was good to be out on the water and spend some time with little Maxwell. He'll be grown up before I know it, if I don't take the time to do things with him. You too. I've hardly seen you at all since I got here. Let's have a real family day tomorrow."

"What about the Picardis?" I asked, as Dad took two glasses from the cupboard.

"I have to tell you that I'm getting a bit tired of them. Frank wants to buy the Farrencrow property with his two friends in there. His plan is to build a huge mansion right next door to us, then subdivide the rest of the property into little lots, so we'll have twenty or thirty new neighbors. I don't think I could bear it. I haven't had a minute alone so I can get the Farrencrows' phone number. I want to buy the land, if they'll sell, just to keep it open space, but I don't know if I have the same kind of money Frank and his friends have. They might be able to make an offer the Farrencrows can't refuse."

I didn't know what to say to all that. Dad plunked ice cubes into the glasses and searched the crowded refrigerator for some soda.

"How can you stop them?" Muffy asked. "If they have so much money and the Farrencrows want to sell, what can you do?"

"I think I'll get religious and pray!" he laughed, handing Muffy her drink.

"That sounds good to me." Muffy smiled.

"It would!" I said. "You can pray, but Dad, you have to do something to stop them." Why was my father talking about religion? That never happened in our family. We Parkers handled our own problems. God wasn't part of the Parker equation.

"God can tell you what to do," Muffy offered meekly.

"I wish he would," said Dad. "Because I don't know what to do. I need help. I can't even find out what Frank does for a living. I'm beginning to think that John Seymore is right about him being involved in money laundering. Oh! I shouldn't have said that!" He gave Muffy a guilty look.

"She already knows," I said. "I told her."

Dad looked surprised, but continued, "I think Frank might basically be a good guy. If he really is honest, I could overlook his crudeness. We grew up together, in the same neighborhood. I don't know how he got mixed up in this...whatever it is, but if he's the man I think he is, or the man he used to be, he ought to get himself out of it."

"But what if they won't let him go?" Muffy asked. "What if he knows too much? His yucky friends might be afraid he'll go to the police."

"If they bring their dirty dealings to Massachusetts, it will be the F.B.I. who will have to investigate. Maybe the best thing I can do is talk some sense into him before it's too late. He's really not so bad."

I didn't think so, but I took my soda from Dad, and we returned to the living room.

"What took you so long, Eddy?" asked Mr. Picardi. "We were thinking you slipped out on us. Ha ha!"

Dad gave Mr. Picardi a sharp look. "I wanted to spend a little time with my daughter. I don't get to see my family very much. In fact, I'll be spending the day with them tomorrow while you go on the seal watch. Why don't you come over later for a barbecue?"

"But I thought we were all going to the seal watch!" exclaimed Mrs. Picardi.

"I'll go with you, Joan," Mom interjected. "Ned, why don't you and Frank watch the boys? Mollie and Brittany can go with us too. Won't that be fun?"

No! I didn't want to spend the day with Brittany again. I had to think fast. Going on a seal watch with a bunch of tourists was another thing I wanted to avoid. The Girls and I had work to do. We had four missing persons and their robbing kidnappers to find. I didn't have time for Brittany Picardi.

"But what about our family time?" asked Dad in what sounded like a defeated voice. The fancy men were observing the scene with amusement. I wondered if they had families, and if they did, if they liked to spend time with them. I didn't want to think that much about them, so I turned my thoughts back to the conversation.

"We'll be together tonight and tomorrow night," Mom reminded Dad encouragingly. "Now, would Georgie like to stay over here tonight?"

Georgie and Maxwell started cheering as they gave each other shoves and bounced over the couch. What little brats they were!

"It's time for the band concert," announced Dad. He had given up his dreams of "family time" without much of a fight. I didn't exactly love "family time," because it meant I had to be with Maxwell, but I would like it if it meant getting rid of the Picardis.

"The kids gotta eat," announced Mrs. Picardi.

"Some of the local organizations sell hot dogs and popcorn in the park," Mom said. "Then they love to visit the candy store. They won't go hungry."

"Let's load 'em up!" Mr. Picardi practically shouted. Mrs. Picardi and Mom ushered the boys and Brittany through the house and out the front door. The fancy men stood, but they lingered in the living room. Muffy and I sat still to listen. This ought to be interesting, I thought.

"So," began Elbert. "You in with us, Eddy?"

"I think not," said Dad, looking him in the eye.

"What's wrong with you?" Silverson questioned in an impatient way. "Don't you think we'll give you your commission?"

"I'm sure you could use the money," Elbert said. "Braces for the kids, new car for the wife, big boat for you."

"I have enough money," Dad snapped. "The fact is, I don't fancy twenty new neighbors. I bought this property so I could have some peace and quiet. I want to look out my windows and see trees, nature, water views. I like it the way it is."

"You mean you don't want me for a neighbor?" asked Mr. Picardi, as if his feelings really were hurt.

"It's not that," said Dad, though I was sure it was. "It's not that I don't want you in particular—I don't want anyone. And your plan calls for twenty other houses in addition to yours. There are plenty of other lots where you could build and find the same solitude that I have here. I'm sure you could use some peace and quiet."

"I like having my neighbors close," Picardi stated. "If they're far away, how can you borrow a hammer or talk over the back fence? I'd be lonely off in the woods all by myself. Tomorrow I want you to call up some of those swanky yacht club friends of yours and see who's selling. We want all the prime lots we can get. With your influence, I'm sure you can get a bunch of them to sell."

"There are plenty of realtors in town," Dad responded. "You could—"

"I told you, we don't want any of those types involved," said Elbert, cutting Dad off. "Tell your friends we're willing to pay cash. That ought to get them going."

"And just how is it that you happen to have so much cash?" asked Dad, revealing his suspicions.

"We've got friends," said Silverson, putting his arm around Dad's shoulders. "And they've got plenty of money they like to invest in real estate. We help them out and we get our cut on the deal. You can get a cut too. So wise up, Eddy boy."

"I don't want anything to do with your scheme," said Dad, shaking Silverson's arm off his shoulder. "And I'm not going to change my mind.

I don't want to hear any more about it. I'm not going to involve my friends in any of your real-estate deals. Some of them already know you, Frank, and I have to tell you, you have a bad reputation. You'll have a hard time involving any of the yacht club crowd."

"They don't know anything!" shouted Mr. Picardi. "It's lies! All lies!"

Elbert and Silverson burst out laughing. Muffy and I were glad that the men seemed to have forgotten that we were still there. "Yeah, Frank." Elbert chuckled. "You're squeaky clean!"

"No one has anything on me," he said defensively.

"Oh, no, not you," said Silverson. "You're as pure as the driven snow. You should have been a nun!"

"Shut up!" shouted Picardi. "I'm sick of you guys. I don't need you."

"Whoa!" exclaimed Elbert. "Wait a minute, Mr. High and Mighty. All of a sudden you're better than us? You're too good for us? Just because you don't want our money anymore, you think you don't need us and you're going to throw us away like a filthy rag?"

"You're the ones who need me," Mr. Picardi countered. "I'm the only legitimate one in the bunch. You need me because I'm honest."

The two fancy men guffawed, then grew very serious. Silverson said, "It's not that easy, Frank. You can't just walk out on us."

"I have my own investments," Mr. Picardi said. "I don't need you, and I'm through with the both of you."

"All right, Frankie, all right," said Elbert, with mock understanding. "We'll just tell Mr. Big that you couldn't take it any more and that you quit. Maybe you aren't as clean as you think, old buddy boy. Mr. Big might want to send you a little message one day."

"And what do you mean by that?" asked Mr. Picardi, clenching his fists.

"You might get to feeling like you want to share your thoughts with someone, if you know what I mean. There's nothing like an accident to make you get laryngitis."

"Are you threatening me?" Mr. Picardi's face was bright red, and he pushed his chest up against Elbert's, as if he would go berserk. Dad looked terribly pale.

"Me?" asked Elbert. "Why, I'd never do a thing like that! Come on, Silverson. They think we're not good enough for them. See you around, Frankie."

The two men nodded good-bye to Dad, but they didn't bother to shake his hand. Dad followed them through the hallway and watched them exit the front door. They slid into their red convertible and sped out of the driveway, making their tires squeal as they hit the road at the end of the driveway. Muffy and I stood in the living room doorway. We could see Mom, Mrs. Picardi, Brittany, and the boys sitting in the car waiting for us. Mom had a puzzled expression on her face.

"Everything O.K.?" she called out to Dad.

Dad's expression showed relief. "We'll be right there," he answered.

Mr. Picardi seemed just as tense as before. "I always hated those two," he mumbled. "I'm glad they're gone, but I don't trust them."

"Is there something you should tell the police?" Dad asked.

"They're not doing anything illegal," Mr. Picardi insisted. "It's Mr. Big who's the real crook, but I never met the guy. Don't even know his real name or what he does to make his money. And I don't want to know."

"They threatened you," Dad said quietly.

"Yeah, I know. But I won't go to the police or the feds. Everything we do is legal. The only way to get Mr. Big is through Elbert and Silverson, and they'd never talk. Besides, they might not even know any more than I do. There's probably a middle man between them and Mr. Big too."

"Come on!" Mom called from the car. "It's getting late, and the boys are out of control!"

Dad raised his index finger in a "just a minute" gesture.

"Whose name are the investments in?" Dad asked.

"It's a trust."

"Hurry up!" hollered Mrs. Picardi. "The boys are hungry, and I can't take them anymore!"

Dad and Mr. Picardi stepped outside. Muffy and I followed them. Dad spun around. "Where have you been?" he asked in surprise. "You weren't in the house, were you?"

We nodded yes.

"You heard our conversation?" We nodded again. He paused and gave us a worried look, then continued on to Mr. Picardi's car.

"We'll take these two girls," Mr. Picardi announced to Mom and Mrs. Picardi. Muffy asked if she could put her bike in the back of the car. She would need it to ride home later, after the band concert.

Mr. Picardi and Dad kept up their conversation. They instantly forgot about us and talked as though we weren't there. Soon Mr. Picardi was parking behind the Nor'easter and helping Muffy unload her bike. Dad handed me some money for food. Muffy and I pushed her bike across the street and bought hot dogs from some kids raising money for a church mission trip. We needed fuel for this evening. The Eel Grass Girls had serious work to do!

Chapter Thirty-Two

Muffy parked her bike against a "bed and breakfast" on one side of the park, and we wove our way through hordes of people filing in. She and I stepped over blankets and dodged lawn chairs until we found Abigail, Laura, and Louie. They were sitting in our regular spot on a red plaid blanket, but they were not alone. Abigail's grandmother, Uncle Jack, and Freddy Frisket were seated on the blanket with them. That was fine, I supposed, but how were we going to talk with them there?

"Hi!" I greeted the crowd.

"I hear your dad has some friends who'd like to meet me," said Freddy.

I gave Abigail a questioning look. I suspected had told him something about Dad's awful acquaintances. She gave an innocent shrug.

"Uh... I think they've changed their minds," I stammered. "If I were you, I'd send them to Muddy River if you have the misfortune of meeting them."

"Oh," said Freddy. "Not the type to be interested in my renovated antique beauties?"

"They're the type to rip down any antique beauty and subdivide the entire lot to build six or seven new houses in its place," offered Muffy.

"You can't tear down anything over fifty years old," said Mrs. Lincoln. "It's a town ordinance."

"They can find a way," Laura said. Her father was a builder, and she had heard all the tricks of unscrupulous contractors. "Either they accidentally yank it down or have a convenient fire."

"No!" Abigail was horrified.

"Let's discuss more pleasant things," Mrs. Lincoln said soothingly. "Tell us about your day."

"We had a nice day," said Muffy. "Billy Jones took us out on his boat."

The town band, ensconced in the well-lit bandstand, struck up a lively waltz.

"May I have this dance, Mother?" Uncle Jack asked Mrs. Lincoln. He helped her get up from the blanket and led her to the dancing area around the bandstand.

Freddy Frisket stood up. "I'm in the mood for popcorn! I'll be right back."

As soon as he had disappeared into the dark, Laura said, "So? What happened?"

"You won't believe it!" Muffy answered. "When we got out to Freeman's Island, the castaway was sick in bed, so we ran back to the shore and built a fire to get Billy's attention, only Howie Snow was passing by. He saw our fire and came to help."

I continued the story. "Howie came ashore, but by the time we got back to the hut, the old man was gone!"

"Gone?" repeated Laura.

"How could that be?" Abigail asked. "You said he was sick."

"He *was* sick, so sick he didn't even seem to be breathing!" Muffy said. "The gypsies came and kidnapped him as soon as we went to the shore to get help."

"My goodness!" said Abigail. "That's just terrible."

"But where were the gypsies?" Laura queried.

"They were hiding somewhere on the island, ready to snatch the old man as soon as we weren't looking," Muffy answered.

I took up the story and gave them every detail of the saga, including the arrival of the castaway's daughter. "And that's not all!" I told them about Mr. Picardi's argument with the fancy men.

"Mr. Picardi's going to change?" asked Abigail. "And be good from now on?"

"Humph!" I snorted. "We'll see how good he becomes, but the fancy men threatened him."

"How?" asked Louie, finally joining in.

"They said 'an accident' might happen," Muffy said. "If they do something terrible and it appears to be an accident, they'll never get caught."

"It would be almost impossible to convict them," Abigail put in.

The waltz was over. Abigail's grandmother and uncle returned to our blanket. Freddy also reappeared, with his arms full of popcorn boxes. The buttery snack was still warm and tasted yummy.

"What's the latest on the kidnappings?" asked Mrs. Lincoln. "I didn't get to read the Hyannis paper tonight. The local paper came out yesterday, and I saw that they still have that theory about aliens, if you can imagine!"

"It's odd that there haven't been any ransom letters, as far as anyone knows, though sometimes they're kept secret," said Uncle Jack. "The victims have vanished without a trace. If the kidnappers don't want money, why on earth are they abducting people?"

"Gypsies have been persecuted for hundreds of years," Muffy stated. "Maybe they just want to get back at the Westerners for all the misery they've suffered. They could have chained up their victims and made them into slaves."

I had to roll my eyes at that! But it just might be true. That would explain why there were no ransom notes.

"Gypsies?" asked Mrs. Lincoln. "What are you talking about?"

"There are three trawlers full of gypsy fishermen moored in Yacht Harbor," Laura explained. "They've been dumping garbage, camping in the woods, and stealing from houses and boats. They're the ones doing the kidnapping too."

"Oh, my goodness!" exclaimed Mrs. Lincoln. "If that's true, why don't the police arrest them?"

"The gypsies claim that they've been robbed as well," I said. "And no one knows where they're keeping their victims."

"Well, if the police don't catch those kidnappers soon," said Freddy, "no one will want to vacation in this town, and my new business will never get off the ground. Everyone will be buying houses in Muddy River instead."

"What's that?" asked Muffy.

"What's what?" I asked, looking around. There were crowds of people seated on blankets and in lawn chairs. I couldn't see anything out of the ordinary.

"It felt like a raindrop," she said. "Maybe I'd better head home now. I don't want to have to ride my bike in the rain."

"We'll give you a ride home," said Uncle Jack.

Just then Maxwell appeared. "Mom says it's time to leave," he announced as if he were giving me bad news and was very happy to do so.

"I'll be right there. Good-bye!" I said to him, giving him an evil stare until he retreated. Then I said to the Girls and Louie, "Tomorrow I have to go on a seal watch with Brittany and our mothers. I might not be able to get away, but let's call each other if we find out anything, O.K.?"

"Agreed," said Laura. "If nothing comes up, we'll meet here at the bandstand on Monday morning."

A big drop of rain splashed against my cheek. "Hey! It really *is* raining!" I looked up to the dark sky, where a string of colored balloons stretched upward as far as I could see. There was no moon and no stars, but I couldn't see any clouds. Yet they must have been there, because rain began to pelt us.

"I think it's time to leave," said Mrs. Lincoln. We gathered up our popcorn boxes and helped her fold the blanket.

"My parents are here somewhere," Laura said. "There they are, on the other side! See you Monday." She dashed across the dancing area to the spot where Mr. and Mrs. Sparrow were gathering up their blanket.

Louie nodded good-bye and disappeared into the crowd. I said good night to Muffy and Abigail and the adults, then wandered over to my parents. The Picardis had left already, except for Georgie, who was spending the night.

"Joan and Brittany will be over early so we can go on the first seal watch," Mom said as she and Dad folded our blanket. "Boys, don't get lost. Come along. Stay with us."

The rain was falling steadily. The town band played on as families collected their belongings and scrambled to their cars. The few that had rain ponchos or plastic shower curtains—yes, you heard me, shower curtains—covered up and stayed to the bitter end. Some people, without any protection, ignored the rain and were determined not to let the weather spoil the highlight of their vacation. We hurried through the park.

"Where are those boys?" asked Mom. I spotted them near the cotton candy cart, which was out of operation and being wheeled toward a parked van. Dad called to them, and they ran toward us. We crossed the street together with the assistance of Officer Lopez, who was on Main Street traffic duty. He smiled at us as we passed by him, before we raced through the rain toward our car.

It took forever to maneuver out of the parking lot. It took even longer to get onto the street. Streams of traffic lined Main Street in both directions. Then we crept along until the end of Main Street, where it ran into Lowndes River Road.

The cars thinned out after that, and we drove along, the windshield wipers slashing away at the rain, which was by now falling in torrents.

"There won't be any seal watch if this keeps up," Mom observed. That was fine with me. I didn't want to be stuck in a big, open motorboat with a bunch of tourists, especially if one of them was Brittany Picardi.

Dad drove carefully along the harbor and then up our long driveway, pulling into the garage. We made a mad dash for the house. Mom rushed around closing all the open windows and doors. Dad followed her around with a towel, wiping up the puddles of rain on the counters and floors. Maxwell and Georgie raced around the living room, whooping and screaming.

I headed for bed. I had had enough of the Picardis for one day. They were causing not only disruption and discomfort (two more of my vocabulary words), but they were also causing serious problems. I had no idea, as I lay down in my own bed (Mom had definitely changed the sheets), that the problems of the coming day would be far worse!

Chapter Thirty-Three

"Mollie, dear! The Picardis are here. Wake up and come along! We'll be waiting for you in the car."

I heard Mom's voice through a thick fog of sleep. I knew I was in my own bed and that I was about to face a long day of boredom, or so I thought.

I hopped up, threw on some clothes, and dashed down to the kitchen to grab a granola bar and glass of juice. Looking through the doorway to the living room, I could see Dad and Mr. Picardi seated on the patio with their coffee cups and newspapers while Maxwell and Georgie tore around the yard. I was not excited about going out with Brittany, but I didn't want to stay around those boys, either.

Mrs. Picardi and Mom were in the front seat of our car. I sat in the back with Brittany.

"Good thing that storm blew over," said Mrs. Picardi. "I was so afraid we wouldn't get to go out and see those adorable seals today. Aren't you girls excited?"

Brittany stared straight ahead. She didn't look excited. "In a foul mood" would be more accurate. Brittany had "attitude," as they say. I would make the most of the situation, but I sure hoped that no one I knew would see me on that bright-yellow seal watch boat. Seal watching was for tourists only. All anyone who wants to catch a glimpse of seals has to do is walk along the beach in front of the lighthouse. The water there is full of all the seals you would ever possibly want to see.

"I've always wanted to see those seals," Mom was saying. "I just love their whiskers. They look almost human. I'm so glad we have an excuse to go. It's the sort of thing I keep putting off because of all my tennis matches and Maxwell's play dates."

Mom drove the short distance to the town parking lot next to the yacht club. It looked as if some of the little kids were having private sailing lessons. They were just off the club dock with a couple of junior instructors, zigzagging back and forth in Sprites.

After parking, we stood in line to buy tickets and lined up again to wait for boarding. The huge motorboat was tied up at the town dock, just opposite the yacht club pier. I felt so embarrassed. A woman in a skimpy top and tight blue jeans stood next to me. An obnoxious child whined to his father, who wore the worst thing possible: socks with his sandals. Everyone was carrying a camera, including Mrs. Picardi.

We were given big orange life jackets and herded like a flock of sheep onto the boat. As soon as the passengers filled the boat to capacity, we set out into the choppy waters. The children squealed as the salt spray hit them in their faces. The seas were always high and turbulent after a storm. *Turbulent* was one of my vocabulary words at school this past year. The constant bouncing up and down was not agreeing with my stomach, but I did not want to puke, especially in front of Brittany.

A good-size motorboat overtook us. I could see Gilly and Harvey in the bow. Naturally they looked over, and their mouths fell open when they recognized me. I stared them down, but they had to tell their parents, who stared as well. Mr. Seymore gave a polite wave to the captain of our boat as they pulled around on our starboard side and motored through the channel ahead of us.

The gypsy trawlers were on the town moorings, as usual. Their laundry was flapping in the breeze the same, as always. At least they liked their clothes clean, even though they didn't mind dumping their garbage in the water and woods.

It made me angry that they had kidnapped four people and, just because they claimed that one of their boats had been robbed, they were allowed to stay in town and get away with more stealing and more kidnapping. They had fished the local waters and moored on the town moorings, but felt that they didn't owe the community anything. They took what they wanted and did what they pleased!

I glanced at Brittany. She had turned a sickly shade of green and was clutching her stomach. Her mother didn't look well, either; neither did my mom. Some of the children began to whine and complain. Before long they and some of the adults were leaning over the sides of the boat to vomit. Brittany soon joined them. Her mother held her hand and wiped her face.

I gritted my teeth and kept looking toward Womponoy. I would not puke. I would not puke.

Out through the cut we went, heading to the east side of Womponoy Island. The swells were much bigger outside the harbor. The harbor had been choppy, but in the Sound, the waves were really rolling in. Up and down, up and down we went, gliding up one side and pounding down on the other. It was not pleasant. I was going to puke, but I forgot all about it as we rounded the island.

The sight before us was amazing—the entire beach was absolutely covered with big, dark shapes! At first I couldn't tell what they were, but as I saw a little movement here and there, I realized that they were zillions of seals, sunning themselves on the sand! The Eel Grass Girls had been to Womponoy before, and though we had spotted an occasional seal here and there in the surf, we had never seen so many seals at once, anywhere, ever! I had to admit it was awesome. Mrs. Picardi snapped some shots.

The captain of the boat gave us some seal history and facts, none of which I had known before. It was actually interesting. The tourists and my mom ooooed and ahhhed. We cruised along the island, as close as possible, but not so close as to frighten the seals and send them galumphing back into the water.

As I watched the bulky forms lying about like so many black garbage bags, I saw a quick movement in the beach grass, beyond the shore. It looked like someone hiding, but the image vanished before I could tell what it really was. Probably it was just one of those rare shore birds, the kind that's protected by law. It had most likely risen up and dived down again to its precious nest in the sand. Or it could have been a birdwatcher lying in wait on the island, trying to spot one of those protected birds.

I dreaded the choppy return to the harbor, but the trip had been worth it. The sight of all those seals was really something, though I wasn't about to admit it to Mom or the Picardis. Actually the ride back wasn't so bad, and before long we were taking off the ugly orange life jackets and wobbling onto the dock. My stomach settled almost instantly, but I was looking forward to getting home.

I was glad that the outing was over. I couldn't understand how bouncing around in a sailboat didn't bother me at all, but a motorboat, rough water, and the smell of gasoline was such a sickening combination.

Brittany's normal color returned to her frowning face, but she smelled like vomit. I gave her credit for not complaining, though. We drove home along the harbor, the sun glittering on the little waves. Through the pines we went and up the driveway. Mom and Mrs. Picardi were discussing Dad's barbecue and deciding who would make what.

Inside the house, Mom took some sandwiches out of the fridge and poured some milk for us. Mrs. Picardi must have bought the food in town and brought it over this morning. We ate at the kitchen table.

"Mollie," said Mom as we finished eating. "Why don't you and Brittany go play on the beach?"

Ugh! I didn't want to go anywhere with that sourpuss! And *play* on the beach? That had to be a joke, only I knew it wasn't. I walked through the house and out onto the patio. Brittany followed like a puppy dog. Dad and Mr. Picardi were still there. They had finished their coffee and newspapers and were now talking. It seemed to be a serious discussion, so I didn't want to interrupt. We would have passed on by, but Mr. Picardi caught a glimpse of us.

"How was the whale watch?" he asked.

"It was a seal watch," Brittany corrected him. "I puked my brains out, but other than that, it was good."

"See any seals?" Dad asked.

"Tons," I said.

"Your tennis teacher called," he added. "She said she couldn't get any answers for you. I don't know if she was talking about tennis or not, but she said you'd know what she meant."

"Sure," I said, thinking that a great idea had come to nothing. There still had to be a way to find out more about Sammy's connection with the gypsies and the robberies. He was our only contact. It would be best to concentrate on him.

Maybe he would be the one to help us get the evidence we needed to "crack the case wide open," as they say. If the police could catch Sammy, he'd turn the gypsies in, I was sure. Then the police could arrest the whole bunch. I continued across the lawn toward the steps.

"The boys are on the beach having a picnic," Dad called after us, as if I cared. We descended the wooden steps to the shore. Last night's storm had tossed heaps of eel grass onto the beach, making a stinky, slimy mess for us to walk through.

I walked toward Howie's landing, which was to the right. I had never walked beyond his landing before. It was in the opposite direction from Laura's house and the yacht club. There was nothing down there, but we were less apt to run across anyone I knew. I didn't want to be seen with Brittany Picardi.

Soon we were at the bluff where the Girls and I had found the gypsy footprints, the scene of the kidnapping. That poor girl! And that man and woman! It made me angry. I felt so frustrated, but it made me even more determined to solve this case. Those bums wouldn't get away with it! I kicked at the piles of eel grass as we plodded along.

Before long we found ourselves approaching Howie's landing. I stood still and listened. I didn't see anyone, but I heard voices. Was it those gypsies in the woods again? No. I recognized one of the voices—Howie Snow.

I looked up and saw Howie's truck on the bluff and Howie and Connie walking down.

"Hey, little neighbor!" he called out to me. Connie waved, but her face was sad and tense.

"This is Brittany Picardi," I said, pointing to my acquaintance. "This is Howie Snow, and this is Connie Dill."

Connie seemed frantic. "I'm so worried about Daddy! He was out all night in that horrible storm. I doubt those kidnappers are taking care of him. Oh, what will become of him?"

Brittany's face had a questioning expression, but I didn't stop to explain. I didn't want her to know our business. Whatever our business was, Eel Grass Girl information wasn't for outsiders. Brittany Picardi was definitely an outsider.

"He'll show up," Howie reassured her. "Any time now, we'll find 'im."

Connie wrung her hands. "Are you sure?" To me she said, "We're going out to look for Daddy now. We've been on the telephone with the authorities all morning long, but it hasn't done a bit of good. No one knows a thing!"

"I'll let you know if we see or hear anything," I promised.

We said good-bye and continued walking toward Smith's Landing. The beach was desolate. The Farrencrows' property seemed to go on forever. I knew that the Smiths owned the next property. Their house was over in the woods somewhere, beyond the trees. We came across their path, coming down to the beach, and marked by dinghies and a mountain of beach chairs.

The beach narrowed and became muddy. Brittany didn't complain as our feet sank down into the squishy mire, which actually pulled my flip flops off a few times before we got to sandy beach again. Smith's Landing was as far as I wanted to go. Three trucks and two cars filled the small parking lot. I walked over to the boat shed and peeked in. Nothing could be seen through the windows. A sunfish sail had been pulled in front of one and a canvas tarp hung over the other.

A jeep pulled up and stopped behind one of the cars. It was Mr. Seymore!

"Hello, girls," he said, not sounding very friendly. "Aren't you the Parker and Picardi girls?"

"Yes," I replied.

He went over to the shed and unlocked it.

"Is this your shed?" I asked.

"Would I be unlocking it if it weren't?" he retorted. I didn't answer. He didn't have to be so mean about it. I moved around so I could see inside the door of the shed. It was just as the police had described—full of junk of all descriptions, but nothing that looked like stolen property.

"Where the heck did that good-for-nothing boy put my oars?" he muttered, rummaging through the debris. "It looks as if he's trying to hide something in here, the way he's covered the windows," he said as he ripped the sail and canvas down. "So dark in here, I can't see a thing!" He pushed the door open wide and continued to look around. I assumed that he was complaining about his nephew, Sammy Boucher.

Suddenly he whirled around. "What are you two staring at?" he yelled. "Go on, get out of here!"

"There're some oars over in the corner there," I offered, pointing to the far side of the shed.

"But they aren't *my* oars!"

"Sammy might have left the oars in your motorboat," I said.

"How...? What do you know about Sammy?" he demanded.

"I don't know much, except that he and his friends use your boat sometimes."

"What friends?" he asked, suspiciously.

"I don't know for sure," I began, not knowing how much I ought to tell.

"Well, I'm going to change the padlock on this shed. That way he and his friends won't be able to get the oars to row out to the motorboat and then he won't be able to use the motorboat anymore either." He kicked over a milk crate full of junk. It was the kind of crate that has "Thou shalt not steal" printed on the sides. Something shiny fell out onto the floor. It looked like a fancy fish lure, the kind my father liked. He was a sucker for the latest fishing gimmick. I think I mentioned that he had an enormous collection of shiny metal, sparkly plastic, and neon "bobbers" and "poppers," as he called them.

Mr. Seymore didn't seem to notice it. He threw some burlap sacks around in disgust before slamming the shed door shut with a bang. He padlocked it and stomped over to his jeep, jumped in, recklessly backed up, and sped away.

"Whew!" exclaimed Brittany. "What's the matter with him?"

I shrugged my shoulders. I wasn't going to tell her what I thought.

"He talked to us as if we're criminals, or ticks, or something nasty," she continued. I didn't respond, because I agreed with Mr. Seymore—about Brittany being something nasty, that is.

I didn't want to walk home on the beach, so I led the way up the road. I had had enough mud for one day. It would probably be shorter to go home by the road, anyway.

As we walked along, I heard a truck in the distance. It was coming our way. When it got close enough, I could see that it was Sammy Boucher in his old truck. He turned into River Lane, just ahead of us. I turned into the lane too. I didn't have a plan yet, but I was sure I could think of something.

Chapter Thirty-Four

Sammy had already disappeared inside his cottage, the *Robin*, by the time Brittany and I got to Miller's. I walked up to his truck and looked in. A pile of dirty canvas tarps was heaped in the back, behind the cab. I boldly approached the *Robin* and knocked at the rickety screen door.

"Hello!" I called out. "Hello in there!"

"Pipe down," came a voice from inside and instantly Sammy appeared at the door. "My roommate's sleeping. What do you want?"

He gave me a puzzled look, then one of recognition. "Weren't you here yesterday morning?"

"Yes," I said pleasantly. "You see, my friends and I need to make some money, and since you don't need a babysitter, we were thinking that we could do some house cleaning or scrub the barnacles off your boat or something."

"Uh...our house is perfectly clean, and I don't have a boat," he said. I looked past him and observed clothes, beer cans, and pizza boxes strewn all over the floor, but I decided to let that go.

"You don't have a boat?" I asked. "I thought I heard that you took your friends out on your boat all the time. And my tennis teacher, Lizzie Winkle, told me that her college friend lives in one of these cottages, and that..."

"Lizzie? You know Lizzie?" he asked eagerly.

"Yes. She's my tennis teacher," I babbled on. "She's so pretty and so nice. I really need a job."

"I don't have a boat, like I said, but my uncle lets me use his. I'd really like to hire you girls, but I...uh...I know! I have a boathouse that needs cleaning. I need more room in it, I mean it has plenty of room, but there's so much junk in it. You could move everything to the sides, so the middle is clear. That would really help me out a lot, and I'll give you five dollars for it."

"Five dollars? Is that all?"

"Sure, it won't take you long and there're two of you. And when you come back here to get paid, we can talk about you getting me a date with Lizzie Winkle."

"O.K.," I agreed. "It's a deal."

"Now, here's the key to the shed. It's at Smith's Landing. Do you know where that is?"

I nodded.

"Good! Now get going. I need that space for...later."

I thanked him and led Brittany back to the road.

"What was all that about?" asked Brittany. "You aren't really going to clean out that awful shed, are you?"

"We both are," I told her. She said no more.

At Smith's Landing, I unlocked the shed. We set to work, and I directed Brittany. Surprisingly, she pitched in and worked steadily without objecting.

First of all, I wanted to find that shiny lure. It sure did look like one of my dad's. With an old rag, I picked it up and carefully wrapped it. I didn't want to get hooked on the sharp barbs. Then I put it down near the door, where I wouldn't forget or lose it.

It didn't take long to move all the junk to the edges of the small building. The oil drums weren't heavy—neither were the kayaks—but the outboard motor and dinghy were. We left them where we found them. Soon everything else lined the walls. When the job was finished, I picked up the lure and locked the door.

We started walking, but when we passed River Lane, Brittany asked, "Aren't you going to return the key?"

"Not until I make a copy."

Her eyes widened. "But that's stealing!"

"I'm not stealing!"

"But I saw you steal that fishing thing and now you're going to steal that boy's key. I don't know what you're going to—"

"Hold on a minute!" I shouted. The Eel Grass Girls did not steal. I didn't like Brittany, but she had just helped me clean the boat shed. I supposed that I did owe her an explanation. I had to be fair.

"Four people have been kidnapped in this town in the last few days. The men who've done it are also stealing equipment from boats in the harbor. And they've been breaking into houses and stealing money. We saw them unload equipment and put it in that shed.

Sammy Boucher is working for them, and we're going to prove it."

Brittany stared at me, but didn't say a word. I started walking again.

"And don't you tell a soul a thing I just said!" I added.

She blinked and still said nothing. We continued our walk home. There weren't many houses around. Pines and oaks spread out on either side of the road. It was quiet, except for occasional rustling noises in the dry leaves, probably made by rabbits.

Finally we reached my house. Upon entering the kitchen, we were surprised to see our parents there, looking very worried.

"Thank goodness you're home!" cried Mom. "Are the boys with you?"

"No," I answered. Why would those brats be with me?

"They're not?" Mr. Picardi screamed. What was his problem? "Where are they?"

"I don't know," I replied, looking to Mom for a clue as to what was going on and why they were so frantic.

Mrs. Picardi became very dramatic, getting down on one knee and grabbing hold of Brittany's arms. She was trembling as she looked up into Brittany's face. "Tell me, Brit, when was the last time you saw little Georgie?"

She shrugged her shoulders. "I don't know. I guess it was this morning, when we first got here. I saw him and Maxwell running in the yard."

"And you?" asked Dad, beads of sweat forming on his forehead. "When did you last see the boys?"

I thought for a moment. "I guess it was before we left for the seal watch. I can't remember seeing them when we got back."

"They weren't at the beach with you?" asked Mom, her voice rising. She looked kind of panicky.

"No," I said. "We walked on the beach toward Smith's Landing. Then we came back on the road. Did you check the beach?"

"We've been all up and down the shore, both ways! From the yacht club all the way to Howie Snow's, and there's no sign of them anywhere!" said Dad. I had never seen him look so worried before.

"Well, you know Maxwell," I said. "He could have wandered off anywhere."

"What do you mean?" demanded Mom, tensing up. "Maxwell never wanders off. He's always with me. Your father wasn't paying attention and without any adult supervision..." Her voice broke off and ended in a sob. Mrs. Picardi looked as if she would cry, and began to sniffle. Then she broke down as well.

"What's all the fuss about?" I asked. "Those two are around here somewhere. Maybe they're just hiding. Did you check the house and look in the woods?"

"We've looked everywhere!" Mrs. Picardi wailed. "If only you guys could have kept an eye on them!"

"They were here one minute and then gone the next," Dad said sheepishly.

"How long ago did you notice they were missing?" I asked.

"When we got home!" snapped Mom. "But your dad said they were on the beach."

"Get your car, Frank," said Dad. "We'll split up and search the roads. Call all the neighbors, Gabby."

"Shouldn't we call the police first?" Mom asked. "With all those kidnappings, I'm afraid the boys have been snatched."

"What kidnappings?" asked Mrs. Picardi, her face turning pale.

"There're some gypsy fishermen in the harbor who've been kidnapping people and robbing houses," I said.

"We haven't heard anything about that," Mrs. Picardi said. "Tell us about it."

"It's been in all the local papers," said Mom, dabbing her eyes with a tissue. "Everything has gone wrong since those gypsies came to town."

"There's never been anything like it here before," Dad said. "It's absurd that those gypsies can cause so much trouble, but the authorities don't have enough evidence to arrest them."

"Actually, they don't have any evidence at all," I said.

"Well, let's not sit around here doing nothing," said Mr. Picardi. "Let's go get those gypsies and teach them a lesson. They can't kidnap our sons and get away with it!"

"Call the police, Gabby," Dad said to Mom.

It was then that I unwrapped the fishing lure I had found in the boat shed and held it up for Dad to see. "Is this yours, Dad?"

"What has this got to do with anything?" he asked, reaching for the shiny metal gadget.

"Don't touch it!" I quickly pulled it away from his hand. "Is it yours?" I repeated.

"Of course it is," he answered. He was obviously puzzled by my question. "It's one of the new ones I ordered from Oregon. That was custom-made for me. I asked for this neon fin and this white-speckled feather, but why can't I touch my own lure and why are you asking me about it at a time like this?"

"I found it in the boat shed at the end of Smith's Landing. The gypsies have been unloading their stolen boat equipment and storing it there. If this lure has the gypsies' fingerprints on it, maybe the police will be able to catch them now. The police will have a reason to search their boats and force them to tell where Maxwell and Georgie and all their other victims are."

Mr. Picardi glanced at Dad. "Let's go and search the roads just in case they haven't been kidnapped," he said. "But call the police anyway."

He and Dad stalked out of the house. I heard the cars speed out of the driveway and onto the road, going in opposite directions. Mom grabbed the phone.

"Tell the police to search Snow's cranberry barn too," I said. "Some of the gypsies have been camping in the woods near the barn, and that's where they may have stuck Maxwell and Georgie."

Mom dialed the police and was calm enough to give them all the information. Then we heard her say, "Now you listen to me! You get a police car over here right now. My son has never been out of my sight. He's a good little boy and wouldn't dream of playing a prank like this on me." There was a pause, then she said, "You might think that all little boys do that sort of thing, but my Maxwell is not that sort. Of course he's full of energy and likes to play, but he's never caused us any trouble, ever."

I'm sure she thought she was telling the truth, but I wondered what child it was that she had been describing to the police. Maxwell had never caused any trouble? Oh, well. She hung up the phone and seemed a little less distraught. She must have thought that the police would come and be able to find the boys right away.

"They'll be here any minute," she announced.

I had to get to town to make a copy of Sammy's key. I considered leaving the lure with Mom for her to give to the police, but she might forget about it or she might get the story all mixed up. And if the police didn't realize what the lure was, the fingerprints might be ruined, so I decided to take it to the police station myself. I grabbed my backpack from the peg near the door, took some change that was lying on the counter, then started for the back door.

"Where are you going, Mollie?" asked Mom.

"I've got to go to town," I said.

"Be careful, dear. We don't want to lose you too."

"Can you take Brittany with you?" asked Mrs. Picardi, who had stopped crying and was blowing her nose.

"She can't ride a bike," I said and flew out the door. Not being able to ride a bike is a real handicap. I rode to town by way of the yacht club. Billy Jones's truck was parked out in front. There were no classes on Saturday, so I wondered what he was doing there. I rode my bike up onto the lawn and propped it against the rope fence.

Since I didn't see Billy down below, I entered the clubhouse. He was hanging a clipboard on a nail in the wall. He looked up at me, but didn't smile.

"Your mom just called."

"It's no big deal," I said. "Maxwell will turn up. He's too dumb to get lost."

"He's not lost, Mollie. He's been kidnapped by those bums out there." Billy nodded his head in the direction of the three trawlers, a blot on the beauty of our harbor.

"I'm not worried," I rejoined. "He'll turn up. I think the gypsies have been kidnapping people, but not Maxwell. What would they want with him?"

Billy didn't answer, but his face was grim. Then he said, "I heard there's still no word on Mr. Dill."

"Yeah. Nothing," I answered.

We walked out to the deck. Something caught my eye. It was the Coast Guard launch chugging around the corner of the town pier into the channel, followed by Jake Rison.

"Looks like they've called out the cavalry," he said, clasping the deck railing.

"Huh?"

"They're taking Maxwell's disappearance seriously. They must have a search warrant for the trawlers. Want to take a ride out and be there when they find Maxwell?"

"Mom and Mrs. Picardi are at home waiting. I don't need to get involved. There's too much crying and carrying on."

"I understand, I think," Billy mumbled.

"That boy is such a nuisance," I said. "But if his getting lost can help us find the other victims and put those darned gypsies behind bars, then he's O.K."

"The police will make the gypsies talk and then return the stolen goods," Billy declared. "I'll be glad when life in this town returns to normal."

"That reminds me," I said. "I've got to get to town."

"Want a ride?" he asked. "I was just leaving."

"Sure."

Billy locked up the clubhouse and helped me get my bike into the back of his truck. We cruised past the marina and over the bridge, where the tourists were catching the usual crabs and sea robins. Around the lighthouse we went, and on to Main Street. As we pulled into the Nor'easter parking lot, I could see a familiar red convertible. The two fancy men stood near the kitchen door, talking to the same aproned young man who had accepted money from them before.

"Oh, no! I don't want those men to see me!" I slouched down in the seat. Billy drove to the far end of the lot.

"What's the matter? You know those guys?"

"They're friends of Mr. Picardi," I explained.

"I've heard from my brother that those men are asking anyone and everyone if they have land or houses to sell, but I don't think people like them much. They sure are persistent."

"Annoying is the word I would use," I said. Billy lifted my bike out of the back of his truck and set it down. "There you go. Have you found any clues?"

"I think I've got some evidence to convict the gypsies of those boat robberies and to connect them to Sammy Boucher," I said.

"That's great! I won't ask for details, because I'm sure it's top secret," he said with a wink.

"I suppose it's secret," I said. "I'm taking the evidence to the police station now."

"Well, keep safe. This old town isn't what it used to be," was his wistful reply.

I jumped on my bike and rode down a lane at the end of the parking lot, behind Muffy's Aunt Ella's shop, as far away from those fancy men as I could get. I didn't want anything to do with those creeps.

I cut back to Main Street at the church and pedaled to the hardware store. I parked my bike out front and entered the store. It smelled like boat varnish and birdseed and was filled with building things, yard stuff, and house junk. I stood in line at the counter behind a man buying a plastic trash can and a clothesline.

When it was my turn, I handed the clerk the key and asked for a copy.

"Hey, you little twerp!" An angry voice behind me made me jump. I swung around to see Sammy Boucher!

Chapter Thirty-Five

Oops! The clerk was staring at me. So was everyone else in the store.

"That's *my* key! What do you think you're doing?" he demanded.

"*Your* key?" I asked, my voice dripping with innocence. "Are you sure? I thought it was the one my dad gave me to have copied."

I showed him the key and Sammy frowned. He suddenly wasn't so sure.

"Then where's my key?" he asked, hands on his hips.

"I think I left it in my other pocket," I said with a big smile. "I'm sorry. I forgot to give it back to you, but I'll bring it by your cottage just as soon as I get home."

"Well, all right. But don't forget!" He turned on his heel and strode to the back of the store, where I hoped he would stay for a while. Whew! That was close!

I smiled brightly at the clerk, who made a nice clean copy of the key for me. I hurriedly paid for it and exited the store. The sooner I got away from there, the better. I hoped that my trip to the police station would go more smoothly.

I made a right at the rotary, then a left at the ball field. As I parked my bike out front, I wondered who would be on duty. When I entered, I saw Officer Hutton at the desk.

"Mollie Parker," she said, as if she had been expecting me but wasn't pleased that I had shown up. "What brings you here today?"

"Didn't you hear that my little brother got kidnapped?" I asked. Not that I was very concerned about Maxwell, but I was annoyed by her attitude. She should have felt sorry for me, even though I didn't feel sorry for myself.

"Yeah. Jake Rison actually got search warrants for those gypsy trawlers, and he and the Coast Guard are doing a thorough search. They've probably found your brother by now."

Officer Hutton wasn't impressed. "We checked out those footprints. Nothing. Checked out the fingerprints. Some of them belong to your family, but not all. We don't know who the other fingerprints belong to."

I waited for her to say more, but she didn't, so I said, "I brought you something else to fingerprint." I took the lure out of my backpack and unwrapped it. The police officer stared at it, without any expression on her face. "It's my Dad's lure. I found it in the boat shed at Smith's Landing. I'm sure it has the robbers' prints on it."

She called Officer Lopez over her intercom. He appeared from a door at the back of the station. After he nodded a hello to me, Hutton told him about the lure. At least *he* seemed interested. He carefully picked up the rag and took the lure into the back, where I supposed the lab was.

"You think they're gypsy fingerprints?" Hutton asked.

"Yes," I replied. "But someone else is working with them, you know."

"Got any suspicions?"

"Sammy Boucher, of course."

"Sammy Boucher," she repeated, leaning back in her office chair. "Sammy Boucher, the speed-demon party animal?"

"I don't know about that, but he has a key to that boat shed, access to the motorboat the gypsies have been using, and a pickup truck at Miller's Cottages."

"Can't just bring him in for fingerprinting," she continued. "But the gypsy troupe will be spending the night in jail, I expect, so we can match up their prints."

I realized that Sammy's prints had been on the key to the shed, but they were gone by now, covered up by mine and the hardware store clerk's. It was still worth a try. Officer Lopez was called back out and took the key. I waited.

"Have a seat," offered Officer Hutton. I looked around. There was nowhere to sit. I read all the "Most Wanted" posters on the bulletin board and found out all you could ever want to know about dog licensing. Finally Officer Lopez returned. He gingerly handed me the key, still covered with white powder.

"I have to keep the lure for evidence. There's a thumbprint on it which matches one on the handle of your sliding glass door in the living room of your house," he said.

"So there's your proof!" I shouted.

"When the gypsies come in, we'll fingerprint them and arrest the one with the match. Then he'll squeal on his friends, and we'll have the whole lot of them. They'll tell us where they're hiding the kids and the other victims, we'll rescue them, the town's reputation will be cleaned up by Labor Day, and we'll all live happily ever after."

"Sounds wonderful," I said. It did sound good, but I wondered if it would really be so easy. "Thanks." I put the key in my backpack and let the door slam behind me. I would stop by Sammy's on my way home. Dad's barbecue would be cancelled because of Maxwell, but I didn't care. It wouldn't be fun with the Picardis there. I had to call the Girls and let them know what was going on.

As I pedaled past the rotary and toward Small Pond, I could hear police sirens. Two cruisers sped by—on the way to the harbor, I supposed. When I got to the spot where Lowndes River Road connects to Yacht Harbor Road, a Coast Guard van tore around the corner. They must have been going to arrest all the gypsies and transport them to the police station.

At the town pier I paused to watch the Coast Guard launch pull into the pier and tie up. The police and petty officers were prodding the gypsies and their big black dog off the boat and into the waiting cruisers and van. I wondered what they would do with the dog.

I waited, but I didn't see Maxwell and Georgie. I admit I felt a little disappointed. Maxwell was a pain, but the weekend would be ruined if they weren't found. Then it occurred to me that Jake Rison must have taken the boys to my house already. Mom and Dad and the Picardis would have watched the whole proceeding from the beach and were now having a happy reunion with the little devils.

There was always the possibility that the gypsies had held them at the cranberry barn, and the police had searched it and found them there. I wasn't one hundred percent certain that the gypsies had kidnapped the boys, but Maxwell wasn't the type of brat to stay away from his mommy for long. I supposed Georgie was the same way. Wherever they had been, they were most likely home by now.

I got back on my bike and rode up the hill while the cruisers and van sped back toward the police station. As I rode on, I remembered that I should call Louie. Then I thought about Sammy: What would he do tonight if his friends were in jail? He would be waiting at the cottage, but no one would come to announce that the stolen property had arrived at the boat shed. His gypsy friends would never arrive.

Pedaling along, I passed my driveway and headed toward Smith's Landing, turning off onto River Lane. Approaching the cottages, I could see Sammy's truck and a few small cars parked under the trees. Wet bathing suits and towels hung on a clothesline and over lawn chairs. A barbecue grill was smoking. A row of hot dogs waited for the heat to rise.

I parked my bike beside the *Robin* and knocked at the screen door. There was a scuffling noise inside. Then a girl appeared. She wore a thin cotton dress, and her scraggly brown hair hung limply around her face.

"I'm looking for Sammy Boucher," I said.

"What'dya want?" she snapped. She was definitely hostile, but she didn't scare me.

"I need to see Sammy. His truck is here, so where is he?"

She gave me a nasty glare and faded back into the darkness of the cottage. I waited. Sammy shuffled to the door. He had taken his shirt off, and his skinny chest looked as white as a fish's belly.

"Oh, it's you," he said pushing the screen door open. He held out his hand, and I dropped his key into it. He turned and let the door slam shut in my face.

"Wait a minute," I said. "Where's my five dollars?"

"You didn't think I was really going to pay you, did you?" he asked, retreating into the cottage.

"Of course I thought you would," I shouted. "Don't you think my friend and I have anything better to do than clean up your mess? Give me my money!"

He came back to the screen and pulled his pants pockets inside out. "I don't have any."

"You think you're smart, don't you? I tried to get you a date with Lizzie Winkle and now this? She'll never want to go out with you after she hears…"

The girl was back. "What's this?" she snarled at Sammy. "You tried to get a date with someone else?"

"Uh…No! She misunderstood. I don't want to go out with anyone

226

except you, Honey." Sammy turned to a table near the door and frantically rummaged through the rubbish covering the top. He found some money and opened the screen to hand me two five-dollar bills. "Here you are, kid. Thanks a lot. Now get going."

He took the girl's arm and led her back into the darkness. I had made twice as much money as I had expected and now knew what kind of character Sammy Boucher was—a Grade A, Super Deluxe creep!

The shadows were lengthening, and the air felt cool as I rode my bike back home. The Picardis' car and Dad's were parked in the driveway beside Mom's.

From the kitchen I could hear voices in the living room. There I found my parents and the Picardis. Brittany was sitting in a corner, a grim expression on her face. There was no Maxwell or Georgie!

"Mollie, the police just called us," Mom said. Her eyes were all red and her face was puffy. She must have been crying.

Dad said, "The Coast Guard and harbor master searched the trawlers and that barn you told them about, but they didn't find a trace of the boys."

"Those gypsies say they don't know a thing about the boys," Mr. Picardi said, pounding his fist on the coffee table.

"The police have got to make them talk," wailed Mrs. Picardi. "They have to tell us where they've hidden our boys!"

The phone rang. We all jumped. Dad lunged for it. "Hello? Hello?... Yes, this is he...Excuse me?...I'll tell her...All right...You what?...Don't you think..." He nearly slammed the receiver down.

"What is it?" asked Mom, standing up and moving toward Dad.

"They've let them go! Can you believe that? They fingerprinted the whole gang of them and then just turned them loose!"

"Why?" Mr. Picardi sprang to his feet, his face purple with rage. "How could they do that?"

"Maybe the police think the gypsies will lead them to the children," Mom said hopefully.

"They said they have nothing to go on, so the gypsies are free to leave town." Dad shook his head in dismay. "They're pulling out tomorrow morning."

"Tomorrow morning?" shouted Mr. Picardi. "But this is an ongoing investigation! The police have got to make those guys stick around until someone finds our kids!"

"Why don't those horrible gypsies just tell us what they want?" asked Mom. "We would pay them whatever they ask, if only they would release the boys and not hurt them!"

Mrs. Picardi suddenly turned white as a sheet. She looked at her husband and shrieked, "It's them! It's those lousy bums you were doing business with! They're the ones who've taken the boys! You told them you're not going to do business with them anymore. That's the way they operate. Once you start working with that type, you can't stop. I told you..."

"Shut up!" hollered Mr. Picardi. Mom and Dad became stiff as statues.

"I won't shut up! You've got to tell the cops! Those snakes have got my little Georgie, and I'm never going to see my little baby again!"

She began sobbing uncontrollably. Brittany just stared at her, but Mr. Picardi calmed down a little. He put his arm around her shoulder and said in a totally unconvincing voice, "No, no, Joan. It wasn't them. The kids just wandered off, the way they always do."

Mom looked up, but didn't say anything. I knew she wanted to make her speech about what an angel Maxwell is and how he would never wander away, but she kept quiet. Maybe she was thinking about Mrs. Picardi's theory. So was I.

Could it possibly be true that the fancy men had kidnapped the boys? Did that mean that they had kidnapped all the other people too? Their reason for kidnapping Mr. Dill could have been because he wouldn't sell them his land! Was there a real-estate connection to the others? The man and woman both lived on Yacht Harbor, on prime real-estate lots with water views worth millions of dollars. Maybe Mrs. Picardi was right!

I had no idea if the missing girl had some link to real estate, but I had to call the Girls and tell them about this new theory. I didn't want to dismiss the gypsies. The Girls and I had to come up with something.

Dad faced me. "The police said that there were other prints on my lure that you took to them, but none of the prints matched any of the gypsies'."

"Really?" I was shocked. How could that be true? I recovered and said, "That doesn't mean anything. Those are probably your prints, and maybe the gypsies wore gloves when they stole the lure from the garage."

Big deal! Whether the gypsies were the kidnappers or not, we knew for sure that they were the thieves. We had seen them stealing in the harbor with our own eyes.

Tonight would be our last chance to catch them. They would strike again. The police had released them. Now they were free to do as they pleased, and it would please them to steal some more and maybe try another kidnap, if they were the kidnappers. All the money they had lost by not fishing they had made up by stealing. They would use their last night in the harbor to loot a few more boats, and the Eel Grass Girls would be ready for them. The police were letting those hoodlums slip through their hands, but they would fall into ours.

But we needed a plan. All we needed was a way to trap the gypsies while they made their rounds in the harbor. They might break into another house or go after another innocent victim, but whatever they did, they would start from their trawlers. All we had to do was keep an eye on them. From the shore near my house, we had a perfect view of the entire harbor. That was where we would set up our watch. Or maybe we should just wait at the boat shed, because they would surely end up there.

"The police are requesting a dog from Hyannis to help find the boys," said Dad. "A few officers will be over to help us with our search. Let's go out and look in the woods again," he said to Mr. Picardi.

"Don't you wish you had lots of neighbors now?" Mr. Picardi asked. "Searching would be so much easier if we could go door to door rather than wandering through that forest."

Dad didn't answer. He might have been thinking that Mr. Picardi was right in this situation.

"We'll stay here," Mom said. "We'll wait for the police to arrive. I'll telephone all our neighbors and the yacht club members who live around the harbor."

Speaking of calling, I had to phone the Girls and Louie. When I turned to go upstairs Dad said, "Please, stay off the phone, Mollie. Your mom needs to make those calls."

"I have to talk to my friends," I said.

"Use my cell phone," offered Mr. Picardi. "You'll need it more than us."

I didn't want to use his phone (or correct his English). If they hadn't come to visit, none of this would have happened. My little brother would be tearing around the house annoying me and we could get on with our summer vacation, but no. Dad had to invite this dolt and his awful family to visit us to ruin our weekend and lose my brother. Not that I really cared about Maxwell, but it was affecting my life, and I didn't like the inconvenience.

Mr. Picardi handed me his cell phone. "Here. Press that button to turn it on. Then after you dial, wait and press this button. Got it?"

What did he think I was, a moron? I thanked him and raced up the stairs. I sure hoped the phone worked. It was such a disappointment when technology lets you down, such as in the case of Abigail's cell phone.

I dialed Muffy first. "Muffy, wait 'til you hear this!" I told her about Maxwell's kidnapping, the gypsies being set free, the lure, Sammy Boucher, and Mrs. Picardi's theory about the two fancy men.

"I'm sorry about Maxwell," she said.

"You don't have to be," I replied. "Maxwell will take advantage of the situation to get every ounce of sympathy he can out of it. Once we find him, he'll be even worse than ever. Take my word for it. So, can you meet me later? If the gypsies are leaving town tomorrow morning and the police don't suspect them anymore, they'll want to commit all the crimes they can tonight. We can go down to the harbor to wait for them. Maybe we should split up. Two of us can wait at the boat shed."

"I don't know," said Muffy. "Mom and Dad said something about going to the movies, but when they hear about Maxwell, I'm sure they'll want to join the search party."

"Dad and Mr. Picardi already left to look for the boys in the woods. They've looked everywhere already. Those brats might be hiding on purpose. The police are on their way over too, and they're bringing a dog. Let me know if you can come. Call me as soon as you talk to your parents." I hung up. Abigail was next.

"Oh, Mollie! You poor thing."

"How soon can you come over?" I asked her.

"We were going to watch home movies," she said. "Freddy said he wants

230

to see what Uncle Jack looked like as a baby, but they won't care about movies once they hear that Maxwell's missing."

"Dad is looking in the woods, and the police will be here any minute. If the fancy men have the boys and all those other people, then we have a different problem on our hands. Their motive isn't money, not directly, but revenge, so they might really hurt them."

"This mystery seems so much more difficult than our others!" said Abigail. "The robberies aren't so serious, compared to the kidnappings."

"Even if they're not connected, we have to catch those gypsies tonight," I replied. "It's the only way to convict them of anything."

"I'm sure you're right about all of that," Abigail said. "Freddy and Uncle Jack have gone out to look at houses for Freddy's new business, but they'll want to join the search party as soon as they get back. We can come over then and help look for Maxwell."

"But can't you come over now and help me?" I asked. "The gypsies are leaving tomorrow. We have to act tonight."

"Let me ask Grammy." I waited.

"Grammy said she'll leave a note for Uncle Jack and Freddy, but she and I will go to town to look for Maxwell and Georgie there. She thinks the boys may have wandered in and could be at the toy store."

"Good grief!" I was exasperated. "I need you to come here, not to hunt for Maxwell in town!"

"But Maxwell's lost, and Grammy said that's more important than—"

"Oh, fine!" I hung up the phone. There was no point arguing with Abigail. Mrs. Lincoln was doing what she thought was right, but she was making a mess of our investigation. Family was important, but I just couldn't believe that Maxwell was really in danger. I could be wrong, very wrong, but I knew for sure tonight would be our last chance to solve our mystery of the thefts. If the gypsies were the kidnappers, then solving the thefts would lead to solving the kidnappings.

I dialed Laura. There was no answer. The moment I hung up, I heard the phone ring. Not the cell phone, but our telephone.

"Mollie! It's for you," called Mom. I picked up the receiver.

"Mom and Dad will be right over." It was Muffy. "We just spoke with

231

your mom and she asked them to scour the beach beyond the yacht club and follow it along the dyke road out to Deer Island. They want me to go with them! I tried to tell them that we have something important to do, but of course I can't tell them the details. You know that. I'm sorry."

"Then I'll just have to catch those gypsies myself," I said.

"What about Louie?" she asked.

"I'll call him now, but it's not the same. I want the Eel Grass Girls to be with me. We have to put those gypsies behind bars. Any ideas on what to do about the fancy men?"

"They're really bad news. You have to be careful if you run into them. Be careful, promise? We'll be in touch about Maxwell. Anyway, I'll see you Monday," she said before she hung up.

So much for the great Eel Grass Girls—plural. I hoped Louie would be home. He was my last resort. I used the cell phone again. Louie's mom answered. He was at a ball game with his brother. Rats! I decided to call Howie and Connie to fill them in on the gypsy situation, but there was no answer there either. Then I had a thought: Brittany. She wasn't my favorite person, but I had to admit that her attitude had changed. Her visit to Cape Cod just might turn out to be of some use after all. I had a feeling that this was not going to be the long and boring evening I had anticipated.

Chapter Thirty-Six

I changed into a long-sleeve navy blue T-shirt and jeans. I tried to remember what Brittany was wearing. Something dark enough, as I recalled. If we would be slinking around the beach and woods tonight, we had to blend into the background.

I snatched up my backpack and dashed downstairs. Mom was at the back door directing two police officers to the woods. She was handing them two T-shirts, which I presumed were Maxwell's and Georgie's, so the huge German shepherd they had with them could get the boys' scent. Hopefully the dog would do a better job of finding the boys than Dad and Mr. Picardi had.

Mom wearily turned to me. "I hope they'll find the boys soon. That dog ought to be able to track them."

Brittany sat glumly at the kitchen table, but looked up hopefully as I entered the room. Mrs. Picardi sat beside her with the phone and yacht club directory.

"I think we've called every club member within a hundred miles of here," Mom exclaimed.

"Those boys have to turn up soon!" Mrs. Picardi exclaimed.

"Oh, the Cortezes have offered to help join the search party," Mom said. "They're going to scour the beach beyond the yacht club. I don't think anyone has searched over there yet. Of course, the boys may have boarded a boat—"

"Oh, don't say that, Gabby!" wailed Mrs. Picardi. "Little Georgie doesn't know anything about boats!"

I thought I heard another car enter the driveway. A knock on the front door signaled someone's arrival. I dashed to the door to see our pizza deliveryman. Mom joined me and took two huge boxes from him as Mrs. Picardi took a twenty from her wallet. The four of us ate in silence around the kitchen table.

I quickly finished and asked, "Mrs. Picardi? Could I borrow Mr. Picardi's cell phone tonight?"

"You're not going out, are you?" Mom looked worried.

"Yeah. I thought I'd show Brittany around. We'll be safe, don't worry."

"Sure you can use the phone," Mrs. Picardi responded. "It will help you to stay safe."

I dropped it into my backpack, which already contained my flashlight. Mom and Mrs. Picardi decided that we should all go down together and check the beach again. I didn't mind. It was early to begin our gypsy watch, but it was growing dark and soon we might be able to spot some gypsies. It would be their last night, so would they alter their usual schedule? The fireflies were slowly making their way over the lawn, through the cool air.

"Aren't they pretty?" Mom asked.

Mrs. Picardi didn't answer the question, but said, "You know, Gabby, I don't trust those guys from Jersey. I think they took the boys all right. Our husbands won't find the kids in the woods or on the road. Where would those two bums hang out in town, if they wanted to meet people and try to get them to sell their real estate?"

"The Nor'easter," said Mom. "That's the restaurant where we had dinner and where we ran into them the first time."

"Then let's go!" said Mrs. Picardi, grabbing Mom by the hand.

"I don't know, Joan." Mom hesitated. "What would we say to them?"

"I know!" I shouted. "You could pretend that you didn't know the men had an argument with Mr. Picardi. You weren't even in the house at the time, remember? You were waiting in the car. Pretend that you found a friend who wants to sell his property. Say that Dad doesn't really have as much money as he says he has, and that we need more. You could say that you want a commission, or whatever they call it."

"She's a real smart kid!" exclaimed Mrs. Picardi.

"But then what?" Mom asked, still doubtful.

"Then mention that the boys have wandered off and gotten lost. See what their reaction is. Find out where they're staying. You'll think of something," I assured her. "Maybe they'll let the boys go if they think you'll do business with them."

"Genius!" gushed Mrs. Picardi. "Then we're going to town now. When we get back, I'm sure we'll have the boys with us, or at least some

234

idea of where they are. I hope we're clever enough to figure out what to say to get them back."

"You'll do fine," I said encouragingly.

Mrs. Picardi dragged Mom across the lawn toward the driveway. Brittany and I continued toward the steps and down to the beach. We turned right toward Smith's Landing. I decided that my best course of action would be to stake out the boat shed. Regardless of who the kidnappers were, the gypsies would make another raid tonight and take their loot to the shed.

Brittany and I walked along the deserted beach. The sand felt cold on our feet, but that was nothing as long as the bugs didn't come out. The mosquitoes could be bad, but the nosee'ems were worse. They nibbled you with pinprick bites, all over your exposed skin, including in your hair and up your nose. Ugh! But we were spared this evening.

"It's awfully dark," said Brittany. I suppose she was complaining, but I didn't answer. Of course it was dark. It was nighttime. I had my flashlight, but we didn't want the gypsies to be able to see us. That was also the point of our dark clothes. We kept going.

"Here's five dollars from Sammy Boucher. He gave me two fives for our work on the boat shed." Brittany took the bill and stuffed it in her shorts pocket.

After a while she stopped. "What's that?" she asked, grabbing my arm. I shook her off as I scanned the beach, not expecting to see anything scary. She wasn't used to the beach. But something was there. Something big and black bounding straight toward us! It looked like a bear!

Then I saw what it was and relaxed. It was just a dog. But it wasn't the police dog. In the fading light, its dark shape made it seem bigger and more menacing than it really was. I could see a couple walking their dog on the beach. They were probably neighbors helping to look for the boys. We continued toward them, but as we got closer, I recognized the "couple"—it was two of the gypsies and their dog!

"Don't say a word," I whispered to Brittany.

We neared the two, clad in their ridiculous clothing—one even wore a scarf around his neck. Didn't he know it was summer? The other man's head was topped with a patterned cap, and both wore multicolored and patterned sweaters. Up close we could see that their pullovers were full of holes. Everything about them was a mess. I wondered what they were doing here. Had they spotted the police? Or had the police seen them?

If they were looking for houses to rob or people to kidnap, we now had our chance to follow them and catch them in the act. We had Mr. Picardi's cell phone and could call the police if we saw them try anything. But we were alone on the deserted beach. I didn't know how close the police really were. What if they had already finished searching the woods and were back at the station? I felt that our main concern was getting as far away from them as possible, before we became their next victims!

I hoped they wouldn't try anything. I held my breath as we passed by. What was there to stop them from kidnapping us? They would have no trouble grabbing us. Even if we screamed our heads off, no one would hear or come to our aid. Mom and Mrs. Picardi were at the Nor'easter by now. Howie and Connie were off somewhere. And even if Louie's mom or someone on a boat happened to hear us, they would probably think it was only kids playing.

Our eyes met. The gypsies' piecing glares bore into us, but they walked on by. They neither paused nor slowed down. Brittany and I quickened our pace, and Brittany turned back to make sure they weren't following us.

"What happened to them?" she asked in surprise.

"What?" I spun around to see that they had vanished from the beach. "They must have gone up the bluff and into the woods," I speculated.

"Why would they do that?" she asked.

"I'm not sure," I said. "I'd like to follow them, but it's getting dark and it won't be easy to track them through the woods." Not to mention dangerous. If the Girls and Louie had been there with me, we'd have followed the men, but with only Brittany and me, I thought we should get away from them. I felt frustrated about it, but what could I do?

We were passing through the muddy section of beach, and I didn't relax until we reached Smith's Landing. There I felt safe in the light of the single street lamp illuminating the little parking lot. We climbed the low hill overlooking the beach and sat down on the soft pine needles to wait. From there we had a good view of the water and the boat shed. It wasn't much fun being with Brittany. If the Eel Grass Girls had been there with me, we would have plenty to talk about. Brittany was silent, but at least she wasn't complaining. She did have a few virtues.

It wasn't very long before we heard a motorboat putt-putting up Small Pond River from the harbor. We strained to see if it was the gypsies, but from the conversation floating over the water, we could tell it was three men who were fishing. Someone had told him that the big bass come into the river at night. Maybe it was true, but I wished they would go on and get out of our mystery. They were making so much noise I wondered how they expected to catch anything. Something moved in the bushes behind us. Brittany practically jumped into my lap. We didn't hear it again, so our concentration returned to the river.

After a while we could hear the boat coming back down the river. Those goofy fishermen had stopped their chatter and neared the shore. It seemed they had given up on trying to catch anything, because they were mooring their motorboat and unloading their gear. When they rowed in and came to the shore, it was only then that I realized that it was the gypsies! It wasn't their gear they were unloading, but someone else's!

Brittany and I didn't move an inch while they unlocked the shed and hauled in their plunder. Soon they had locked the shed and disappeared into the woods opposite our hiding place.

"Come on!" I whispered and dashed across the parking lot. I pulled out my copy of Sammy's key. Obviously Mr. Seymore hadn't followed through on his threat to change the padlock. I had been hoping he hadn't, or else neither the crooks nor I would be able to unlock the shed door. As it was, they had been able to hide their loot, and I was going to be able to see it and make sure they got arrested.

There was enough light from the street lamp for me to see well enough to unlock the door. Then I flicked on my flashlight to view the goods the gypsies had stolen tonight, but suddenly Brittany shoved me so hard that I fell face forward onto a pile of hard, metal objects! What was wrong with her?

"Ow! What...?" Before I could finish, Brittany landed on top of me, and I squirmed to get out from under her. I saw the shed door closing and heard the padlock click. Who had done this to us?

"Of all the—!" I didn't finish. Brittany and I scrambled to our feet and I shined my flashlight at the windows to get a look at our attackers, but the panes were so dirty, covered with cobwebs and gook, that all we could see was the glare of the flashlight's reflection.

"Open the windows and let's get out of here," I shouted, whipping out Mr. Picardi's cell phone and dialing 9-1-1. I rubbed my shins and elbows as I gave the report to the police. I could see Brittany tugging at the windows. With the aid of my flashlight we could see that not only had both windows been nailed shut, but long pieces of wood had been wedged into the top sections so that they couldn't be raised. We would be trapped until the police car arrived.

Soon we heard a siren blaring in the distance. Why did they do that? Didn't they know they shouldn't announce their arrival? Within seconds, a police cruiser screeched into the parking lot, and an officer broke the hasp from the door. Brittany and I burst out.

Quickly I panned my flashlight over the stolen goods, which included a small outboard motor, several boxes of fishing tackle, a few rods, and some sort of electronic equipment. The officer, who I didn't recognize, wanted to make a list, but I told him we'd better hurry to River Lane before the gypsies got away.

"But unless they're deaf, they'll know you're on the way," I said, hoping he would realize that he'd made a big mistake by using his siren.

Brittany and I jumped into the front seat of the car. The officer kept the siren turned off for the short drive to the bird-named cottages. Two of the cottages were lit up. The open area between them was filled with cars, including Sammy Boucher's truck. Deafening music made the officer cringe as we pulled in. The lights on top of the cruiser were whirling and blinking. It was then that I noticed that the *Robin* was the cottage that was dark.

"The gypsies should be in that cottage," I whispered to the officer, pointing to the *Robin*. He got out of the cruiser and approached.

"I don't think they need to know Brittany and I are here," I told him as Brittany and I slid down in the car seat. I peeked through the open window, though, to see what was happening. Several college kids came out of the cottages when they saw the red and blue lights. The music suddenly stopped.

A young man appeared at the door of the *Bluebird*. "Sorry, officer," we heard him say, as he came out through the screen door onto the little front porch. "Did the neighbors call? We'll keep the volume down, I promise. We were just having a little fun. Sorry."

Inside the *Bluebird* we could see Sammy Boucher and his girlfriend, as well as a crowd of other college kids. Where were the gypsies? The police siren must have scared them off. Why would they hang around when the police were on their way? They were most likely hiding in the woods, waiting for us to leave. The officer returned to the car.

"They must be hiding," I said in an undertone.

"I don't have a search warrant," said the officer, also in a quiet voice, "I could make some arrests for underage drinking, if there's any of that going on here."

"Forget the drinking," I said quickly. "You've seen the stolen goods. This is your last chance to catch those gypsies! They're leaving town tomorrow, so if you don't do something now, they'll get away!"

"What can I do?" he asked.

"Is there something wrong?" the young man inquired. He was still standing on the porch.

"Keep it down," said the officer in a gruff voice. He got back into the cruiser.

"Let's go," he said. What a waste!

"If you hadn't used your siren, you would have caught them," I said, accusing him.

"Just following orders," he blandly replied. "Where d'you live?"

"Just drop us off here," I said, as we drove out of River Lane. "I live nearby, and my mom will be worried if I arrive at home in a police car."

Brittany didn't say anything. The car drove off. We walked back to Smith's Landing and our hiding place in the woods. Sitting on the pine needles again, we waited for the gypsies or Sammy Boucher to come get the stolen property, but no one came.

"I think the gypsies will go back to their trawler, and Sammy will wait until tomorrow night to move the loot. Their routine has been upset, and they're afraid because of the police."

"They might think that it was just a noise complaint," offered Brittany, "and that it had nothing to do with the robberies."

She was right, but I didn't say anything. We waited. Before long we could hear a vehicle approaching. It didn't turn into any of the driveways along the way, but it came straight down to the parking lot and switched off its headlights.

A man sprang out of a jeep and strode directly to the boat shed. He paused, realizing that the padlock hasp had been broken. He had a flashlight and switched it on, then entered the shed. Coming out again, he went to his vehicle. Instead of driving away, he pulled the jeep up close to the shed. Then he began loading it up with the stolen property. I couldn't see him very well, but I had a suspicion that it was Mr. Seymore!

I dialed 9-1-1 again. This time, though, all the cruisers were out. There was a barking dog complaint and a minor traffic accident. The officer on duty said that there weren't any cruisers available, so we would have to wait.

"Curses!" I exclaimed. Mr. Seymore was finishing his work and closing up the shed doors. He got into his jeep and drove off.

"If only we had our bikes, we could follow him!"

"If only I could ride a bike!" muttered Brittany.

We had to walk home. We began trudging along in the pitch dark. Mr. Seymore was getting away! As we reached the intersection with Yacht Harbor Road, we could hear the rumbling of an old truck. A street lamp high on a telephone pole illuminated the corner, so Brittany and I leapt out of sight behind a clump bushes. When the truck came into the light, I could see that it was Billy Jones!

I jumped out of the bushes and waved my arms frantically. "Stop! Stop!" I cried.

Billy swerved to the middle of the road and slammed on his brakes.

"You almost got us all killed!" he hollered. "What's wrong?"

"Do you know where the Seymores live?" I pushed Brittany inside the cab of the truck and hopped in behind her.

"Don't tell me!" he sighed. "I have to take you to the Seymores' right away."

"Right! Let's go."

"Should I ask what you're doing wandering around in the dark?"

"What about you? Why are you wandering around this neck of the woods?" I countered.

Billy sighed. He drove past the yacht club and took a right onto Lowndes River Road. "O.K. I'll go first. I had a date and took her home."

I didn't make any remark. I didn't care whom he was dating. Since I was silent, he continued, "And what are we going to do once we get to the Seymores'?"

"We'll corner Mr. Seymore and call the police," I said.

"Oh, great! Just what I need—for me, a lowly sailing school instructor, to corner one of the yacht club executives and turn him over to the police like a common criminal! May I ask what he has supposedly done?"

I very patiently explained about the gypsies locking us in the Seymores' shed, the police rescuing us, and later witnessing Mr. Seymore in the act of transferring the stolen goods from the shed to his jeep.

"Wow! So he's the one working with the gypsies?" Billy was flabbergasted.

"Yes," I said as we approached the lighthouse and swung down to the right toward Deer Island. "Sammy isn't the one involved at all. He may be a yucky person, but he's innocent. Mr. Seymore is the guilty one. It was just a coincidence that the gypsies went into the woods near Miller's Cottages. One of their campsites must be nearby."

Billy parked his truck in front of one of the huge houses along the shore. Even though it couldn't have been very late, the house was completely dark. There were two cars in the driveway, right in front of the garage. I bolted out of the truck. Brittany was behind me. We peered into the garage windows. There we saw two other cars, but no jeep!

We rushed back to Billy's truck. "Where's the jeep?" I asked. "Where did Mr. Seymore go?"

"Maybe he's meeting whoever buys the stuff from him," Billy speculated. "Uh...I have an early meeting with the sailing master tomorrow morning before the Sunday races, so if you don't have any other mysteries to solve, I'll drive you two home."

I was stunned! Where was Mr. Seymore? How could we catch him now?

And how would we ever find out who was buying his stolen property?

"Brittany, where do you want me to drop you off?" Billy asked.

"She's with me," I said. Billy drove us to my house and dropped us off at the end of my driveway. I thanked him.

"Sorry I couldn't help," he said. I was disappointed, but I didn't know what to do next. This mystery wasn't easy, especially trying to solve it on my own! Brittany had gone through the adventures of the evening with me, not making a single complaint, but I wasn't ready to trust her. I didn't want to trust her.

I could see a light on in the house as we walked up the driveway. Brittany and I found Mom and Dad in the living room, asleep in their chairs. I woke them.

"We'll see you in the morning," Mom said as she yawned.

"I'm glad to see you home safe and sound," Dad added. He and Mom followed us upstairs, where Brittany and I fell onto my two beds. All thoughts of the robberies, gypsies, and kidnappings slipped from my mind as I fell asleep instantly.

Chapter Thirty-Seven

I awoke with a furry feeling in my mouth and remembered that I hadn't brushed my teeth before I fell asleep. The events of last night raced around my brain. I wanted to telephone the Girls and let them know about Mr. Seymore, but they would all be in church. That's what they did on Sundays. The Eel Grass Girls took the day off from our mysteries, anyway. Of course, we kept working if we could, but we didn't get together unless we were allowed to have a Saturday night sleepover, which didn't happen often.

Brittany was still asleep. I rolled over and thought evil thoughts about Mr. Seymore. What a louse! And he was the one telling tales about Mr. Picardi. Who did he think he was? I would have to wait until tomorrow to talk it over with the Girls, but we would figure out a way to catch him. After the gypsies left town, he would need to find someone new to do his stealing for him.

Maybe we would be able to persuade Louie and his brother to approach Mr. Seymore and offer their "services." Hopefully we'd be able to trap him that way. And to think that Sammy Boucher was innocent!

I heard Brittany moving around. She was awake. We got up and went downstairs to eat breakfast. Mom was in the kitchen making coffee. The house was quiet. Probably it would be until the boys were found. Brittany and I sat at the kitchen table. Mom joined us, looking exhausted.

"How did it go last night?" I asked.

"The Cortezes and a group of yacht club members hunted for the boys all over the beaches and Deer Island," Mom answered. "They even searched the harbor, but there's no sign of Maxwell and Georgie." She sighed. "Joan and I went to the Nor'easter, as you suggested, but those two characters weren't there. We waited and waited, but they never showed up. We felt we were wasting our time there. It was just awful—so loud and noisy—and with all those drunks leering at us! But it was a good idea. I only wish it had worked."

I did too. "What did you do then?"

"Jack Lincoln and his friend Freddy came over just as we got back here," Mom said. "They drove around the neighborhood for a while. Some of the yacht club members came over too. They went from house to house all around the harbor, the neighborhood, and all the way down to Pine Street. Mrs. Lincoln and Abigail searched along Main Street, but no one has seen the boys."

"Are the police going to question those nasty developers?" I asked. Brittany didn't respond, but that was O.K.

"Joan thinks we should keep quiet about them and not tell the police at all. She says it would put the boys in danger. I just don't know what to do! Poor little Maxwell!" she choked back her tears.

"There must be a way to track those men down and find out where they've hidden the boys, if they really are the kidnappers," I said, feeling sorry for her.

"We're going to check the morning papers," Mom said, as if they might really have some vital information, which I doubted. "Afterwards, we'll drive around again."

I stood up to get some granola bars from the cupboard. Brittany got up as I handed one to her. Mom's mouth fell open. I didn't know what was wrong with her. "Mollie! Brittany! What happened to you? What are all those scrapes and bruises?"

I had forgotten about our wounds, even though I still felt sore. "Brittany and I fell over something in the dark last night." We hadn't bothered to clean up, but I suppose we should have. "We'll clean up after breakfast."

Brittany wasn't cut and bruised as much as I. Mom poured us some orange juice. Dad wandered in.

"I just put in a call to the police," he said. "Still no word. They're going through the entire town, and it'll be in all the papers this morning."

He walked out the back door to pick up the newspapers at the end of the driveway. Mom took some buns out of the freezer and popped them into the microwave.

"How about some nice hot, fresh buns?" she asked, trying to sound cheerful, though her face was lined with worry.

"Sounds good," I said, tossing the granola bars back into the cupboard.

"You two were out awfully late last night," remarked Dad, when he returned with the paper. His face was very sad. I really didn't like my little brother, but my parents were just miserable. It was only natural for them to be so worried and distraught, fretting about Maxwell.

Where was that little brat? Who could have kidnapped him? The gypsies or the fancy men? I couldn't understand what the gypsies would want with him or his friend Georgie, but I was sure that they would set them free before they left town. If the fancy men had them, then we might have a good reason to worry.

The buns were done and smelled great. Brittany and I took our food to the patio. Mom and Dad followed with their coffee and newspapers. We sat so we were facing the harbor. It was a beautiful, clear morning. There was the usual early morning activity on the water, but I noticed some of the gypsies boarding a rowboat and beginning to row. I watched their progress as I munched on the hot pastry, wondering where they were headed.

Today was the day they were to leave town. If they were smart, they would depart before they were arrested. But they weren't so smart. The longer they stayed, the more apt they were to make a mistake and get caught. Yet I was surprised when it became obvious that they were rowing straight in to our beach!

"I've had enough of this!" I declared. I stood and headed across the yard. Brittany was right behind me. Mom and Dad didn't look up from their newspapers. They were engrossed in the news about Maxwell and Georgie, trying to find some new information, something to give them hope.

At the top of the steps I stopped. Three gypsies were pulling their rowboat onto the shore. Their furry black dog was with them again. They secured the oars and looked up at us. They gave us the same cold stare and marched off down the beach. What did they think they were doing? Where were they going? Were they going to commit another crime in broad daylight?

I felt angry. If we didn't hurry up and find some evidence to convict them, they would get away with all those robberies and just cruise out of the harbor later today, completely free. It just wasn't right.

Whether they had Maxwell and Georgie or not, they were most likely the kidnappers of those other missing people. Would they release their victims before they left? What good were those victims to the gypsies, anyway? They hadn't received any ransom money from the victims' families.

Then we had to consider that it might be the two fancy men who were the kidnappers. Two horrible little boys, a man, a young woman, an older woman, and an old sick man! I couldn't imagine keeping all those captives hidden away, day in and day out.

It was a whopper of a mystery. Up to now, the gypsies and Mr. Seymore had slipped through our fingers, but I hoped that the gypsies would make a mistake before they left and give the police a reason to arrest them. We knew they were the robbers, anyway.

I started down the steps. Brittany followed. We walked slowly along behind the gypsies. Just to appear that we weren't tracking them, we stopped now and then to look at shells or pick up a bird feather. The gypsies didn't look back.

Before long, their dog had raced up a cliff and begun sniffing around a huge rock formation sticking up at the top of the hill. The men climbed up too and walked along the ridge towards the dog. I had never noticed those rocks before, but Cape Cod was like that. Though it wasn't a rocky kind of place, there were some really big rocks lying around. Laura told me some-thing once about how Cape Cod was formed. She had learned in school about a glacier leaving stones around and making bogs, but that was a long time ago.

We walked on, but the gypsies were no longer visible at the top of the bluff. Where had they gone? Why were they snooping around the woods again? It seemed strange that they would try to rob Howie or the Smiths again, when we had clearly seen them and they had seen us. Were they try-ing to lure us into the woods?

I didn't want to follow them too closely, but when we had climbed the bluff, they had vanished. There was no trail, but we entered the woods. After a short distance, we came to the trail between my house and Louie's. We still couldn't spot the men, so we stopped and listened. There was no sound. It seemed that they had melted into the woods. We could go back to the house and wait for the gypsies to return to their boat. I led the way along the path. Dad was on the phone when we entered the living room.

"Brittany, we're meeting your parents at the Nor'easter for lunch," Dad told us as he hung up the receiver. There went our plan to spy on the gypsies.

"I don't feel like eating," said Mom, who was standing at Dad's side. She probably hadn't touched her breakfast. Brittany and I had eaten all of ours, and it seemed a little early for lunch. Nevertheless, I didn't mind eating again, if we were going to the Nor'easter. I liked their food.

"None of us feels like eating," said Dad, "but we ought to get out. Maybe we can pick up some information in town."

First I dragged Brittany into the downstairs bathroom to clean up our cuts. We didn't need to attract attention to ourselves in town. We might have work to do, and it was better if we looked like normal kids, not kids who had been in some kind of accident. We all piled into the car, and Dad drove to the restaurant. Mr. and Mrs. Picardi were waiting on the bench outside the Nor'easter when we arrived.

We parked out back and when we rounded the corner to the sidewalk, Mrs. Picardi rushed to Brittany and exclaimed, "Oh, Brittany! At least I got one kid left!" She gave Brittany a big hug, but Brittany was as stiff as a board.

We were given a table right away and sat at a round booth table again. Our mothers made sure Brittany and I sat side by side. We ordered ginger ales and waited for our sandwiches to arrive.

Suddenly Mr. Picardi jumped up, knocking his beer all over the table! We were shocked to see him lunge across the room to where his two former friends had just walked in from the bar area.

"I'll get you for this!" he screamed, grabbing Elbert by the neck and sending Silverson to the floor with the whack of his backhand. Women screamed, a waitress dropped her tray, chairs scraped the floor as patrons struggled to avoid the melee. Mr. Picardi and Elbert were really fighting now, swinging their fists, punching, and even kicking.

Dad started toward them, but Mom held onto his arm. He pulled free and caught Silverson, who was struggling to his feet. Dad grabbed his arms and held them behind his back, so he couldn't hit Mr. Picardi.

The fighting continued, with Mr. Picardi flattening Elbert. The man groggily tried to get up from the floor. Officers Nick and Lopez rushed in through the front door and quickly assessed the situation. They must have recognized Dad and Mr. Picardi, but Officer Nick grabbed Mr. Picardi as Lopez took Silverson from Dad.

"They kidnapped my son!" screamed Mr. Picardi, wrestling to break free. "They threatened me. Make them tell you what they've done to my kid."

"You've lost your mind, Picardi!" said Silverson. Blood trickled down his forehead into his eye. "We don't know anything about your son."

"We'll handle this," said Officer Nick. He helped Elbert up from the floor and led the three men outside, where two patrol cars with flashing lights were blocking the narrow street. We filed out of the restaurant. A huge crowd formed around us.

"We know you're shook up about your son, Mr. Picardi," Officer Nick said sympathetically, "but you have to let us handle the investigation."

"You don't know these guys," shouted Mr. Picardi, whose face was beginning to swell. "They don't play fair. They go after your wife and kids."

Officer Nick grew serious. "Now why would they want to do a thing like that?"

"We were doing business together and I quit," explained Mr. Picardi. "They didn't like that." At this, he gave his two ex-business associates a sneer.

"He tried to kill us!" exclaimed Elbert.

"Yeah!" agreed Silverson. "He's an animal—dangerous! He needs to be locked up!"

"Do you want to press charges?" Officer Nick asked.

"I feel sorry for the guy," muttered Silverson in mock concern, but I don't think anyone was convinced by his act.

"Let him go," said Elbert, rubbing his bruises.

"You have to arrest them," Mr. Picardi demanded. "They're the ones who kidnapped our sons!"

Dad stepped forward. "Those men did threaten Frank."

"Let's take a little ride to the station and you can make a formal accusation there," Officer Nick told them.

"I want to pay for the damage first," said Mr. Picardi, motioning toward the restaurant. Officer Lopez accompanied him back into the Nor'easter, where I saw him give a big wad of money to Billy Jones's brother, who had stepped out of the restaurant office to help clean up the mess.

Officer Lopez put the two fancy men into one of the cruisers and drove off. Nick turned to Dad. "Bring Picardi to the station, and we'll see what we can do."

Officer Nick left, relieving the congestion his double-parked cruiser had caused on Main Street.

"Better go home and wait," Dad told Mom and Mrs. Picardi. We all walked out back together. Mr. Picardi seemed ready to explode. Dad drove him to the police station, and Mrs. Picardi drove us to my house in her car.

"Girls," Mom began as we parked near the garage, "why don't we play a game while we wait? It will keep our minds off everything. We've searched everywhere for the boys. I don't want to give up, but I don't know what more we can do."

"I want to go see Howie," I replied as we got out of the car. "He might have some information."

"Really?" asked Mom. "The police have been over there several times already, but you go on. You never know." I didn't want to explain about the castaway, Mr. Dill. "Let's eat something first. We never got our lunch."

Mom and Mrs. Picardi made sandwiches and soup. It wasn't long before we were eating, and soon we were ready to leave. I saw my backpack on the bench near the back door and remembered that I still had Mr. Picardi's cell phone. I handed it to Mrs. Picardi. Brittany and I exited through the back door. We hiked down the driveway, veering to the left, to Howie Snow's. Connie Dill's blue sedan was still parked in front of his house.

I walked up and knocked on Howie's front door. We heard a noise inside and waited. After a moment, Howie swung the door open.

"Hey, little buddy!" he said. "Come in."

We entered the cluttered house. It was an old house full of antiques, nothing fancy. Everything was worn out. Piles of tools, jars of bolts and nails, boat parts, glass milk bottles, and newspapers covered the tables, chairs, and floor.

He led us through the house to the kitchen, where Connie was seated at the table, sipping tea.

"Hello, girls," she said, looking up wistfully from her cup. "We can't find Daddy anywhere. He's gone without a trace. And we heard about the boys too. It's just awful! What kind of beasts are those gypsies? Kidnapping innocent children and sick old men?"

"The worst part is that the police have let the gypsies go," I told them. "They're leaving town today."

"How can they let their prime suspects go free?" asked Connie.

Howie was stunned. "That don't make no sense!"

"The Picardis suspect that those developers with the red car have kidnapped the boys," I told them.

Connie's eyes flashed. "Could they have something to do with Daddy's disappearance?" she asked, turning pale. "Those men are just awful, but kidnapping is a serious offense. How would they have known Daddy was out on that island? How would the gypsies have known, either?"

"Them two wouldn't know, but them gypsies are another story," Howie said. "They've been fishin' the area all summer. They'd know."

"Howie is going to take me out again to look for Daddy," Connie told us. "We've got to find him!"

"Don't worry," I consoled her. "He'll be found."

Brittany and I said good-bye and left. I decided to take the path behind Howie's house through the woods. It was perfectly still and quiet except for a blue jay calling and another bird hopping through the dry leaves, or maybe it was a rabbit. We took the path that led to the beach. I pointed out the gypsies' campsite to Brittany.

We came out on the bluff and looked over the harbor. What a gorgeous day! It was the perfect kind of day for a sail. Too bad I didn't have a boat, but this wasn't the best time to sail. Our mysteries needed solving.

Brittany and I walked along the beach and back to my house. No one was home when we got there. All the cars were gone, so I assumed that Mom and Mrs. Picardi had been called to the police station. I hoped that Mr. Picardi wouldn't have to go to jail for making a mess at the Nor'easter and fighting with those fancy men.

If only the Eel Grass Girls were with me, we would be able to think of something to do. We would be out on our bikes, looking for clues— but then, we weren't usually together on Sundays, anyway. What was I going to do with Brittany?

"Want to hit tennis balls?" I asked.

"Sure," Brittany replied. I took Maxwell's racket from the hook near the back door and picked mine up from the bench. Brittany took the container of pink balls, and we went outside to hit them off the side of the garage for a while. If only we had a tennis court, we could have played a real game, but we kept on hitting for a while. Brittany hit fairly well. I practiced my backhand, my forehand, and serve.

When we tired of tennis, we went inside for a drink of water. Mom had left some cupcakes on the counter. I gave a package to Brittany, then opened one for myself. We sat down at the kitchen table to eat. Then I heard something.

"Uh-oh!" I said. We slipped from the table and crept to the hall doorway. Standing at the sliding door in the living room were two men! Gypsies! They were peering inside, and one was opening the door!

I rushed into the living room. "Get out of here, you dirty rotten creeps!" They turned and ran over the lawn and down the steps to the beach.

"Wow!" exclaimed Brittany. "You sure are brave!"

I didn't answer. I was fed up with those men. We had been right about them. They had gone out last night for one last robbing spree in the harbor. We had seen them hide their stolen goods, and they had trapped us in the boat shed. Now they were stealing from a few houses before they left town! I hoped that they would leave, but we needed to find certain missing persons first. Maybe I shouldn't have yelled at them. Maybe I should have called the police. Rats! The only thing left to do was follow them now.

"Come on!" I said to Brittany as I bolted out through the sliding door across the lawn. We raced to the top of the stairs, where we slunk behind the bayberry bushes. On the beach, three gypsies stood arguing. Their big black dog bounded over the mounds of eel grass, probably chasing sand fleas. The men looked very angry, and one pointed toward my house. Then they boarded their rowboat and headed out toward the trawlers.

Brittany and I continued to watch. The sun had receded behind a cloud, and the sky was clouding over. The air had become a little cooler. A fog bank hovered over the Sound.

"Boo!"

I nearly fainted! Brittany's eyes almost popped out of her head! I twisted around to see Louie laughing hysterically at us!

"Ha, ha! Gotcha!" he chuckled.

"This is no time to fool around," I scolded him. "The gypsies just tried to break into my house!"

I told him about seeing Mr. Seymore last night and about Mr. Picardi's fight at the Nor'easter.

"It's getting serious," he said. "We've got to track the gypsies and those developers. If we watched them every second, they'd lead us to the victims. Trouble is, we only watch them now and then. That'll never work."

"They're pulling out of the harbor today," I reminded him. "Once they've left, we'll never be able to find out where they've hidden all those people."

"I wish I had a boat," he lamented. "A rowboat's not good enough."

We looked out and saw the fog bank rolling in as far as the cut and the old lighthouse beach. Before our eyes it swept across the harbor.

"It'll be hard to track them in this fog," he added. I agreed. Pretty soon, we wouldn't be able to see a thing out there.

"But I thought your brother had a motorboat," I said.

"Nah. But this fog is good. If we can't see them, they can't see us," he replied.

"But if we don't have a boat, what good will the fog do for us?" I wondered.

He had no answer. Soon whiteness enveloped us. The mist felt cool against my bare arms and legs. We didn't know then what mysteries lurked within it.

Chapter Thirty-Eight

Louie, Brittany, and I sat on the steps. This was the worst mystery we had come across. Six people had already vanished, and no one could find a trace of any of them. Maybe it *was* aliens who'd done it!

Just then we heard something—footsteps! Someone was coming up the stairs! The gypsies must have decided to take advantage of the fog and come back to rob the house!

We sprang to our feet and dove into the bushes. Brittany grabbed onto my T-shirt. We listened. The movement was slow, one step at a time, each one falling heavily after the other on the treads of the wooden stairs. He, or she, was moving up, closer to us with each footfall.

He was at the top of the stairs now, pausing. Why had only one gypsy come back? We peered through the fog, but it was too thick to see him. We heard his breathing, then a sigh. Through the milky whiteness, we saw a form. Could he see us? He was coming straight at us. It looked like an old man with a beard! Ruben Dill?

"Aaaah-eeek!" Brittany squeaked.

"Shut up!" I hissed.

"Who's there?" he called. His hands were stretched out in front of him, groping nearer.

Louie boldly stepped out of the bushes. "It's me, Louie Stello," he fearlessly announced, standing in front of the ragged man.

"Boy, I'm Ruben Dill. You've got to contact my daughter, Connie. I have to let her know I'm alive!"

"Mr. Dill," I said, coming out of our hiding place. "What happened to you? How did you get away? Are you all right?"

"Get my daughter and get the police!" he shouted frantically, not answering my questions.

"Your daughter's at Howie Snow's," I said, but instantly realized that he wouldn't know who Howie was or where he lived. "She's just next door. I'll go get them. Oh, no! I just remembered they went out in Howie's boat to look for you."

"Maybe they didn't go out when they saw the fog rolling in," Louie suggested.

"O.K. I'll go see," I said. "You two can take Mr. Dill to my house and call the police from there."

I ran over the damp lawn and thought of cutting through the woods. It would be quicker than going around to the driveway. I started in. It was pea soup, as they say, but the path was straight, and I knew Howie's was the only path off to the right. I jogged along until I heard voices. I stopped in my tracks and listened. Nothing. I thought of calling out but restrained myself. It could have been some of the gypsies, and I didn't want to meet any of them in the woods.

The wind in the pines above me made a swishing sound. Far off in the distance I heard a foghorn groaning. Silence. I continued on. I should have come to Howie's path by now. Maybe I had missed it. I must have. I turned back. Something rustled on my left, then on my right. I stopped and stood still. I really didn't think there could be so many wild animals in the woods. It was something else—someone else—and they had surrounded me!

I slowly crept on, one little step at a time. Finally I could see Howie's path and raced down to it. I would get to his house before they could catch me, whoever they were. But when I got to Howie's, no one was home! Both the car and truck were gone! I couldn't imagine where they could be. They were supposed to be out in the Sound, or the harbor, looking for Mr. Dill. And if they had decided not to go out because of the fog and had gone to town, why would they take both cars?

I could hear someone running up the path behind me! I turned abruptly, took the driveway, and ran as fast as I could toward my house. I didn't know who was following me, but I wasn't going to hang around there to find out. I didn't like the thought of confronting them on my own, alone in the fog.

Finally I reached my back door and slammed it shut after me. I locked it and ran around to the front door, shut and bolted it, entered the living room, slid the sliding glass door shut, and flipped the latch to lock it. Louie, Brittany, and Mr. Dill were sitting on the sofa, staring at me.

"What's wrong?" asked Brittany.

"Someone was following me in the woods all the way to Howie Snow's. Howie and Connie are gone, but I'm sure they'll be back soon, Mr. Dill. Did you call the police?"

"The phone's not working," said Louie.

"What do you mean?" I asked, picking up the receiver on the table beside the sofa. The line was dead. "It's been cut!"

We heard a sound in the basement. The cellar door—I had forgotten to lock it! I dashed to the door just as it opened.

Silverson and Elbert forced their way into the hallway! Elbert grabbed my arms so tightly I couldn't move.

"Louie! Brittany! Get out! Get away quick!" I screamed, but it was too late. Silverson had rushed into the living room, snatched Brittany, and knocked Louie to the floor! Elbert dragged me in and, before I knew it, our hands and mouths had been bound with duct tape. Mr. Dill was so shocked that he was easily subdued and also bound.

"Thank you for locking all the doors," said Silverson. "Now, down into the cellar we go." He pushed us ahead of him so we almost tumbled down the basement stairs. The lights were on, and the air was stuffy. The men marched us into the game room.

"A squirrel made a nest in your exhaust pipe," Elbert said. "So carbon monoxide is building up in your game room. It doesn't have any odor, so you and your friends didn't notice that when you came down here to play table tennis." He pointed over to the table and paddles next to the furnace room.

"I can't explain the old man being here, but that's not my problem," Silverson added, with a glance toward Mr. Dill.

"We'll just wait upstairs," Elbert continued. "I hope you don't mind, but four senseless deaths is enough. We have important work to do for Mr. Big. He has several loads of dirty bills that need laundering in real estate."

Silverson added, "But as soon as you pass out, we'll slip down and rip the duct tape off your wrists and mouths, otherwise it wouldn't look like the accident it is."

"Bye-bye," said Elbert cheerfully. He closed the game room door, and we heard them clomp up the stairs. Brittany's terrified eyes met mine. Elbert was right—the carbon monoxide didn't smell, but the air was turning foul and toxic. We had to get out of there—quick!

I scanned the room for a pair of scissors, a tool, or any sharp object, but of course there was nothing. It was the game room, and I was sure that nothing sharp existed in the entire basement. Mom didn't have anything in our house that Maxwell could hurt himself with. I was beginning to feel dizzy. This was bad, very bad.

Louie was squirming and leaning his head toward his right side. I suspected that he had something in his pocket. I wiggled over to him and I turned my back toward him so I could get my hands into his pocket. It was next to impossible because my hands were taped together, but with a lot of contorting I was able to get one hand into his pocket deep enough to feel a jack knife and get it out.

I held the knife while Louie pulled the blade out. He deftly slit the tape around my wrists. I ripped the tape from my mouth and freed Louie. He set the others free one by one as I untaped their mouths. Mr. Dill was nearly unconscious. Louie and I pulled him toward the door.

Oh, no! Elbert had locked the door! I took hold of the doorknob anyway and realized that it didn't even have a lock on it. Good old Mom and Dad had thought of everything. They wouldn't want Maxwell to lock himself in the game room. I suppose I should have been thankful for that. I flung the door open and helping Mr. Dill, we rushed out, gasping for oxygen. I closed the door behind us.

We dragged Mr. Dill toward the stairs and were glad when he began to recover. But we had a problem: The only way out of the basement was through the house. What were we going to do? We stood at the bottom of the stairs.

"Let's go," said Louie in a whisper.

"I'm sure the door will be locked," I said.

"Nah," said Louie. "They're too sure of themselves. It'll be unlocked."

"They won't get the better of us this time," said Mr. Dill, getting to his feet. He was wobbly, and I wasn't sure if he could even get up the stairs.

"I wish we had Dad's cell phone," Brittany whined.

"What's our plan?" asked Louie. He wasn't the type to rely upon technology, anyway.

"Each one of us should head for a different door," I said. "One of us, at least, should be able to get away."

We decided that Louie would go for the front door. I told him how to unbolt the lock. Mr. Dill would go with Brittany to the back door. I would head for the living room, the room where those two were most likely hanging out, or maybe not. They might be in the kitchen, watching for our parents. Whoever escaped would run out to the road and head to Laura's or Louie's house.

We started for the stairs, carefully creeping up. Slowly I tried the knob, holding my breath. What if this door were locked? I let out my breath when I felt the knob turn in my hand. Louie had been right: The two fancy men hadn't bothered to lock it.

A few lights were on in the house. We paused, listening for voices. They were still there. We could hear them in the kitchen.

"O.K." I whispered. "Go!"

I raced through the hallway, across the living room, to the glass doors. All I could see outside was the white haze of fog that had descended upon the house. I fumbled at the latch of the sliding glass door, pulled hard to open it, flung the screen aside, but stopped short. Something was blocking my way! I froze!

"Oh, no...!" The two men were standing in front of me! How did they get out of the kitchen and around to the patio so fast? Completely confused, I stared up at the dark figures enshrouded in the thickest fog I had ever seen.

"Out of my way, you creeps!" I yelled, giving one of them a good kick in the shin. He hopped back as he cried out and said something I didn't understand. I ducked out of his partner's reach, to race around the house to meet my friends, but he somehow caught my ankle and brought me down. I hit the grass with a thud.

"Let me go, you loser!" I screamed, kicking with all my might.

"Be quiet down, Miss," he said earnestly. "I am not here to harm you please."

Why was he talking that way? I flipped over so I could face him. "Let me go!"

"Please to help you," the other man said. He leaned toward me. I didn't see Silverson, or Elbert, but two gypsies!

"What do you want?" I demanded as I struggled to get free. "Why are you here? Are you trying to rob us again? Or kidnap me?"

"We have robbed no ones or stealed from nothing," the first gypsy said. He wore a cap. "We have napped no kids or any peoples. We try to help."

I was really confused now. They appeared to be so sincere. Were they? Or was I being set up? Should I trust them? I had to make a decision fast.

"If what you're saying is true, help me now," I said, taking the risk that they were serious and being honest with me. "There are two bad men in the house. They're trying to kill me and my friends."

The other gypsy let my foot go. Together we snuck around the outside of the house, close to the shrubbery, looking for Louie, Brittany, and Mr. Dill. Near the front door Louie sprang out in front of us.

"There you are!" I said, wishing he wouldn't leap out of nowhere like that. My heart was beating even faster than it had been. This mystery work was sure hard on a person's health.

"They've got Brit and the old man! Who are these guys?" he asked, looking at the gypsies and stepping back.

"They say they want to help us."

"We help," the capless one stated. At least the two of them could speak enough English so they could communicate.

"All right, but be careful. They might have guns," Louie told them.

"I be careful," the capped one said.

"If you go through the back door," I said, "the rest of us can go back around to the sliding door, get in the house, and sneak up behind them while you distract them."

He nodded.

"I'll go with the other gyp...man," said Louie.

"Then I'll stay here," I announced.

It seemed strange to suddenly trust these men after all they'd done. Why were they helping us? Were they working with Elbert and Silverson? Were we going to end up back in the basement? I didn't have answers, but for now we were putting our lives in their hands.

We waited for Louie and his gypsy to get into position. Then my gypsy stepped up to the back door as I hid in the shrubs. He boldly knocked. "Hello! Hello! Come out! We need help!"

There was a scuffling noise inside the door, and it slowly opened. I could see Silverson peer out.

"What'dya want?" he asked angrily. "Go away and leave us alone!"

The gypsy grabbed him by the collar and swung him through the doorway and outside onto the ground in one swift movement. With the wind knocked out of him, Silverson just lay there. It was long enough for the gypsy to give him such a whack in the face that he was knocked out cold! The other gypsy could be seen tossing Elbert out through the doorway. He literally flew through the air and landed beside his pal. My gypsy finished him off the same way. I wondered if they would now turn on us, but they didn't.

Brittany and Mr. Dill ran out, followed by Louie. We wrapped the fancy men's wrists, ankles, and mouths with the duct tape in Elbert's pocket. We weren't sure what to do with them, so we left them in the yard, after first making sure they didn't have any knives or other weapons in their pockets.

Louie said we had to do something with them. When they regained consciousness, they might get back into the house and get a kitchen knife. I suggested locking them in our garbage bin. Louie and I took the garbage cans out of the bin, which ran along one side of the garage. The gypsies and Mr. Dill, who turned out to be quite strong once he had recovered from the carbon monoxide, dragged the two over and tossed them into the bin, slamming the lid down and locking it.

"We have to fix that furnace," said Mr. Dill. He was able to find the shut-off valve for the gas. We then aired the house by opening up the game room door and all the windows and doors in the whole house. "I ain't a homeowner for nothing," he said. "This house could blow up any minute."

"What's that supposed to mean?" I asked him.

"A gas build-up could blow your house to smithereens," he said. "We'd better get out of the vicinity for a while, until the gas dissipates."

"We find something," said the capped gypsy, abruptly changing the subject. "In woods. Come see."

I wasn't so sure. What could they have found in the woods? Louie seemed eager to find out. Brittany looked at me for direction. I had trouble completely trusting the men responsible for so many robberies and kidnappings. Why had they suddenly decided to help us? It just wasn't normal and it didn't make any sense.

"What did you find?" I asked.

"Come see," the man repeated. "Bring light."

"You mean a flashlight?" asked Louie.

I stepped inside the back door and grabbed my backpack. My flash-light was still in it.

The gypsies started across the yard. The fog was beginning to lift, but we could only see a few feet ahead of us. I couldn't believe that I was allowing these men to lead us into the woods. But we jogged along behind them. Mr. Dill was able to keep up. Traveling the path to Louie's house, we then turned off toward the harbor. You'll never believe what we found there!

Chapter Thirty-Nine

We found ourselves at the huge rock formation Brittany and I had seen earlier. What was it that the gypsies wanted to show us? From somewhere the capless gypsy produced a huge coil of thick rope. I stepped back. They were going to hang us, or at last tie us up! We had jumped out of the frying pan into the fire!

The gypsies did not hang us or tie us up. The capless gypsy dropped the end of the rope, and it disappeared into the ground! Whoa! This was freaky! The other gypsy wrapped part of the rope around his waist and slowly vanished into the base of the rock!

Louie knelt down and looked on as the gypsy sank into the ground. "There's a big hole here!" he exclaimed. "Where does it go?"

"Cavern," said the gypsy. "You go too."

"Be careful, children," said Mr. Dill. He had had a lot of excitement for one day, and I couldn't wait to find out how he had escaped. He didn't seem to be afraid of the gypsies and was even helping the capless gypsy to hold the rope. We were all going to remain confused until we had a chance to talk. But now wasn't a good time for chitchat.

Louie held onto the rope and in an instant was also gone.

"No! Louie! Don't do it!" I called out, but it was too late! I saw a gaping hole at the corner of the rock and felt a cold blast of air blowing up from deep below.

After a moment I heard Louie yelling up to me, "Mollie! Mollie! Your brother! Maxwell's down here! And his friend!"

"What?" I glared angrily at the gypsy. "You kidnapped my brother! You beast!"

"No! No! I did not! Your brother he fell to hole. We find and tell you."

"So you say," I retorted. "Louie, are they all right? Can you get them out?" I called down.

"It's dark down here," he said. "You've got to come down. Bring your flashlight."

"O.K." I whispered to Brittany, "If I never come up again, you've got to go for help."

"But I might get lost!" she whispered back. "What about Mr. Dill? Couldn't he go?"

"He's too old. Leave him here. Just head for the beach. Run to the left until you reach the steps. Maybe our parents will be home. If they're not, go back to the beach and keep going until you find a house where someone's home. You have to get help."

"Come on, Mollie!" I heard Louie call. "I think some of that stolen stuff is down here too. I can't see it that well, but I can feel boat stuff all over the place."

"What?" I asked.

"Get down here and you'll see!" he yelled.

I nodded to the gypsy and grabbed hold of the rope. He gently lowered me down into the cavern. Was I ever surprised! It smelled of seaweed and saltwater—a sour, dank smell. When I hit the ground, I fished my flashlight from the backpack and switched it on. Wow! This was unreal! I shined the light all around. We were in a large cave. Maxwell and Georgie were huddled together on a big, flat stone. They were weak from hunger and fright, but otherwise they looked O.K.

"Mollie!" Maxwell whimpered. "Where's Mommy?"

"Uh...Don't know. But we'll get you out of here."

"I want my mommy and daddy!" cried Georgie.

"Did you boys get hurt when you fell into this place?" Louie asked.

"We found an old tree that had blown over in that storm," Maxwell explained. "We put it in the hole and climbed down, but when we tried to get out, the tree broke in half and we were trapped."

The two halves of the tree lay on the floor of the cave. I scanned the layout and couldn't believe all the new-looking electronic equipment, fishing gear, outboard motors, and other boat things stacked all around. It was the type of stuff we had seen in Mr. Seymore's boat shed!

"Louie! Do you think this is where Mr. Seymore has been hiding the things the gyp...someone has been stealing?"

"Sure looks like it," he responded.

"We'd better get these boys out of here," I said. "Let's try to make a harness out of my backpack."

We were able to rebuckle the pack so that it held Maxwell. The gypsy helped us attach it to the rope. The knot-tying I had learned in sailing school sure came in handy.

"One of the boys is ready," I called up. "Pull!"

Maxwell went up first. Next we attached Georgie, and he, too, was pulled up. I went next, then Louie, and last, the other gypsy.

"Thank you," I said, once we were all out of the cave and standing on solid ground near the big rock. I looked the gypsies in the eye. "We were wrong about you. I'm sorry, but I still don't understand how all that stuff got to be in the cave. What do you know about it?"

"Bad persons taked it. Stealed," said the capped gypsy. "Many things from our boats. Police tell us many persons robbed."

Did this mean that these were the "good" gypsies and the "bad" gypsies had done the stealing? These two men should know. "Do you know who did it?" I asked them.

"We not know," said the other man. "We not know laws of this place," he explained. "We make mistake. But we no steal. We..."

"That's all very nice," said Mr. Dill, impatiently. "But I need to contact my daughter and the police. I know who stole those things. I saw them last night when I was hiding on Deer Island. Fortunately they didn't see *me*, but I watched them go from boat to boat, taking things."

"Who was it?" I asked. Now this was amazing. Mr. Dill must have seen the other gypsies on their robbing spree, just before our encounter with them at the boat shed.

"A boy and a girl," he replied. "Their names are Sammy and Honey."

"Sammy and... and...Honey?" I stammered. They were the robbers? Those two had done it? I was so sure that they had been only receiving and selling the stolen goods, not actually doing the stealing. "Are you sure?"

"Of course I'm sure!" Mr. Dill seemed offended. "I heard them and I saw them clearly, though I don't know why they were dressed in caps and old sweaters. Kinda like what you menfolks are wearing now," he said to the gypsies.

Then I put two and two together! "That's it!" I shouted. "Sammy Boucher and his skinny girlfriend were committing the robberies all along! With the help of Sammy's uncle, Mr. Seymore! And the two of them dressed like gypsies so if anyone saw them, they wouldn't recognize them, but think they were seeing gypsies! And it worked! They tricked us!" We thought that catching the thieves would lead us to the kidnap victims, but it hadn't exactly turned out that way.

"We have to tell the police," said Mr. Dill.

"We can go to my house," said Louie. "Our phone is working."

"Howie Snow's is closer," I said. "But maybe we should go to my house. Our parents must be home by now. We can use your dad's cell phone, Brittany."

"I want Mommy!" whined Maxwell.

"Me too," sniffled Georgie.

"Let's split up," Louie suggested. "Just in case there's another problem. I'll go home and call the police. Mollie, you go to Howie's and see if he's home and if Connie's there. Mr. Dill, you and the others go back to Mollie's house and we'll meet you there just as soon as we can."

One gypsy picked up Maxwell and the other carried Georgie. Brittany appeared to be unsure of what to do, so I said, "You can come with me."

The whole group of us turned back into the woods, still filled with thick fog. At the fork, Louie took a left to his house, Brittany and I found Howie's path, and the gypsies, with the boys and Mr. Dill, retraced their steps to my house.

I wished the Girls were with me. It seemed so strange to be having this adventure without them. I had never had an adventure, before this summer, but the Eel Grass Girls always had exciting times together. Now here I was sharing this excitement with Brittany Picardi. I had never expected that!

It was one thing to have Louie Stello be part of our mystery, but Brittany was another. As we trotted along the narrow path, I had to admit that she wasn't all that bad. She could have been much, much worse. She knew how to keep quiet and mind her own business. But I couldn't think about her now. Connie Dill's blue sedan was up ahead, and Howie's truck was near the barn.

I pounded with all my might on the weather-beaten door. "Howie! Open up quick! Emergency! Emergency!"

The door swung open. "What's the matter, little buddy?" asked Howie, looking surprised to see me so upset.

"We've found Mr. Dill! Where's Connie?" I spluttered.

"Found Ruben Dill? Where? How?" He turned and called urgently into the house, "Connie! Come here! Hurry! It's your dad!"

Connie appeared at the door. She was obviously flustered, and her eyes were wide.

"Daddy? Where is he?" she looked out, expecting to see her long-lost father on the doorstep.

"He's at my house! Come on!" Brittany and I started down the driveway. Howie and Connie hurried behind us through the fog, which was just beginning to blow off.

Both of our cars and the Picardis' car were in the driveway. I didn't know where everyone had been when we needed them, but they were all there now. When we got to the living room, two happy reunions were in full force. Mom and Dad were sobbing over Maxwell, and Mr. and Mrs. Picardi were locked in a group hug with Georgie. The gypsies were standing beside the two family groups looking both proud and ill at ease. Louie was already there, beside Mr. Dill, who looked up to see Connie.

"Daddy!" Connie shrieked, lunging for her father. They clung together. Police sirens pierced the air, and two cruisers screeched into our driveway. Officer Nick raced into the living room from the kitchen as Officer Lopez appeared at the sliding glass door.

"Everyone all right here?" Officer Nick asked, surveying the room. We didn't know what Louie had said when he called 9-1-1, but Nick sure was trying to figure out exactly what had happened. It was quite a sight! Maxwell and Georgie had obviously been found, as well as our castaway, Mr. Dill, who had been reunited with his daughter, Connie.

Lopez and Officer Nick were clearly surprised to see Howie Snow and Louie, but were shocked to see the gypsies. They couldn't imagine why we were all together in one place without any fighting or arguing. Then everyone began talking at once. No one could understand a word!

Chapter Forty

"Hold it! Hold it!" commanded Officer Nick. "Everybody, just calm down. One person at a time!"

Everyone started babbling again.

"Quiet, please," Nick said. "I want to get this straight—the two boys fell into a cave?"

"Yes," I replied. "The gypsies found them."

"That's very good news," Officer Nick said with a smile. "And I have some news for you too. We've just had a piece of information come in at the station that I'm sure will interest you all. You remember Millicent Bartles, who disappeared from Deer Island last week?"

We all nodded, though Mr. Dill didn't know what we were talking about.

Nick continued, "Well, it turns out that she's been over in Hyannis on a drinking binge."

"Huh? Of all the nerve!" I said in disgust. "After the worrying we've done! She was out drinking and having a good time?"

"Mollie, dear," said Mom. "Some people have a problem with drinking. You must learn to be more sympathetic. She probably wasn't having such a good time. Think of her poor husband."

"That's the thing," continued Officer Nick. "Her husband knew that she had a drinking problem and, of course, he knew that the car was gone, but he didn't give us all the details."

"Is she all right now?" asked Connie.

"Oh, yes," replied Nick. "Her husband has put her in a special hospital to dry out, as they say. She'll get all the help she needs there. And the other guy, Otis Wilton, ran off with another woman. Same thing. The wife knew perfectly well what he'd done, and with whom, but didn't want it in the papers."

"And?" I asked, wanting to know the outcome.

"Oh, he's come back. It's hurt his reputation, of course. He's supposed to be a model of virtue, but he's going to try to patch things up with his wife."

"So no one's missing?" asked Mrs. Picardi. "Everyone's been found?"

266

"We've still got that teenager who hasn't turned up," he said. "But we've got it all wrapped up concerning you folks." He glanced around the room, making a note, I'm sure, to get back to the gypsies and find out what they were doing in my living room.

"Mr. Dill has some information for you," I said.

All eyes were upon the disheveled form of Mr. Dill. I wanted to know who had kidnapped him, but instead of telling us, he related the story of how he had witnessed the robberies committed by Sammy and his girl-friend, "Honey." The gypsies were interested in how the two had dressed in multicolored sweaters and caps.

"And Sammy's uncle Mr. Seymore is in on it too," I informed the police.

"Not exactly, but we'd better go over to Miller's Cottages again," Officer Nick said. "O.K., Lopez. Let's go."

"But first we have to tell you how Elbert and Silverson tried to asphyxiate us," I said.

"What?" cried Mr. Picardi. "They tried to hurt you?" He grabbed Brittany, and she nodded slowly.

"I told you those two were no good!" shouted Mrs. Picardi, taking Brittany in her arms and hugging her again. Brittany actually spoke up and told everyone about how we had escaped. She concluded the tale"They're outside in the garbage bin."

"Oh, I've got to see this!" roared Mr. Picardi. Everyone traipsed through the kitchen and out to the garage. Dad unlocked the bin, and our families and the police were shocked to see the two former "fancy men" lying in the garbage bin. Dad and Mr. Picardi helped the officers pull the crooks out and thrust them into the patrol cars. They sped off to jail.

"This calls for a celebration!" cheered Dad. "Let's have a barbecue tonight—the one we cancelled last night. Mollie, invite your friends and their families and let's celebrate! And you men," he said to the gypsies. "Invite all your buddies. The whole bunch of them. We'll eat here tonight!"

"We get our friends," said the capped gypsy. "We bring food."

"No, no. You don't have to bring a thing," said Dad. "This is our party for you! We want to thank you for finding our children. If you hadn't found them, I don't know what would have happened."

"We thanking you," said the capless one. He and his companion bowed and cut across the yard, disappearing down the steps toward the beach, into the lifting fog. It looked as if it would clear soon.

Howie and Connie decided to take Mr. Dill to Howie's house to get cleaned up. The old man needed some clothes, but Howie was twice his size, so Dad gave him an outfit to wear. We were sure Dad's clothes would be too big too, but anything would be better than the filthy rags Mr. Dill was now wearing.

Louie said good-bye and promised to come back soon with his brother and parents. He jogged off toward the path through the woods and was gone. Dad and Mr. Picardi took the charcoal out of the garage and wheeled the grill around to the patio to prepare for the barbecue.

I ran inside to phone my friends, but as I picked up the receiver, I remembered that the phone lines had been cut by Silverson and Elbert. I went back outside to ask Mr. Picardi if I could use his cell phone again.

"I don't have it," he replied. That's right—Mrs. Picardi had it. Back inside, I found Mrs. Picardi in the kitchen. She and Mom were feeding the boys, who were sitting at the kitchen table as docile as kittens. Just wait until they had eaten. I knew they would be little monsters again!

"Here it is," she said, taking the phone from her purse. I went into the living room to make my calls. Brittany was sitting there alone. It finally occurred to me that her parents probably ignored her the way mine ignored me. Both couples gave all their attention to their darling little sons. I guess Brittany and I did have something in common.

I rang the Girls, one after the other. "We almost got killed!" I told them. I briefed them on how we had found the boys and the stolen goods. It seemed that our mystery had been solved. "The gypsies helped us!" I exclaimed. The Girls had so many questions, but I invited them to come over with their families to the barbecue, where everyone would have their questions answered. Each one of us would have the chance to tell our story.

They couldn't say no to that! They all promised to bring something yummy to eat, so we wouldn't have to suffer too much with my father's cooking. It would be a really fun party.

I motioned to Brittany to come with me, and I took the cell phone out to Dad, who first called the gas company to check the furnace. Then he phoned Jake Rison and invited him to join us. Dad lured him with a promise that he would hear all the details about the boys' rescue and Mr. Dill's adventure. Even we hadn't heard Mr. Dill's story yet. Jake agreed to join the party.

Dad then telephoned the police to give them Mr. Picardi's cell phone number, just in case they needed to call us. He asked them to fill us in on any new information as it came in. He left an invitation for Officers Nick and Lopez to come to our party too. They were still on duty, but promised to come over as soon as they were off.

Brittany and I went back to the kitchen, where I pulled the phone book from the kitchen drawer and dialed Billy Jones. He needed to be included after all he had done to help us with this mystery. I had a difficult time tracking him down, but I finally found him at the Nor'easter. After a long wait, he came to the phone.

"Don't tell me the whole story now," he said, sensing that I couldn't wait to explain all the drama and excitement. "I get off work in twenty minutes. I'll be over then. I can't wait to hear what happened!"

I needed a quick shower and a change of clothes. I was feeling grungy after all the running around and climbing into that stinky cave. Brittany and I took turns in the shower, and I lent her an outfit to wear. By the time we were clean and dressed, I heard a car drive up. We looked out my window to see the police again, then raced downstairs to see why they had returned. I was the first one to the door.

Officer Lopez was at the screen. "Hi," he said. "We need someone to show us where that cave is." I looked out to see two other officers with him.

"I think I know an easy way to get there," I said. "We can take your car."

Mom came to the door at the same time Dad and Mr. Picardi came around from the patio. I explained the situation. Dad wanted to come along, but thought he should stay and get ready for his party. Brittany and I hopped in the back of the cruiser and directed the police to the street, where we took a left.

I knew that the next driveway was Louie's, but I suspected that there were a couple of little dirt roads going through the woods to Howie's landing and maybe to one or two others. I was right. We took the first one and found ourselves only a few yards from the big rock formation. This was the same road Mr. Seymore used to bring in the stolen goods. We got out of the car. I led the police to the rock, where I pointed out the opening of the cave.

"Here it is," I said. It's full of equipment stolen from boats in the harbor."

"You were right about Sammy Boucher and his girlfriend," said Officer Lopez. "But his uncle isn't part of it. John Seymore arrived at the station late last night with a jeep-load of stolen property. He accused his nephew and friends, but by the time we got to Miller's, we had nothing to go on. The kid and his girlfriend were gone. We just picked them up now. It turns out she's the missing teenager!"

"What? Say that again!" I was shocked.

"The last 'kidnap' victim is Sammy Boucher's girlfriend," he said. "Sammy met her—her name's Lucinda Swift—at a bar over in Hyannis. She decided to run away from home and came over here. She and Sammy then started robbing houses in the neighborhood and boats in the harbor. They put the goods in the boat shed, then transferred them to this cave until they had buyers or a way to dispose of the stuff."

"You mean that skinny girl is the one we've been searching for and fretting about?" I couldn't believe it! What a waste of time it had been!

"That's right. Well, we'll send some boys over tomorrow to clean this cave out and notify the rightful owners. Anything else we need to discuss?" he asked as we got back into the cruiser. "'Cause I'm off duty now and I'd like to go home before we come back to your party."

"I'm glad you're coming," I said.

"Me too!" echoed Brittany. I was surprised that she said something. She was turning out to be almost normal.

"I've had a lot of excitement for one day," the officer replied. "There're a lot of loose ends that need tying up, so I'm looking forward to a recap tonight. My buddies here are working the next shift."

We got back into the police car. Lopez backed it up, turned around in the little clearing, and drove us to my house. "Just drop us at the end of the driveway," I said. I thanked him and the other officers as we hopped out. Brittany and I walked in silence toward my house.

I heard a car behind us, and we turned to see Abigail and her "family" coming toward us. Uncle Jack was driving, and Mrs. Lincoln sat in the passenger seat. Freddy Frisket and Abigail were in the back. We stepped aside and stood near the fence to let them pass. Uncle Jack stopped and Abigail jumped out.

"Hi!" she said. "You have to tell me everything! I can't believe you two solved the whole mystery in one afternoon!"

"You'll hear everything, don't worry!" I laughed. "Mr. Dill never told us who kidnapped him and how he escaped. The gypsies didn't do anything bad! It was all Sammy Boucher and the 'kidnapped' girl from Hyannis."

"No!" Abigail couldn't believe it.

When we got to the house, Mom was at the front door greeting the Lincolns. Maxwell and Georgie were sticking their heads out the door too. They were all bathed and cleaned up and looking their evil little selves again. Mom led the Lincolns to the patio. We followed them around the house.

When we went to the kitchen to get them something to drink, we heard another car drive up. It was Muffy and her parents. Next Laura and her mom and dad arrived, coming up from the beach. Her father carried a huge platter, which turned out to be meat that he had marinated in his famous sauce.

Someone was coming through the woods. It was Louie, his brother, and their parents. Next Howie, Connie, and Mr. Dill came along the driveway, just as a huge band of gypsies came up the beach stairs, trailed by their big black dog. Mr. Dill sure looked strange in Dad's khakis cinched in at the waist and his big Oxford shirt billowing out around him. He had shaven and it looked as if Connie or Howie had cut his hair.

The gypsies must have rowed over from their trawlers. It was difficult to accept them as our friends after hating the sight of them for days on end, but it was a relief not to have any enemies anymore. They carried a few fresh fish and a guitar. They also produced some strange-looking musical instruments and a couple of tambourines.

The fog was completely gone by now. It was a clear and cool evening, just perfect for a cookout. Jake Rison and his wife drove up and crossed the lawn to join us on the patio, followed by Officers Nick and Lopez. Billy Jones was the last one to arrive. He brought a plate of cooked lobsters.

Several tables and every single one of our chairs covered the patio and part of the yard. All the food was piled on the tables, as well as drinks, silverware, plates, and all that sort of stuff. Once we were all assembled, Dad said, "I want to thank everyone for helping us to search for my son and his friend. You are all the best neighbors in the world! And I especially want to thank our new fishermen friends not only for finding the boys, but also for saving the lives of our daughters, Louie Stello, and Mr. Ruben Dill!"

Mr. Picardi led us in giving the gypsies three cheers. At least a few of them spoke a little English and could translate for the others, so they knew how much we appreciated their help. Maxwell and Georgie were cavorting over the grass with the big black dog. I hate to say it, but I was glad the little monster was back.

I decided that I should make a speech too. "We've had a rough week," I began. "A lot of unusual things have happened in our little town, and we made a lot of assumptions about exactly what was happening. All of those assumptions were completely wrong. A whole bunch of us have worked together to find the truth. Now we're going to hear what really has been happening. Almost every person here has a story to tell. We'll let the boys go first."

Maxwell and Georgie stopped playing and were thrilled to be the center of attention. They gave a garbled and distorted account of falling into the cave. Everyone clapped when they finally finished. The boys cuddled up to their moms and dads while Officer Lopez explained the true fate of the missing man and woman. It was a relief to know that they were "safe" and were working out their personal problems.

Then Jake Rison took over. He began, "I want to thank each one of you for your part in solving these two mysteries. We thought we had kidnappers here in town and we're sorry we were suspicious of you fishermen." He directed that statement toward the gypsies, who shyly smiled.

"We've had a rash of burglaries on and off the water," he continued. "And we've discovered that a summer kid, Sammy Boucher, and his new girlfriend from Hyannis, Lucinda Swift, the runaway, nicknamed 'Honey', did it all themselves. They heard about the gypsies having problems in the harbor, so they dressed up in colorful sweaters. They thought anyone seeing them would think they were seeing some of these fishermen here. But those two kids won't be going back to college this fall—they'll be going to jail."

I related our confrontation with the two fancy men and how they tried to kill us. Louie and Brittany helped tell the tale.

"What's going to happen to Elbert and Silverson?" Mr. Picardi demanded.

"Oh, they're going to jail too," answered Officer Nick. "You won't be bothered by them for a long time, because they're accused of four counts of attempted murder. But what I want to know is what happened to Mr. Dill? How on earth did he turn up here? And where has he been for the last couple of days?"

That was what we all wanted to know.

Chapter Forty-One

"It's not really such an interesting story," Mr. Dill began, though we were sure it had to be.

Mom and Mrs. Picardi were still serving drinks. Dad glanced at the grill every now and then, giving the meat and fish a poke or a flip. The food situation was under control.

Mr. Dill continued, "After the little girls visited me, and I explained why I had left my home, I got to thinking that I had left the whole mess—the property, the taxes, and the shady developers—to my dear daughter. It wasn't fair to her and it wasn't the right thing to do. I decided it was time to go back and face my problems. Talk to Connie about what could be done. Work together on our future."

He stared intently at the four of us. "I want to thank you girls. You helped me, but I must confess something: When you came to visit me the second time, I pretended to be asleep."

"You what?" I gasped. "How could you?"

"Calm down, Mollie," said Howie gently. "Let him finish his story."

"I didn't want you to interfere with my decision," he said.

"Why would we do that?" asked Muffy, confused by his remark.

"I don't know." Mr. Dill hung his head and shook it. "I wasn't thinking straight. As soon as you left, I jumped up, ran down to the shore, and hid. You returned quickly, but as soon as you were on the island, I dove into the water and swam for Womponoy."

"You swam all the way from Freeman's Island to Womponoy?" Jake Rison couldn't believe it.

"Yup, I did," affirmed Mr. Dill. "It was a good long swim, but I was out of sight by the time you all came back to the east side of Freeman's. I hid on Womponoy and crept onto Deer Island at low tide. It was from there that I saw those kids stealing from the boats in the harbor. I worked my way around the harbor. The fog sure helped keep me hidden. It was a lucky break that this home was where I came up from the beach."

"It was a miracle!" exclaimed Connie, giving him an embrace. "A bona fide miracle! Oh, Daddy, I'm so glad that you made it. Now we can go home and work all your problems out. I never knew how overwhelmed you were with the taxes. I think we should crusade against taxes on vacant lots. That way people won't be tempted to sell their land. It would be the best thing for Cape Cod."

"I agree wholeheartedly!" said Mr. Picardi. We looked at him in surprise. Had he suddenly changed his opinion about buying and developing land? "High taxes make a breeding ground for sharks like Elbert and Silverson. I'm ashamed that I had anything to do with them. Freddy and I have been talking." He gave Freddy a slap on the back. "And Freddy here is going to find me a nice old place, fix it up real good, and sell it to me for a lot of money!" He laughed so hard that his face turned red! All the men were laughing, but I didn't understand what was so funny.

"As long as it's really your money," said Freddy, "I won't overcharge you too many millions."

They all chuckled again. I felt that it was my turn to make another speech regarding the gypsies. "I want to apologize to you fishermen. We misjudged you. We're really sorry."

Jake added, "We should have given you the benefit of the doubt. You were new in town and didn't know the ropes, so it seemed that you were the cause of all the problems that just happened to crop up when you arrived in the harbor."

"We make mistake," one of them admitted. "We break laws and no speak good English."

"You kept our laws, once you knew what they were," Jake consoled them. Then to the rest of us he said, "In the meantime, I've found out that the owner of the trawlers hasn't been paying these men their share for the fish they were catching. Back in New Bedford, the owner took all the money and paid them less than their agreement."

"That's not right," said Howie. "Every man gets a share."

"Correct," Jake said. "Then the men were sent to Cape Cod, to Muddy River Cove. At first they thought it would mean that they would get their share, but the owner was still the one who collected the money. They moved on to our harbor, but they stopped fishing rather than fish and not get paid. The owner thought he could get away with it because the men don't speak English very well and he thought they would be too shy to complain. I found out about it, and now the owner has agreed to pay them what he owes them. They'll be leaving tomorrow, but they would be welcomed back here any time."

"We like to come one time back," said one of them.

"Thank you so much for finding our boys!" said Mom. Dad stood and threw his arms around each and every gypsy. Mr. Picardi copied him. Mom and Mrs. Picardi asked each gypsy his name, and Mom even wrote their names down on a piece of paper. Mrs. Picardi got her camera and began taking photos of the whole crowd.

"And I want to thank the Girls, Louie Stello, and Brittany Picardi for all their help," I announced, ending my speech.

The Girls surrounded me. Muffy said, "Oh Mollie! God answered our prayers!"

"Huh?" What was she talking about?

"Remember?" Laura asked. "We asked God to find the kidnapped girl and keep her safe."

"And?" I asked, not understanding the connection.

"God helped us find her," Abigail stated. "And she was safe."

"Are you serious? She's going to jail!" I said.

"She'll be safe in jail." Abigail smiled.

"And the bad guys got caught," added Muffy. "Thank God!"

"Mr. Dill is the one who found out that Sammy and whatever her name is were the robbers. It wasn't God. And the gypsies' dog found the boys. I don't know why you all have to be so religious."

"Do you think it was just a coincidence?" Laura asked in surprise.

"Yes," I replied. "I do." The whole mystery, in all its parts, had just come together. Everything fit in the end, the way it always did. That's just the way life is. I don't know why it's like that, but it just is.

Hmmm. If life were just a series of coincidences, then things should work out only half the time—that's the law of averages—half good and half bad. I'm not saying that everything always works out perfectly, but things usually work out fairly well. What did that mean? I didn't think that it meant there's a God, but it had to mean something. I didn't have time to think about it now, yet I would have to think about this later. Maybe I was wrong about this God stuff. I had to be logical, even if it meant that I'd been wrong.

I noticed that Brittany had joined us, and then Louie. We watched the fireflies glide over the lawn as the darkness surrounded us. Mom had turned on the outside lamps and had set candles on the tables and patio walls. It looked nice.

The gypsies began singing—that weird wailing we had heard in the woods, but it sounded good, with all the instruments and tambourines. It was different now, knowing who was singing and why. A few of the men began dancing. These strangers had become real friends. Without them and their big dog, I don't know how we ever would have found Maxwell and Georgie. We had needed them.

"We're leaving early tomorrow morning," said Brittany. "I hope I'll see you in New Jersey sometime."

"Sure," I replied. "And thanks." I noticed a teeny, tiny smile cross her face.

"You're *it*," said Louie, slapping me on the back and dashing off into the dark yard.

"Oh, yeah?" I raced after him. The Girls and Brittany followed. Even Maxwell and Georgie appeared from somewhere and joined in. They raced after us. Brittany wasn't so bad. Maybe I wouldn't mind her coming over, once I was back home.

But I wanted our summer to go on forever. There was only one more week of sailing classes. We'd attend the Captain's Ball next Saturday and then what? I didn't want to think about, you know what, the "s" word—school. When would I see my Eel Grass Girl friends again? The Eel Grass Girls would have to see each other on Cape Cod for Thanksgiving, Christmas, New Year's, Easter, Memorial Day...

But was Cape Cod the only place we could be together? Would we find mysteries over the holidays? Or would we find mysteries back in our home towns? Could we get together at Muffy's apartment in New York City, at my place in New Jersey, or Abigail's home in Connecticut? Could Laura visit us? My thoughts returned to our game. I tagged Maxwell.

"You're it, you little creep," I shouted as I zipped away. He tagged Georgie, of course, who was right beside him, the easiest person to get. It felt good to have my family back to normal. Maxwell's disappearance had been a strain on my parents. If they weren't happy, I couldn't be happy and life didn't feel right. I was glad that all the mysteries were over.

After playing for a while, we all fell on the ground, laughing. The two little monsters ran off to make a fort under one of the long tables covered with platters piled high with goodies. Brittany wandered off to her mother. Louie vanished, then reappeared beside his older brother.

"Before we came over tonight, I telephoned my parents," said Abigail. "Mom said that she saw a light in our barn last night."

"So?" I asked. "Is that unusual?"

"Of course it is." She seemed upset. "Our barn is just full of junk. There's no reason for a light to be turned on at night. Dad went out to shut it off, but a little later they noticed that it was back on again. The next day an electrician came to check the wiring and it's fine, so they suspect someone's getting into our barn, but they can't imagine who or why."

"So what are they going to do about it?" Muffy wondered.

"They don't know what to do," Abigail replied. "But I was thinking, Columbus Day isn't that far away. Maybe we could confer over the telephone and e-mail each other. Connecticut isn't that far away. Maybe you could all come and visit me."

"Confer?" I laughed.

"Yes!" Abigail smiled. "Please?"

"You had the last mystery," said Muffy. "It's not fair for you to get the next one." I was sure Muffy was just teasing.

"I can't help it," Abigail said. "I didn't want to have another mystery, ever. The light keeps coming on and we have to find out why. Say you'll come to Connecticut and help me."

"You want us to come all the way to Connecticut just to check out a light bulb?" Laura laughed.

I said, "Dad will want to come up here for that weekend."

"He can drop you off on the way," said Abigail. "He'll have to drive right through Connecticut."

"I don't know," said Muffy. "Maybe I could take the train from Grand Central Station."

"How about you, Laura?" I asked.

"I've heard there's a bus from Hyannis," she said. "I think my parents would let me go."

"Good," said Abigail. "I need Eel Grass help and I need you Girls."

She was right. We needed each other and we had to keep in touch—forever.

Glossary of Sailing Terms

Aboard — on a boat

Alongside — close beside

Bail — to remove water from a boat

Bailer — a device used to remove water from a boat

Bar — a raised line of sand, usually parallel with the shore, causing shallow water

Below — under the deck of a boat

Bilge — the lowest part of a boat's interior

Bow - front end of a boat

Buoy — a floating marker

Capsize — to turn a boat over in the water

Cast off — to push away from and release lines holding boat to mooring

Channel —a body of water deep enough for navigation in an area otherwise not suitable

Choppy water — water covered with small, disordered waves

Close hauled — sails pulled in tight to sail toward the wind as much as possible

Come about — change direction

Dock — n. a pier or wharf; a wooden structure built over the water supported by pilings; v. to bring a boat to such a structure

Gill netter — a fishing boat using nets to catch fish

Head — v. to go in a certain direction

Head off — to go away from

Head up — to go toward

Jibe — when the mainsail moves from one side of the boat to the other with the wind coming over the stern

Mark, Marker — a buoy

Mooring — a buoy attached to a line, which is attached to a submerged cement block and used to tie up and secure a boat

Onboard — aboard, on a boat

Pier — a wooden structure built over the water, supported by pilings

Pin — mark representing the end of the starting line

Pitch — to be thrust suddenly in any direction

Port - left side

Rig — *v.* to put sails and other equipment on a boat

Starboard - right side

Stern - back end of a boat

Tack — *v.* to change direction when sailing upwind

Thwart — a seat on a boat that extends from side to side

Trawler - fishing boat using a large dragnet

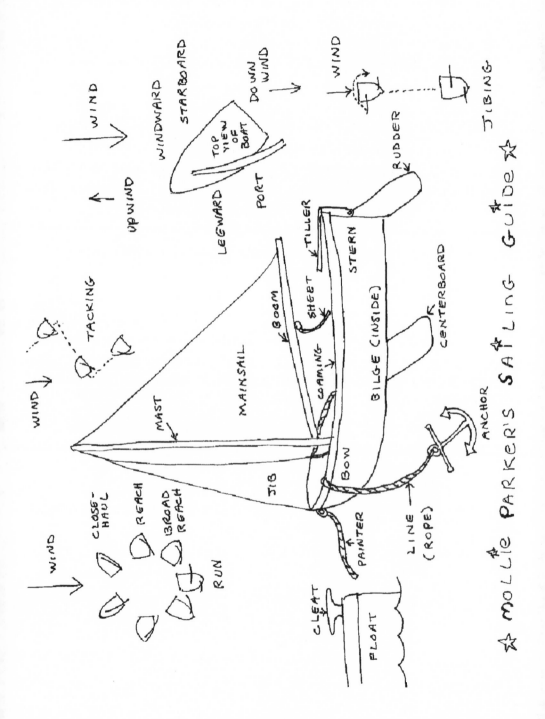

WIND

UPWIND

WINDWARD

STARBOARD

TOP VIEW OF BOAT

DOWN WIND

LEEWARD

PORT

WIND

RUDDER

JIBING

WIND

TACKING

SHEET

TILLER

STERN

BOOM

CENTERBOARD

MAINSAIL

COAMING

BILGE (INSIDE)

MAST

WIND

CLOSE-HAUL

REACH

BROAD REACH

RUN

JIB

BOW

ANCHOR

PAINTER

LINE (ROPE)

CLEAT

FLOAT

☆ MOLLIE PARKER'S SAILING GUIDE ☆

282

Read All the Eel Grass Girls Mysteries

Book 1 *Murder Aboard the California Girl* Paperback 1886551073
Rachel Nickerson Luna $7.95
Mora Cortez and her yacht club friends discover a dead body on a fishing boat. When the body disappears and no one in town is missing, the Eel Grass Girls embark on their first mystery.

Book 2 *The Haunting of Captain Snow* Paperback 1886551081
Rachel Nickerson Luna $11.95
Four feisty pre-teens solve a century-old mystery involving a sea captain and his strange family. Laura Sparrow, the young sailor who tells the story, is shocked to find skeletons in her own closet.

Book 3 *The Strange Disappearance of Agatha Buck* Paperback 188655109X
Rachel Nickerson Luna $11.95
An apparition is seen in Abigail Lincoln's summer home. Is it a ghost? When food is missing, the Eel Grass Girls suspect a homeless woman, but they discover someone truly incredible!

Book 4 *The Desperate Message from Freeman's Island* Paperback 1886551103
Rachel Nickerson Luna $12.95
A stranded castaway's message in a bottle sends the Eel Grass Girls on their fourth adventure. As Mollie Parker organizes a rescue, townsfolk and even her little brother disappear in this nautical mystery.

Join the Eel Grass Girls Mystery Club

It's Free!

Send in your name and address
and we'll send you
an Eel Grass Girls Mystery Club card
signed by
all four of the Eel Grass Girls!

Emma Howard Books
PO Box 385
Planetarium Station
New York, NY 10024-0385

Visit our Web site, send us an e-mail, or order a
Deluxe Eel Grass Girls Gift Bag

EelGrassGirls.com

Author Rachel Nickerson Luna

After graduating from art school, Rachel Nickerson Luna and her sister opened an art gallery. Luna later moved to New York City, where she exhibited her collages in a one-woman show. She worked in graphics for the clothing industry, then began to create picture books. Now she pens the *Eel Grass Girls Mysteries*, and when she is not writing she can be found rollerblading in Central Park, golfing, sailing, kick-boxing, or hosting literary salons.